Mended

A SWEET HOME DIXIE NOVEL

Kayla Marie

Kayla Marie
www.kaylamariebooks.com/contact

Publisher: Kayla Marie
Mended/Kayla Marie – First Edition
Printed in the United States
ISBN-10: 069280367X
ISBN-12: 978-0692803677

For Elijah. You light up my life. Always remember, you can do anything you set your mind to.

Acknowledgements

First and foremost I'd like to thank you, reader. Thank you for giving my debut novel a chance. I hope you enjoy reading it as much as I enjoyed writing it.

I want to thank my wonderful husband for supporting me and helping me to achieve my dreams no matter how difficult. Thank you for always believing in me. I love you.

I want to thank my little boy, who's a constant reminder of what the important things in life are and for teaching me how to love someone more than I love myself.

I want to thank my friends and family for all your love and support. A big thank you to my editor, Nikki Busch for all her great guidance. And a thank you to all of the wonderful writers, editors, and mentors out there who provided a multitude of information and support to help me make my dream of creating and publishing my first book a reality.

CHAPTER
ONE

STONY SILENCE FILLED the air as Ashley and her son made their way down the rural highway. Though hours had passed since she'd packed their belongings and forced Emmett into the car, he still seemed to simmer with resentment. She could feel the displeasure radiating from him as he sat like a martyr in the backseat. It didn't take much to set him off these days and he was now an expert at holding grudges. A brew of negative emotions constantly churned inside him and it seemed like everything she did just made things worse.

She was saddened by the turn their relationship had taken. As she watched the expanse of highway ahead of her, she daydreamed about the connection they used to have: cups filled with dandelions picked just for her, curling up on the couch sharing popcorn as they watched his favorite movie for the hundredth time, talking, laughter, hugs. Now instead of joy and love, their interactions were filled with arguments and tension. He used to share everything with her—no secrets, nothing held back. But, he'd become a stranger to her, a boy who shut her out and treated her like dirt. He acted like she was his enemy when she was just trying to do what she thought was best for him.

Some people might say Emmett was just being a teenager, but Ashley knew it was more than that. He was only nine when the unspeakable incident happened and he'd never been the same since. She'd tried almost everything to help him, but nothing brought back the boy he was before. Still, she loved him with all her heart. She would do anything for him. Which is why she'd sat in this car for the past eight hours—butt numb, back aching, hungry, tired, and cranky—as they drove toward what she hoped would be the answer she was searching for. Even though he resented her for it.

Ashley studied Emmett in the rearview mirror. He'd been so upset with her when they left he refused to sit next to her in the passenger seat. He was wearing his earbuds, no doubt listening to the disturbing heavy metal music he'd recently grown accustomed to. His auburn-blond hair—messy and too long—hung haphazardly over his hazel eyes as he glared out the car window. His lips were pressed firmly together in that familiar look of disapproval most often found on the faces of sulking teenagers.

He could condemn her all he wanted, but he had only himself to blame. Maybe if he hadn't added new violations to his rap sheet at every opportunity, failed school, or hung out with kids whose greatest achievement was stealing cigarettes and alcohol from the local liquor store, she'd have considered staying. He'd made his choices and now she made hers. She loved him too much to let him throw his life away. Hopefully he'd understand someday, but she wouldn't hold her breath.

She remembered his shock when she told him to pack his things and get in the car. Shock soon turned to rage, which never led to anything pretty. The appalling and hurtful things he said to her in his desperation would stagger nerves of steel. Despite his painful verbal blows and empty promises, she stood her ground. His poor life choices forced her hand and she refused to compromise on this. She did what she thought was right for him, even if he hated her for it. After all, she was the parent and he was a thirteen-year-old boy heading toward a life in prison if she didn't take drastic action.

Not wanting to think about her little boy living out his life in a cell, she shook off the image and turned her attention to the landscape around her. Lush green fields decorated with blooming yellow and purple wildflowers surrounded her. In the distance lay the Appalachian Mountains, their peaks still frosted with snow from the recent winter. The grassy fields below were dotted with grazing cattle and wooden farm shelters. In the distance, just off to the right of the two-lane highway, stood a faded red barn nestled among fields of cotton.

Though the scenery was beautiful, she had to admit she was going to miss the amenities city life provided. She certainly wasn't going to be able to get Chinese takeout in the middle of the night where they were headed.

Was she crazy? The city had been their home and she'd left it behind—left Jeff behind—all in hopes of fixing what was broken in her life and putting an end to Emmett's pattern of destruction. Moving away meant she could no longer visit Jeff's gravesite whenever she needed to. Or trail her fingers over the ridges of his name engraved on his headstone as she cried for him. She knew it was morbid, but it was the closest she could get to touching him. Even so little a connection wouldn't be possible now. Their new home was too far away. The thought sent a sharp pang through her heart and she curled inward in agony. Tears welled in the corners of her eyes and her throat constricted as she struggled to hold back her grief.

She ached for the life they once had together. It had been the three of them against the world: her, Emmett, and Jeff. Her Jeff. As she thought of him, she absentmindedly twirled the diamond-studded band she still wore on her finger, letting her tears slide down her cheeks.

He'd been gone four years now. Four painful, troublesome years. She feared she was starting to forget him. Every day she struggled more and more to remember him—the way he smelled, the sound of his voice, how it felt to have his strong, loving arms wrapped around her. No matter how desperately she tried to hold on, all his idiosyncrasies she had fallen in love with were fading with each passing day and she felt helpless to stop it. Her regular visits to his gravesite were one of the few connections that remained, yet she gave it up.

Ashley gripped the steering wheel with white knuckles as an agonized sob escaped her throat. Her shoulders shuddered and her vision blurred until she could barely see the road ahead. The realization of what she was leaving behind made her ache to turn the car around and go home. Only her thoughts of Emmett prompted her to keep driving. He needed to get out of there and a part of her needed to as well. It was too painful living so near to the place where her husband had lost his life, the familiarity around them a constant reminder of the life they'd shared together and all they had lost. She cleared her throat and brushed her hair out of her wet eyes, willing her grief to pass.

No matter how painful it was to leave their old life behind, she didn't have much of a choice. Living in the city was expensive and she didn't make a lot of money. They could only afford to live in less-than-desirable neighborhoods, which meant crime always lurked nearby. Somewhere along the way, Emmett had begun hanging with the wrong crowd and making his own criminal contributions. His actions became more and more serious, granting him numerous stays in juvenile detention centers and an extensive criminal record. Once he spiraled out of her control, leaving was the only way to stop him. Even that might not be enough.

On the road ahead was a sign advertising a roadside diner a few miles up. As if her stomach had a mind of its own, it rumbled uncomfortably. The long trip and painful silence helped her work up an appetite and a hot meal would do a lot for her weary body. She waved at Emmett to get his attention and he grudgingly pulled out one of his earbuds without looking at her. "There's a diner up ahead. I was thinking we should stop to get something to eat," she said.

Emmett tore his gaze away from the window and gave her a disgusted look. His hazel eyes, so much like his father's, narrowed in distaste. "There's no way I'm eating anywhere while we're in the ass-end of hickville. They'd probably try to feed me squirrel or something." His freckled nose wrinkled in revulsion.

"Yum, squirrel, the other white meat," Ashley teased.

Emmett sent her his usual derogatory look that informed her he thought she was the stupidest person on the planet.

"If you're really that worried about it, you could always go vegetarian. There's plenty of wildflowers and grass to choose from. If you're lucky, one of the cows might share some of its milk with you. Do you want me to pull over so you can try? That heifer over there looks pretty docile." She used her hands to milk an invisible cow.

Emmett scoffed and gave her one of his derisive eye rolls before returning his gaze to the window.

"Squirrel diner it is then."

"I'm not eating there!"

"Suit yourself. But I'm hungry so I'm stopping. You can sit in the booth with me and drool over my dinner." A few minutes of tense silence later, she sighed as she gave in to her mother's instincts. Not wanting Emmett to go hungry just because of his stubbornness, she picked up her bag of cookies from the seat next to her and offered it to him. It wasn't the best thing for him to eat, but it was better than nothing. "Consider it a peace offering."

Without offering a thank-you, he bitterly ripped it of her hand. She heard the distinct crinkle of the bag opening, followed by the sound of chewing. Deciding not to fight this battle, she swallowed her irritation and continued driving toward the welcome promise of warm comfort food in her belly.

A few miles down the road, Ashley and Emmett sat at a booth in an old roadside diner.A handful of truckers and other weary highway travelers occupied nearby booths and stools, eating their hearty plates of comfort food. Ashley looked hungrily at the menu while she pretended not to see Emmett taking peeks at his from its place at the edge of the table.

As she contemplated her options Emmett picked at the yellowed foam padding protruding from the ripped vinyl bench. He let out a labored sigh and placed his elbows on the table-top. He scowled as it wobbled beneath his weight and muttered his discontent about it being sticky. She didn't need to hear him to know he'd rather be anywhere else right now.

When she stood to place her order at the counter, Emmett stayed behind to pout in his seat. Despite his obvious hunger—characterized by the audible grumbles of his stomach—his pride seemed to get the better of him and he ordered nothing. He was so like his father in that way—self-sacrifice for the sake of his pride.

Fortunately for Emmett, Ashley knew how to handle him. She ordered an extra cheeseburger and fries for herself, which she later slid over to him after clutching her belly in fake stuffed agony. She knew he saw right through her game, but she also knew he could never resist a cheeseburger sitting in front of him.

After a tasty squirrel-free meal, they were back in the car, ready to hit the road again. As she backed out of their parking spot, she was pleased Emmett had chosen to sit next to her in the front seat this time. She knew from experience he wasn't done punishing her yet, but she had obviously earned his favor with the whole cheeseburger incident. It was a start.

After Emmett resisted her repeated attempts at conversation, he returned his earbuds to their place of residence and they drove on in silence. Trying not to let his rejection get to her, Ashley turned her attention back to the expanse of highway ahead. The breathtaking stretch of land—or as Emmett had so gracefully put it, "hickville"—surrounding their car captivated her. It may not be the city, but country life had its benefits: fresh air, wide-open spaces, and less opportunity for hoodlum-induced trouble, all things that could do a boy like Emmett some good. They could build a decent life for themselves here. She snuck a glance at Emmett beside her. He may not be talking to her, but at least he seemed to be less pissed off at her than he'd been at the start of the day. He would come around eventually. He just needed to give things a chance.

On the shoulder up ahead she saw a green road sign with fancy white lettering that read: Welcome to Alabama the Beautiful. It wouldn't be long now. They would soon find out what their new life had in store for them. She was ready for change; she just hoped the change would be for the better.

Mended

CHAPTER
TWO

WADE HUDSON PULLED his truck into the Butterfield Correctional Facility parking lot. Once parked, he turned off the engine and sat in silence for a moment as he examined the prison grounds.

Closest to him was the visitors' entrance—a grey concrete building emblazoned with the Alabama state seal. Cement steps covered with worn, charcoal-colored carpet led up to the steel double doors. Two rows of tall chain-link fence topped with gruesome-looking barbed wire jutted out from the sides of the visitors' entrance and surrounded the prison's perimeter. Tall guard towers with windows on all sides stood intermittently throughout the grounds.

Wade ran his fingers through his hair, making the longer hairs on top stick up at odd angles. Although he'd been here many times before, it didn't get any easier. The familiar knot of guilt forming in his stomach reminded him of what had been lost and of his failure to change the course of events that led to his monthly visits here.

He took another deep breath and stepped out of his truck. As he crossed the parking lot, he looked to the sky. It was a grey and gloomy day; the rays of the sun remained hidden behind dark clouds. The bleak weather above and dreary colors of the prison in front of him mirrored his somber mood. With a weight in his chest, he crossed the parking lot and climbed the six steps to the double doors of the visitors' center.

As he waited for his turn to clear security, he saw a number of people sitting in the waiting room. Most portrayed the nervous body language of someone who feels ill at ease—fidgeting, foot tapping, pacing.

Wade understood all too well how they felt. He was always uncomfortable when he came here, although his reasons were probably different from theirs. He was the reason his brother now called this dreary place home. If he'd done a better job, his brother could've been a successful businessman or a mechanic, instead of inmate number 549. "Next!" Wade heard the security officer's shout and stepped up, emptied his pockets, and spread his arms out to the sides.

After Wade passed security and checked in with the less-than-congenial female officer at the front desk, he found himself sitting at a cold metal table, facing a wall of windows and thick steel doors that led to the inside of the prison. Despite the fact that the room was full of people waiting to see their loved ones, there was a hushed silence filled with anticipation and unease.

Correction officers wearing khaki shirts, utility belts, and no-nonsense attitudes stood strategically throughout the room. Two of the biggest, meanest-looking officers guarded the exit, blocking the thick steel door with their rhinoceros-sized bodies, hands poised over their weapons.

A loud buzzer sounded and Wade could see the inmates in their denim jumpsuits lining up outside the room. A few moments later he heard another loud buzzer and the audible click of the heavy door unlocking. The inmates filed slowly into the room, their hands behind their backs like model citizens, while the correction officers watched them intently, ready to take action at the first sign of trouble.

Wade's eyes widened and his breath caught in his throat when he caught sight of his younger brother's face. Patches of purple-and-black bruises, still puffy and swollen from recent blows, surrounded Ford's left eye and jaw. Worse was the line of black stitches holding together the mangled flesh on his neck. He had clearly been in a fight recently and the outcome was one of the worst since Ford had been there.

As Ford approached the table, Wade assessed his features beneath his injuries. Ford's forest-green eyes, once bright and full of life, were now dulled and hardened. At the ripe age of twenty-one, a whisper of worry lines was already taking up permanent residence across his forehead as if relief was no longer a possibility. His jaw, once slack and prone to smiles despite life's disappointments, was held taut in a hard line—a sign prison was taking its toll on his innocence.

The foreign, hardened man who used to be his innocent little brother sat down at the table across from Wade. "Hey, man. It's good to see you."

Speechless since he noticed his brother's disturbing appearance, Wade cleared his throat to recover. "Hey, Ford. I wish I could say that you looked good, but then I'd be lying."

Ford laughed without humor. "Oh, you mean this," he said, pointing to the bruises on his face. "It's nothing. You should see the other guy. He was in the infirmary for a week."

"What happened?"

"This fool decided I was done with my lunch, but I disagreed. So, long story short, he got his ass handed to him."

"How did you get that?" Wade gestured to Ford's stitches.

Ford shrugged his shoulders. "He pulled a shank on me, but I turned it on him and ended up giving him one bigger than mine," he said with a forced smirk.

Feelings of rage, horror, and again guilt—the guilt was always there—bubbled up inside Wade and threatened to spill out. He took a few deep breaths and pushed his feelings back down in hopes of keeping them contained. It might add fuel to the fire raging inside him, but he had to know. "So how much time did they add for that?"

Ford shrugged casually. "Six months, but it was worth it. Now that fool and whoever watched me kick his ass won't bother me again."

There was something Ford wasn't telling him. "What about the guy's friends? I bet they weren't too happy about what you did to their buddy."

"Yeah, but they're too chicken to do anything. Even if they did, I could take them." Ford spoke tough, but Wade could see what lurked underneath. Ford was afraid. Wade opened his mouth to say something, but Ford continued before he found his words. "So, how's Dad?"

"Oh, you know Dad. Always drunker than the day before."

Ford smiled but it didn't reach his eyes. "Yeah, if there's anything you can count on Dad for, it's being bombed out of his mind."

Although he tried to hide it, Wade could see Ford's pain. His heart clenched for his sad baby brother who had desperately wished for a stable home and loving parents. Wade had wanted that for him as well—more than anything—which is why he'd tried so hard to fill the role himself. But, despite all his efforts, he fell short.

"How's business going?" Ford asked.

"It's going well. I just finished doing a master bathroom remodel for the Campbells and now I'm putting on a new roof for Mrs. Clemons."

"Get laid recently?" A smug grin spread across Ford's face.

"The look on your face tells me you clearly already know the answer to that question."

"Oh, come on, man. What's your problem? You need to get yourself some. I'm sure there are plenty of hot, loose chicks with brain damage who are just dying to make your acquaintance." Ford feigned a serious face. "Wait. Are you gay, bro? Because that would explain a lot. It's okay, Wade, I'm your brother. You can tell me."

"Ha-ha, very funny. That joke never gets old. Dating hasn't exactly been on my list of concerns since you've been here. I don't get why you're so smug about it anyway. I highly doubt you're getting any in here. And if you are I'd seriously question your sanity. I know you've never played for team sausage."

"You're right. I'm a ladies' man through and through. But if I did decide I wanted a little action I bet I could get laid easier in this hellhole then you could if you hosted ladies' night in your pants and handed out free liquor and hundred dollar bills."

Wade chuckled and reveled in the hint of the satisfied smile on Ford's face. He'd missed this side of Ford. The funny, cocky kid brother he used to know didn't come around very often anymore. Fond memories of playing pranks on one another came to mind: putting worms in each other's shoes, filling the yogurt containers with mayonnaise, putting salt in the sugar bowl, and of course the classic plastic wrap over the toilet bowl. Sometimes things got a little out of hand, but most was all in good fun.

"How's the work program going? Have you been able to go to any interesting places or learn some new job skills lately?" Wade asked.

Ford shifted uncomfortably on the slick metal bench. "I kind of got kicked out of the work program. Something about my 'behavioral misconduct'" Ford used air quotes.

Wade noticed the familiar feelings of exasperation bubbling up inside once again. He took yet another deep breath to collect himself—he'd needed a lot of deep breaths today. He gritted his teeth to keep from yelling. "So, what do you plan to do instead? Are you at least trying to get your GED?"

"And what would I do with a GED, Wade? In case you forgot, I'm stuck in this shit hole for at least the next four years of my life. The way things are going, I'll be lucky if I get out at all."

Wade couldn't contain his anger any longer. "Stop saying crap like that. You need to change your attitude. If you're really motivated, you'll have the possibility for early parole. Try to better yourself and do your time so you can get on with your life. This doesn't have to be it for you. You have so much potential and it kills me to see how you keep throwing it away."

Ford squared his shoulders as he sat up straighter. "When are you going to get it through your thick skull that this is my life, Wade? I'm not you. Mind your own damn business and live your own freaking life."

"I want more for you, Ford! Why can't you want it for yourself? When are you going to stop being so irresponsible and grow up? Stop making such stupid choices. Do you want to be a loser your whole life?" The words came out louder and harsher than he wanted, but it was too late to take them back now.

Ford narrowed his eyes and lowered his voice until Wade could barely hear him. "Somehow it always comes to this. If that's the way you're going to be, then stop coming around here. I don't want to see you anymore. Leave. Me. The. Hell. Alone."

"Ford, come on. I just want what's best for you. Can't you see that?" Wade's question was met with silence and Ford's averted gaze. "Mom would be ashamed of you." It was a low blow, but that didn't make it untrue.

Ford pretended not to hear him, but Wade could see him stiffen at his words.

A correction officer's booming voice broke the silence: "Visiting time is over. Inmates line up by the door with your hands behind you back." Without giving him a second glance, Ford stood and walked away.

"If you won't do it for me or for yourself, then do it for Mom!" Wade called after him, but Ford kept moving toward the line of inmates filing out the door as if he hadn't heard him. "I want my brother back," Wade called desperately.

Ford stopped in his tracks but didn't turn around. When he spoke, his voice was cold as ice. "I'm not sure if I ever had a brother." With those words, Ford took his place in line and filed out the door.

***

Back in the driver's seat of his truck, Wade let out an exasperated sigh as he thought about the intense visit with his brother. It seemed like he never got anywhere with Ford. They kept having the same conversation to no avail. No matter how hard Wade pushed, Ford refused to change. If anything, Ford was worse since his incarceration last year. He had more attitude and less concern for his own well-being than ever before.

Wade cringed as he pictured Ford's gruesome new injuries. It seemed like he acquired new cuts and bruises every time Wade saw him, but his most recent ones were by far the worst. The cut on his neck looked serious. He was probably lucky to be alive. Ford needed help, but what could Wade do? Talking to him never seemed to work. He had to think of something. Giving up on him certainly wasn't an option.

Wade thought about what he'd said to Ford today and wondered if he was too hard on him. He only said those things because he cared about him and wanted him to see the error of his ways, but Ford probably didn't view it that way. Wade was never good at expressing his feelings, but his brother should already know how much he loved him. Why else did he keep pushing Ford to do better for himself? Wade knew he'd made a lot of mistakes with his brother, but caring about him wasn't one of them. If only Ford would see it.

Wade's guilty conscience, always lingering in the back of his mind, shoved its way front and center. If his mom could see him right now she would be so disappointed in him. He should have been able to keep his brother from a life like this.

The thought of his baby brother, with his dark curls and toothy smile, living out the rest of his days behind bars made Wade shudder. He hoped it wasn't too late for Ford. Pulling away from the prison, he began the long drive home. He needed to find a way to help his brother. At the very least, to knock some sense into him. He had to. Ford's life depended on it.

.

CHAPTER
THREE

ASHLEY HUMMED CHEERFULLY to herself as she unpacked the last box of their belongings. They'd arrived at their charming southern home in Mason, Alabama last week and she was pleased to be settling in.

Their new home was even more alluring in person than in the pictures she'd seen online. The soft white of the painted wood panels complemented the charming royal-blue shutters that framed the home's double-hung windows. Two wooden patio chairs, matching the ruby red of the big front door, were nestled under the overhang of the wraparound porch. They revealed a perfect view of the beautiful yard.

A blanket of lush, green lawn surrounded the home. Mature magnolia trees, pink with spring blossoms, stood on either side of the porch, framing the house. A huge elm tree stood behind, towering over the roof of the small, single-story home.

From the moment Ashley pulled into the driveway of her new picturesque home and heard the crunch of gravel under her tires, she fell unequivocally in love. She was shocked when she found out how affordable the rent was. Because she lived in the city most of her adult life, she was familiar with the concept of paying outrageous prices for closets advertised as apartments. In the city, a house this size would cost more per month than she made in six. Not to mention the lot would be a fraction of the size. With the amount she'd save on rent, she would finally have money left over at the end of the month. For once she could start saving for the future and even start a college fund for Emmett. She smiled at the prospect.

If Ashley was charmed by her new home, she was utterly captivated by the town of Mason itself. Quaint Victorian and ranch-style homes lined the quiet residential streets, all with impressively sized, unfenced yards. The downtown area was filled with small family-run shops and diners that wafted mouthwatering smells of southern home cooking. The streets of the town were clean and well maintained, and the traffic could be considered nonexistent to a city girl like her.

The people living there were the best part of all. Strangers made eye contact with her, smiled, and said hello as she walked down the street. They stopped to make pleasant conversation with one another as if they were old friends; in a town this small, they probably were old friends. All week long people had welcomed them, bringing fresh-baked pies and homemade baked goods to their door. She felt safe here. Time would tell for sure, but she was already confident she made the right decision coming here. A community like this was exactly what they needed.

Their first week in their new home went better than Ashley expected. Emmett helped her unpack some of the boxes and set up their furniture. He went with her to explore their new town with less grumbling and complaining than expected and even participated in some outdoor excursions with her.

Ashley smiled as she remembered the long hikes they took together and the day they spent at the river. They enjoyed most of the hiking in silence, but she hoped it was an appreciative silence rather than an irritated one. Maybe he didn't harbor the enthusiasm he once had when they used to do things like this together, but at least he kept the eye rolling and insensitive comments to a minimum.

She was nearly certain Emmett had enjoyed the day they spent at the river. She relished the memory of seeing his rare smile as they zipped down the river in their paddle boat, and later, when they splashed around in the cool water. She wanted things back the way they were four years ago, but she was willing to accept any improvement he offered. Small successes were still successes.

If she ignored the fact that Emmett spent the majority of the week alone in his room or that his general irritability was now the standard by which all other behavior could be compared, she'd say that they were almost getting along. Well, as long as she didn't count the fight they were having today. At the very least she could say things were better than expected considering their tense drive down here.

Suddenly Emmett stormed into the room, rousing Ashley from her glass-half-full thoughts and declaring for the third time that afternoon, "I still don't understand why I have to go to some stupid after-school program. I'm not a little kid! I can stay here alone until you get home from work."

"Emmett, we've been over this. The terms of your probation specify that you can't be without adult supervision. So unless you can find some other kind of adult-supervised activity that your probation officer and I approve of, you are going to that after-school program." She wanted to add, "And frankly, I don't trust you to go anywhere without a responsible adult," but her blunt honesty was not very well received these days.

"This is such crap." His face reddened. "Why can't I just come home after school?"

Ashley took a deep breath to steady herself. "Emmett, I'm not talking about this anymore. This is what is happening. You need to accept it and move on."

"This sucks," he yelled as he moved toward the front door of the house.

"Emmett, stop." Her voice rose. "You can't just leave. You need to tell me where you're going."

"I'm just going for a walk. Don't get your panties in a twist."

His disrespectful attitude was downright offensive. Was every thirteen-year-old boy this rude to his mother? She didn't think so and it made her bitter. After a few deep breaths, she counted backward from ten. When she felt calm enough to avoid yelling, she said, "You may go for a walk but you have to stay in the neighborhood. And take your cell phone with you."

"Whatever." He continued moving toward the door.

"And if you're not home in twenty minutes, I'm calling your probation officer."

"Okay! *Chill out*, Mom." He stormed out of the house and slammed the door behind him.

Ashley's gaze caught the potted houseplant by the door. It rattled in its dish, its leaves trembling as if a train was rumbling past. As she placed her hand on the pot to steady it, she caught her reflection in the mirror on the wall beside it. Her ocean blue eyes looked weary and troubled and her long golden hair was frazzled from tugging at her roots. Her ivory cheeks were flushed with irritation and frown lines lay between her eyebrows. Life hadn't been easy without Jeff.

Emmett never used to get this angry just because he didn't get his way. He was never one of those kids who rolled on the floor, kicking and screaming when he didn't get something he wanted. Occasionally he would let out a few whines or an "it's not fair," but most of the time, he either accepted it or calmly tried to compromise. Lately, though, any little thing could set him off into an overblown fit of anger. At least this time he had the sense to walk away and cool off instead of continuing to scream at her. *I guess you could call it progress.*

After what happened to their family, she understood he needed time and support above all else. He also needed structure and a firm hand, but that wasn't her forte. She was good at being Mom, but still hadn't quite grasped how to fill the role of Dad. If she was certain about one thing, though, it was that no matter what, she loved Emmett more than life itself, and she would never stop trying.

***

Emmett stomped down the street with all the fury of an angry teenager in the middle of a full-blown tantrum. *First I had to leave my friends and move to the middle of nowhere and now I have to go to some stupid after-school daycare because my mom thinks I'm some big baby. She's so annoying!* He kicked the metal pole of the street sign in front of him. A sharp pain consumed his toes and shot up his leg, further increasing his anger. He shook the pole furiously as he let out a yell of outrage, causing onlooking squirrels to scurry away and birds in nearby trees to take to the air in fright.

He continued his outburst until the end of the next street and flopped down to sit on the curb. "This sucks!" He wondered what his friends were doing in that moment. Maybe they were skating at the park or lifting alcohol or cigarettes. Whatever they were doing, Emmett was certain they weren't sitting on a curb in a quiet, annoyingly picture-perfect neighborhood with nothing better to do. He wished he could talk to them, but unfortunately his probation officer and his mom forbade it. In spite of the rules, he'd tried reaching them, but his mom had turned on the parental controls on his cell phone and computer, so he couldn't. Just another reason why his life sucked.

Emmett looked up and down the quiet street. An old lady walked—or shuffled—her dog at a snail's pace a ways down the street from him. A middle-aged couple lounged in wooden chairs on their front porch, seemingly asleep. The smell of charcoal burning and the distant sounds of idle chatter and laughter drifted to him from backyard barbecues. What was he supposed to do for fun in a boring town like this? He admitted the food at the downtown diner was pretty tasty, the hiking wasn't so bad, and he actually had a little fun at the river, but other than that, this place sucked big-time. It could never compare to what city life had to offer. Although, maybe a safe unsuspecting neighborhood like this did have an upside.

No anticipated crime also meant not a lot of cops on patrol. He looked at the grey-and-white house behind him and noticed that the unattached garage was open. Parked inside was a grey, lifted, heavy-duty diesel truck with built-in toolboxes along the sides of the bed. Leaning against the wall were two rusty dirt bikes that looked like they belonged at the dump. The shelves of the garage held various expensive-looking tools, spare parts, and boxes of unidentifiable things. Emmett had been sitting there for a while now and the occupant of the house was still nowhere to be seen.

People were so trusting in a small town like this. That should make this easy. He looked up and down the street once more. There was no sign of cars and the few visible people appeared to be half-dead. A grin spread across his face. It looked like he might be able to have some fun after all. He stood up and walked tentatively toward the open garage. After scanning his surroundings one last time, he went inside to search for valuables.

CHAPTER
FOUR

WADE RUMMAGED INSIDE his refrigerator for something to eat. It was slim pickings as usual. After deliberating between a jar of pickles and a slice of cheese, he gave up, grabbed his last Coke, and closed the refrigerator. He was hungry for a home-cooked meal, but because his cooking skills were limited to heating something up in the microwave, he was going to have to settle for something else.

It looked like he would be dining at The Fried Pickle yet again tonight. It was the best place in town for comfort food that came close to the quality of a home-cooked meal. It's not like no one had ever cooked for him. His mom had cooked of course and there were times when he'd been in a few long-term-almost-serious relationships with women who liked to cook. But, his mom was long gone, and Wade had been too concerned about Ford since he was sent to Butterfield last year to care much about dating. Sure, Wade could try to cook something for himself, but from his experience that always turned out to be the worst option. Unless his cooking skills miraculously improved or he developed a taste for burned and unappetizing food, he was better off with The Fried Pickle or the frozen foods section at Hardy's Grocery Store.

Wade popped open his Coke and took a long draft. The sweet, fizzy liquid slipped enjoyably down his throat. Since giving up drinking, Cokes had become his replacement. It wasn't the same, but it would have to do. He felt his phone vibrate in his pocket and he pulled it out. Wade looked at the number on the screen and contemplated not answering. Whenever Myra called, she either asked him to do something for her or talked his ear off as she gossiped shamelessly about this or that. As it almost always did, chivalry got the best of him.

"Afternoon, Myra," he said into the receiver.

"Wade, it's Myra," said the shaky, raspy voice of Wade's eighty-one-year-old-neighbor.

"Hello, ma'am. What can I do for you today?" He braced himself for what was to come next.

"Well, I was out walking Avery a little while ago when I saw this young man sitting out front of your house. Now, I usually don't think the worst in people but I've never seen this boy before and it seemed like he might be up to no good. I've heard that a woman and her teenage son moved to town last week. You know, the city folk? I thought maybe he was one of them. Those city folk can be terrible, so I thought I should watch him. I kept my eye on him all the way home then sat in my chair and kept on watching because you never know what those city scamps are going to do. Do you know what I saw? I saw that boy walk straight into your garage and start rummaging through your things! Can you believe that? He's in there doing God knows what as we speak. I was going to call the sheriff, but I thought I should call you first."

Wade hesitated for a beat as he looked out his kitchen window and saw the lanky boy with the reddish-blond hair, who was indeed rummaging through his garage. Wade had never seen him before, and he knew just about everyone in this small town. Despite the circumstances, Wade thought he looked completely harmless.

"No need to call the sheriff, ma'am. That's just my buddy's boy. He's staying with me while his dad runs a few errands in town. I just asked him to get some tools for me so I can fix a hinge on one of my kitchen cabinets," he lied.

"Which friend is that?" Myra asked skeptically.

"Just a buddy of mine from my early college days. We haven't seen each other in years and he wanted to come by to catch up. He's not from around here."

"Oh, good. I just thought I saw something fishy and I wanted to be a good neighbor. You know me."

"Thank you for looking out for me, ma'am. Have a nice afternoon."

"While I have you on the phone, I was wondering if you could do something for me…"

After agreeing to fix Myra's stuck window and leaky kitchen faucet free of charge, Wade hung up the phone and looked through the window into his garage. The boy was currently rifling through his toolboxes. He'd better go find out what his story was before the kid took something valuable. To avoid scaring the boy off before he had a chance to talk to him, Wade went around back. When he reached the garage entrance he took a moment to observe.

Up close the boy was taller than Wade first thought but had the scrawny appearance of a budding teenager who was still too young to put on any muscle. The glimpse of white socks in the gap between the bottom of his generic jeans and the tops of his dirty sneakers indicated what was likely a recent growth spurt. His hair was wavy and wild like that of a nomad. Taking a closer glance, Wade could see styling product held strands of hair firmly in place as if the messy style was intentional.

"Find anything good?"

The boy startled and slowly turned around. He wore a black T-shirt with an angry yellow smiley face. His hazel eyes assessed his chances of escape as they darted between Wade and the space from the open garage door.

"You can try to run if you want, but I'm pretty fast," Wade said.

The boy's eyes widened slightly and narrowed in defiance.

"My dad knows where I am, and if I'm not home in ten minutes he'll come looking for me." The boy breathed in and out in a rush. "He was in the Marines for eight years and he isn't afraid to use his gun," he added hastily.

Wade held up his hands in a peaceful gesture. "Relax, I'm not going to hurt you. I just want to talk to you for a minute. You are in *my* garage, looking through *my* stuff if you hadn't noticed."

The boy shrugged and relaxed slightly.

"What's your name, son?"

"I'm not your son, but my name is Emmett."

"I would rather have met under different circumstances, Emmett, but it's nice to meet you nonetheless. I'm Wade Hudson."

Emmett looked at Wade's outstretched hand and defiantly stuffed his hands in his pockets.

Wade dropped his hand unfazed. "I haven't seen you around here before. Where are you from?"

"New Jersey."

"A city boy like you must be out of his element in a quiet town like Mason."

"If you mean bored out of my mind, then yes."

"I bet you'll realize this place isn't so bad once you get used to it. Most folks never want to leave once they catch sight of our little town."

"Well, good for them." Emmett's words dripped with sarcasm.

"How old are you?" Wade asked.

"Thirteen. Can I go now?"

"Sure. After you tell me what you were doing in my garage."

Emmett looked down at his shoes and started kicking invisible stones. "I don't know. I was just mad at my mom and I was bored and saw that your garage was open…"

"And because you thought you could get away with it," Wade finished.

Emmett's forehead lifted in surprise, but he quickly shrugged it off. "I guess. I've never really thought about why I do it."

"Emmett, you seem like a good kid. You'd do better if you stopped doing things like trespassing and stealing."

"I didn't take anything, I swear," Emmett said innocently.

"Would you have?"

"Maybe. It depends on what I found."

Emmett's arrogant attitude and the smug grin on his freckled face reminded Wade of his cocky little brother. "I think I'm pretty safe to assume this wasn't your first rodeo. Am I right?"

"I've been to juvie a few times, and I've lost count how many times I've been arrested."

"That's nothing to brag about. If you're not careful, you may find yourself somewhere you don't like so much. I'm sure that a lecture from the likes of me is going to go in one ear and out the other, but do me a favor and hear me out for a minute. I know someone who used to be a lot like you—breaking all the rules, not a care for the consequences of his actions, thinking he was a big shot. He continued down the path you seem to be on, and now he may not have much of a life left to look forward to. Just keep that in mind, will you?"

"Yeah, yeah. Whatever gets me away from you."

"There's the door," Wade said as he stepped aside.

Wade watched as Emmett's gaze lingered on the dirt bikes in the corner before making his way toward the open garage door.

"You like dirt bikes?" Wade asked.

"I've never ridden one before, but I always wanted to. My dad used to have one, but we sold it before I was old enough to ride it," he said wistfully. "But those look like junk. Do they even work?"

"No. I planned to fix them up with my brother, but we never got around to it."

"Why do you still have them, then?"

"Well, I hoped to still have the opportunity someday, but the way things are going I'm thinking it's most likely not going to happen." The thought tightened Wade's stomach into knots, urging him to change the subject. "I assume your dad or your mom are waiting for you so do me a favor and head on home. I have eyes and ears all over this neighborhood so I'll know if you don't."

"You're not going to call the cops?"

"That depends. Am I going to find you uninvited in my garage again?"

"No…"

"Well then, I guess you'd better head home. Try not to rob anyone on the way."

Emmett snorted. "I think I can manage that. Thanks for being so cool about this."

Wade nodded. "See you around, kid. Take care of yourself, and think about what I said." He watched as Emmett gave him a half smile and walked away.

Nice kid. Hopefully he would stop making bad choices unlike someone else he knew. Ultimately it didn't matter what he hoped. Emmett was not his kid so it was none of his business. Besides, he was sure the kid's dad would straighten him out.

CHAPTER
FIVE

ASHLEY LOOKED AT the clock for the third time in the past minute. Twenty minutes had come and gone, and Emmett still wasn't home. She looked at the clock again. Twenty-five minutes now. Why couldn't he just do what he was supposed to? She didn't want to have to do this, but she had to hold him accountable for his actions. As she reached for her cell phone to call his probation officer, the front door opened and in walked a much more relaxed Emmett. Not wanting to bring back the yelling and arguing that so often plagued their home, she decided not to tell him he was late.

"Did you have a good walk?"

"Yeah, it was fine," he said. "I'm getting hungry. Can we go to that diner downtown for dinner tonight? I really liked their fried chicken last time we went."

"Sure, if you want. As long as we're back home by a decent time. I want you to be rested for your first day of school tomorrow."

"Ugh, school." He slouched on a bar stool at the kitchen island and put his head down on the counter. "I hate starting at a new school. I don't know anyone."

"Starting a new school can be tough, and it's completely normal to feel uneasy about a new situation. Just be friendly and open and I'm sure you'll make new friends." She rested her hand on his shoulder and he shrugged it off.

"You don't know that."

"You've been the new guy before, and you've always made new friends pretty quickly."

"Back home, maybe. But if you haven't noticed, we're in hillbilly central now. People here are…"

"Different," Ashley finished. She knew "different" wasn't the word he was looking for, but it was a much better alternative than the possible adjectives he was thinking. "People are different here, yes, but that might make it even easier to make friends. I've felt like everyone has been very friendly and welcoming so far, don't you?"

"Maybe."

"Just don't joke about drinking milk straight from a cow while you make milking motions in the air. The last time I did that, it didn't go over so well."

Emmett rolled his eyes. "That's because you're a huge dork."

"Maybe dorks have more fun. Have you ever thought of that?" She sang, "Dorks, they want to have fuh-un. Dorks just want to have fun!" She was far less musical than Cyndi Lauper.

Emmett pushed himself away from the counter. "There you go again. I'm out of here."

"Emmett Thomas, is that a smile I see on your lips? Did your old, dorky mother actually say something amusing?"

"Don't flatter yourself, Mom. I'm laughing at you, not with you."

"You can try to hide it, but I know better. I see right through you." She winked.

He tried to hide his amusement with a shake of his head, but she knew otherwise. Her heart felt lighter than it had all day.

***

Ashley and Emmett sat at a rustic oak table near the front entrance of The Fried Pickle. The front door was propped open, and she was grateful for the cool breeze from outside. The restaurant was crowded and noisy. The sounds of animated chatter, lighthearted laughter, and bluegrass music from the vintage jukebox in the corner made it feel even more crowded than it was. Ceiling fans rotated above, attempting to circulate the warm, stuffy air caused by so many breathing bodies.

The smells of cooking oil and comfort food drifted to the dining room whenever anyone opened the swinging kitchen door. Delicious, savory smells wafted from the steaming plates of barbecue and fried foods the servers carried out to the tables. The walls of the dining room were lined with red brick and decorated with framed photographs of the town and its residents. The high ceilings were adorned with exposed ductwork and chandeliers that gave the restaurant a warm glow.

A long metal bar with brown leather bar stools stretched the entire length of the far side of the room. Behind the bar was a wall of mahogany shelves lined with strings of white lights that illuminated the multitude of liquor bottles resting there. Lively music, good food, and an abundance of booze gave the restaurant a fun, relaxed atmosphere.

Ashley looked over the menu options and was impressed by the sheer number of fried foods and food slathered in gravy. Everything looked so good. If she wasn't careful, she might have to start exercising.

She deliberated between the array of mouthwatering, artery-clogging, happy-in-your-belly dishes and the few more sensible options. After a moment, she opted to embrace all aspects of their new southern home and decided to order family-style fried dill pickles, fried chicken, mashed potatoes and gravy, skillet corn bread, and coleslaw. If they weren't completely stuffed from dinner they might have to try the restaurant's famous banana pudding and vanilla wafer cookies.

As they waited to place their order, a man in a leather jacket and ripped jeans swaggered over to their table. His alluring amber eyes scanned her body up and down, making her feel naked and exposed. He had a short scruffy beard and unkempt dirty blond hair that hung over his forehead. As he approached, he smiled at her seductively in invitation. He looked sexy and dangerous, and he screamed promiscuous bad boy.

"You know what's good on the menu here, Me-n-u." His voice sounded as sexy as he looked, but Ashley had no desire to play along.

"Huh, that's weird. We must be ordering from different menus because I don't see that on mine." She held up the menu, making sure he could see the wedding band on her finger. She watched as his eyes flickered to her ring and then back to her face. To her dismay, he continued his pursuit without so much as a flinch.

"You must be new in town because I know I wouldn't pass up meeting a sexy temptress like you." His words slurred slightly as if he'd been drinking. "I would love to show you around the town sometime. Show you all of what Mason has to offer. Maybe we could grab a drink and get better acquainted." As he leaned toward her, she noticed the strong smell of whiskey and too much cologne.

She was getting irritated now. Usually men backed off once they saw her wedding ring. This guy clearly had no shame. "I can see for myself all about what Mason has to offer, thanks."

"Oh, come on now. I think we could have a lot of fun together. All I'm asking for is one drink. Just give me a chance. I promise you won't regret it." On the last word, he leaned in farther and slightly brushed her shoulder with his. He smiled a heart-stopping smile that Ashley was sure had melted the resolve of many women before her. Not her, though. She made a point of avoiding players like him. Well, all men, really, but especially men like him.

She was about to put an end to his game when a deep, smoky voice with a thick southern drawl spoke for her. "Are you quite finished, Reid? You clearly don't have a chance with her. Look at her. She's obviously way too good for you and too smart to fall for your questionable pickup lines."

"Aw, Wade, you're such a cock-blocker. No matter. Watch and learn. I was just about to ask her if it hurt when she fell from heaven."

"Yeah, yeah, and when God made her he was showing off, right?" Wade said. "Reid, why don't you get us a table and I'll come join you in a minute."

"Fine. But, my game was working and you know it. You're just jealous."

"You got me there. I'm a regular green-eyed monster. I can't stand to see you score with such a beautiful woman when I wish she'd pick me instead."

Reid nodded like this was the most reasonable thing he had ever heard. "For the sake of our friendship, I won't turn you into a third wheel tonight. I'll leave this angel to her meal." Reid turned to Ashley and winked. "If you decide you can't live without me tonight, I'll be over by the bar." With that final unwelcome invitation, he turned to leave.

The stranger with the striking, coffee eyes and the dark brown hair looked down at her apologetically. He was tall. Her five-foot-three frame would probably barely reach his chin. A thin layer of dark stubble caressed his jaw and upper lip, making his handsome face appear even more rugged and distinguished. She watched as his lips parted and he drew in a sharp breath as his eyes locked with hers.

He seemed to realize they were staring at each other in silence because an embarrassed smile spread across his perfectly crooked lips. "I'm sorry about Reid. He can make an ass of himself sometimes, but I promise he's completely harmless." He stuck his hand out to her. "I'm Wade Hudson."

His hand was warm and rough with calluses, like someone who worked with their hands all day. "I'm Ashley Thomas and this is my son, Emmett."

Emmett looked at Wade and seemed to stiffen. Eyes wide, he sat still and said nothing.

After a pause, Wade smiled politely and shook his hand. "It's nice to meet you, Emmett."

"Is that Reid guy really your friend?" Ashley asked.

Wade's jaw tightened at her words. "Yes. We go way back and he's a really good person."

"I'm sorry. I didn't mean to offend you. I was just taken aback by his bluntness. He did come on a little strong. The fact that I'm wearing my wedding ring and sitting with my teenage son didn't even faze him."

Wade relaxed almost imperceptibly. "Yeah, sorry about that again. He's always been charming and flirty but never so direct and borderline inappropriate. That's a fairly recent change. Is your husband here with you tonight?"

"No…"

"That's good. I'd hate to see Reid get his ass kicked tonight. Although, that might be just what he needs to knock some sense into him. Well, I don't want to keep the two of you. I hope you enjoy your dinner, and I promise I won't let Reid bother you again."

"It was nice to meet you, Wade. Bye." As he walked away, she noticed his grey plaid shirt covered strong broad shoulders and visibly toned arms. Washed-out jeans hugged low on his hips and continued down to his brown leather work boots. He was fit, rugged, and dangerously handsome. *And he thinks I'm married.*

"Mom. Can we order now?" Emmett's voice startled her from her reverie.

"Yeah, sweetie. I was thinking of ordering family-style fried chicken and sides. How does that sound to you?"

"Good. I'm starving."

CHAPTER
SIX

"RISE AND SHINE sleepyhead. It's time to get ready for school." Ashley's words were met with groans and a string of unintelligible words. She sat on the edge of Emmett's bed and gently pulled the covers off his face. He grumbled angrily and threw them back over his head.

"Come on, Emmett, please get up. You can't be late for your first day of school." She walked over to his window and opened his curtains all the way. Bright spring light flooded the room, making him groan louder and wiggle deeper under the covers. "I've been lenient with you all morning, but you have to get up now. We need to make sure we have time to check in with the office before your first class."

Muffled unintelligible words emanated from under Emmett's comforter. Ashley walked toward him and moved to pull the covers off again, but he held on tight and they wouldn't budge. She pressed her lips together. "Emmett, I'm not going to fight you on this. If you're not in the kitchen, dressed, and ready to go in five minutes, you won't like what happens." Hoping to avoid a fight, she walked out of his room and into the kitchen.

In four minutes, she finished packing both of their lunches and Emmett's breakfast and gathered their belongings. With ten seconds to spare, Emmett shuffled into the kitchen wearing jeans, a wrinkled T-shirt, and a sullen expression. His bed head wasn't much messier than the way he usually styled his hair and Ashley hoped no one at the school would notice. She wished he would make himself look more presentable for his first day, but they were late and she didn't have time to make him change. He was ready and mostly willing to go to school this morning. That would have to be enough.

"You just made the deadline. Did you remember to brush your teeth?" she asked.

"Yes."

"That's good. All of the cute girls at your school will be glad you did that." She was rewarded with a classic Emmett eye roll. "Your lunch is in your backpack, along with your cell phone. Here's your breakfast." She handed him an egg sandwich and a smoothie. "Are you ready to go?"

"As ready as I'll ever be," he sighed.

"Don't worry, honey. It'll be okay. And remember, there are only twelve weeks left in the term and then it will be summer."

"That long?" he whined.

"It will go by fast, especially once you get settled and make some friends. Maybe you can even join a club or one of the school teams."

He gave her an exasperated look. "Clubs? Sports? You know that's not how I roll."

"I'm well aware of how you used to 'roll,' but things are going to be different here. And hey, you were looking for a way to get out of having to go to the after-school program. Doing something extracurricular at your school would get you out of that."

"I know, Mom. I'm not an idiot."

"I never said you were. I was just trying to be helpful."

"Let's just go."

They arrived at Mason Middle School minutes before the bell rang. Emmett was just finishing his breakfast as they climbed the steps and reached the front entrance of the school. Students were milling about, talking animatedly to one another—most likely catching up and talking about their spring break activities.

When they stepped inside the school's front office, the plump and cheery woman at the front desk smiled warmly at them. "Good morning. I'm Lou Ella, and you must be Ashley and Emmett Thomas. Welcome! We're so happy you'll be joining us." She pulled out a piece of paper from a manila file on her desk and handed it to Emmett. "Here's your schedule, sweetie. Students here go to all their classes every day so you never have to worry about what day it is. Do you have any questions about your schedule?"

Emmett gave it a cursory glance and shook his head.

"Great. If you have any questions, don't hesitate to ask." She gestured to the boy making copies behind her. "This is Carson. He has volunteered to show you around the school and help you find your classes."

Carson smiled kindly at Emmett. "Hi, Emmett. I'll make sure you know where to go, where to hang out at lunch, and what food to avoid in the cafeteria. And you should definitely hang with me and my friends at break times too if you want."

"Sure," Emmett said reluctantly.

Ashley turned toward Emmett, suddenly feeling like she was dropping him off at kindergarten for the first time again. "I'll pick you up a little after five. Call me if you need anything, okay?"

"This is actually a cell phone-free school, but Emmett is welcome to use the office phone if he needs to reach you for any reason," Lou Ella said.

Ashley heard Emmett mutter under his breath almost unintelligibly, "It just keeps getting better and better," and hoped no one else heard him.

"Okay. Bye, Emmett. Be friendly and behave yourself and try to have a good day. I'll see you after." As she said her good-byes, she noticed how much he'd grown since the start of this year. All of a sudden she was looking up at him instead of down. When had that happened? His boyish features were starting to harden, his voice deepening. She couldn't believe he would be a high school student in the fall. Where had the time gone? She swallowed back her nostalgia and blinked the blurriness from her eyes. She moved to hug and kiss him, but he strategically dodged her, much *unlike* his first day of kindergarten.

"Don't embarrass me," he said in a harsh whisper.

She hid her hurt with a small smile. "It's my job, remember?"

"Well do a worse job at it."

Ashley chuckled. "Okay, honey, bye."

Emmett traipsed away and Carson followed, talking animatedly as he pranced along beside him.

"Mrs. Thomas, if you could stay for a moment, the principal would like to have a word with you. I promise it won't take long," Lou Ella said before Ashley could leave.

"Okay."

"Go head on back. Her office is through there."

Ashley walked past Lou Ella's desk and into the principal's office. The small room was fully furnished with a small denim sofa, two wine-and-gold-colored chairs, and a modest ash desk. Natural light streamed in through the windows, making the room feel warm and welcoming.

Upon entering, she saw a slender woman in her late fifties seated behind the desk, studying some papers. The woman wore her light brown hair in short curls that barely reached past her ears. Thickly framed glasses slipped down her prominent nose as she lifted her head and peered at Ashley over the top of them. With one finger, she pushed them up so they framed her warm chocolate eyes, which crinkled at the corners as she smiled.

"Mrs. Thomas. Welcome, and thank you for meeting with me. My name is Luann Montgomery. Please call me Luann." She rose from her chair and offered her hand. Her handshake was firm and professional despite how thin she was. "I'm sure you need to get to work soon, so I'll be brief. Please have a seat." She gestured to the padded chairs in front of her desk.

"I wanted to talk to you about Emmett's transcripts. I'm sure you know that Emmett's grades are poor. If he doesn't achieve passing grades by the end of the school year, we recommend he attend summer school."

"What if he goes to summer school and still doesn't pass?" Ashley asked though she already knew the answer.

"Then I'm afraid he will need to repeat the eighth grade."

"I know Emmett has been struggling in school for a while, but nothing has worked so far. I try to help him with his homework when I get home from work, but I can only do so much without doing it *for* him."

"We have excellent tutoring services as a part of our after-school program. I see that Emmett is already planning to attend. I recommend signing him up for the tutoring portion of our program. They help with every subject, focusing more heavily on the areas that need the most work. If he enrolls, our tutors ensure he completes and understands all of his homework and classroom material before he participates in the other more recreational aspects being offered."

"We've tried tutoring before, but the tutors never seemed to motivate Emmett to work very hard."

"Our tutors are all highly trained, certified educators, and they have experience working with students who have all ranges of difficulties. However, they can't perform miracles. Emmett will have to try if he wants to do well. That being said, I still highly recommend the program. It has helped a great number of our students become successful in school."

She knew he wouldn't like this, but he needed to pull his grades up. "We could give it a try. I want to give him all the help he can get."

"Wonderful. Now, there is a fee for the tutoring services, but I can check to see if you qualify for the scholarship program first, if you wish."

"No, thank you. I'll pay for it myself. Just tell me how much," Ashley said as she took out her checkbook. Now that her expenses were affordable, she wanted to pay her own way. Government assistance programs had been helpful at times, but she was eager to be self-sufficient.

After signing papers and settling the fees for Emmett's tutoring, Ashley walked to her car with a spring in her step. Not only was Emmett going to get the help he needed, but she could also afford it. Feeling cheerful, she climbed into her car and drove to work.

***

Ashley took a long drink from her iced coffee as she sat at the picnic table outside the veterinary office where she worked. The morning had gone quickly and more smoothly than expected for a first day at a new job. Everyone at the office was friendly and helpful, and she already felt right at home. Dr. Miller, the veterinarian, insisted she call her Maggie and treated her more like a sister than her subordinate. Ashley had successfully assisted the doctor with animal patients all morning long, including a minor surgery on a Labrador retriever. They certainly kept her busy today, which was exactly the way she liked it.

Maggie's three o'clock appointment canceled, giving them the opportunity to enjoy a much-deserved break in the fresh air.

"In need of a pick-me-up, huh? Did we wear you out today?" Maggie asked as she sat down at the picnic table across from Ashley.

"Maybe a little, but mostly I just like iced coffee on a warm, spring day," Ashley said. "Besides, being a little worn out is a small price to pay for a great job. Thank you for giving me this opportunity and making me feel so welcome here."

"Oh, come now. You don't need to suck up to me. I already liked you from the moment I met you."

"Then I guess I don't need to share one of these with you." Ashley pulled two huge chocolate-chip cookies from her lunch bag and handed one to Maggie. "I made these yesterday. Do you like chocolate chip?"

"I guess a little sucking up never hurt anyone." Maggie bit into one of the cookies and moaned. "Dang, girl. You sure know how to win over this woman's heart. I can tell we're going to be good friends."

Maggie ran her clinic in a rather unconventional way. She treated her entire staff as though they were a team—equals— instead of her subordinates. She made them feel like family.

Ashley glanced at the woman sitting across from her. Maggie was in her late thirties with wild black curls and bold emerald eyes that twinkled whenever she spoke. Like everyone around here, she spoke with a thick southern drawl, though her voice was more melodious than most. She was a free spirit and had a heart full of love.

"We're having a barbecue at our house next Saturday night. You and Emmett should come," Maggie said.

"That sounds really fun."

"I'm sure Carson would love the opportunity to spend some time with Emmett. He was so excited about volunteering to show 'the new kid' around school this morning. We don't get many new families moving here with kids his age. I think he wanted to claim Emmett for himself before anyone else got to him."

"How sweet. Carson was so nice when I met him this morning. It would be great to give them the opportunity to spend some time together. He could use a friend like Carson. What are the odds that Carson was the one who volunteered to show Emmett around this morning? What a small world."

"The odds are better than you think in a town as small as Mason."

"What's it like living here? Raising a family here?" Ashley asked.

"Everyone knows everyone else. So, naturally that means that everyone knows everyone's business. It's a safe place and people are there for each other, but it's hard to keep a secret around here. Some people are just nosy, but for the most part, people want to know what's going on with you because they care. So don't tell anyone anything you don't want the whole town to know."

"What have you heard about me and Emmett so far?"

"Apart from what you've told me, not much beyond the basics."

"Which are?"

"You're in your early thirties, you're a veterinarian assistant, you live in the white-and-blue house on Magnolia Street, you make excellent chocolate-chip cookies—that one was newly discovered about two minutes ago—and Emmett's daddy isn't in the picture. No one knows for sure why, but there are some theories. Overall, you have done a fine job at keeping the big stuff quiet so far."

Ashley sagged with relief. "Well, I haven't really gotten close to anyone yet."

"Just know, if you ever decide to tell me anything, the rest of the town won't hear your secrets from me. So don't you worry about that."

"Thanks, Maggie. So what are some of the theories on Emmett's dad?"

"Oh, they range from the generic scumbag who left his family to the heroic Navy Seal killed fighting for his country. My favorite is the one where he's a secret agent who blew his cover and had to leave you and Emmett behind to keep you safe."

Ashley laughed. "Very creative. Those theories are better than the truth."

"What is the truth?"

Ashley looked into Maggie's kind, searching eyes. As great as Maggie was, Ashley wasn't ready to share the story of her husband's passing just yet. People always treated her differently when they found out, like she was some victim of a heinous crime. At first they would look at her with pity as they offered their condolences; then they would slowly distance themselves from her, unsure what to say or how to be around her anymore. "I think I'll keep everyone guessing for a while longer," she said.

Ashley's cell phone rang, interrupting the conversation. It was a number she didn't recognize. "Hello?"

"Hi. Is this Ashley Thomas?"

"Yes..."

"Hi, Ms. Thomas. This is Lou Ella from Mason Middle School. I'm calling about Emmett. His tutor informed me that he never showed up for his session today. I just wanted to call to check if you had decided to pick him up early today."

Ashley's blood ran cold. "No. I'm still at work. I've been here since I dropped him off this morning."

"Is there anyone else who might have come to get him instead?"

"No. It's just me."

"Oh dear. Do you want me to call anyone for you?"

"No, thanks. I've got it."

"Okay. I'll ask around here to see if anyone might know where he went. I'll call you if I find out anything."

"Thanks. I appreciate it." She clicked off her phone, her face a mask of worry.

"What's wrong, Ashley? You look pale," Maggie said.

"Emmett ditched his after-school program and I have no idea where he is. He could be anywhere. What if something's happened to him?"

"Hold on, take a breath. Has he ever done something like this before?"

"Yes. More than once. And he always ended up in trouble somewhere. I have to go look for him."

"Of course. I'll cover for you. Call me if you need anything."

Ashley stood up and haphazardly shoved the remains of her cookie into her bag and went to find her son.

CHAPTER
SEVEN

EMMETT STROLLED DOWN a quiet residential street, which he hoped was somewhere near his house. He hadn't wanted to go to the after-school program today, so he ditched it and headed home on his own. He might get a slap on the wrist for it, but it was worth it. All day long he had met all kinds of new people and was coerced into sharing details about himself over and over again. Carson and his friends seemed nice enough, but they didn't go to the after-school program, and Emmett didn't feel like explaining his life story to any more curious teenagers. He'd had enough for one day. Leaving seemed like a good idea. The problem was, he was having some trouble figuring out how to get home.

He walked to the end of another block and decided to turn right. So far, not much seemed familiar. Most of the houses looked the same to him: single story with big porches surrounded by green grass and colorful flowers. At the end of yet another street, he turned right again. He stood on the sidewalk and looked up and down the street to try to get his bearings. Maybe the grey-and-white house across the street looked familiar, but he had passed by others that were similar. Maybe leaving hadn't been such a good idea after all.

He'd been wandering around, trying to find his way for over an hour now, and wasn't sure if he was any closer to figuring out how to get home. He sighed and pulled out his cell phone. Calling his mom to come get him wasn't exactly high on his wish list. He would have to admit that he'd left school without permission and had gotten lost. The school had likely called her by now anyways and she was probably panicked with worry. He kicked the pavement, not wanting to do what he knew he should. Things would only get worse the longer he waited. He guessed he didn't have much of a choice.

***

Wade put down his paintbrush and wiped the sweat from his brow. His old, worn kitchen had needed a makeover for some time now, and since he was currently in between jobs, he finally had some time to work on it. Today he finished putting in the new laminate flooring and started on the cabinets. In the past few hours he removed, cleaned, prepped, sanded, and applied a primer to every kitchen cabinet and drawer. Once they were dry, he would sand them again and give them a nice layer of fresh paint. But now, he needed a drink and something to eat.

He opened his refrigerator and pulled out a Coke and the extra chili he ordered at The Fried Pickle last night. Even though his kitchen was currently in shambles, Wade made sure to keep his microwave hooked up. *A man's gotta eat.* As his food was heating, he took a long draft of his refreshing Coke and looked out the window.

Across the street, he saw a teenage boy pacing back and forth on the sidewalk. His messy auburn-blond hair and lanky gait seemed familiar. Suddenly, a name came to mind: Emmett. That was the boy he caught looking through his garage yesterday—the same boy he saw again at The Fried Pickle last night. Three times in less than twenty-four hours seemed like more than a coincidence. He hoped Emmett's presence was innocent. He seemed like a good kid, and Wade didn't want to see him get into any more trouble.

Wade deliberated whether he should mind his own business or go outside and confront him. Emmett didn't seem to be making any mastermind plans of thieving or otherwise. If anything, he appeared to be troubled about something. Maybe he needed help. If that was the case, Wade could hardly ignore him. He put down his drink and went outside.

***

Emmett watched as a tall, toned man with short dark hair trudged purposely toward him. His ripped jeans and white T-shirt were dirty and splotched with paint. Emmett began to feel afraid and wondered if he should run, but something about the man looked familiar. He'd seen him somewhere before. As the man approached, his face registered a name: Wade. Why did he keep running into Wade?

"Emmett, so we meet again."

"It must be my lucky day," Emmett said sarcastically.

"You look troubled. Is everything okay?"

"Not really. I was trying to go home, but I kind of got turned around. But now that I know this is your house, I think I can find my way."

"What's with the death grip on the cell phone?"

Emmett looked down at his knuckles, turned white from clutching his phone. "I was thinking about calling my mom for help. But, she's at work and I didn't want to bother her on her first day. I guess I was trying to decide what to do."

"She had you walk home on your first day at a new school, in a new town, on an unfamiliar route you never walked before?" Wade asked skeptically.

"Yep." Emmett could see Wade saw right through his lie. Usually, he would stick to his story, but something about this man compelled him to tell the truth. After all, he had been really nice about the garage incident, and he didn't tell his mom about it when he saw them last night. "No. She doesn't know where I am," he confessed.

"Where does she think you are?"

"At the after-school program. She's supposed to pick me up from there around five."

"I'm guessing the school has already called to tell her you never showed up. She's probably really worried about you."

Emmett looked at his shoes. "I know. That's why I was thinking about calling her."

"Why don't you call her and ease her mind?"

***

Ashley anxiously drove up and down streets, trying to think of anywhere she hadn't looked. Emmett wasn't at home, school, the park, or any of the convenience stores in town, and she was running out of ideas. What if he ran away, caught a bus that would take him back to the city and to his delinquent friends who were nothing but trouble? He couldn't afford to make any more mistakes. Palms sweating and heart racing, she started to panic just as her cell phone rang. She rushed to pull it out of her pocket and let out a sigh of relief when Emmett's name flashed across the screen. "Emmett, thank God. Are you okay?"

"Yeah, Mom. I'm fine."

"I've been worried sick about you. Where are you?"

"I'm sitting out front of Wade's house."

50

"Wade? Who's Wade?"

"We met him at The Fried Pickle last night, remember?"

"I remember, now. What are you doing at his house?"

"I was trying to go home, but I got a little lost and ended up in front of his place. He saw me and came out. No big deal."

"You ditched school to go wander around town and then you got lost. It certainly is a big deal, Emmett."

"I told you I didn't want to go. Besides, you didn't say anything about having to go to tutoring."

She could hear his defenses rising. "We will talk about that later. Tell me where Wade lives and I'll come get you."

***

Emmett put his phone back in his pocket. "She's on her way to pick me up. Can I stay here and wait for her?"

"Sure, I'll sit on the porch with you. Do you want a Coke?"

"Okay."

"I'll be right back."

Wade returned shortly, carrying two bottles and his heated bowl of chili. He handed a Coke to Emmett and sat down next to him.

"That smells good. Did you make it?"

Wade barked out a laugh. "Only if you count heating it up in the microwave making it. If I'd actually cooked it, you'd be able to tell by the burned smell."

"What do you eat if you can't cook?"

Wade held up his bowl of chili. "Things I order from restaurants, selections from the frozen food section, or the occasional casserole brought over by a friend."

"That's pathetic. Aren't adults supposed to be able to feed themselves?"

"I can feed myself. It's called reheated cuisine. Besides, I bet you don't know how to cook, either."

"I'm a kid. I've never had to worry about that. I could learn if I wanted to. But why learn when my mom cooks the best stuff?"

"So that you don't end up like me." He took a bite of his chili and chewed. "For now, consider yourself lucky. Anyway, why did you leave the after-school program?"

"I just didn't feel like going. I didn't know anyone, and I was tired of having to tell strangers about my life. I just wanted to go home and get some time to myself, I guess."

"I can understand that. What are you going to do tomorrow?"

Emmett slumped in his seat on the porch. "I don't know. My mom says I have to go unless I can find some other kind of suitable 'adult-supervised' activity," he said using air quotes. "In other words, I have to be babysat until my mom gets home from work, which is complete BS. I'm thirteen, I'm not a baby."

"It sounds like there's more to it than what you're telling me."

Emmett's eyebrows lifted in surprise. Why was it so easy for Wade to read him? And why was Emmett so willing to be honest with him? "Thanks to my probation, I have to have an adult with me at all times, kind of like a toddler. They don't trust me not to get into trouble again."

"Are they wrong?"

"Yes… No… I don't know. I guess I have gotten into some trouble. Maybe I'm just a bad kid."

"I don't think that's true at all."

"You don't even know me."

"You're right. But, from the little I do know about you I can tell you're not a bad kid. I think maybe you have something going on with you that compels you to make some poor choices, but I think you're a good person."

Emmett shook his head. "If you got to know me, you'd see I'm not. Good people don't do the things I've done."

"Even the best people do bad things from time to time. It doesn't make them bad people."

Emmett studied Wade. No adult besides his mom had ever given him the benefit of the doubt. Not only had Wade not called the cops when he found him trying to steal from him, he also treated him like a respectable person, not like the no-good, not-to-be-trusted scoundrel most adults saw him as. "So what are you working on over there?" Emmett gestured to the cabinets laying out in the sun..

"I'm updating my kitchen. The cabinets were in decent shape and I liked the style, so I repaired them. When the primer's dry I'll give them a fresh coat of paint. I also put in a new floor and plan on replacing the countertops."

Emmett suddenly felt nostalgic. "My dad used to do stuff like that."

"Used to?"

"He died when I was nine."

"I'm sorry to hear that. I lost my mom when I was eighteen. Losing a parent can be really hard on a person. Especially, someone as young as you were."

They continued their conversation until an old white sedan pulled up along the curb in front of Wade's house.

"That's my mom. Thanks for letting me wait here."

"Anytime, Emmett. I enjoyed it."

Emmett watched as his mother stepped out of the car and made her way toward the porch. She wore athletic shoes and shapeless medical scrubs, her long blond hair haphazardly tied back. As she powered up the driveway, her face was tight with anger as her blue eyes focused on him.

"It's time to go. You and I have a lot to talk about, young man." Her features softened slightly as she turned her attention to Wade. "Thanks for sitting with Emmett and making sure he was okay. That was very kind of you."

"It was my pleasure. He's a great kid. Can I get you something to drink? It looks like you've had a rough day," Wade offered.

"No thanks. We need to get going. Emmett, get in the car." She gave Emmett her "I dare you to argue with me" look and he stood and went to her side.

"Yeah, okay. Do you think we can hang out again sometime, Wade? I'd love to see what you're doing with your remodel," Emmett said.

Through gritted teeth, she said, "I told you to get in the car."

Wade seemed about to say something but held off. "Maybe we can talk about that another time. You should listen to your mom now," was his only response.

"Okay, later." Emmett looked at his mom's clenched jaw, narrowed eyes, and tense shoulders and knew he was in big trouble. He had screwed up and he was going to get an earful about it. At least she wasn't as mad as the time he was caught stealing those laptops from school. Still, things weren't looking good for him.

CHAPTER
EIGHT

ASHLEY LAY IN the darkness of her bedroom listening to the slow, quiet breathing of the man she loved as he slept peacefully next to her. The sound brought her comfort after so many nights alone. She shifted closer and draped her arm over him, pressing her body against his warm skin.

As she pulled in a deep, blissful breath, the alluring scent of his spicy aftershave filled her nose. Whenever he had been away for too many months, she would take the bottle out of the medicine cabinet so she could appreciate its familiar scent. For a moment, she could pretend he was here with her, keeping her bed warm, instead of fighting for his country thousands of miles away. His aftershave smelled much better on his skin than it did from inside the bottle, and she snuggled into the curve of his neck and took it all in.

As she lay there, sensing the steady rise and fall of his chest, she felt safe and protected. His warmth comforted her, and she let out a deep breath and started to drift off.

Suddenly, his entire body tightened against hers, and she was thrown on her back. His weight pressed her into the mattress, his knees painfully digging into her sides. Terror and confusion replaced safety and bliss. She called out to tell him he was hurting her, but strong hands closed around her neck, cutting off her words and her breath. Pain exploded in her throat as it was crushed under the strength of his grip. White spots danced in front of her eyes, clouding his dark silhouette poised above her. She scratched at his hands and tried to throw him off, but he was too strong. Her lungs burned from lack of air, and she felt herself slipping. She raked her nails against his skin as she tried to pry his hands off of her. She fought and she struggled until her strength left her, and she sank into darkness.

Ashley awoke with a start. Her heart was beating frantically and her sheets were soaked with sweat. She brought her hands to her throat, feeling for damage as she drew air too quickly into her lungs. Her ears were ringing and she felt dizzy as her vision darkened. She feared she would pass out and find herself back in the nightmare. Desperate not to let that happen, she forced herself to slow her breathing until her head cleared and the darkness dissipated. When she had calmed, she could see the grey light of the early dawn spreading across the sky outside her bedroom window. It was morning and she was safe in her bedroom in Mason. It was just a nightmare. She knew the words were true, but she still had to check.

She climbed out of bed and walked to the bathroom. Breathing deeply she prepared herself and stepped toward the sink. When her eyes met her own reflection in the mirror, she was relieved to find no trace of the bruises she expected to see coloring her neck. Though she had seen the proof herself, her gut still wrenched with unease and her limbs shook with fear. She turned on the shower as hot as she could tolerate until the bathroom was so full of steam, she could no longer see her own reflection.

She stepped into the tub and thrust her head underneath the stream, allowing the burning water to cascade over her face and throat. With eyes closed, she let the hot water wash away any lingering effects of the nightmare. As her body and mind relaxed, her thoughts drifted to Emmett.

Last night had been emotional for both of them. In their anger, they'd said things they hadn't meant, and Ashley was already wishing she would've been more patient with him. As she turned around to let the water wash over her back, she recalled one of their exchanges from last night.

"What were you thinking, Emmett? Leaving school without permission to go wander around town. Anything could've happened to you. I was worried sick!"

"I thought the whole reason we moved to this stupid town was that it's supposed to be *so* safe." His voice rose. "So why would you worry about something like that?"

"That's not the point. You didn't do what you were supposed to. You left without permission and without telling anyone. I drove all around town looking for you. Do you have any idea how scared I was?"

"I didn't want to go to tutoring, so I went home," he said matter-of-factly.

"You mean, you tried to go home, but you got lost. Luckily Wade found you before anything bad happened."

"Shut up! I could have found my way back on my own eventually."

"We'll never know, will we? You're always saying how capable you are and that I should trust you. But, how can I when time and time again you don't do what you're supposed to, and you get yourself into bad situations?"

"I was fine. Nothing bad happened to me."

"It could have."

"I can take care of myself. I don't need you always getting in my business. I'm not a little kid."

"Sorry, but that's not going to happen. I'm your mom and it's my job to be in your business. If you want to stop being treated like a little kid all the time, then stop acting like one. Start taking responsibility for your actions and do what you are told."

Emmett balled his fists, his face reddening. "How can I do what I'm told when the things you tell me to do are stupid?"

"I don't ask that much of you. All I want is for you to stay out of trouble and bring your grades up." Ashley crossed her arms. "So from now on, you will go to school, you will go to tutoring, and you will stay at tutoring until I come to pick you up."

"I hate you!"

***

Emmett took the consequences as she'd expected: with excessive amounts of arguing, yelling, and slammed doors. Lately, it seemed like he always reacted this way, which only made things worse for him. Now instead of just no TV for one week, he had earned himself no screen time of any kind for two. He'd also added to his list of extra chores. Thanks to his temper, she didn't have to clean the bathrooms or do the dishes for the next two weeks. That seemed great in theory, but she would much rather he just did what he was supposed to in the first place. She would gladly scrub toilets for the rest of her life if it meant Emmett would stay out of trouble.

He eventually calmed down about his punishments, but he seemed to have a new mission. He had always been known for his successful negotiation tactics, which often scored him what he wanted without having to do much more than what was already expected of him. When he was little he would use his skills to get things like an extra bedtime story, the chance to watch another episode of *Power Rangers*, or an extra cookie. Maybe it was because he was the son of a Marine or maybe it was just a natural gift. Whatever the reason, his tactics usually worked on her.

This time, Emmett negotiated that after tutoring every day, he should be allowed to spend the rest of the afternoon with Wade.

Without quite understanding the reasons behind his request, Ashley went along with it. By the end of the conversation, she found herself agreeing that if Emmett was still at school when she picked him up after work today, they would stop by Wade's on their way home and invite him over for dinner. If Wade got her stamp of approval, they would negotiate something that worked for all of them. So essentially, if Emmett did what he was supposed to in the first place, he would get something extra.

Ashley shut off the water and climbed out of the shower to dry off. Before long she was sitting at the kitchen counter, dressed and ready for work. As she sipped her steaming cup of coffee, Emmett strolled into the kitchen looking awake and ready to go. He grabbed the remaining half of her bagel and stuffed it in into his mouth.

"Were you going to eat that?" he asked, his mouth full of her bagel.

"Does it matter? Do you want my peaches too?"

He either missed her sarcasm or didn't care because he grabbed her plate and inhaled the peach slices in a few bites. "Thanks. So is our deal still on?" he asked.

"I'll hold up my end if you hold up yours."

"I will."

***

After dropping Emmett off at school, she parked her car at the clinic and walked inside. Maggie immediately rushed over and gave her a hug. "How did everything go yesterday? Is Emmett okay?"

"Yes. He called me after I left. Sorry I didn't tell you. We spent the majority of last night talking about what happened and working things out."

"Of course. If my Carson had pulled a stunt like that, he would be grounded for a month. At least. But luckily for me, Carson has

59

learned by now not to mess around with the rules. My husband Robbie has always been able to keep him in line one way or another."

"It can't hurt that Robbie is a deputy."

"True. He's used the role to his advantage before, not that I condone him doing that. I'm just glad I'm not the one who has to do it. I don't know how you raise a teenage boy all alone. I admire you, Ashley."

Ashley thought of Emmett's rebellious nature and unstable emotions and felt like she didn't deserve anyone's admiration. She tried hard, but she wasn't sure she was doing such a good job with him.

"We have a pup here that has been having some tummy issues. Can you help me examine him?" Maggie asked.

"Sure thing, Dr. Miller."

Maggie gave Ashley an irritated look. "Don't start with that Dr. Miller crap."

Ashley laughed. "Yes, Maggie."

The morning went smoothly and passed quickly into afternoon, thanks to the cheerful environment and good company. Ashley and Maggie chatted about various things as they looked after their furry patients. If it weren't for the tiredness creeping back into her body from her poor night's sleep or her thoughts about the whole Wade thing, she may have considered it a good day. As Ashley prepped the vaccines for their next patient—a floppy cocker spaniel puppy named Floyd—she couldn't put a stop to her need for information. "So, Maggie. What can you tell me about Wade Hudson?"

Maggie looked at Ashley and a knowing grin spread across her face. "Does someone have a little crush on the town's sexy contractor?"

"What? Of course not."

"Don't be afraid to admit it, girl. You wouldn't be the first one to fall for my cousin's perfect manners and even more perfect body."

"Wade is your cousin? I guess Mason really is a small town."

"You haven't even scratched the surface. What do you want to know about him? Wait, before I say anything you should know that Wade hasn't shown much interest in dating lately."

"It's a good thing I'm not looking to date him then. I'm not interested for me, I'm interested for Emmett."

"You're going to have to give me more information."

Ashley chuckled as Maggie's eyebrows furrowed in confusion. "It's not what you think. When Emmett ditched the after-school program yesterday, he was trying to find his way home, and he ended up in front of Wade's house. They must have talked or bonded or something because now Emmett wants to spend his afternoons with him until I get off work. I don't get it. And I don't know how I feel about it."

Maggie laughed at the concerned expression on Ashley's face. "I can see you're thinking the worst."

"Candy in a van did cross my mind, no offense to your cousin or anything. Where I'm from, you have to be cautious if you want to be safe."

Maggie chuckled and shook her head. "I can guarantee Wade isn't trying to lure Emmett in for any reason. Wade is one of the most genuine, trustworthy men I know."

She wasn't convinced. "But don't you think it's weird he would bond so easily with a thirteen-year-old boy? I mean, Emmett never asks to spend his time with a responsible adult. So my thought is that Emmett really doesn't want to go to the after-school program or he sees Wade as an attractive alternative for some reason."

"It could be a mix of both, but he's your son, not mine. You'll have to find out from him if you really want to know."

"I tried. But all I got from him was that Wade seemed cool."

Maggie chuckled. "Oh, the thorough explanation of the teenage boy. But to answer your question, no I don't think it's weird for Wade to bond with Emmett so easily. Wade pretty much raised his brother all on his own. Ford had a lot of run-ins with the law and eventually landed himself in prison. The whole thing has been really hard on Wade. You've said Emmett has been getting in trouble with the law for the last few years too. Maybe he reminds him of his brother."

"First of all, I don't see how he could possibly know about Emmett's past. And second of all, are you saying Wade might see Emmett as some kind of charity case or person he can fix? Because if that's the case, there's no way in hell I'm letting him spend time with my son. Emmett doesn't need some so-called male role model telling him he isn't good enough!"

"Ashley, if you don't relax, you're going to pop those syringes, and I don't think you want rabies vaccine all over your hands."

Ashley loosened her grip and blew out a breath.

"Besides, I wasn't saying anything of the sort," Maggie continued. "You drew that conclusion about Wade all on your own. Wade is a good guy. You can trust him."

"But is he responsible?"

Maggie gave her a look. "At the age of eighteen, he stepped up to be a father for his three-year-old brother. What do you think?"

"But his brother is in prison. What does that say about Wade as a parent?"

"Please don't make me say it."

"Say what?"

"Emmett has been to juvie and arrested. Many times. Does that make you a bad parent? Of course not. Sometimes kids go astray no matter what you do."

"I guess you're right," Ashley admitted. "I just need to protect him. I can't stand the thought of him getting hurt." *Not after what he's been through,* she finished silently.

"I get it. You're looking out for your son. But you have to let go at some point. You can't protect him from everything."

Ashley knew that better than anyone.

Mended

CHAPTER
NINE

ASHLEY FROWNED AT herself in the car mirror. Her blond hair was tied back in a messy ponytail. Wisps of hair stuck out at various angles thanks to a busy day at the clinic and the southern humidity. She groaned and tried to smooth it down without success. Her hair had always had a mind of its own. Why would today be any different? Most of her light makeup had worn off by the end of the day, and all she had in the way of touch-up was some cheap tinted lip balm. She put that on and gave the mirror a pouty look.

Feeling ridiculous, she flipped the mirror closed and gave herself a mental slap across the face. It didn't matter how she looked anyway. It's not like she was trying to impress anyone. Just because Wade was handsome, it didn't mean she had to make herself look good to talk to him. Not like that was even possible today with the way her hair was behaving. Never mind that she was wearing shapeless scrubs covered in little dog biscuits. She loved her job, but the wardrobe was not at all flattering.

Ashley watched Emmett as he moved toward her car, his backpack slung over one shoulder. He looked bright and lively today, which probably had something to do with the fact that he was getting his way.

"Hey, sweetie. How was school today?"

Emmett climbed in the car beside her and tossed his backpack into the back seat. "Fine."

"How did tutoring go?"

"Fine."

"Did you finish all your homework."

"Yep."

"Do you have any more studying to do?"

"Some."

It was like trying to get information from a parrot. She recalled a tip she'd learned from a past counselor about asking open-ended questions to try to engage further conversation. "What do you have to study for?"

"Math."

Well, she tried.

"So, I went to tutoring. That means we're going to ask Wade if I can hang with him after school, right?"

"We'll stop by his place on our way home and invite him to dinner so I can get to know him. I'll talk to him about the rest of it if I feel comfortable with everything. And you won't be spending time with him until after your tutoring sessions every day," she clarified.

"Ugh. Fine."

"Why do you want this so much?"

"I told you. He's cool."

"That's what I've heard, but that doesn't really give me much to go off of."

"You wouldn't understand."

"Try me."

"I don't know. I guess I feel like he doesn't judge me. He listens to me and tries to understand me instead of just forming his own opinion about me, unlike most adults."

"I listen to you."

"Yeah, but you're my mom. It's not the same thing."

"Okay, any other reasons?"

"He knows a lot about building and fixing things, and I thought maybe he could show me how." He averted his gaze. "You probably think it's stupid."

Emmett had always loved helping his father fix things around their house. When Emmett was six, Jeff had bought him his very own tool kit. Equipped with the basics—hammer, screwdriver, level, wrench—Emmett had loved using his tools to help Jeff hang pictures on the wall, tighten loose screws, change the batteries in his toys, and help with other basic home repairs. The memory of a six-year-old Emmett wearing an oversized tool bet made her smile.

"I don't think it's stupid at all. I wish you wouldn't think so little of me. I'm sure if you like him, I'll like him too," she said.

"Yeah right. You didn't like any of my friends."

"I think this will be different. Do you want to come with me to ask him?"

"No. I'd rather you do it."

"Okay. I'll be right back."

As Ashley stepped out of the car and walked to Wade's front door, a disconcerting thought crossed her mind. Here she was on her way to ask a very attractive man over for dinner while she looked like a mess from work. It wasn't as though she was asking him out on a date or anything; this was merely an innocent, "get to know you dinner." But what if he got the wrong idea? It's not like she could keep pretending she was still married forever. Suddenly feeling nervous, she hesitated before knocking on the door. *This is for Emmett.* As she waited, she repeated the mantra in her head, hoping to gather strength from it.

"Just a minute!" a deep, muffled voice called out from somewhere in the house, followed shortly by the sound of boots on wood floors.

The big black door in front of her opened to reveal a sweaty, mouth-gaping, turn-your-head-to-stare, dirty Wade in ripped jeans and an old plaid shirt. A range of emotions flitted across his face as he took in his unexpected visitor: surprise, worry, and pleasure? "Ashley. Is everything okay? Did something happen to Emmett?"

"No, no. It's nothing like that. Emmett's fine."

He visibly relaxed. "Good. What can I do for you? And sorry about the mess. I've been working on my kitchen." He gestured to himself.

"I'm sorry to just drop by like this, but I didn't know how else to reach you. Usually I would call first, but since I don't have your phone number, I didn't see how I could do that very easily. So, I just decided to stop by on my way home from work. I hope that isn't rude." *Oh. My. God.* Why was she rambling so much? She was babbling like an idiot in her dog biscuit scrubs. Emmett was right, she was embarrassing. *Get to the point.* "I stopped by to invite you over for dinner tonight."

His eyebrows lifted in surprise. "Dinner? Tonight? With you?"

"Yes. If you're not busy."

"Like a date?"

"No. God, no. Not a date. I just wanted to repay you for what you did for Emmett yesterday. And I thought it would be nice to get to know one another since we seem to keep running into each other. Not a date. Just a home-cooked meal. With me. And Emmett. Emmett will be there too. If you don't have any dinner plans already." *Oh my God. Stop talking.*

A smile played on the corners of his lips. "I don't have any dinner plans tonight. And a home-cooked meal sounds a whole lot better than what I planned to eat tonight."

"Okay. Great."

"Great."

"Then we'll see you tonight."

"What time do you want me to come over?" he asked.

"Oh, um how does six thirty sound?"

"Sounds good."

"Good."

"Where do you live?"

Why was she being so awkward? "Sorry. 1211 Magnolia Street. We're the white-and-blue house at the end of the street."

"I'll see you at six thirty. I promise I won't come over smelling like this."

"You smell fine." What was wrong with her?

He gave her a polite smile. "I'll see you tonight."

"Oh, I almost forgot. Do you have any kind of dietary restrictions or anything?"

"No. I'll eat pretty much anything."

"Okay. That makes it easy. See you soon. Bye."

As she turned and walked back to her car, she was dumbfounded by her level of awkwardness. What had happened back there? Maybe it was just general discomfort about the whole situation. It wasn't like she had much, or any, practice inviting strange men over to her house for dinner. She was probably just nervous because she didn't want Wade to get the wrong idea and think she was looking for a romantic relationship. That part of her life was over. Or maybe it was partly because she was self-conscious about her after-work appearance. Whatever it was, she needed to get herself together. Tonight was about figuring out if letting Emmett spend time with Wade was a good idea. She needed to at least be able to form intelligent sentences.

Mended

CHAPTER
TEN

ASHLEY GREETED WADE with a warm smile. In place of the scrubs, she wore a striped top and dark-wash blue jeans that hugged her curves. Her long, golden hair hung in waves around her shoulders and down her back. The blue stripes on her shirt brought out her eyes, which glimmered like the sea in the late afternoon sun. Even angry and wearing shapeless scrubs, she was beautiful. But now, she took his breath away.

"I'm glad you could make it. Please come in."

Ashley's home was warm and inviting, decorated with curtains and mismatched furniture that somehow fit together despite the differences. Simple touches—fresh flowers in decorated pots, a colorful rug, pictures in frames, and various knickknacks—added color and hominess and gave Wade some insight into the person who put them there.

"You have a lovely home," he said.

Her full pink lips curved up into a smile, and her big blue eyes lit up as she looked around the room. "Thank you. I just love it here. It feels like home, you know?"

"You have good taste."

"Thank you. I bought most of the furniture at garage sales and secondhand stores. But you can find some really great things if you know where to look."

Wade picked up a framed photograph from the beech wood bookcase. Ashley stood next to a man in a military uniform. His arms were wrapped around her in a warm embrace, and she leaned her head on his shoulder. Between them, a young boy with reddish-blond hair stood, clinging to the man's leg. All of them wore elated smiles, their joy clearly evident. "Is this your husband?" he asked.

"Yes. That's my Jeff."

"What branch of the military was he in?"

"Marines. This picture was taken right after he finished his first tour."

"Did he die in action?" Wade asked with sympathy.

"I never told you he died. How did you know?"

He looked at her apologetically. "Emmett told me."

"Oh."

Wade thought she looked surprised.

"No. He was retired from the military for almost two years when he died."

Wade knew grief when he saw it. It was the eyes. They always looked so hopeless. "I'm sorry for your loss. That must have been tragic. You all looked so happy."

"We were."

He studied the picture more closely. "Wow, Emmett looks so much like him."

"Yeah. Except for the hair color, he looks exactly like a younger Jeff."

Wade put the picture gently back in its place on the bookshelf with all the others. "It smells delicious in here." He was so hungry, his stomach rumbled in anticipation.

"Thank you. It's just about ready. I made us chicken pot pies. I make them small so we can all have our own. That way we get more crust."

"I like the way you think."

"Why don't you have a seat and I'll bring everything out."

"Let me help you."

"You're our guest. I insist. Plus, I have Emmett to help me. He's my own personal slave for the next two weeks thanks to his choice to ditch school." She smirked a bit. "Please sit. The dining table is right through there. I'll be right back."

Ashley returned shortly, carrying pot holders and two single cup-sized chicken pot pies. Emmett trailed behind her, carrying a third, along with a casserole dish.

"Nice to see you, Emmett," Wade said.

Emmett nodded in greeting.

Ashley carefully placed a steaming pie in front of him. "Be careful. It's really hot."

After she and Emmett made a few more trips, the table was filled with delicious-looking food: individual chicken pot pies, green bean casserole, fresh dinner rolls, and a pitcher of sweet iced tea. "Please eat. Let me know if you need anything else," Ashley said.

"Everything looks so delicious. Thank you." Wade took a bite of his pot pie and almost moaned out loud. It was the best he'd ever tasted. She had beauty, charm, and skill in the kitchen. He was in trouble if he wasn't careful. Everyone knew that the fastest way to Wade's heart was through his stomach. "This is delicious. I could eat about four of these."

She gave him a genuine smile. "I was hoping you'd say that. I made extra."

"You really didn't have to go to so much trouble for me."

"I'm happy to. It's nice to cook for someone else for a change. It helps to get an outside opinion."

"Well, my opinion is I will eat whatever you put in front of me."

He wasn't kidding. Three pot pies, three servings of green bean casserole, two glasses of sweet ice tea, and two dinner rolls were stretching the clasp on his jeans to the max. Wade wiped his mouth with his napkin and suppressed a belch. "That was the best dinner I've had in as long as I can remember." He also couldn't remember the last time he'd been so full.

The company had been a close match. A certain level of awkwardness is usually to be expected when dining in the home of a virtual stranger, but surprisingly, there hadn't been any. The conversation had flowed easily between Ashley and him as if they'd known each other their whole lives.

They'd covered the basics of a "get to know you meal," but the conversation also went deeper than that. Wade usually didn't like talking about himself much, especially the aspects of his life that were personal, but somehow she made him want to talk about it. Something about her kind smile, genuine interest, and understanding demeanor made him comfortable. Emmett had seemed interested in his work and what he knew about dirt bikes. His eyes had lit up when Wade told him how he used to race them when he was Emmett's age.

"I don't want to impose upon you any further. I'll just clear my dish and move on out. Thank you for your hospitality," Wade said.

"Emmett will clear the dishes. I was hoping that you and I could talk over dessert. I made homemade ice cream for our apple pie."

Despite the uncomfortable fullness in his stomach and the indigestion creeping into his chest, he was tempted. "That sounds delicious, but I think my stomach might kill me if I try to cram anything else in there right now. I'd love to take some home with me for later, though, if you don't mind."

"Sure. You're welcome to take the last pot pie home with you too. But, if you could stay just a few more minutes I'd really appreciate it. I have something I'd like to talk to you about."

He was intrigued. "Okay, no problem. What is it?"

She glanced behind her to make sure they were alone and turned to him. Before she spoke, she started playing with her hair. "This is probably going to seem like a weird request since we just met and all, and you're under no obligation to say yes. But you seem like a great guy... and I know Emmett likes you. And, well, he begged me to ask you this."

She was rambling again. He put his hand gently on the one in her hair and she stilled and put it in her lap. "Sorry. Nervous habit. Anyways, Emmett and I were wondering how you'd feel about him spending some time with you in the afternoons after tutoring."

"Emmett asked about this?"

"Yes. Which is absolutely huge for him. He must really like you."

"What did he say exactly?"

"He said he thinks you're really cool and he likes that you seem to know your way around a power tool. His dad was always Mr. Fixit and would often let Emmett be his assistant. I think he misses that. But, ultimately he wants to learn how to fix things. He's always expressed an interest in it, but I could never show him how. I have to hire someone to change a lightbulb."

Stunned, Wade didn't know what to say. Emmett wanted to hang out with him because he reminded him of his dad? How could he possibly fill that role? He wasn't father material. Sure, Emmett was a great kid and he wanted the best for him, but could he give him this? He'd tried playing dad before and it hadn't turned out so well. He wasn't exactly thrilled about the idea. There were too many unknowns.

He must have been quiet for some time because Ashley said, "I'm sorry. I know it's a lot to ask. You don't have to answer right now. I don't want to pressure you."

"I'm flattered, really I am. Emmett is a great kid, but I don't think I'm the right person to ask. My schedule is so unpredictable. Sure, I'm in between jobs right now, but I could get hired for a new project tomorrow and I wouldn't want to make plans I'd have to break."

"I'd be happy to compensate you for your time."

"It's not about that."

"Okay. I understand. No hard feelings." She said the words, but the look on her face told a different story. "Thanks for considering it. I don't want to take up any more of your time. I'll just wrap up your food and then you can be on your way."

"Thanks. I appreciate it. And I'm sorry." Her generosity and kindness made him feel guilty.

She came back minutes later with his leftovers and a worried look on her face. A door slammed shut down the hall and shook the small house. "Here you go. It was nice getting to know you."

Wade recognized the dismissal. "Thank you again for dinner."

As he started his walk home, he tried to convince himself that he'd done the right thing. Ashley might not see it now, but if she knew him better she wouldn't have even asked him to mentor her son. He wasn't the right person for that kind of role. Just look how his brother had turned out.

He pictured Emmett sprawled out, angry and disappointed on his bed. He understood that feeling all too well. The boy needed a positive male role model in his life, but Wade just wasn't the right person for the job. He'd done the right thing saying no. As he walked home, a gnawing thought consumed him: if he had really done the right thing, then why did he feel so terrible right now?

CHAPTER
ELEVEN

AFTER A LONG week, Ashley was glad it was Friday. Ever since Wade's rejection, Emmett's behavior had been worse than usual. Ditching classes, giving her attitude, leaving his assignments incomplete, and violating his probation were all on the list. Yesterday she'd been called down to the school after he was caught trying to steal a wallet from a student's backpack.

The thought of something like this happening had kept her up at night. Emmett was a sensitive boy and rejection could have a drastic effect on him. Aware of the risks, she'd made the mistake of asking Wade anyways.

She truly thought things were going to be different here. Unfortunately, Emmett seemed motivated enough to find ways to get in trouble no matter where they lived. His behavior drew the attention of his probation officer, which meant a meeting with her next week. Ashley worried what that might entail and hoped Emmett wasn't heading toward another trip to juvenile detention.

Spending time there always made things worse. She needed to find something to help snap him out of it.

When Ashley pulled up to Emmett's school, she turned to him before he could open the car door. "No more detentions today, please. I'd like to make it through one day without getting a call from your school."

"I can't make any promises," he said.

"If you get through the whole day without starting any trouble, we'll go out for ice cream after I pick you up."

He looked insulted. "I'm not five. You can't bribe me with ice cream anymore."

"Is there anything I can bribe you with?"

"Don't make me go to that stupid barbecue tomorrow."

"We were both invited to the Millers' house, so we are both going. Besides, Carson is really looking forward to spending some time with you."

"Great," he said sarcastically.

"What's wrong with Carson?"

"He's such a nerd."

"Hey! He's a nice boy. Give him a chance."

"Like I said, he's a nerd." He moved to get out of the car.

"I'll pick you up a little after five. Please try to have a good day. It's Friday!"

He frowned and slid out of the car. Ashley watched as he trudged to the front of the school, his backpack slung over one shoulder. *Let it be a good day*, she silently pleaded.

***

"Is there anything I can bring tomorrow?" Ashley asked Maggie as she took a blood sample from a massive orange tabby cat on the exam table.

"You can bring your beautiful self and that handsome son of yours," Maggie said.

"Are you sure? I always feel weird coming to a party empty-handed."

"You're my guest. I don't want you to lift a finger. Besides, you've had a rough enough week as it is. Just come over, relax, and have a good time."

"Thanks again for the invite. I've really been looking forward to it. I'm hoping it'll give Emmett a chance to get to know Carson a little better."

"Carson said that Emmett's been a little distant at school. He's nice enough to him—he just seems like he doesn't want much to do with him."

"I'm sorry about that. It's not Carson's fault. Emmett tends to only show interest in the 'cool kids,' which basically means the troublemakers. He tends to push away anyone he thinks doesn't fit into that category. That's why the whole Wade thing surprised me so much."

"It was too bad Wade said no. That could've been good for Emmett."

"He took the rejection pretty hard. But you already know all about that because of all the calls I've been getting at work," Ashley said apologetically.

Maggie waved her hand away in a dismissive gesture. "How is all of that going to affect his probation?"

"I talked to his probation officer at lunch and she agreed not to have him arrested for now. We have a meeting next week to talk about a possible house arrest, but I don't know for sure. She did say this is his last chance. If he gets into any more trouble, she'll take him into custody. I'm freaking out. I don't want him to go back there."

"That sounds stressful. Does Emmett know how serious all of this is?"

"Yes, but it doesn't seem to change his behavior. He's been through all of this before. I don't think he wants to go back there, but I'm worried the threat of that place might not be enough."

"You're doing all you can. The choice is really up to Emmett now. I wonder if this would have happened if Wade had agreed to take him on."

"I don't know." Ashley shrugged. "This is just how Emmett has been the past few years. There was a moment when I thought he was changing, but maybe I was wrong. Maybe having a positive role model like Wade would've helped, maybe it wouldn't have. He said no, so I guess it doesn't matter much."

"I honestly thought Wade would have at least considered it," Maggie said thoughtfully. "Did he tell you why he said no?"

She told her Wade's explanation as she stroked the cat's soft orange fur.

Maggie furrowed her eyebrows. "That sounds like an excuse to me. I'll talk to him and see if I can figure out what's going on."

"Please don't." Ashley shook her head. "I don't want to make things awkward."

"You could ask him about it. He's going to be there tomorrow."

"Seeing him after his rejection might be awkward enough as it is. I don't want to make things worse."

"Something else is going on here and someone should find out what it is. I'll talk to him."

"Maggie, don't. Please leave it alone."

"It won't be a big deal." She placed a hand on Ashley's shoulder. "He's used to me pestering him about his business. Don't worry, I'll make sure he knows you had nothing to do with it."

"It's not like Wade is obligated to spend time with Emmett. It's not like he owes us something. If anything, I overstepped by asking him. Wade doesn't even know us," Ashley countered.

Maggie pursed her lips. "That's not the point. Wade wasn't completely honest with you about his reasons, and I want to find out why."

Ashley sighed. "I don't even know if spending time with Wade would make any kind of positive difference."

"But, it probably wouldn't have hurt, either," Maggie said. "Look, I understand how you feel, Ashley, but I'm not talking to him only for your and Emmett's sakes. I'm also doing it for Wade."

Mended

CHAPTER
TWELVE

IT WAS A warm, breezy Friday afternoon: the perfect conditions for enjoying an ice cream at the park. It turned out that even though Emmett wasn't five anymore, he could still be enticed with the promise of ice cream before dinner. Ashley was just grateful to have made it through the day without a call from Emmett's school. As long as she didn't bring attention to the bribe she had made him this morning, she was safe to enjoy the creamy treat with her favorite boy.

The park surrounding their seat on the bench hummed with activity. Children laughed as they climbed, swung, and chased each other on the playground. Parents ran around with their children, playing games and chasing escaping toddlers. Families seated at picnic tables talked and laughed while they enjoyed their food. Couples held hands as they strolled through the park, basking in the glow of romance.

In the center of it all, a local band played live music from a stage underneath a white gazebo, filling the park with their lively honky-tonk music. People milled about, enjoying themselves as they danced energetically to the music.

Being here reminded her of the days she had spent with her family at the park. Emmett would race her and Jeff to the swings, his little legs pounding the ground as quickly as he could make them go. She remembered his proud, toothy grin and the rapid rise and fall of his little chest as he reached the swings first and tried to catch his breath. Seconds later, she and Jeff would jog up behind him, pretending to huff and puff and grab the fake stitches in their sides, further widening Emmett's grin.

Jeff would push Emmett on the swing until he reached a height that made her shudder with worry. All the while, Emmett laughed and squealed with delight as he begged Jeff to push him higher.

The three of them ran around together, playing games like hot lava monster or jet pilot until they all collapsed on the grass, completely spent. Sometimes she and Jeff sat together as they watched Emmett collect park treasures, the weight of her husband's arm resting comfortably around her shoulders. If she closed her eyes, she could almost feel his warm breath in her ear when he whispered that he loved her. The welcome melodies of their family's laughter and delight filled her ears often those days. Now, hearing those sounds coming from other people's families made her heart ache for what she no longer had.

Ashley watched Emmett eat his ice cream cone while he silently observed the activity around them. His face and body language suggested he was relaxed, but when she looked closer she could see an underlying sadness there. "What are you thinking about?" she asked.

He turned toward her, his bright hazel eyes glistening just a little and his mouth downturned. "Being here reminds me of when we used to go to the park with Dad."

"I was actually just thinking about that too. We had a lot of fun together on those days, didn't we? Do you remember when Dad got that remote-control helicopter?"

"Oh yeah. What happened to that thing?"

"The first time he tried to fly it he got it stuck in a tree. There must have been a nest up there because as soon as he started climbing the branches to get it, two mockingbirds swooped down and started pecking at him. They chased him all the way to the other end of the park."

A small smile played on Emmett's lips. "Wasn't it stuck up there for a while?"

"Nearly a week. Every time he tried to get it, the birds would launch a full-blown attack. It took five days and two bird-induced bald spots for him to think to put on a helmet. Luckily, his pride wouldn't allow him to be thwarted by a couple of little birds, so he eventually got his helicopter back. He was always careful about where he flew it after that." She smiled as she thought about her heavily muscled, six-foot-three Marine husband cowering in the tree as the little birds dove at him, his light brown hair clutched in their beaks. "Whenever anyone asked about his bald patches, he'd always tell them an old barber dozed off during his haircut."

"Oh yeah, I remember that. But Dad didn't go to a barber so everyone knew he was lying."

"Yes. That, and we made a point of telling everyone about the killer mockingbirds."

They laughed together. Ashley watched as Emmett's smile slowly changed back to a frown. "It's okay to feel sad," she said. "Sometimes talking about him makes me smile, but other times it can make me want to cry. It's hard to be the ones left behind."

Emmett swallowed and looked down at his sneakers. His breath caught on his next inhale and wavered as he exhaled.

"Do you want to talk about it?" she asked.

He shook his head and kept his eyes on his shoes as he kicked the pavement.

"I miss him so much. We were happy, you know? The three of us. He was a good man and he loved us very much. Sometimes life can be so cruel." Tears welled in the corners of her eyes and rolled silently down her cheeks. There were times when her heart still ached for the only man she ever loved. Although time continued to heal her, she had lost a part of herself the day he died—a piece she wasn't sure she would ever regain. She thought of the horror the night Jeff died and chills ran down her spine. She could have lost everything that night. She turned toward Emmett and gently placed her hand over his. "I'm thankful every day I still have you."

At her words, Emmett ripped his hand away from hers. When he turned to her, a mixture of anger and pain crossed his face. "Then why are you always so sad that he's gone?" His voice rose. "How can you still cry about him after what he did to you, to us?"

"He's your father, Emmett. I will always love him. He didn't mean to do what he did. He loved us. And in the end, he did what he had to do to protect us."

"You're delusional." Emmett pounded the bench. "He's not some kind of superhero, no matter what you say. A hero wouldn't have done what he did."

"He was sick, Emmett. You need to cut him some slack."

"No, the problem is you cut him too much slack. You did it then, and you're still doing it now."

"Emmett, he's your father. He loved us more than anything."

"I don't want to talk about him anymore," he yelled. Fists balled, he shook his head furiously as if he were trying to forget and took off running, disappearing into the crowd.

CHAPTER
THIRTEEN

ASHLEY NO LONGER heard the noises around her. It felt as if she was in a fog, as if nothing here was real. The only thing that mattered was finding Emmett. She ran every which way, pushing her way through the crowd as she called his name. Her own voice sounded distant to her. She continued to search for him, but she was becoming more frantic with every minute. It was difficult to focus. Her breath came in short gasps and her stomach churned. People in the crowd began to stare at her. She vaguely heard concerned voices, asking if she was okay or how they could help, but she was too panicked to hear them.

Suddenly, warm, strong arms caught her, and a deep smoky voice called her name. She tried to shake off what was holding her, but the more she struggled, the more it tightened around her, refusing to let her go. She felt herself being spun around and looked into familiar dark brown eyes full of concern.

"Ashley. Tell me what's wrong." Wade's words woke her from her trance.

"Emmett's gone. He was really upset and he ran off. I can't find him anywhere." Her voice caught and she bit her lip. Tears splashed over her warm cheeks.

"Which direction did he go?" Wade asked.

She turned in all directions to find the bench where they'd been sitting. Emmett's ice cream cone lay broken on the sidewalk, leaving a puddle as it melted in the warm afternoon. She pointed to a spot to their left. "He disappeared into the crowd over there."

Beyond the spot she indicated lay a line of thick foliage.

"I'll go look for him," Wade said.

"I'll come with you."

"I think it would be better if you waited here in case he comes back."

"He's my son. I can't just wait around here and do nothing. I have to find him."

"I know the area better than you do. I think I'll be able to find him faster on my own. Do you have your cell phone with you?"

"Of course," she said as she pulled it out for him.

He quickly entered his phone number and handed it back to her. "Send me a text so I have your number and call me if you need to get a hold of me. Okay?"

"Okay."

"Call the sheriff if you don't hear from me in ten minutes."

Her eyes widened. "What? The sheriff? What's in there?"

"Everything will be fine," he said, but his furrowed brow said something else.

"Stay here. Don't go wandering in those trees, or we may end up with two people to find." With those words, Wade walked purposely to the woods and disappeared among the trees.

***

Walking past the line of trees was like entering a different world. The music at the park, blaring in his ears only moments before, now sounded like a distant whisper. The bright rays of the warm afternoon sun were blocked by a canopy of trees, making the light around him as dim as dusk. Bird songs resounded from the trees around him. The sounds of excited chatter and rustling of small animals filled the air as they moved through the thicket. The air was cooler here, by ten degrees at least, and a gentle breeze tickled his skin. The fresh smells of dirt, lush greenery, and sap filled his nose as he breathed it all in. Rich, earthy, and sweet mingled together to create the pleasing smell of nature.

Somewhere among the thick rows of trees around him lay the steep banks of the creek. If someone unfamiliar with the area wasn't paying close attention, they could easily fall the twenty feet down to the creek bed. When Wade was a kid, he was playing with his mom at the park when their dog got loose and chased a squirrel into these trees. They found him in the ravine of the creek, his neck broken. Wade's throat tightened. He needed to find Emmett quickly.

Thick in the undergrowth, he looked around to get his bearings and assess his surroundings. His phone vibrated in his pocket and he pulled it out to look at it. He had a text from Ashley that read: "Any sign of him?" He quickly texted her back: "It's only been two minutes. I'll let you know when I've found him." He put his phone back in his pocket and started his search.

He trudged through bushes and over rocks. Low hanging branches and sticks in bushes scratched at his skin, and the silk of spiderwebs clung to his face and neck. Up ahead, he saw muddy shoe prints leading toward the hidden edge of a cliff. Beyond, was a sheer twenty-foot drop to the creek below. A broken tree branch, stripped of its leaves, swung in the slight breeze on the brink. *No, please no.*

He treaded carefully as he approached the edge. He grabbed hold of a thick tree branch and tested it to see if it would hold his weight. Gripping it tightly to steady himself, he held his breath as he leaned forward to peer over the edge.

Nothing lay below him except the trickling creek and the vegetation growing on its banks. He called out Emmett's name. The only response was the echo of his own voice and the sound of flowing water over rocks. He slowly backed away from the ledge and blew out a relieved breath. Moving away from the cliff face, he continued his search.

A few yards ahead, he caught sight of more muddy shoe prints. As he passed through the next line of trees, he saw him. Emmett sat hunched on a fallen tree, his elbows resting on his skinny knees, his hands knotted in his rust-blond hair. "Emmett," Wade called.

As Emmett looked up, Wade caught a brief glimpse of inner turmoil. Pain turned to recognition, which then turned to irritation. Emmett quickly wiped the tears from his cheeks and scowled. "What do you want?"

Wade held up his hands and approached him cautiously as if he were a skittish doe who might flee at any moment. "I ran into your mom at the park and she told me you ran off."

"So she sent you to find me?"

"No. I offered to look for you. She wanted to come, but I told her to stay at the park."

Emmett glared at him. "Why the hell would you do that? You don't care about me."

"Your mom was in need of a friend, and I wanted to help. But I also did it because I do care about you, Emmett. I don't want to see you get hurt."

"Bullshit. You don't want anything to do with me. You made that very clear."

"That's not fair. I think you're a great kid, Emmett. Like I told your mom, as an independent contractor, I never know when—"

"That's a load of crap and you know it," Emmett snapped, cutting him off. "I didn't believe your lame excuse then and I'm not buying it now. I'm not going to sit here and listen to your crappy lies." He stood and made a move to push past Wade. "I'm out of here."

Wade grabbed hold of his arm to stop him. "Emmett, wait!"

Emmett threw off his hand and whirled to face him. "Why? So you can feed me more lies? I'm not stupid, you know."

"No. You're clearly not stupid. But your mom is worried sick, so please come back with me."

"I'm not going anywhere with you," he said defiantly as he threw himself back down on the fallen tree.

Wade approached him slowly and sat down next to him. "You're right, I did lie to you before."

"Duh."

"If I tell you the truth, will you walk back with me?"

"That depends on what the truth is."

Wade inhaled and blew out a breath. He couldn't back down now. If he did, he ran the risk of Emmett not trusting him, and he wasn't sure he wanted to close the door on that just yet. "Okay, give me a minute to collect my thoughts, all right?"

"I'm not giving you time to make up another lame excuse. It's now or never."

Emmett's piercing stare told Wade everything he needed to know: he was serious. "Fine. When your mom asked me about mentoring you I panicked so I made up an excuse to get out of it."

"So it is because you don't want anything to do with me. I knew it." Emmett moved to stand, but Wade put out his arm to stop him.

"No, I didn't say that. Let me finish. I panicked because I was worried that I wouldn't do a good job."

"A good job at what? It's a few hours a week in the afternoons. It's not like you're adopting me."

"I know that. But, if you're going to hang around with me, I want to make sure I can be a good role model for you. I don't want to screw it up."

"What do you mean?"

"I've already told you I have a brother. Our mom died of a heart condition when he was three and my dad became useless because of it. So I pretty much raised him all on my own. I must have done a pretty poor job at it too because he's in prison."

"Oh." Emmett paused for a moment to take in the news. "Well, you can't screw me up. If I end up in prison, it won't be because of you."

"What if it is because of me? Would you really want to take that chance?"

Emmett scoffed. "Don't flatter yourself, dude. You have less influence than you think."

Wade shot Emmett an amused look, the corners of his mouth turning upward. "Well, you really know how to kick a man when he's down, don't you?"

"What I'm saying is, I can think for myself. I'm not a gullible little baby."

"Why do you want to hang out with me anyway?" Wade asked.

Emmett's gaze shifted to his hands as he fiddled with his fingers. "I thought you were cool. You know, before all that cover-story crap. When you found me in your garage, you could've treated me like a criminal like everyone else, but you didn't. You didn't even turn me in. You talked to me like a real person and made me feel like you actually cared. I just thought maybe you liked me too and that you might be willing to teach me a little about fixing or building things."

"I do like you, Emmett. That's why I said no because I didn't want to risk hurting you."

"You hurt me by lying."

"I can see that now. I wouldn't mind having you around and teaching you some things from my trade."

Emmett seemed to perk up. "Once I learn a few things, I could help you on some of your house projects or something. Or I could help you fix up those old dirt bikes in your garage."

"I'm not one to deny free labor."

"Does that mean you'll do it?"

"I'll think about it."

"Dude, all you have to do is make sure I don't kill myself or do something illegal."

"I said I'll think about it. I'll talk to your mom about it at the barbecue tomorrow. Maggie said you guys are coming?"

"Yeah." Emmett's phone buzzed in his pocket and he pulled it out. "It's my mom. She's been blowing up my phone for the past twenty minutes."

Twenty minutes? Crap! Wade pulled out his own phone and saw four texts and two missed calls from Ashley. He must have accidentally put his phone on silent when he answered her last text. "What are you waiting for? Answer it."

As Emmett talked to his mom, Wade sent her an apology text and let her know he was with Emmett.

"Yes, I'm fine." Emmett's shoulders slumped. "I'm sorry. I didn't want to worry you. I just needed some space. Okay… Yeah, I'm with Wade." He held out his phone to Wade. "My mom wants to talk to you."

Wade reluctantly took the phone and put it up to his ear. "Ashley, I'm sorry I didn't call you, my phone was on si—"

Ashley's irate voice cut him off and poured into his ear. "I haven't heard from you in almost twenty minutes, Wade. Twenty minutes!" Her voice was shrill. "I almost called the sheriff. For all I knew you were dead and my boy was lost, or worse. I was worried sick. Why didn't you call me back?"

"I found Emmett a few minutes after the last text I sent you. We started talking and lost track of time. I must have turned my phone on silent by accident."

"How can you be so careless? I can't believe I ever thought I could trust you with my son. If you'd actually said yes, I'd be changing my mind about it right now."

"Ashley, you're obviously upset. Why don't we talk about this when Emmett and I are back at the park."

"If you're even capable of bringing him back in one piece." She was practically growling.

"We're leaving right now," he said calmly. "We'll see you in about ten minutes."

"Turn your ringer on this time, or I swear to God—"

"It's on. We'll see you soon." He made sure the ringer on his phone was turned on and shoved it back in his pocket. "Why do I feel like a toddler who was just caught flushing Mommy's best makeup down the toilet?"

Emmett gave him an understanding look. "She has that effect on people."

"Do me a favor and don't worry your mom like that again. If we're going to be spending time together, you need to behave yourself. I don't want to find myself at the front end of an angry mother grizzly bear again anytime soon."

"Okay, if she even lets that happen after today," Emmett said dejectedly.

"How did you…?"

"I heard her on the phone. Her voice carries when she's mad."

Wade thought of the ringing sensation in his ear and couldn't agree more.

***

As Emmett had sat alone in the woods that afternoon, he was consumed by unwanted thoughts about his dad. The harder he tried to push them away, the more they haunted him. He hated his dad. He hated him for what he became, for what he did to them, and for what he did to put a stop to it all. He had acted so quickly as if he didn't think of them at all. Emmett remembered how his mom cried every night, missing him, how she was so stricken with grief she could barely function. He did that to her, and Emmett hated him even more for it. Most of all, he was angry at himself for missing his dad so much despite everything he hated about him.

All these thoughts had tormented him as he sat on that rotting log like they did whenever his mom talked about those final days. Despite what his dad put them through, his mom still missed him and always spoke so fondly of him as if none of the bad things happened, as if everything was perfect up until the end. He was angry at her for pretending that was the truth and for making Dad out to be some kind of hero. He wished she could see things for what they were so they could get on with their lives. He didn't want to harbor these thoughts anymore, but he feared that until she moved on, he wouldn't fully be able to either.

He let out a sigh where he sat slumped in the easy chair in their living room, his eyes following Ashley as she paced back and forth in front of him. She had been dangerously quiet throughout the drive home and Emmett braced himself for the worst. But instead of the expected scolding and irate lecture, she surprised him by bursting into tears and rushing over to hug him.

"I was so worried. I thought something terrible happened to you," she cried.

He patted her arm. "I'm fine, Mom. Everything is okay."

"You really scared me, Emmett."

"I'm sorry. I didn't mean to. I just needed some space."

She let go and looked at him. Her eyes were red and puffy from crying, and tears smeared her cheeks. "Why did you run away from me?"

"I don't like talking about what happened with Dad. I just had to get away."

She placed a hand on his shoulder. "Oh, honey. I understand it's hard. It's hard for me too, but you can't just run off because you don't like something. You need to start thinking about how your actions affect others. Not to mention you had no idea what was in those woods. You could've been hurt."

"But I wasn't, Mom. You need to stop babying me. I'm thirteen. I don't need you for everything."

"I need to know where you are and that you're safe. You're all I have left, Emmett." Her voice caught and fresh tears rolled down her cheeks.

"Geez, Mom. Don't cry."

"You are so important to me. I can't lose you."

"You're not going to lose me, all right?"

"Sometimes the things you do make me worried that I already am losing you. I try and I try, but you keep pushing me away. I love you so much, Emmett. I just want to be close to you again."

Emmett looked down at his shoes as guilt overcame him. On almost a whisper he said, "I'm sorry. I'll try to be better."

She sniffed and wiped her tears away. "Oh, Emmett, it's not like that. All I want is for you to let me in. Let me be a part of your world."

Emmett fiddled with his fingers as he sat in silence. She shifted toward him and wrapped her arms around him. As she lay her head on his shoulder she said, "I will always love you, no matter what. Nothing you can do will change that."

He stiffened at her admission and slowly relaxed and leaned his head against hers.

"Whenever you're ready to talk about what happened in the park, or about anything else, I'll be here for you," she said.

"I know, thanks. I'm pretty tired. Can I go to my room now?" he said.

"Or we could order a pizza. Maybe watch a movie?"

"I'm not hungry."

"Are you sure?"

"I just want to be alone right now."

"Okay. I'll come check on you a little later."

Emmett gave her a grateful look and headed to his room.

As Ashley sat on the couch, her mind wandered to the events of this afternoon. When she thought something bad had happened to Emmett, it flipped a switch in her brain. Suddenly she was this crazy, hysterical lunatic. It was like she was in a haze and the only thing she could focus on was making sure her son was safe. She worried something was wrong with her. Clearly this wasn't normal behavior, was it? Maybe Emmett was right and she needed to let go a little. She could still be a caring and committed mom without going into a complete frenzy whenever something went a little wrong. There was a difference between concern and distress.

She cringed as she remembered how she treated Wade. He had stepped up and helped her, and she didn't even thank him. Even worse, she yelled at him, scorned him, and possibly even made him regret helping her. He was there for her and she metaphorically spit in his face. She needed to apologize to him. She thought about calling him but decided that her horrendous behavior deserved an apology face-to-face.

Mended

CHAPTER
FOURTEEN

WADE WAITED ON the covered porch of the two-story Victorian home. It's fresh robin's egg blue paint matched the color of the cloudless sky. The shingled roof, the same grey as a nimbus cloud, pointed steeply up toward heaven. A tall, slender woman with curly black hair and striking features opened the door. As she smiled at him, her green eyes crinkled at the corners and laugh lines etched her high cheekbones. "Wade, you're early."

"I told you I was coming over early to help, Maggie," he said.

"Help or play with Carson?" she asked, gesturing to the mystery paper bag Wade held.

A grin spread across his face. "Both."

"What did you bring him this time?"

"Shock springs for his dirt bike."

She smiled and shook her head. "You're spoiling that boy, but I guess I can't complain since it's coming out of your pocket and not mine. Carson will be ecstatic."

"It's fun for me too. I get to help him put them on."

"Oh, I'm well aware," Maggie said, snickering.

"Are you going to let me in, or not?"

She eyed the foil-covered tray he held with suspicion. "What's that?"

"Chicken wings."

"Did you make them? I need to know whether I can serve them to my guests or not."

Wade clutched his chest in feigned injury. "Ouch. What about the fruit salad I made before? That turned out all right."

"You cut your finger preparing it and had to go to the emergency room."

"Yeah, but it's not like any of me ended up in the salad."

"You left the peels on the banana slices and didn't take the pits out of the cherries. We had to Heimlich Carson."

"Maybe he should've spit them out like everyone else," he countered.

She placed her hands on her hips. "He was three."

"It's ten years later and you're still holding that against me. You never give me any credit."

"I give credit when it is deserved." Maggie grinned. "Now, I'll ask you again, did you make those chicken wings?"

Acting resigned, Wade sighed. "I picked them up from the hot food section at Hardy's. Happy? Am I allowed in now?"

She gave him a satisfied smile and stepped aside. He moved past her and put the tray of wings on the kitchen counter. As Maggie put the tray in an insulated bag to keep the wings warm, Wade admired the newly remodeled space.

Beige countertops glistened under hanging double-sconce lights with opal glass shades. Additional single-wall sconce lights with a shiny chrome finish brought light and warmth to the antique-white Victorian style cabinets. Custom arched shelving held decorative vintage plates and bowls. A row of cabinets with glass panel doors displayed ceramic serving dishes and mugs. Golden oak hardwood floors gleamed underfoot with its beautiful natural grain.

"This kitchen is the perfect mix of modern and antique. It really fits the style of the rest of the house. Just look at those beautiful hardwood floors. Your contractor clearly knew what he was doing." Wade quirked a brow.

"Yes, but he's kind of conceited about it."

"Maybe if you would admit it on your own you wouldn't force him to go fishing for compliments. What about your whole speech a minute ago about giving credit where credit is deserved?"

"Using my own words against me? Fine, you did a great job, Wade. Everyone knows it."

"If you're not careful your nose will start turning brown."

"Are you done? See, this is why I don't give you compliments."

He was grinning ear to ear. "I couldn't resist. I owed you from letting you harass me about the chicken wings."

"If you keep this up, I might decide to hire out when we remodel our master bathroom."

"You and I both know you'd never do that because I'm the best around."

"That, and you're cheap."

"I call it being fair." He held up the paper bag with Carson's gift. "Is Carson around?"

"Carson, Wade's here!" she called up the stairs.

Right on cue, Carson pounded down the stairs and slid to a stop in front of Wade. "Hey, Uncle Wade. Is that for me?"

Wade handed over the paper bag and Carson dug inside. He pulled out two yellow coils. "New shock springs. These are the best. You can drive on the bumpiest terrain and barely feel a thing. I figured you needed these since you wanted to start practicing your jumps," Wade said.

Carson's eyes lit up with delight. "Awesome! Can we put them on now?"

"My tools are in my truck."

"You're the best. Thanks, Uncle Wade!" Carson practically jumped on him as he gave him a huge hug and dashed off to the garage.

"I'll meet you out there," Wade called after him.

Maggie grabbed his arm as he turned to leave. "Before you two start foaming at the mouth over those coils, I wanted to talk to you about something. I heard you turned Ashley down when she asked if you'd spend time with Emmett after school. Something about your schedule? What's that about?"

"I know you already have your theories."

"Yes, but I want to hear it from you."

Wade sighed. "After what happened with Ford, I'm worried I'll make the same mistakes again."

"What mistakes are those?"

"That's the thing. I don't know which of my mistakes caused him to end up the way he did, so I wouldn't even know where to start. Though, I know what didn't help the situation..."

Maggie held up a hand to stop him. "It's not your fault Ford ended up in prison. You did the best you could under the circumstances." She pursed her lips in irritation. "We both know Roy was no help. Besides, even if you had anything to do with it, you're not the same guy you were back then."

"You don't know that."

"Yes, I do. But the issue here is Emmett's a good kid and I think he would really benefit from spending some time with you. He needs a good man like you in his life. You did a great job with Ford under the circumstances and you will do a great job with Emmett too."

"You always think you know everything."

"That's because I do. Don't turn this down, Wade. I think you'll regret it. That's all. Go enjoy your time in the garage. I'm sure Carson is eager to get started."

Wade hated that Maggie was always right. He already regretted saying no in the first place, and now Ashley was mad at him for yesterday and would probably rescind the original offer. There had to be a way to change her mind.

***

"I told you not to bring anything," Maggie scolded, her hands on her hips.

"I couldn't help myself. I told you I can never come to a party empty-handed," Ashley said. When Maggie continued to look at her without amusement she quickly added, "They're my chocolate-chip cookies."

Maggie perked up. "The ones you brought on your first day of work?"

Ashley knew she had her. "The very same."

"I guess I can let it slide this one time," she said as she reached her hand into the basket of cookies on the kitchen counter. She took a slow bite and closed her eyes in obvious enjoyment. "Before I sit here and eat this entire basket of cookies myself, let me introduce you to everyone. Emmett, why don't you go meet up with Carson. He's in the garage with Wade right now."

"Okay, I guess," Emmett said.

Maggie linked arms with Ashley's and led her out the kitchen and through the living room. "You have such a lovely home. I just love the mix of vintage and new age and how everything has so much character. You really have some great taste."

"Aren't you sweet. We love it here. Wade remodeled our kitchen a few months ago. I'm so in love with it. Don't tell him I told you or he might let it go to his head." Maggie grinned. "Everyone is out back. I better introduce you now before the game starts. Once the game's on, their behinds are glued to the sofa and their eyes to the big screen."

"Game?"

Maggie gave Ashley an incredulous look. "It's Saturday. That means football around here. We're all about the Crimson Tide in this house. They're playing USC so it should be a good game. Through here."

They stepped through the sliding glass door and onto a covered flagstone patio. A white wicker couch and two wicker chairs with floral patterned cushions stood on a natural-colored area rug. All of the seats were taken by smiling, chatting guests clutching their glasses of sweet tea or bottles of Coke or beer. A wrought iron table with intricate vine-like and floral accents stood as the centerpiece of the sitting area.

Beneath the overhang were ceramic pots filled with vibrant red royal catchflies and purple false indigo, their petals open to soak up the warm Alabama sun. Beyond the patio lay a lush green lawn and paver stepping stones that led to cedar raised beds filled with growing vegetables. Smoke and the smell of smoldering charcoal rose from the big black barbecue on the edge of the flagstone patio. A sturdy man with dark hair streaked with grey manned the grill, using massive tongs to turn over what looked like entire chickens.

Maggie, her arm still linked with Ashley's, led them to the man responsible for the savory smells of grilled meat. "Robbie, I want you to meet my friend and colleague, Ashley Thomas. Her son Emmett goes to school with Carson. Ashley, this is my husband, Robbie."

When he turned around, Ashley could see that he wore an apron with the words: "Try my meat stack" printed across the front. "Ashley, I'm glad to finally meet you. Maggie won't stop yapping about you. I hope you like chicken because I have an entire coop here," he said.

"I can see that. It smells delicious. I can't wait to try it," she said.

"Just wait until you try it with my secret white barbecue sauce. Family recipe. My wife can't get enough," he said as he gave Ashley a wink.

"Robert! What have I told you about saying it like that? It sounds dirty," Maggie said, smirking.

"I know. That's why I say it that way."

"Get back to the grill, you dirty, old man." As she turned to walk away, Robbie gave Maggie a slap on the butt. When she turned around to give him a playful shove, he pulled her in and slopped a big wet kiss on her mouth before pushing her away and giving her another slap on the butt. Ashley couldn't miss the bright red blush that warmed Maggie's cheeks or the grin she was trying to hide. "I'm sorry about him. He has no manners," Maggie shot the words at Robbie over her shoulder, earning her another wink.

"I like him. I think your other guests enjoyed the show as much as I did." Everyone's eyes were turned on Maggie and they all wore the same amused expression as Ashley. One of them even whooped. "Maybe you should take a bow," Ashley said.

"That's enough out of you." Maggie turned to address her guests. "All right, show's over. Go back to sipping my drinks and eating my food."

"Will there be another showing later?" said an overly attractive man with dirty blond hair and smoldering amber eyes. Ashley instantly recognized him as the bad boy who'd shamelessly hit on her at The Fried Pickle last weekend.

"You'll be the star of a different show if you don't shut your mouth, Reid. Everyone, this is my friend Ashley," Maggie announced. She gestured to the cute middle-aged couple sitting on the wicker sofa. "Ashley, these lovely people are our neighbors Peggy Sue and Hardy Joe Davison. They own the grocery store in town. You know, Hardy's? Next to them is Tucker Brown. Robbie and Tucker played together on the Mason High School football team and have been reminiscing 'the good ole days' ever since."

The introductions continued. Ashley exchanged greetings and pleasantries with each of Maggie's guests in turn. She chatted cordially with them as they exchanged polite compliments, minor details about themselves, and bad jokes. They all seemed like good people, and Ashley was already enjoying herself.

"And this sorry excuse for a man, is my annoying little brother, Reid," Maggie said as the alluring ladies' man in the leather jacket and the dark stone-washed jeans made his way over to them.

"We've met," Ashley said.

"I'm sorry to hear that," Maggie retorted. "Reid, be good. I need to start bringing out the other food." Before Ashley could offer to help, Maggie was halfway to the house, leaving her alone with the town's player.

Reid slid over to her and put his arm around her shoulders. "It's a pleasure to see you again, beautiful. You look stunning in that dress. Like a fresh spring day under the romantic light of the late afternoon sun."

Ashley couldn't help but laugh. "I'm sorry, but does that crap actually work on women?"

Reid shot her an amused smile. "You'd be surprised how often it works. But I can see I'm going to have to step up my game if I want to win the heart of a smart, charming, all-American girl like you. You have high standards and I admire that."

"It's possible I've heard worse lines."

"You're just being nice. Even I gagged a little on that 'romantic light of a spring afternoon' crap. You really do look great, though. Yellow is definitely your color."

"Thank you. I have to say I find you more attractive when you're not stinking of liquor and spouting embarrassing pickup lines."

His warm amber eyes danced with amusement. "I've found that my looks aren't the problem, it's when I open my mouth that I drive away the good ones."

"So just keep your mouth shut around me, and we'll be all right," she teased.

He chuckled deep in his throat, a gruff appealing sound. "I knew I liked you, Ashley."

"In all seriousness though, Reid, I'm sure you're a great guy. We all know you're very attractive and I'm learning you're also sweet and funny, but I'm not interested in being anything other than friends."

"Fair enough. Friends it is." Reid removed his arm from her shoulders and held out his hand for her to shake. As they shook, she didn't see that Wade had stepped out onto the patio and was watching them. Nor did she notice Reid's eyes flicker to where Wade stood behind her.

Recognizing Wade's reaction for what it was, Reid made a split-second decision to test the waters. He laced his fingers with Ashley's and wrapped his other hand around hers in a gentle caress. Looking deep into her blue eyes, he leaned toward her until their lips were only a few inches apart. As he spoke, his voice was a seductive whisper. "But who am I to deny the role of the little brother crushing hard on his big sister's best friend."

Mended

CHAPTER
FIFTEEN

AS WADE STEPPED onto Maggie's back patio, he was immediately drawn to the golden-haired beauty in the yellow sundress. Ashley looked more stunning every time he saw her. Her lovely features shined with delight as she chuckled at something the man next to her said. *Wait, man?* Having been captivated by Ashley's appearance and the sound of her throaty chuckle, Wade hadn't noticed the man standing next to her with his arm draped over her shoulders. *Reid.*

He felt like he'd swallowed a boulder. Its heavy weight pulled deep in the pit of his stomach and anger swirled inside him. His breath became harsh and shallow and his hands curled involuntarily into fists, just aching to punch the smirk right off Reid's stupid face. He watched as Reid removed his arm from her shoulders, only to lace his fingers with hers as they stared deep into each other's eyes, an alluring blush coloring her lovely face. *Get your hands off of her. She's mine.* His sudden possessiveness surprised him. For a moment, it almost felt like he had feelings for Ashley.

Still surprised by the sudden onset of jealousy churning inside him, Wade approached the happy couple. His presence must have broken whatever spell was cast on them because Ashley turned her glazed eyes to his bitter ones and pulled Reid's hand off of hers.

"We were having a moment here, Wade. Do you mind?" Reid said without taking his eyes off Ashley.

"There was no moment, and you're not interrupting," Ashley said.

"You have your story and I have mine."

Reid had used up what was left of Wade's tolerance. "The Crimson Tide's cheerleaders are warming up right now. I know how you would hate to miss out on watching them do their stretches up close and personal on the big screen, Reid."

Reid didn't even flinch. "I'm fine right where I am, thanks."

"Actually, I'd like to talk to Wade for a minute, if that's okay," Ashley said.

Wade's heart soared at her words. Now it was Wade's turn to shoot Reid a triumphant look. To his dismay, Reid appeared unfazed.

"No problem, baby. The game's starting soon. I'm going to grab a plate of food and find a seat inside. I'll save you a seat next to me… or on my lap, if you prefer." Making sure Wade was watching, he leaned in to give Ashley a kiss on the cheek followed by one of his panty-dropping smiles. *Bastard.* Under Wade's death stare, Reid swaggered away, clearly pleased about something.

"That was awkward," Ashley said apologetically.

"For who? It seemed like I interrupted something pretty significant."

"It's not what it looked like. Right before you walked up, I actually told him I wasn't interested."

Wade wasn't buying it.

"I'm serious! I told him I just wanted to be friends, and he just came back with some line about how he can't help but fulfill the stereotype of having an all-consuming crush on his big sister's friend."

"Now, that I believe. Reid isn't one to take no for an answer, especially from someone as appealing as you." Wade felt an unexpected pull toward her as the entrancing blush colored her cheeks once more and a shy smile played on her shiny pink lips. What was happening to him? "What did you want to talk to me about?" he said.

"Oh, right. First of all, I wanted to thank you for bringing Emmett back to me safely yesterday. And also, I'm so sorry about how I treated you. You went out of your way to help me and I turned on you like a vicious beast. I'm really embarrassed by how I acted."

"No need to be embarrassed. We've all done things we regret when we're upset, me probably more than most. I'm glad I could help."

Maggie's voice called out from the patio, interrupting them. "Food's ready and the game's about to start. Grab a plate and find a place to park yourselves."

***

"Before we go in and watch the game with everyone, I had something I wanted to talk to you about," Wade said to Ashley. "After you get something to eat, do you mind sitting out here with me for a few minutes?"

"Sure." As Ashley moved to the line forming at the grill, Emmett walked toward her with a bounce in his step, his eyes bright with excitement.

"Mom, Carson has a dirt bike! It was his dad's, but since he got it he's been pimping it out. He just had some awesome new coil shocks put on. He wants me to come with him to try it out at half-time. Can I go? He says there's a dirt course set up right down the street. Please?"

"It's really close. I already told Carson I would take him. You and Emmett can ride with me if you want," Wade offered.

Ashley could feel Emmett's excitement and see his hope for the answer he so desired. Who was she to deny him this kind of happiness. "We'll all go."

"Yes! He even said he would show me how to ride it sometime."

"We'll have to talk about that later. Today is for watching only."

"Fine." Emmett raced back to Carson, whose head was peeking out the sliding glass door to the house awaiting the good news. She watched as Emmett gave Carson a thumbs up, which Carson reciprocated with a high five. She felt the stupid grin plastered on her face as she watched their interaction. She was elated. Emmett was making a friend here and was excited about doing something constructive for a change. Above all else, it felt good to see him so happy. "Make sure you eat dinner, please, Emmett," she called to him. He gave her a thumbs up too and started filling a plate with mountains of food. Apparently instructing him to eat wasn't necessary.

"We should get something to eat too," Wade said.

Ashley nodded and followed him to the table.

Platters of appetizing food were laid out on a large folding table adorned with a blue-and-white-checkered tablecloth: spicy chicken wings, baked beans, buttery grilled corn on the cob, potato salad, garlic bread, and in the spotlight were Robbie's chicken pieces grilled to perfection and covered with his secret white barbecue sauce. A smaller table close by held enticing desserts and baked goods. Unable to decide what to get, Ashley took a little of everything but steered clear of the desserts.

As she carried her plate to the wrought iron table, it bent precariously under the weight of her dinner. She sat in a wicker chair and eyed her plate with mixed feelings of desire and guilt.

She bargained with herself, deciding that if she ate all of this, she would skip dessert tonight and make herself exercise tomorrow. Happy with her compromise, she dug in. Wade joined her at the table, carrying his own towering plate of food, its contents stacked to an impressive height.

"You can't possibly eat all of that," Ashley said.

"Challenge accepted," Wade replied.

She chuckled. "Seriously, though. How could you possibly eat that much food?"

"I'm a starving man. I haven't had a real meal since your pot pies."

"You're kidding! That was more than a week ago."

Wade shrugged. "I'm a lousy cook, and food from the prepared section at Hardy's has lost its luster. Once I tasted your food it became the standard I hold all other food to. My usual pickings just can't compete."

"How did you get all that food on one plate?"

"Lots of practice. Do you want to know my secret?"

"Enlighten me."

"The first thing is to make sure you use a minimum of two plates to avoid the classic rookie mistake of compromising the structural integrity of your foundation. Once you have a solid foundation, you can start building upward from there. Start with your heavy stuff on the bottom; in this case your meats or your corn on the cob. You can do one, or if you are ambitious like me, you can do two layers of that. Next comes the glue. This would be your potato salads, baked beans, sauces, those sorts of things— basically any kind of kind of food that has a cohesive quality to it. Those fill in the gaps and create a unique flavor combination when they mix, so make sure you get glues that complement your bottom layer. Last would be your toppers, which are your lightest foods: your garlic bread, pastries, cookies. And there you have it. A feast fit for a king without having to burn any calories getting up for seconds."

"Impressive. Maybe you should patent your idea."

"What's impressive to me is your plate. I love a woman who isn't afraid to eat."

"Oh, I'll be paying for this later with plenty of self-loathing and forced physical activity."

"Seriously? Look at you. And in that dress, no wonder Reid couldn't stay away."

Ashley nearly choked on her food. They were heading toward dangerous territory and she needed to put a stop to it. "What did you want to talk to me about?"

"I guess we're getting right down to it. Would you reconsider letting me spend some time with Emmett after school? I know last night it seemed like you had changed your mind about me, but I was hoping we could work something out."

"Please forget anything I said last night. Clearly, I wasn't in my right mind. But I thought you said your schedule changed a lot so you wouldn't be able to commit."

"I did say that. And my schedule does fluctuate a lot. But, since I run my own business I have the luxury of making my own schedule."

Ashley lifted a brow. "I don't understand. What's the problem then?"

"The reason I gave you for why I said no wasn't the whole truth."

"Okay…"

"I'm sure you know by now that I had a big role in raising my brother Ford. And I already told you he's in prison…"

"And?"

"And I feel like I must have gone wrong somewhere to push him in that direction and I don't want that to happen with Emmett. So, I thought it was better I didn't take the chance."

"And now?"

"I'm still worried about it, but I really like him and I think there's a chance this whole arrangement could have some benefit. For him and for me."

"I agree. And I don't have any reservations about you. From what I've seen, you're going to do a great job with him."

"So, are you saying yes?"

"There's something I should tell you about Emmett first."

"What's that?"

"Things have been kind of rocky since his dad died. He's gotten into some trouble the past few years. He served some time for some of his more major offenses and he's still on probation."

"He told me."

Her eyes widened. "He did? And it doesn't bother you?"

"Not at all. I trust him."

"Okay, then all that's left is working out the details. I want to compensate you for your time, of course"

He waved the idea away. "That won't be necessary."

"You're doing both Emmett and me a huge favor. I insist."

"Ashley, give it a rest. I'm not going to take your money."

"Okay, how about this. I cook you dinner every weeknight. I can bring it over to your place or you can come over and eat with us."

"I can't say no to that. You've got yourself a deal. It looks like everyone has gone inside to watch the game. Do you want to bring our food inside and try to find a seat?"

"I've never really watched football," she said.

Wade looked around him as if to make sure they were alone. "Don't let anyone else in this town hear you say that. People here may be nice, but they take their football seriously. Come on, we'll hover in the back and I'll teach you the basics. They'll all be so focused on the game they won't notice us."

With his major-league barbecue skllls, he balanced his massive plate in one hand and used his other hand to lead her into the house. His hand was warm and strong and felt comforting in hers. As he gently wrapped his fingers around hers, she felt an unexpected flutter in her belly, something she hadn't felt in a very long time.

CHAPTER
SIXTEEN

ASHLEY SLUMPED ON her comfy lime-colored sofa. Her belly full to bursting from her massive plate of food and the dessert she'd promised herself not to eat, she'd thrown herself on the couch as soon as they arrived home from Maggie's barbecue and she hadn't been able to move since. Emmett was in his room, probably paging through the dirt bike magazine Carson gave him.

Emmett and Carson—and Wade for that matter—had all been so enthralled with how the dirt bike handled with the new shocks, they missed the second half of the football game entirely. Not that she was complaining. She'd never been into football, but thanks to Wade's secret corner football class, she at least knew enough to blend in with the other more die-hard fans of southern Alabama. At the very least Wade taught her enough to know when to cheer or act disappointed.

The best part of their secret corner hadn't been learning about football; it had been Wade. He was helpful, personable, and funny. She laughed so hard at one of his jokes that beer came out of her nose, which was both unattractive and uncomfortable. Lucky for her, he was a good sport about it and pretended not to notice. She recalled how her heart picked up speed whenever he leaned in to whisper a football fact in her ear and how a swarm of butterflies took flight in her belly whenever he brushed against her. To top it off, he was fit and handsome with an adorable crooked smile. He was attractive with a personality to match, and she was struggling to keep herself from falling for him.

It had truly been a great day. She couldn't remember the last time she enjoyed herself like that or ate so much. She clutched her swollen belly and wished there were antacids nearby. Sitting in the silence of her living room, rehashing the pleasures of the day, she realized something: this was the first day since Jeff died that she hadn't thought about him. Not once. She wasn't sure if she should be glad or sad about that.

Jeff would have loved trying out Wade's food-stacking strategy for himself. You would never know it by looking at his toned Marine body, but Jeff was always known to pack away impressive amounts of food. He had that in common with Wade. Jeff would have gotten along great with Robbie too. He used to have the same dirty sense of humor. She could picture them both standing around the grill, cackling as they exchanged inappropriate jokes. Jeff would have begged to know where Robbie got his novelty apron. He'd have searched the web for one of his own as soon as they arrived home. She imagined Jeff and Robbie standing side by side wearing matching aprons as they manned the grill, exchanging dirty jokes and heckling each other about their grilling abilities. With these pleasant thoughts, she drifted off to sleep.

***

The house was dark. The only light streamed out from the crack under the closed door of the study. She moved toward it, trailing her hand along the wall as she went. As she moved closer, she heard Jeff's gruff voice from inside. It was distorted with emotion. As she waited at the door his voice became louder and more desperate. She heard a commotion from inside, thumping, shuffling, and the sound of objects hitting the floor and breaking. Something was after him. She could hear the fear in his voice clearly now. Someone was trying to hurt him. "Jeff!"

She felt afraid and alone in the dark hallway, but she was more afraid of what she would find on the other side of the door. Gathering her strength, she grabbed the handle and threw open the door. The room was in shambles. Books, papers, and broken glass were strewn across the floor. The lamp lay in pieces, it's shade bent at an odd angle. The window was shattered, the curtains billowing in the wind from the raging storm outside. Jeff was alone in the room. His back was to her where he crouched, his shoulders shaking with uncontrollable sobs. His fingers were curled tightly around the black pistol in his hand. Blood flowed in dark crimson streams from a gash on his arm and dripped to the floor with a sickening splat.

"Jeff!" She ran to his side and clung to him. Upon contact, he whirled around and hit her with the butt of his gun. Pain exploded in her head and she was momentarily blinded. She crashed into the desk, which knocked the wind out of her and she fell to the floor. She curled into a ball, clutching the sharp pain in her side as she struggled to force air back into her lungs. When she looked up, Jeff stood over her, his eyes wild with terror. He was disoriented, his mind clearly somewhere else. "Jeff! It's Ashley. I'm your wife!" She tried to scream, but her voice was merely a breathy whisper. He looked at her without recognition and lifted the pistol in his hand. She cringed and shut her eyes until she heard the voice behind her. "What are you doing?"

Emmett had come. She heard the sharp click as Jeff aligned the bullet, ready to take the shot. "Dad! Stop!" Emmett yelled out and charged him. Jeff seemed to notice him then and turned the pistol on Emmett, aiming at his heart. Emmett stopped in his tracks and held up his hands, pleading as Jeff stared at him, his eyes black.

Through the pain and fear, Ashley managed to find her voice again. "No! It's Emmett, Jeff, it's your son. Stop!" Despite her cries, he continued to hold the gun steady on him, his face hard, his eyes wild. His finger twitched as he put pressure on the trigger. "No!" She threw herself at Jeff, knocking him off balance as she heard the crack of the gunshot.

Ashley jolted awake. Her pulse pounded wildly and she was drenched with sweat. It took her a moment to figure out where she was. It was still dark outside and the clock in the living room told her it was only four. Still, there was no chance of falling back to sleep now. She sat up on the couch, her yellow sundress clinging uncomfortably to her body. She must have fallen asleep on the couch after the barbecue last night. She wiped the tears from her cheeks and wrapped her shaking arms around her knees, rocking back and forth to calm herself. When she felt able to stand, she headed to the shower in hopes that the hot water would help calm the trepidation currently racking her body from the terrifying memory.

CHAPTER
SEVENTEEN

WADE STOOD OUTSIDE Mason's little white chapel watching the other churchgoers mingle as they drank their coffee and ate pastries after the Sunday service. He spotted Reid as he exited the church and waved to get his attention. Something had been bothering him since yesterday and he needed answers.

As soon as Reid was within earshot, Wade started in on him. "What was your deal at the barbecue yesterday?"

"What are you talking about?" Reid asked.

"Why were you all over Ashley?"

"She's hot and has a great personality. Can you blame me for trying?"

"Did anything happen between you two? It seemed like I interrupted something."

Reid gave him a knowing grin. "Wade, you know it's not polite to kiss and tell."

Wade ran a hand through his hair. "You're killing me, dude."

"Nothing happened. I swear. It was just harmless flirting. Why? Did it bother you?"

"What? No. No, of course not," he said, shaking his head.

"Come on, Wade, just admit you like her. I know you do."
Wade opened his mouth to protest, but Reid cut him off. "Don't
bother denying it. I know you. You're into her. Why do you think
I've been flirting with her so much?"

"Because you're a sex addict?" Wade suggested.

Reid frowned. "I was trying to make you see how much you
liked her. It worked too. I saw how jealous you were when I had
my arm around her yesterday."

"You saw me watching you guys?"

"Why else would I try to make a move right after she rejected
me? That was purely for your benefit. You'll thank me later."

"And I'm sure you kissing her on the cheek and offering her a
spot on your lap to watch the game was for my benefit as well?"

Reid grinned. "That was for both of us."

Wade shook his head. "You're a pig. So… she actually did
reject you?"

"True story. She's not into me. Maybe she has a thing for
contractors. You should go for it, man."

"I can't do that."

"You're both single and attractive people and you want her
bad. Why the hell not?"

"I'm going to be mentoring her son. Wouldn't it be like a
conflict of interest or something?"

"You're not the kid's shrink. You're just hanging out with him
after school. Sounds kind of perfect if you ask me."

"No one asked you."

"Whatever, dude. It's your loss. I would have gone for her in a
second if she would have let me, and if I knew you weren't into
her…" Reid finished after seeing the fierce look on Wade's face.
"Chill out, dude. I'm just messing with you."

"Just promise me you'll stop pursuing her."

"Flirting with beautiful women is in my nature. I can't promise I won't flirt, but I will promise it will be innocent… mostly," Reid said with an arrogant smirk.

"You're the worst."

"You love me."

"You're my cousin. I have to. Well, I better get going. I have to stop at the store to pick up supplies before heading to Roy's place." Every Sunday after church, Wade visited his dad to check up on him, clean his trailer, and stock his fridge and liquor stash. It was either that or risk him getting behind the wheel drunk. Although Wade had taken his dad's car away months ago, the old man was resourceful, and Wade wouldn't be surprised if he convinced a neighbor to let him borrow theirs for a booze run. It wouldn't be the first time.

"Tell him I said hi. You know I was just messing with you about Ashley, right? I promise I won't pursue her. I know you like her and I don't want to get in the way of that. I think she'd be good for you." Reid slapped him on the back.

"We'll see. See you later tonight."

"Good luck with your dad today."

"Thanks, I'm going to need it. I'm going to ask him if he'll come with me to visit Ford. I think it would be good for both of them."

"Don't you ask him that every Sunday?"

"Yep. And he always says no. That's why I need the luck."

CHAPTER
EIGHTEEN

THOUGH THE HOT shower had soothed the tremors, Ashley still felt uneasy. The nightmare was so real it brought on a stream of unwanted memories that left her on edge. Encouraged by the bright and sunny morning and pleasant thoughts of her time spent with Wade yesterday, she decided to try to cease her morbid thoughts by keeping busy.

Before Emmett woke up at ten o'clock Sunday morning, Ashley cleaned the kitchen and bathrooms, planned her menu for the week, went for a run that nearly killed her, and took a much-needed second shower thanks to the jog of death. She considered cutting back on all of her future indulgences because they just didn't seem worth it. If she had to endure that amount of pain every time she tried to burn the calories off, she'd rather avoid them in the first place. Her legs already felt heavy and she was pretty certain that walking would be near impossible tomorrow.

Emmett trudged to the kitchen, yawning and rubbing the sleep from his eyes.

"Good morning, sleepyhead. You slept in pretty late. Did you have a late night?" she asked.

"I stayed up a while reading the magazine Carson gave me. Did you know that Carson competes in dirt bike competitions?"

"Maggie mentioned something about it."

"Carson said it's really cool. They have these events where you race against people on different courses depending on your skill level. Some of them are pretty advanced and have some crazy terrain like big jumps and ditches and stuff. Carson's thinking about trying to move up to one of the more difficult tracks this summer."

"I take it you also stayed up talking to Carson last night."

"We were instant messaging on my computer, but I waited until super late so my grounding was pretty much over. Are you mad?"

"I'm more impressed that you got me on a technicality as usual. You're still on extra chore duty for a while, though."

"I know."

"I'm glad you're making a friend here. Carson is a great kid."

"He invited me to watch him practice his riding with a few of his other friends on Friday after school. He said I could spend the night after too. Can I go?"

"As long as things go well this week, then I don't see why not."

"Cool. I wish I had my own dirt bike, though. Then, I could ride with them instead of being lame and watching from the sidelines."

She held in her smile. Emmett may be a good negotiator, but he needed to work on his subtlety. "I've actually been thinking about that. If you start working harder in school, bring your grades up, and follow the rules, then we'll go about finding you a dirt bike and getting you some lessons on how to ride it."

"Really? That would be so cool! I'll do better, I promise."

"Show me that you're serious and we can talk about it."

"I will. Thanks, Mom."

"That brings me to the next thing I want to talk to you about. Your probation officer called me after you stole that boy's wallet from his backpack the other day. We have a meeting with her tomorrow."

His shoulders slumped. "Is she going to send me to juvie?"

"Not this time, but any more probation violations and she will."

He blew out a breath. "I don't want to go back there."

"I don't want you to either, but it's pretty much up to you at this point."

"What do you think she's going to say?"

"I won't know until we talk to her tomorrow. It could be any number of things from community service to house arrest."

"That's crap!"

"What did you expect, Emmett? You can't just steal from other students and ditch school without there being any consequences. You're lucky she's giving you another chance. You know your last probation officer wouldn't have."

"That's because he was a narc."

"Be grateful she's giving you another chance and use it. Make good choices and you won't have any more problems."

"Is she going to let me go to Wade's after school?"

"I've already talked to her about it and she thinks it's a good idea. She was actually pleased you'd suggested it."

"Okay, well I'm glad I get to do that."

"The more you show me I can trust you to make good choices, the more freedom you'll have. You do realize that, don't you?"

Emmett huffed and rolled his eyes. "I know. I already said I'm going to try."

"I don't need you to tell me, I need you to show me. We also need to talk about your grades. I know you don't want to be stuck in summer school so let's make a plan to help you keep your freedom this summer, okay?"

They discussed which areas needed the most work and came up with a doable study schedule to share with Emmett's teachers and tutor. With the threat of house arrest or juvenile lockup hanging over his head and—on the other end of the spectrum—the promise of getting his own dirt bike and having more freedom, Emmett willingly agreed to follow the plan they laid out. For the first time in a long while, it seemed like he truly wanted to do better.

After breakfast Emmett went to his room to study and work on any remaining homework while Ashley finished the rest of the household chores. After a trip into town for groceries and other household supplies, she was exhausted but prepared to start the week. Once she finished correcting Emmett's practice tests, she would finally be able to relax for the evening.

She said a silent hallelujah as she wrote down Emmett's scores. "You got a seventy-six percent on the English practice test and a seventy-nine percent on the math. Please show these to your tutor tomorrow so you can focus on the things you missed. If you do that, I don't see why you can't do great on your tests next week. I'm proud of you, Emmett. You showed a lot of improvement today."

"Thanks. I want to do anything I can to stay out of summer school."

"That's the spirit."

"It actually wasn't as hard as I thought it was going to be."

"I've always known you were smart. I'm glad you see it too. Keep up the good work. Do you want to go out to dinner tonight? I'm pretty beat." Just the thought of cooking tonight made her want to take a nap.

"Can we go to The Fried Pickle?"

CHAPTER
NINETEEN

WADE PERCHED ON a stool at the bar, sipping his Coke and chewing his country-fried steak. Days like today made him wish for an ice cold beer. Although visiting his dad was never easy, today had been particularly rough. In addition to refusing to go with him to visit Ford in prison and the usual stink and mess he had to clean up in and around his dad's trailer, Roy had also complained about a pain in his side. By the look of his yellowing skin and the fact that he'd been an alcoholic for the past eighteen years, Wade worried his condition was serious.

He tried to convince Roy to see a doctor, but the stubborn old man refused even though Wade offered to pay for a house visit. He would schedule the appointment anyways if he thought Roy would let the doctor run some tests. Maybe if he held him down for the doctor or waited until his father passed out drunk it would work, but he was pretty sure doing either of those things was illegal. He'd just have to be relentlessly persistent until Roy agreed. *That ought to be real fun.*

At least he would get to have dinner with Ashley every night this week. The prospect of good food and even better company helped lift the heavy weight pressing on his chest. With her kind heart, delicious curves, and fun-loving attitude she was the whole package. He could get lost in her sweet smile forever.

Reid was right, he was into her. He'd better get a handle on himself. It's not like she felt the same way about him anyways. She was still wearing her wedding ring for God's sake. But maybe with time… he pictured himself tucking a loose strand of her hair behind her ear. Her golden strands would feel as soft as silk between his fingers. He would look longingly into her ocean-blue eyes before leaning in for a kiss. It would be soft at first but would quickly grow with intensity until they were both filled with need and aching for more. *Get a grip, Hudson. Not going to happen. She's a sad widow who loves her husband.* He was going to have to settle for being friends.

Distracting himself with safer thoughts about his dad and his plans for his time with Emmett this week, Wade went back to enjoying his meal. As he chewed, he wondered what Ashley's country-fried steak would taste like. Maybe he could ask her if she knew how to make it. Thoughts of Ashley filled his mind again and his blood began to heat once more. He was like a drug addict before his next fix. He just couldn't stop thinking about her.

He needed Reid to come back. It was easier not to think about Ashley when Reid was jabbering in his ear. He wondered what was taking him so long in the bathroom. Whenever he was gone this long it was almost guaranteed Wade would be subjected to another one of Reid's juvenile poop jokes or a fake story about some made-up bathroom sexcapade. Though tonight he would welcome the distraction. Anything to keep his mind off Ashley and the forbidden things they could do together.

The minutes ticked by and thoughts of Ashley crept into his mind yet again. He had no self-control. He put down his fork in frustration and focused his efforts on finding Reid. He scanned the busy dining room until he spotted him wearing his charming "let me take you home" smile and leaning over a pretty blonde. A pretty blonde with a sweet smile and a perfect curvy body. His heart skipped a beat as he recognized Ashley. Sure enough, Emmett sat at the table across from her, eating a cheeseburger. Wade's blood boiled as he watched her laugh at something Reid said to her. *I'm going to kill him.*

Wade stomped over and wedged his way in. "Is he bothering you?" he asked Ashley.

"Oh hi, Wade. No, it's fine. We were just talking about you actually."

Wade's belly flip-flopped uncomfortably. "Me? What about?"

"I was just telling her about some of the family trips to the river we took when we were kids," Reid said. His grin said it all.

Wade shot him a dirty look. Two could play this game. "Did you tell her about the summer you were so afraid of bees you refused to come out of the tent the entire trip?"

"Was that the same summer you got poison oak on your butt?"

"I think it was the summer you were obsessed with NSYNC and you were too busy singing one of their songs in the camp shower to hear Maggie and me take all your clothes."

"I must not have been singing too loud because I heard your lame attempts at pretending to be a bear rustling in the bushes."

"It was good enough to scare you. Why else would you have run buck naked all the way back to our campsite, squealing like a little girl? Or I should say, what you thought was our campsite."

Reid laughed. "Yeah I gave those Girl Scouts quite a surprise. I'll bet they'll never forget that camping trip."

Ashley let out a musical laugh as Emmett snickered into his burger. "Oh no. That's awful," she laughed.

"Thank you for that lovely story, Wade, but I'm going to get back to my dinner before you all start picturing me naked. You coming, Wade?" Reid asked.

"In a minute. I want to talk to Ashley about something first."

"All right, see you in a few. Bye, Ashley. Although it wasn't the thought I originally hoped to leave you with, I'm glad you now have something of me to keep you warm at night," Reid said as Wade shot him a murderous look. "Emmett, good to see you, dude." His eyes twinkled in amusement before he turned to leave.

"Did those things really happen?" Ashley asked after Reid left.

"I wish I could say I made them up. What did Reid tell you about me?"

"Nothing really."

"You're a bad liar."

"He told me you wore arm floaties until you were eight years old even if all you were doing was splashing around in the shallows of the river." Her full pink lips curved into a smile that crinkled her eyes.

"Reid loves making fun of me about that. It didn't help that they were yellow and looked like little ducks." That information earned him another one of her attractive throaty laughs. He felt his responding grin. "My mom made me wear them. It was either wear them and play in the water with the kids or sit out in the hot summer humidity with the adults. There was no dissuading her so I made my choice. Even if it earned me the nickname 'duck wings' until I was twelve."

Once the laughter died down, Emmett turned to his mom. "You could never make me wear something like that."

"Really? If you think about it, your ladybug hat wasn't much different."

"Mom, stop."

"What? I thought it was adorable."

Wade saved him. "I hope that's only your appetizer," he said pointing at the salad greens on Ashley's plate.

"After all I ate on Saturday and the run that nearly killed me this morning, I decided I needed to go light today."

"You shouldn't be so hard on yourself. You look great." If only she could see herself the way he saw her. He was amazed she would have any insecurities about the way she looked. That was one of the things about women he never understood.

"What did you want to talk to me about?" she asked, avoiding his compliment.

"I was wondering if it would be okay if Emmett and me used some of our time together to fix up the old dirt bikes in my garage."

Emmett lowered his cheeseburger mid-bite and his eyes lit up with excitement. "Please, Mom!"

"That sounds like a great idea. I can give you some money for parts," Ashley said.

"That won't be necessary. I already ordered most of the parts I think we'll need. And no, you can't reimburse me either since I know that's what you were about to say next. But I was thinking when we're done I could teach Emmett to ride."

Emmett wasn't finished yet. "Please, Mom!"

"Emmett and I talked about this earlier, actually. If he's doing better in school and staying out of trouble I'm fine with him learning how to ride. You'd really be okay teaching him?" she asked.

"Definitely."

"Then by all means, let me know when they're fixed so we can work out the rest of it. I have our dinner menu for the week planned out already. I don't think you'll be disappointed."

He thought of her pot pies and his mouth watered. "There's no chance of that happening."

"We'll see you tomorrow then."

He looked forward to it for more reasons than just dinner.

CHAPTER
TWENTY

THE SAVORY SMELL of grilled meat and the spicy-sweet aroma of cooked peppers filled the kitchen. Dinner was almost ready, and Wade would be here soon. As Ashley warmed the tortillas, Emmett mashed avocados for the guacamole while he chattered about the progress they'd made on the dirt bikes so far. Nearly a week had passed since Maggie's barbecue, and things were looking up. Emmett's behavior had already improved significantly since the difficulties from the week before, but more importantly, he seemed much happier.

"Did you e-mail your probation officer the essays she assigned you?" Ashley asked as she flipped a tortilla on the skillet.

"Yep. All done. Now I know why stealing is wrong and all the reasons why juvenile detention centers are *so* uncool." Even a dog wouldn't have missed the sarcasm.

In lieu of putting Emmett on house arrest for his probation violations last week, his probation officer assigned him two 1,500-word essays to be completed by the end of the week. She cut Emmett some slack because of the improvements to his grades and behavior he'd made this week. Though he would never admit it, Emmett was lucky she was so reasonable.

"You could've gotten a lot worse than having to write two essays. You know your last probation officer wouldn't have been so compromising."

"Yeah, he was such an ass."

"Language!"

"I speak English, but I could try it in Spanish. He was such a burro."

Ashley shot him a warning look. "At least the essays are finished so you don't have them hanging over your head anymore."

"Since I got Bs on both my tests can I spend the night at Carson's house tomorrow night? You said I could go if things went better this week."

"I know what I said."

"Please? His parents will be there."

"You've been doing very well. Of course you can go."

"Yes! Thanks, Mom. I'm going to go let him know."

"Don't be long. Wade will be here any minute." She smiled as she heard the frantic tapping of his keyboard and the ping of Carson's response, followed by more of Emmett's furious tapping.

Ashley looked at the oven clock as she put the warmed tortillas on a plate. Her heart fluttered in her chest as she saw that it was six o'clock. Wade would be knocking on her door any minute, all handsome and charming as ever. It didn't help that he was so good with her son. Wade treated Emmett like he truly cared for him, like he enjoyed their time together as much as or more than Emmett did. Everything about him drew her to him, but she couldn't go there. She loved Jeff, and she couldn't jeopardize the relationship that was developing between Wade and Emmett. Emmett needed him. Things were finally looking up and she couldn't risk doing anything to ruin that.

***

Showered, shaved, and wearing a fresh shirt, Wade strolled down Magnolia Street. This week had been the best in a long time. He was thoroughly enjoying his time with Emmett and was glad he had managed not to screw anything up yet. The kid had a knack for mechanics and he was learning fast. He was smart and eager for information. The bikes were coming along, but the more they worked on them, the more they realized how much was left to be done. They weren't discouraged, though. The journey was worth just as much as the end result.

As he walked down the quiet residential street, he thought about the past few evenings he'd spent with Ashley. She was hands down the best cook he had ever met. *Sorry Mom.* The conversations always flowed easily between them, and his breath hitched whenever she looked up from her plate and blessed him with her warm smile.

He was finding it hard to control himself whenever he was around her. Last night he ached to tuck the loose strand of hair behind her ear and lean in to kiss her perfect full lips as she said good night to him at the door. The night before that, he almost came unglued when she lightly brushed his arm as she leaned over him to clear his empty plate, her hair smelling of freesia and her breath of fresh peppermint. He couldn't take it anymore. He had to know if she felt the same way. Tonight he was going ask her out, lay it all on the table. At least then he would know where he stood.

Feeling nervous, Wade knocked on the familiar red door. Moments later he was greeted and welcomed into Ashley's home. Tonight she wore a long wrap blouse and dark skinny jeans that could make a man drool. Her hair hung loosely in waves around her face, her delicate features accentuated with light makeup. She looked beautiful as always, and the house smelled almost as good as she looked. Wade didn't know how she always managed to get cleaned up from work and make a delicious dinner in less than an hour. She was amazing.

"I hope you like fajitas," she said.

"If you made them, I'll love them."

"Everything's on the table already."

As usual, the table was filled with what looked like way too much food for three people, but looks could be deceiving whenever Wade came over for dinner. A steaming platter of grilled chicken with peppers and onions sat in the center of a lazy Susan, surrounded by plates of shredded cheese, sour cream, warm tortillas, and homemade guacamole. Wade sat down in his usual seat at the table and happily started building his fajitas.

"So, Emmett, after you left my place tonight, I found someone with a refurbished carburetor in town. Do you want to go with me to check it out tomorrow after school?"

"Heck yeah. I hope it's in better shape than that radiator we found at the junkyard. That thing was a pain to get cleaned up."

"True, but it's in beautiful working condition now, thanks to you." Wade grinned at him. "And now we have extra money in the budget if any unanticipated repairs come up."

"From what I've seen, I think that's pretty much a guarantee."

"That's half the fun of it. So, Ashley, Emmett is becoming quite the mechanic."

"So I've heard. I might have to put him to work the next time my car needs a tune-up."

"I don't know that much yet, but I'm sure I could learn," Emmett said.

"I'm sure you could too." Ashley patted his hand.

"Wade, when do you think the bikes will be ready for a ride?" Emmett asked.

Wade chuckled lightheartedly at Emmett's enthusiasm. "I'm afraid I don't have a different answer for you since the last time you asked me that an hour ago. Like I've said, it's hard to say for sure since unexpected things keep coming up, but if we keep up the hard work, it shouldn't take too long." He turned to Ashley. "How was work today? Anything exciting happen?"

She dabbed at her lips with her napkin. "A corgi came in today with a stomach full of rocks."

"How does that happen?"

"I can only assume he ate them, but you'd have to ask the corgi to know for sure."

Wade laughed as he helped himself to another fajita. "What's the weirdest thing you've found inside an animal?"

She tapped her finger on her chin as she seemed to contemplate his question. "We found forty-one socks inside a Great Dane once."

"Forty-one? I don't even think I own that many socks. Was the dog okay?"

"He was fine. He lived to eat again."

"Hopefully no more socks, though."

Five fajitas later, Wade sat back in his chair stuffed and satisfied once again. Between the three of them—well really just between Wade and Emmett—they had polished off the food in record time. "That was delicious as always, Ashley. Thank you," Wade said.

"Yeah, Mom. It was really good. Can I go watch TV in my room? I finished all my homework."

"After you clear your dish. I'll do the dishes tonight since you did so well on your tests. You just enjoy the rest of your night."

"Cool, thanks," he said as he scurried to the kitchen.

"That's great Emmett has been doing better in school lately," Wade said.

"He really is. And things are going so much better at home lately too. He seems a lot happier this week. That's probably thanks to you. He really enjoys his time with you."

"That makes two of us. He's a great kid."

"Thank you for everything you're doing with him. I owe you."

"You've paid me back plenty already. If it weren't for you, I'd be eating a frozen Salisbury steak the consistency of cardboard tonight. If anything, I'm the one who is in your debt. In fact, to help pay it down I'm helping you with the dishes tonight." He held up his hand as she started to protest. "I won't take no for an answer."

She smiled at him. "I guess I wouldn't mind having the company."

***

Ashley washed the dishes while Wade loaded the dishwasher, all the while making small talk as they worked. It felt nice, casual, routine, like they'd been doing it for years. But there was something else in the air, something electric. As Wade talked about the furniture he was refinishing for work, Ashley happily listened to the drawl of his deep southern baritone. She loved the sound of his voice, how he drew out his vowels, how his lips looked as he formed his words. She could listen to him talk for hours.

She was aware of how close he stood to her in her small kitchen, and she was tempted to reach out and touch him. Her heart skipped a beat whenever his arm lightly brushed hers as he reached for the rinsed dish in her hand. The air between them pulsed with life and seemed to pull her toward him. Did he feel this too or was she losing her mind? She snuck a glance at him and he appeared relaxed and casual as usual. It was just her, then. As he leaned in to grab the next dish from her hand, he exhaled a warm breath that caressed the skin on her neck, causing her to break out in goose bumps.

She looked up and saw him searching her face. He lifted his hand and tucked a loose strand of her hair behind her ear before gently trailing his fingers softly down her cheek. Her gaze moved down to his lips, which parted slightly as he sucked in a breath. He leaned in slightly, his lips poised over hers, the pull toward him growing with every second. She closed her eyes and breathed in his heady scent of spiced cinnamon and sawdust. His hand caressed the back of her neck as he gently pulled her the rest of the way toward him.

Just before their lips touched, she felt the plate slip out of her hand and heard it crash loudly to the floor, startling them both. She pulled away and took a step back to distance herself from the temptation of finishing what they started. "I better go clean that up." She hurried out of the kitchen to get a broom and to calm her racing heart.

She had been about to kiss a man who wasn't her husband, and in that moment she'd wanted it more than anything else. It felt like her body had taken over any ability to think or reason and she was helpless to stop her desire for him. What was she thinking? She couldn't be kissing Wade—not only because she still loved Jeff but also because of Emmett. It wasn't fair to anyone. She would have to be careful not to lose control again in the future. She took longer than necessary to gather what she needed from the hall closet, giving herself time to collect herself.

With a final deep breath, she strode back into the kitchen, broom and dustpan in hand, and tried to act as casual as possible. Wade had finished rinsing the rest of the dishes and was loading them in the dishwasher when she returned. "Thank you for helping me clean up. You really didn't have to do that," she said as she swept up the broken plate.

"I was happy to help. I was starting to feel like you were spoiling me."

"Before I forget, Emmett is going to Carson's house tomorrow night so he won't be here for dinner. They're having a sleepover. You can still come over if you'd like, but I'll probably just be having leftovers, myself."

"You don't have to feed me tomorrow night. I still have some of your leftover lasagna in my fridge. Emmett did say something about hoping to go to Carson's tomorrow. He seemed like he was looking forward to it, although he didn't use the word sleepover."

"Yeah, I guess I like to pretend he's still nine years old. It helps me to overlook the fact that he's growing up and is going to leave home in a few years."

Wade nodded in agreement. "It's hard when they grow up. I remember when Ford became a teenager. It was good-bye I need you, hello independence. It was hard for me to let go of our backyard campouts and *Transformer* marathons." He put the last plate in the dishwasher and dried his hands on a towel as he turned to face her. "So, what are your plans for tomorrow night? I bet it's been a while since you've had an evening to yourself."

"I'll most likely just sit at home in my pajamas and watch a movie while I wait by my phone to make sure Emmett doesn't need anything… Now that I've heard myself say that out loud, I realize I sound kind of pathetic."

"You're not pathetic. You're a mom who loves her kid and enjoys a relaxing evening at home. There's nothing wrong with that. But, if you're not set on those plans, I'd love to take you out tomorrow night."

"Are you asking me out on a date?"

"Yes."

She was quiet for a moment—an uncomfortable, excruciating moment that seemed to drag on forever. "I'm sorry, I can't."

He drew his brows together in confusion. "I thought there was something between us. Did I misread the signals?"

Dodging the question, she said, "Can't we just be friends for a while?"

He drew in a deep breath and exhaled. "I wish it were that easy"—he looked directly at her and held her gaze—"but I'm crazy about you, Ashley. I can hardly control myself when I'm around you."

She froze, her heart racing, unsure of what to say.

When she didn't respond, he continued. "I don't think I can just be friends." He shook his head slowly. "Not right now. I'll still be there for Emmett in the afternoons. I said I would and I won't bail on him, so you don't need to worry about that."

Ashley's stomach clenched and her throat went dry. "Please don't do this, Wade. I don't want to lose you… I just… don't think *us* is a good idea. Not right now… with Emmett and everything."

He looked at her, the light in his eyes now gone. "You don't have to explain yourself, Ashley. It's fine. I understand."

"Can't we just go back to the way things were?" she said, her voice cracking a little.

"Maybe eventually, but not right now. I like you too much to go on pretending that I don't." He moved to leave but turned back, a sad smile on his face. "Enjoy your evening tomorrow. Bye."

Ashley silently watched as Wade closed the door behind him with a thud full of finality. Despite the fact that she wasn't the only one in the house, she suddenly felt utterly alone.

***

Well, that was a disaster. Wade was so sure Ashley had feelings for him too, but he was either wrong or she was denying them. Either way, he'd made a fool of himself. He thought about that moment in the kitchen. He had felt like he was on fire, aching for her so strongly that he needed to kiss her in order to survive, to feel the connection he was so sure they had. Yet she intentionally ended their so-called moment by breaking the plate, and he had still been stupid enough to ask her out anyways. *I'm such an idiot.*

Usually he could brush rejections like this off easily, but it was different with Ashley. He'd never felt this strongly about a woman before, like something was missing when he wasn't with her. He put himself out there and was rejected. It should be simple: you try, you fail, so move on, but somehow he knew it wasn't going to be so easy. He sent Reid a text that he was heading over to his place. Ashley had turned him down and he needed to get over it so they could move on with their arrangement. Reid might be able to help with that.

***

"Thanks a lot for the great advice. I asked Ashley out and she shot me down," Wade said as he let himself into Reid's house and plopped himself down on his couch.

"Really? What happened?" Reid asked.

Wade told him about the incident in the kitchen and their conversation after.

"Do you think it's the dead husband thing? She does still wear her wedding ring."

"I don't know, but I need things to not be awkward between us so I can keep spending time with Emmett. We have a good thing going and I don't want to blow it."

"So suck it up and be friends."

"I can't just pretend there's nothing there between us."

"The way I see it, you can do one of two things. If she actually does have a thing for you, you can go balls deep and not take no for an answer. You know, keep showing her you're not going to give up so easily."

"Or?"

"Or you can brush it off and move on."

"I'm not going to force myself on her."

"Then move on."

"That's easier said than done. She's different, man. I can't get her out of my head." He slouched deeper into the cushions.

"Well, you need to either go for it or try to forget her. Otherwise, you're screwed like me. It's been nearly a year and I still can't let Caroline go. No amount of one-night stands and easy flings can erase that woman from my mind."

He looked at the pained expression on Reid's face, how his shoulders slumped as he said her name. "She's not coming back, Reid."

"I know that!" His tone softened and he seemed to gaze at nothing. "It doesn't change how I feel about her." He cleared his throat, appearing to shake off his inner thoughts. "But, we're not talking about me. We're talking about you. What's it going to be, Wade? Balls deep or walk away?"

"I'm not walking away. I'm just going to pretend tonight never happened and continue my relationship with Emmett."

"Isn't it going to be hard to spend time with her son without being around her at all?"

"Yeah, that's why I'm here asking you about it."

"What you need is a rebound. A good, old-fashioned, casual, build-your-ego rebound. I met some insanely hot girls from California today. They're on their way to Mobile, but they wanted to stop here for a few days first because they heard about our quaint town and wanted to see the charm for themselves. Their words not mine. I told them I'd be happy to show them a good time while they're in town."

"Of course you did."

"Come with me tomorrow night. We'll take them out, have a few drinks, or Cokes for you, and then they'll be on their way. A night to remember, or to help forget someone else, with no strings attached."

"Except maybe STDs."

"You need to relax and have a little fun."

"It's not my thing. I don't do one-night stands anymore."

"So don't. Just come out with us for a while and have a good time. You can always be a square and say good night to her early, leaving me with double the fun." He rubbed his palms together.

"You've become such a pig since Caroline left you."

"Only to hide my pain. So what do you say?"

"If I'm not having a good time, I can leave?"

"Any time you want."

Wade hesitated.

"Come on, man. Be my wingman for one night. It helps me forget what I lost at least for a little while. It might help you, too."

"You just want to get laid."

"That's merely a bonus."

Wade let out a resigned sigh. "What time should I come by tomorrow night?"

CHAPTER
TWENTY - ONE

ASHLEY SAT ON her sofa, her legs curled under her, a big metal bowl filled with buttery stove-top popcorn resting on her lap. Prepared for a quiet night of watching chick flicks, she wore her comfortable purple-and-pink kitty pajamas and fuzzy slipper socks. She crunched her popcorn as she watched the opening credits of one of her favorite romantic comedies.

Emmett was at a sleepover at Carson's house and she had stupidly turned down Wade's offer for a date tonight. So here she sat alone in her childish pajamas, watching people romancing each other instead of experiencing the real thing herself. At least the popcorn was good. Maybe later she would make it a real party and dive into the pint of chocolate ice cream that was currently calling out to her from the freezer.

Should she have gone out with Wade after all? He was great: funny, kind, handsome, responsible, the whole package. Being around him made her heart beat faster and prompted her to think about the possibilities for the future. There was also that moment they had—that almost kiss she wished she hadn't screwed up so it could've turned into a real kiss. She wondered what it would have felt like. Would it have been soft and tentative? Wild and heady?

Slow and sensual? She shook off the thoughts before things got out of hand.

Wade was great, but he wasn't Jeff. Then again, Jeff wasn't Jeff anymore either. There was no Jeff. He was gone and he wasn't coming back, nor would he want her to spend the rest of her life single and lonely. Perhaps it was time to try to move on.

If her regret and overwhelming urge to binge eat were any indication, there was no denying she had feelings for Wade. She should talk to him, tell him she liked him, but she needed to take things slow. That is, if she hadn't blown her chance already. She pulled out her phone to call him but there was no answer. "I guess it's just you and me, tonight," she said hunching over the bowl of popcorn in her lap. With a droop of her shoulders and a remorseful sigh, she settled in to watch the movie, only to be interrupted by someone knocking on her front door.

Maggie stood on her front porch wearing short denim cutoffs and high-heeled cowboy boots. The sequins on her lime-green tank top caught the porch light and glimmered in the evening twilight like fireflies. Matching green eye shadow and bright red lips colored her face and made her features pop. In her hand was a six-pack of beer, still frosty from the fridge. "Pajamas this early on a Friday night? That won't do," she said as she strode into Ashley's house.

"Maggie, what are you doing here—and looking so hot too?" Ashley's voice was full of appreciation.

"I'm here to rescue you from your lonely night at home."

"What did you have in mind?"

"I know a little place where they have a live band and dancing under the stars. It's BYOB." At Ashley's blank look she added, "Bring your own booze. Come on, you went to college."

"I went to night school and I was a single mom with a nine-year-old."

"Didn't you ever party in high school?"

148

"Not really. I was married with a baby by senior year."

"Then you have a lot of catching up to do. So go put on the hottest dress you have so we can have some fun."

"What about the boys?"

"They're fine. They're having a boys' night at the house with Robbie so we might as well have a girls' night out."

"I don't know, I should really be here in case Emmett needs anything."

"He's fine. When I left, they were eating pizza and talking about which action movie to watch. He's having a good time, I promise. But if you're still concerned, then bring your cell with you. Mine is stashed in my boot." At Ashley's reluctance, she added, "You do so much for that boy. It's past time you did something for yourself."

Ashley hadn't been out dancing since, ever, but it had to be better than sitting alone on her couch worrying about Emmett and watching movies that reminded her of what she could be doing with Wade right now. "Okay, I'm in, but I need help deciding what to wear."

***

The *little place* was pretty much just an open field by an old barn lit up with twinkle lights. Rays of yellow, orange, and red shone from lanterns that hung on lines overhead and in the branches of nearby trees. The night was calm and temperate, without so much as a hint of a breeze. The moon was bright and full, though partially hidden by a single wispy cloud that glowed with its white light. The air outside smelled of grass and earth with a trace of distant livestock.

A band played next to the barn, somehow hooked up to enough electricity to power amps that blared their blues guitars into the night. Groups of people sat drinking on the tailgates of their trucks in the makeshift parking lot and stood around in groups talking and laughing with drinks in hand.

Ashley followed Maggie through the crowd to the so-called dance floor, which was merely slabs of pine secured together and laid out on the ground. The crowd on the dance floor was filled with fun energy. People dressed in an array of attire twirled, ground their hips, and stomped to the quick bluegrass music. Ashley smiled as she watched them and felt the involuntary tap of her foot to the beat as she drank her cold beer.

"It's not much to look at, but it sure is a good time," Maggie said.

"Are you kidding? I love it! Jeff would have hated it, though. I could barely get him to dance with me at our own wedding." She thought about their first dance as husband and wife. He'd held her tenderly as he stiffly swayed his uncoordinated body to their song and stepped clumsily on her feet whenever he attempted to spin her around. He may not have been much of a dancer, but all she cared about was being in the embrace of her new husband, the man who loved her completely, who held her like he never wanted to let her go.

Ashley watched as a couple on the dance floor got lost in the music together. Looking deep into each other's eyes, they held one another close as they moved as one. He took her hand and spun her around in a graceful twirl before bringing her close to his chest and wrapping his arms around her again. She wanted that, to feel strong loving arms around her, to be held close like she was precious. She thought of the feel of Wade's soft touch on her cheek and his warmth as he leaned toward her.

"You're thinking about Wade, aren't you?" Maggie said.

"I really blew it, Maggie. What if he won't give me a second chance?"

"Girls' night is not for worrying about men, it's for getting drunk, having fun, and making every man here wish he could put his hands on you. Now, let's put that sexy dress and your to-die-for body to good use."

Ashley finished her beer and let Maggie take the empty bottle and guide her to the dance floor. Maybe a little dancing would help her relax. After all, she didn't put on her best party dress for nothing.

In the heart of the crowd, surrounded by energetic undulating bodies, Ashley followed Maggie's lead and moved her body to the beat, tentatively at first, but more and more confidently as she relaxed until she was lost in the music. She twirled, she shimmied, she shook what her mama gave her until she was out of breath and feeling completely exhilarated. She loved the feel of her ruffled skirt flitting around her legs as she spun, the feel of freedom as she moved her hips and threw her hands into the air.

Maggie yelled in her ear that she needed a break, and Ashley, lungs and muscles burning, followed her to where they stashed their beer. After another beer and a quick break to the ladies' room—which was just a glorified port-o-potty with a sign on the door that said "ladies"—she was back on the dance floor. The alcohol made her head pleasantly foggy, her muscles relaxed, and erased any remaining tension from earlier. Feeling a little tipsy now from her second beer of the night, she swayed loosely to the music, not caring about anything except having fun. "Thank you for bringing me out tonight. This is just what I needed," she yelled to Maggie over the noise. Maggie smiled and gave her a thumbs up.

They danced until Ashley's skin was moist with sweat and her hair clung to the back of her neck. She lifted her thick mane and fanned herself in a poor attempt to cool off. When that didn't help, she tried waving the skirt of her short, ruffled red dress like she was a bird taking flight, trying to get some relief from the breezeless, humid night air.

"If you think this is bad, just wait until summer," Maggie said.

151

"Remind me not to go dancing in summer."

"The first summer here is always the hardest, but you'll get used to it eventually. Well, used to it enough to not let it completely ruin your life."

The song changed to a melodious ballad and people began pairing off for a slow dance, giving Ashley the perfect opportunity to take another break. "I need to go cool off. Are you coming?" They waded through the crowd and found a comfortable spot to rest their hot, tired bodies.

Ashley leaned back on her elbows in the cool grass and tilted her head to look up at the clear night sky. Even with the glow of the twinkle lights and lanterns polluting the darkness, she could see more stars than she ever had before. They glittered and pulsed before her like they were alive, shining luminously in their thousands on the dark canvas they were painted on, like twinkling fireflies trapped forever in a black lake. "It's so beautiful here. I'd love to just fall asleep on the soft grass looking up at those stars," Ashley said.

"It is tempting, but then you'd wake up covered in mosquito bites and scratching like a maniac," Maggie countered.

"So, I'll lay on a blanket and put on bug spray. I still think it would be worth experiencing one time." Ashley sat up and picked up her last beer only to lower it when she realized it was as warm as the night air around them. "I'm really glad I came here. Not just here to the party, but here to Alabama, here to Mason."

"That makes two of us." Maggie clinked her beer on Ashley's and took a swig, making a face as she swallowed. "Beer sure is nasty when it isn't cold."

"Why do you think I'm not drinking mine?" Ashley turned her attention back to the dancing couples where she saw a familiar face. "Is that Reid over there?" She pointed to a man who had his body pressed up against a young, scantily dressed woman with platinum blond hair, wearing stilettos so high Ashley wondered how she didn't teeter over just standing still.

"It appears so, and he looks to have found his conquest for the evening. Her poor unfortunate soul."

Ashley saw the seductive smile on the woman's face and how she pressed herself as close to Reid as possible like she wanted to jump inside of him. "She doesn't seem to mind his attention."

"They all enjoy themselves until the walk of shame the morning after."

If Reid was here, it was possible Wade was too. She searched the crowd involuntarily until she found herself studying the broad shoulders and strong back of a man standing a few yards away from Reid. He wore dark-wash jeans, boots, and a blue-and-white-plaid shirt. Dainty hands with long fake fingernails painted a sparkly ruby red wrapped around his neck. Ashley held her breath as the couple turned in a circle, swaying to the soft twang of the music, waiting for the man's identity to be revealed.

Ashley felt like someone had stabbed her in the gut. Wade's strong hands rested on the hips of a beautiful woman with long fire-red hair that shined in the moonlight. She had a tiny waist, hourglass hips, and long legs that looked like they stretched for miles in her microscopic skirt. The round outline of her perfect butt peeked out from the bottom seam of the red leather, leaving little to the imagination. She wore a glittery white halter top that cut low enough to reveal the crease between her oversized, too-stiff breasts.

A small smile played on her pouty painted red lips as she looked longingly at Wade. She fluttered her fake eyelashes at him as she pressed the front of her body against his hips. Ashley's gut wrenched as she watched her angle her head and part her lips in invitation. She couldn't watch anymore. "I need to get some air."

"But we're already outside. What happened? You look like you're going to be sick." Maggie scanned the area where Ashley was last looking and gasped at the sight. "Ashley, I'm so sorry We can leave if you want. I'll come with you."

Ashley waved her off. "No, it's fine. I just want to be alone for a minute." She turned her back and walked away from the dance floor, away from what she was afraid was happening there. The weight on her chest was crushing her, making it hard to breathe. She was suddenly lightheaded and feared she might fall over. She put her hands against a tree trunk and leaned over as she struggled to pull air into her lungs, to ease the knife in her belly. It was as though she had just run that mile again, the sharp stitch in her side pulsing with every gasp of air, but this time was worse. This time it was her emotions bubbling up and threatening to spill out instead of her breakfast.

She steadied herself as she took small breaths in through her nose and out of her mouth. As her heart slowed and her head cleared, she felt a soft touch on her shoulder. "Maggie, I told you, I'm fine." She turned around and found herself face-to-face with the man she hadn't been able to stop thinking about all day. Her eyes narrowed. "Wade. It's funny meeting you here. Are you having a nice time?" her words were full of loathing.

"I know you saw me with Roxy. You seemed upset so I wanted to check on you. Are you okay?"

Her brows furrowed in anger and her voice turned to venom. "Well, at least you learned her name before feeling her up, so I guess you're not a complete scumbag."

His eyebrows lifted with surprise. Before he could speak, Ashley cut him off. "I don't get it, Wade. Yesterday, you say you have feelings for me and you ask me out for tonight, but then here you are grinding up against some tramp who was practically in her underwear. Not even a stripper would call that a skirt."

Now it was his turn to get irritated. "You rejected me, Ashley."

"And it was a good thing I did because apparently half-naked tramps with plastic boobs and fake eyelashes are more your type. Was that a butterfly tattoo on her back? How adorable," she spat.

"I wanted to be out with you tonight, Ashley"—his voice took on an edge—"but since you turned me down, I don't see how it's any of your business who I go out with."

"I can't believe I spent the whole night wishing I was out with you! I don't know why I ever liked you. But, you're right, it's none of my business. Feel free to go out with any floozy you want. Enjoy those plastic boobs digging into your chest tonight—that ought to be real sexy. Just make sure you use protection. She looks like she has been around the block a few times. You wouldn't want to die from some horrible slut disease." Fists balled, nostrils flaring, Ashley whirled around to storm away when strong hands caught her firmly and tugged her back.

In the next moment, Wade pulled her flush against his body. His hands tangled in her hair and his lips found hers without hesitation. The kiss was fervent and wild, their tongues tangled together in a savage dance. He tasted of peppermint and smelled of sweat, spice, and Wade, a powerful combination that left an ache deep in her belly. Her skin heated until she felt as though she'd catch fire. Her knees were weak like they might give out at any moment. He deepened the kiss further and she wrapped her arms around his neck to pull him even closer, tangling her fingers in his thick dark hair.

Too soon, he pulled away, leaving her panting and desperate for more. She could see the desire carved on his face and his pupils dilated all the way to black."Isn't your date going to be pissed that you're over here making out with another woman?" she asked, breathless.

"Probably, but I don't care. I only went out with her as a favor to Reid so he could have a chance with her friend. And to try to forget you. In case you were wondering, it didn't work."

"It seemed like you were having a good time with her. I saw her try to kiss you."

"Did you also see me turn her down and follow you over here? She means nothing to me, Ashley. You are the one I want, not her. Nothing was going to happen with her tonight, even before I saw you were here." He leaned in and gave her another kiss on the lips, slow and tender this time like she was precious to him. She closed her eyes and melted into the kiss.

"My offer is still on the table. I hope you'll think it over." With those words, he turned around and left her in the darkness.

***

After a cool shower, Ashley lay sprawled on her bed staring up at the ceiling. She had discovered how it felt to kiss Wade tonight and now she only wanted more of it. Her feelings for him weren't going away and she was no longer sure she wanted them to. If she let him go, she would live to regret it. Maybe she didn't have to stop loving Jeff to be with Wade. Maybe it was possible to love them both.

Ashley had been alone, trapped in her own bubble of grief for the past four years and now, she acknowledged how desperate she was to escape it. She didn't want to be dragged down by grief or guilt anymore. Instead, she wanted to live, to love, to have passionate kisses in the dark and gentle caresses, and to stay up all night making love. She wanted going out on dates, romance, and a possibility of a future with someone. She wanted to be free to love again and she wanted Wade. It was time to say good-bye to the past for good.

She rose from the bed and slid open her closet door. Buried behind racks of shoes, hanging dresses, and handbags was a simple wooden box. She pulled it out and carefully set it on the bed. She twirled her wedding band as she looked at the lid and wondered if she had the strength to do this. So many times she had opened this box and studied its contents, but never had it been the last time. Jeff would want her to be happy and this was the only way she thought she could let herself be. It was time. She took a deep breath and opened the lid.

CHAPTER
TWENTY - TWO

ASHLEY SAT CROSS-LEGGED on her bed, looking down at the open box before her. The shades were drawn, her room lit only by the lamp on her bedside table. Though she wouldn't see it until later tonight, the moon was full and luminous above the house, lighting up the darkness outside with a soft eerie glow.

At times she couldn't even look at the contents of this box. Other times she'd needed to stop partway through, sobbing violently and struggling to breathe. Now, as the mementos stared up at her, her shoulders drooped only a little. The rest of her maintained its composure. Her hands were steady, her heart was beating its dependable rhythm, her eyes were dry as they gazed intently at the memories before her. She didn't know when it had happened, but she was ready to say good-bye.

She picked up the stack of some of her favorite photographs and carefully looked through them one by one: Jeff sitting beside her, his hand caressing her pregnant belly; Jeff cuddling Emmett in the hospital on the day he was born, his face lit up with pure joy; Jeff and Emmett sitting on Jeff's dirt bike, his oversized helmet hiding Emmett's eyes. She looked through these photographs and more, studying each one closely as she tried to recall the time they'd been taken. As she stared at the images of their time together, the expected pain didn't come. Though her eyes misted, warmth filled her heart and the corners of her lips curved upward into a smile. Surges of love and comfort overwhelmed any lingering feelings of grief. The notion gave her strength and reaffirmed she was doing the right thing.

Underneath the pile of photographs were Jeff's military dog tags. She pulled them out and cupped the cool metal in her hands, feeling the bumps of the letters on her palms. For nearly their entire marriage they hung on a chain around his neck, pressed close to his heart. He almost never took them off. A warm shiver spread through her as she remembered the chill of the metal brushing against her warm, sensitized skin when they made love. She opened her hands to read the words inscribed on the metal face—his name, blood type, social security number—information that no longer served any purpose. She took a deep breath to ease the pressure on her chest as she ran her fingers over the bumpy surface one last time. Giving them a final squeeze, she laid them on the comforter alongside the photographs.

Next was a pile of creased papers that had been folded and unfolded many times. She tentatively reached inside and pulled them out, setting them on her comforter. She picked up the one on top and slowly opened it, listening to the sound of the paper crinkling between her fingertips. As she looked down at the pages in her hands, Jeff's familiar messy scrawl stared up at her.

The letter she held was one of the last he had sent her before he retired from the military. Over his eight years in the Marines, Jeff wrote her letters as often as he could. Most of the letters contained similar content to the one she clutched now: words that expressed how much he loved her, updates on how things were going, and how he missed her and couldn't wait to be back home. Though she had read the words countless times before, she took the time to go through them again now, saying a final good-bye with every letter added to the finished stack on her bed.

Still in the box was a small leather-bound book: a diary she had kept over the course of their marriage. She skimmed the yellowing pages, urging the memories—both good and bad—of past times they'd shared to sink into her heart. Once satisfied, she flipped to the last few entries. As she read through the final pages, she noticed her hands were shaking. She didn't write much the last year of Jeff's life because she didn't want to remember those dark times that still haunted her dreams. Though jumbled and disorganized like her mental state at the time they were written, the past few entries shared a common theme: terror. She had been terrified of what Jeff might do next and what would become of their family. She'd grown afraid of her own husband, the man she once trusted with her life.

Her nightmares were one thing, but reading the events written in her own words was another experience entirely. Her uncertainty, her fear, her pain, all the trauma she experienced at that time bubbled up inside her as she read through the pages. When she finished, her cheeks were wet with tears and her breaths came harsh and quick. Reliving her terror in her own words was a wake-up call. That year had been awful. Why was she still holding onto a man who made her feel like this?

She dried her eyes and took some deep breaths, calming herself. Jeff wasn't a bad man. He was a good father and a good husband who did some unspeakable things. Still, she knew it wasn't entirely his fault. She was partially to blame for what happened, which was part of the reason she didn't allow herself to move on. Guilt was a powerful thing. So was love. Despite everything that occurred, she loved him still. They had a great life together, but that life was over now. She would always love him, and that was okay, but she needed to stop obsessing. She could analyze everything to death, continue to feel guilty forever, or be loyal to her departed for the rest of her life, but what good would it do now? It was over.

She stilled as she looked at the next item in the box: the sealed oversized envelope of an old piece of spam mail. The advertisement for the local cable company had been sitting unopened on the kitchen counter the day Jeff died. On the back were Jeff's last written words to her, scribbled, barely legible as if he'd been in a hurry.

Despite the morbidity of the moment, a faint smile played on her lips as she pictured Jeff standing in their kitchen, looking frantically for something to write on. Ashley had always made sure to put a blank pad of paper next to the telephone and another one on the fridge to jot down messages, but Jeff rarely used them. Instead, he would write his messages on whatever writing surface was closest to him: magazines, bills, junk mail, his arm. If something wasn't directly in his line of vision—sometimes even that wasn't enough—he wouldn't see it. She called it "man looking," and Jeff was notorious for it.

She picked up the envelope and ran her fingers over the handwritten ink. She didn't need to read the note to know what it said. She had read it countless times in the weeks following his death, forever committing his words to memory. At first she was destroyed, unsure of how she would ever recover. But, she also felt lucky, relieved even, from his admission because it meant she would never have to be afraid of him again. It was the latter that always left her ridden with guilt as though she was a terrible wife for having felt relieved her husband was gone. Guilt had piled on more guilt. That, on top of her unwavering sense of duty and love for the man Jeff once was, had been enough for her to hide the truth from herself.

In her grief she had labeled Jeff's last action as heroic, but now she recognized he was just running away. He could have handled everything better, and if he had there was a chance they would have still been happy today. She could be angry at him, resent him even, as she knew that Emmett sometimes did, but what would it help? In her heart she knew he thought he was doing the right thing and she couldn't fault him for that.

She could dwell on her grief, her anger, her betrayal, her fear, her worship of him, her guilt, and all of the other contradictory emotions she harbored for the rest of her life, or she could let everything go and make room for new emotions, new memories. She could finally leave the past behind her and allow herself to move on. She could allow herself to have a future.

As she set the diary aside, she peered at the last object in the box. Absent of its companions, Jeff's titanium wedding band looked small and lonely. She picked it up and held it gently between her fingertips before sliding it onto the base of her finger.

Even on her thumb, the ring slid around loosely. The grey unpolished surface was riddled with tiny scratches. Jeff had worn it since the day they were married and was wearing it when he died. As she twirled it around her finger, she waited to feel some kind of grand emotion, but all that came was the same heavy ache that had clung to her heart for the past four years.

She twirled her own wedding band, hesitating. Her finger had been its home for the last thirteen years of her life and taking it off seemed foreign. Still, it was the last piece of this journey to say good-bye to her past and she so wanted to let it go. Wedding bands were for married people, and she no longer had a husband.

With a deep breath, she slowly slid the metal off her finger, only struggling for a moment at her knuckle. She pulled Jeff's ring off her thumb and clutched them both tightly in her fist, feeling the hard metals dig into her flesh. Slowly, she opened her hand to take one last look at the bands resting there. They lay overlapping one another, her shiny white gold against his dark titanium as if they were bound together.

As she closed her fist, knowing what would happen next, she felt the emotion building. Though her throat was tight with unshed sadness, her back was straight and her shoulders were square with determination. She lowered the rings into the empty box where they would remain unseen by another living soul.

She blinked back tears, never letting her strength waver as she put the objects in the box. The photographs she would keep— Emmett deserved to hold on to those memories if he wanted to— but the rest of it needed to go. One by one, she put away every memory that had kept her from moving on, from letting herself find happiness. Once everything was stowed inside, she closed the lid with finality. With her head square on her shoulders, she straightened and rose from the bed to finish it.

CHAPTER
TWENTY - THREE

ASHLEY FELT REJUVENATED. Last night had been a rollercoaster of emotions and there were times when she wasn't sure she would make it through. But her determination to be free to find happiness again had surmounted all desire to turn back. Purging herself of the records of her past was her way to prove to herself she was ready to take the next step. Finally she could rid herself of all guilt and sense of duty she harbored for the man she had loved.

With the moon overhead in the stillness of the dark, she had dug a hole in the forest that would become her past's final resting place. As she stood looking down at the box in the ground, there was only a short moment of hesitation. One moment, she wanted to clutch the box to her chest like a child with her treasured teddy bear and return it to the safety of her closet. Like her grief, the moment of hesitation passed, and she covered her past with earth, determined to never let it consume her again. With hope blooming in her chest, she'd said a silent good-bye and refused to look back.

Once home in her own bed, she'd slept a deep and dreamless sleep. When she woke to the birds singing in the trees and her neighbors mowing their lawns in the warm, bright morning, she felt free. Truly and utterly free.

She thought she would feel naked without her wedding band, like something was missing. But once the initial pain of taking it off had passed, she realized it had actually weighed her down. Her actions last night gave her clarity and she was grateful to have had the courage to complete them.

She was finally able to remember the good times she shared with Jeff along with the bad and simply be grateful that she had known him. She would always love Jeff, but for the first time in too many years, there was finally room in her heart for a future.

Ashley looked at her reflection in her full-length mirror. She looked fresh and vibrant, her cheeks flushed pink with excitement. She wore a long flowing skirt that reached her calves, a white camisole accented with lace, and her comfortable flats. Her hair was pulled back in a loose braid and embellished with a flower hair clip behind her ear. Wade had told her to dress casual and wear comfortable shoes for their date, so here she stood in her best attempt to merge comfort and elegance into one. She was thankful her reflection did little to reveal the swirling tempest of nerves within.

While Emmett was with the Millers at Carson's dirt bike competition, Ashley was going on an official first date, her first one in over a decade, possibly even her first one ever. She and Jeff and had been together since high school, so as they got to know each other there were plenty of secret kisses in the hallways, making out under the bleachers, holding hands in the quad, but not much else. Sure, over the years they had their share of date nights, but they were already a couple by then. She was completely clueless about the whole concept of dating. She had no idea what to expect today and her inexperience rattled her. What should she talk about? What if she said something stupid or inappropriate?

What if Wade realized he didn't like her as much as he first thought?

Trying to stay afloat in her sea of self-doubt, she attempted to talk herself down. She and Wade had eaten dinner together every night this week, so she knew she was capable of talking to him. Granted, her son was at the table with them, and dinner at her house with Emmett couldn't exactly be considered a date.

At least they'd already learned some things about each other. Yet Wade had no idea of the kinds of dark things that went on the last year of Jeff's life or about the box of mementos she kept for so many years. What if he thought she was too fragile or worse, crazy? *Not helping!*

They had already kissed and it was amazing. Although, she was a little drunk at the time, and he did most of the work. What if she was a bad kisser or did something to put him off? She was making herself crazy. If she kept trying to reason with herself, she was only going to need to take another shower and she didn't have time for that. She blew out a breath as she smoothed the invisible wrinkles on her skirt. Everything was going to be fine.

The knock at her door made her breath quicken. Giving her reflection one final check, she pulled open the door. Wade was looking as rugged and handsome as always in dark jeans and a white collared shirt. His stubble was gone, smooth tanned skin in its place. Her heart fluttered when he greeted her with a smile that reached all the way to the sparkle in his eyes.

"You look beautiful," he said.

"So do you. I mean handsome. You look handsome." *Please don't be a blubbering idiot today.* "What are we doing today?"

"I know how you said you wanted to keep things quiet until you could tell Emmett about us, so I was thinking a picnic. I know a beautiful place that overlooks the river where no one will bother us."

"Sounds perfect."

He held out his hand and led her to his truck. After opening her door and helping her up into his lifted cab, he went around to the other side and climbed in next to her. Perched on the backseat she saw an adorable wicker picnic basket and a folded blanket. "You have a picnic basket?"

"I borrowed it from Reid."

Incredulous, she asked, "Reid has a picnic basket?"

"Reid was known to be a romantic at one time in his life."

"What happened?"

"That's not my story to tell."

***

They drove out of town and onto a windy gravel road. The hills around them were lush and green from the winter's rains and dotted with pink and yellow flowers in bloom for spring. Ground squirrels darted in and out of their burrows and rolled over each other in play. As they continued driving down the road, the foliage became more dense with mature pine trees. Before long they pulled off the road and parked in a small dirt clearing.

"We have to walk from here. Our spot is straight through those trees," Wade said.

With their picnic basket and blanket in hand, Wade led Ashley through the woods on a thin path littered with fallen pine needles. The tall, dense trees blocked most of the sun's light, leaving the forest floor in shadow. The soft earth beneath their feet, still holding in moisture from the early spring rains, squished softly as they walked. Birds chirped and sang off-key from their unseen perches in the trees around them. The air smelled fresh like dew and sap.

As they moved through the last line of trees, they came to a small clearing. The Alabama River lay straight ahead, its waters calm except for the slow-moving current and the occasional small ripples from fish swimming beneath the surface.

Ashley gasped in awe. "Wow. It's so beautiful here and so peaceful. Why are we the only ones here?"

"I own this land, from where we parked my truck to up along the bank to those trees over there. It's about four acres total. I bought it a few years ago. I'd like to eventually build my own house here. But, for now, I just use it to get away and have a little peace."

"It's such a beautiful spot for it."

Wade laid out their blanket on the soft grass of the riverbank and set up their lunch. Chicken salad sandwiches on puffy croissants, potato salad, pimento cheese and flaky crackers, and a small caramel cake for dessert. "Everything looks so delicious. Did you make it?" Ashley asked.

Wade shook his head. "I got it from Hardy's. Trust me, you wouldn't want me to have made any of this."

"I don't see how you can be as bad of a cook as you say you are."

"I'll make you dinner sometime and then you can see for yourself."

She chuckled and took a bite of her sandwich. "Well, you at least know where to buy a good sandwich."

"Thanks. I've had years of practice. You should try the pimento cheese. It's a southern favorite." He scooped out a spoonful of cheese and put it on a cracker before handing it to her.

When she took a bite, a collection of crumbs dropped to the blanket and her skirt. She brushed them off, her cheeks turning red. "That is good. But if I have too many of those, we may be covered in crumbs by the end of our date."

"On the bright side, you'll feed some hungry birds once we leave."

"I have always had a soft spot for animals," she said as she reached for another cracker.

"Is that why you became a veterinary technician?"

"That, among other reasons. Growing up, I'd always wanted to be a veterinarian. I even planned to go to school for it after high school. But, then I got pregnant with Emmett and married Jeff shortly after, and life gave me other priorities. With Jeff being gone so much, I had to do everything myself, which didn't leave much room for ambition. Between that and moving around every few years, I didn't have an opportunity to go to college or even to have much of a job at all."

"What about your parents?"

Ashley's gaze dropped to the hem of her skirt where her fingers played nervously. "They're not in the picture."

Wade watched Ashley's fingers turn white from their tight grip on the fabric. "Do you mind me asking what happened?"

She tore her hands from her skirt and clenched them in her lap. "They told me to give Emmett up for adoption. When I didn't listen and instead married Jeff without their consent, they were furious. They told me I was making a huge mistake and they refused to have any part in it." Her eyed glistened with tears. "They told me if I insisted on ruining my life, then I would do it alone. That was the last time we spoke."

Wade laid his hand over her fist and ran his thumb across her white knuckles. "You still haven't spoken to them, even after all these years?"

Her brows furrowed in anger as she folded her arms across her chest. "Why should I? They turned their backs on me, their only daughter! And they made it very clear they didn't want to be a part of Emmett's life. Besides, I don't need them. I've done just fine on my own."

He nodded. "I don't doubt that. I just wonder if even though you don't need them, you might still want them to be a part of your life."

After a pause, her shoulders sagged and her fists relaxed. Her eyes softened as she looked at Wade. "I'm sorry. I didn't mean to snap at you. I'm touched that you care, but I'd rather not talk about my parents. I don't want to be angry today. That might turn me into a bad date."

Wade's mouth curved in sympathy as he gave her hand a squeeze. "I understand. Family is a tough subject for me too. I didn't mean to pry. Let's start over." Lightening the mood, he curled his fingers around his chin and leaned toward her in exaggerated interest. "So, you were telling me about why you became a veterinary technician instead of a veterinarian."

Ashley smiled gratefully. "Right. So, life got in the way and school just continued to be put off for one reason or another. When Jeff died, I knew I needed to get a decent-paying job to support Emmett and me, but I didn't have the money or the time for the years of schooling it takes to become a vet. So, I worked at a groomer's during the day and went to school at night and before I knew it, I had my vet tech license and found a job doing that in the city. I wasn't a veterinarian, but it was as close as I could get under the circumstances. And I'm glad I did it. I love my job, especially since I've moved here."

"That couldn't have been easy, working all day, going to school at night, and being a mom everywhere in between. How did you manage it all?"

"I didn't have much of a choice. Living in the city was expensive and we blew through our savings quickly. Supporting myself and my son on a job that didn't require some kind of degree was near impossible, so I knew I had to do more. I'm sure Emmett grew pretty tired of babysitters and after-school programs, and I know I feel like I was robbed of my time with him for those years.

But, I did what I had to and now we are better for it. Sometimes I wonder if my being gone so much had something to do with his growing delinquency. I wasn't there enough to help steer him away from the bad influences around him."

Wade reached over and briefly placed his hand over hers. "You can't blame yourself. Like you said, you didn't have a choice. You had to do what you needed to take care of your family. Besides, Emmett is doing a lot better now."

She smiled. "Yes, he is. And I'm so grateful for that. It seems like moving here was one of the better choices I've made."

"I think so. I know I'm better for it."

She looked up at him shyly through thick lashes and gave him a coy smile. "I am too. Thank you for giving me another chance."

"I'm just glad you came to your senses," he teased. Her laugh was music to his ears. "So why did you decide to leave the city?"

"For a number of reasons, but mainly for Emmett. We didn't live in the best neighborhood so crime was always around. He started hanging out with some older kids in the neighborhood who I think pressured him into doing some pretty destructive things. It started out small: staying out past curfew, trespassing, ditching school, but it quickly escalated from there. Pretty soon he was drinking and smoking cigarettes, vandalizing other people's property, and the police were bringing him home to me nearly every weekend for one thing or another. Things got out of hand pretty fast and before long he was looking at three months in juvie. None of my attempts to steer him in the right direction seemed to work, so I decided I needed to get him away from there."

"Why did you choose Mason?"

"You'll probably think it's weird, but Mason kind of chose me. Emmett had just been sent to the juvenile detention center in Camden County for theft. He stole thousands of dollars' worth of computer equipment from a local private school with his so-called friends. That was the plan anyway, but, they ended up ditching him, letting Emmett take all the blame. He was facing some pretty severe consequences because of his record. An extended stay in lockup, followed by probation, community service, and fines that nearly bankrupted me, to name a few."

Ashley took a bite of her sandwich and swallowed before continuing. "Things were escalating for a while and I had enough. One night I was on my computer searching for, I don't know what, answers maybe, anything that might help our situation. Long story short, I didn't find anything. Frustrated, I went to close the browser but ended up clicking on an advertisement for one of those job search sites by mistake. It turned out that the featured job was the one for Maggie's animal clinic. Something, maybe you could call it fate, compelled me to click on that posting. I decided to do some research on the town of Mason and I fell in love. The next thing I knew, I was putting in my notice at my job and packing my bags." She shrugged. "It's hard to explain. I guess it was more a feeling than anything else. Something about it just felt right. It seemed like the answer I'd been looking for."

"Was it everything you were looking for?"

She gazed at him for a long moment until her cheeks turned pink. "It's too soon to tell for sure, but it looks like it's turning out to be more than I hoped for."

His skin tingled as her sparkly blue eyes searched his. He ached to kiss her and felt himself lean toward her, but she broke their gaze and took another bite of her sandwich, stealing the moment. "That couldn't have been easy leaving everything familiar to move somewhere you'd never been before."

"I'd be lying if I said I wasn't scared." She laughed without humor. "On our drive down here, I almost turned around to go home. But, I felt like I didn't have much of a choice. If we hadn't left… I don't want to think about where we'd be now." She stared at the calm waters of the river appearing to contemplate some unknown scenario. She shook her head slightly as if clearing unwelcome thoughts before returning her attention to Wade and offering him a smile. "Luckily, I won't have to find out."

"I'm really glad you came."

"So am I. Look at me doing all the talking. I think I should give you a turn."

"I like hearing about you."

"I want to know how your dad is doing." She popped the last bite of her sandwich into her mouth.

"Carrying on as usual, except now I'm pretty sure he is drunk in the mornings too. He seems to be going through his booze stash a lot quicker these days. He's been complaining about a pain in his side too, but of course he won't let me take him to see a doctor."

"Oh no. Is there anything you can do to change his mind?"

"Believe me, I've tried. I've even contemplated bending the rules to get some test results out of him, but ultimately it's his body so it's his decision. All I can do is keep riding him about it and make sure he eats and isn't living in filth."

"You do a lot for him. He's lucky to have you looking after him. Has he gone to see Ford yet?"

He let out a pained sigh. "No. Apparently getting his fix is more important than seeing his son. It's getting pretty bad, the drinking. He can barely function anymore."

"Is that why you don't drink? Because of your dad?"

"It's part of the reason," he admitted.

"What's the other part?"

"I think that story is a little too much for a first date," he said, reaching for another sandwich.

"Believe me, I have more than my fair share of demons. I won't judge you. I just want to know more about you."

He studied her for a moment. She seemed curious, eager for information, but also genuine. Ashley wasn't a judgmental person. If anyone would accept his flaws, it would be her. If he wanted things to go further with her he would have to tell her the truth anyways—he wouldn't feel right otherwise. He might as well put it all out in the open now. If she rejected him, it might save him some heartache before he was in too deep.

He took a deep breath, readying himself. "After my mom died, my dad became a useless drunk and was doing Ford more harm than good. At first I dropped out of school to help, but when I saw how bad things were getting, I knew I needed to do more." Wade thought about how he'd come home from work to find his dad passed out drunk and the house in shambles—furniture broken, holes in the walls—and Ford curled up and shaking in the back of the kitchen cupboard, his cheeks pink and stained with dried tears. Even after all these years the image still rattled him.

"So, I coaxed my dad out of the house and I took over as Ford's guardian. I tried my best to raise him, but it wasn't so easy for me. I was young, I had a lot of growing up to do myself, and I wasn't always the best at dealing with the stress of it all." He took a moment to gather himself. Once he said the words there was no taking them back.

Just rip off the bandage. "I'd have a beer in the evenings to help take the edge off. But one beer turned into two, which turned into three. Pretty soon, I was in a bad place, drinking all the time and not being as present for Ford as I should have been. I lost my job and things went downhill from there."

He paused to clear the lump in his throat. "I was stuck in my own head, depressed, and stressed out. I didn't even notice what was going on with Ford. It took a phone call from the county for me to realize. Ford had been arrested for selling drugs and assaulting the officer who arrested him. I was so out of touch with things because of the drinking I didn't even know what Ford was up to. I thought everything was fine. That's when I realized I was turning out to be a lousy, neglectful drunk just like my dad." His hands curled into fists.

"I refused to be like him, so I got help and now I've been sober for almost six years. Still, I can't help but think what happened with Ford was my fault. I was too drunk to notice what kind of trouble he was getting into and by the time I did, it was too late. He had already set that path for himself. I tried to help him from then on, to be there for him, to try to be a good parent for him, but nothing worked."

The lump in his throat grew as he thought about Ford's steadily growing record of misdemeanors. Theft and larceny had been Ford's personal preferences, but he had dabbled in a variety of criminal activities. Wade took a deep breath. "Things progressed and quickly got out of hand. One night Ford broke into his girlfriend's ex-boyfriend's house to rob him and threaten him with a knife. The guy pressed charges and now Ford's spending the rest of his youth in prison. The worst part was, I didn't even know Ford was seeing someone. I'd already lost him by then." His voice wavered. "I failed him." He could no longer swallow past the lump in his throat. When he looked up, Ashley gazed at him with sympathy. "I told you, it was too much for a first date."

"No, I'm glad you told me. And I can actually relate. Whenever Emmett got into trouble, I always felt like it was all my fault. Like, there was something I did or something I didn't do that I should have. You were given a lot of responsibility, and at such a young age. But you stepped up and you were there for your brother. You had some difficulties along the way, we all do, but you worked hard to make it right. Not many people can recognize when they have a problem. But you did, and you were strong enough to fix it. I admire that."

"I don't know if I'm worthy of any admiration, but I appreciate the sentiment. I'm just relieved you're not running for the hills right now."

"I wouldn't do that. I'm happy right where I am." Ashley lightly touched his arm and his breath hitched as she looked up at him through long eyelashes. His pulse quickened as he leaned in to lightly brush his lips against hers. Her lips, which were soft and tasted sweet like the strawberry pink gloss that colored them, parted as he rubbed his thumb gently over them before cupping her chin and pulling her to him for another kiss. When he pulled away, he smoothed his thumb across her cheek, enjoying the silky warmth of her flushed skin. He dropped his hand only to place it in hers, lacing their fingers in an intimate embrace.

"So, you answered a personal question. That means it's my turn. Ask me anything you want," she said.

"You don't have to reciprocate. That's not why I told you about my drinking."

"I know, but it's only fair. Go ahead. Ask." When he hesitated she added, "Please? I want you to."

"Okay… What's your favorite food?"

She rolled her eyes at him. She looked so much like Emmett in that moment he couldn't keep from smiling. "Come on. Ask me something personal," she urged.

"Fine. Tell me about you and Jeff."

She shifted on the blanket. "What do you want to know?"

"What was he like? What were you like together?"

"He was kind, a bit hard around the edges, but he loved us. He was a good dad, always making time to do special things with Emmett like fixing things around the house and teaching him how to play baseball."

"How did you meet?"

"We went to high school together. I was a junior and he was a senior. We fell in love, fast and completely. It was undeniable, and even then I knew I wanted to spend my life with him." She was looking out at the water, a small smile on her lips. "When he graduated, he enlisted in the Marine Corps. People thought that would be the end of us, but we were strong, we made it work.

Then, my senior year I got pregnant with Emmett and the next thing I knew, we were married and raising a family together."

"That must have been difficult, being such a young mother with a husband who was away all the time."

She looked at him. "It was at times, but when Jeff was home, things were really good. We were a family and we were still madly in love. I missed him so much when he was gone and I would worry all the time, but he always came home. People often assume we only got married because I was pregnant. That was part of it, but we were also in love. I wanted to spend my life with him, wherever he was, baby or no baby."

"It sounds like you two were happy."

"We were."

There was something she wasn't telling him, something that made her avert her gaze and her lips tremble, but he wasn't going to press her. She would tell him when she was ready. "How about some dessert?" he suggested.

She looked at him and smiled warmly. "I can never turn down dessert."

"Have you ever had caramel cake?"

The afternoon transpired with the easiest flowing conversation and the most enjoyable company Wade had ever experienced. After a romantic walk along the river and some tender moments beneath the trees, their time came to an end. Reluctantly he drove Ashley home and walked her to the front door.

He couldn't remember a better day, and he knew for certain he'd never experienced a better date than this. Nothing about it had been perfect, and yet everything had been extraordinary. Ashley was sincere and honest, and her heart—though broken by loss— was capable of tremendous love. Love for her son, love for her departed, love for her future and everything in it. He wanted to be a part of her future.

"What are you thinking about?" she asked.

"I'm pretty sure there's nothing that could make me not want you."

"What if I told you I was a man?"

He laughed. "Okay, that might do it, but it would take some serious deliberation. I had a great time today."

"I did too."

"Can I take you out again soon?"

"I'd like that. I just need to find someone to stay with Emmett for me. Hopefully next weekend. Will you have dinner with us this week?"

"You couldn't keep me away if you tried."

"I look forward to it. Just please, do me a favor and don't mention us to Emmett yet. I need to find a way to tell him on my own first."

"Of course. Will I see you at Maggie's barbecue later?"

"I'll be there. To be safe, let's keep our relationship quiet there too. I'd hate for Emmett to find out from someone else."

"Okay, but it's going to be tough to be next to you all afternoon without being able to do this." He leaned in to kiss her, slow and soft at first but quickly growing in heat and intensity. He moved his hands down to her hips and pulled her closer to him. Her intoxicating smell of freesia and hope filled his lungs, sparking an overwhelming sense of affection that spread through his chest and made him weak in the knees.

She rubbed her hands up his back and pressed her body to his, adding desire to the spread of emotions coursing through his body and igniting his blood. Not wanting to lose control, he broke away and pressed his forehead to hers as they caught their breath.

She must have been affected too because when she spoke her voice was a breathy whisper. "We probably shouldn't do that in front of other people anyways. That might be a little too intense for our more innocent viewers."

"For restricted audiences only, got it. I'll see you soon."

"Thank you for today. I had a nice time."

As she stepped inside she turned to give Wade one final look that made his heart leap for joy. The door closed behind her, separating them, and he realized the truth. He had fallen hopelessly in love with her.

CHAPTER
TWENTY - FOUR

THE RAIN CAME down in sheets all day. Streams of water rushed down the gutters to the drain like tiny raging rivers. Massive muddy puddles turned lawns into swamps. The air was warm and humid from the remnants of the tropical storm that had traveled five hundred miles from the coast of Florida to canopy Mason. Fortunately the hurricane's root-ripping, home-destroying, ninety-mile-per-hour winds dissipated before reaching them, leaving a heavy steady rain and the occasional crack of thunder overhead. The storm may not have been dangerous, but it sure was miserable to be stuck outside in it.

Wade stood on the slippery roof, trying to maintain his balance as he worked. He wiped the rain out of his eyes in hopes of seeing better, but fresh drops replaced them almost instantly. His clothes were soaked and clung to his body uncomfortably. He was wet and tired and miserable, but he'd come here to do a job and he wouldn't stop until it was done. Early this morning, he'd received several calls from town residents reporting leaky roofs and clogged gutters. Jobs were jobs and they paid the bills, so he wasn't about to turn anything down, no matter how wretched the circumstances.

Wade pried up another damaged roof shingle and began scraping off the cement underneath. Just a few more hours to go and he would be done for the day, a few hours of back-breaking labor with the rain spattering his face and soaking him down to his bones. The thought darkened his mood. After he fixed this leaky roof, he had a few more gutters to clean before his work was done. He hoped for enough time to enjoy a much-deserved steamy cup of coffee and a hot shower before it was time to pick up Emmett from tutoring.

He'd been dating Ashley for almost two weeks now, and she still hadn't told Emmett about them. Wade understood she was afraid of how Emmett would react, but waiting would only make things worse. Recently, Emmett had been sniffing around, asking him if anything was going on between them. Wade tried his best to avoid telling him the whole truth, but that only made him feel terrible. He didn't want to break his word to Ashley, but he also hated not being truthful with Emmett. He deserved to know the truth. What if Emmett asked him flat out if he was dating Ashley? What should he do then? No matter what he did, someone would feel betrayed. He hoped it didn't come to that.

Wade shook the water out of his hair and cemented a new shingle in place. As he worked, his mind drifted to Ashley. She had him completely under her spell and he never wanted to wake up. He had it bad for her and at this point he knew he could never walk away from her unscathed. Thinking about the feel of her lips on his, the feel of her smooth skin underneath his fingertips, how the sight of her smile warmed him from the inside out, helped lighten his mood as he weathered the storm. He willed his thoughts of Ashley and the promise of a hot delicious meal tonight to help get him through the next few hours.

***

Wade had received an additional urgent work call today for a flooded basement. Drying out the space and sandbagging the entire area had taken the remainder of his afternoon. Fortunately for the owner of the home, there was no permanent water damage, but unfortunately for Wade, taking on the extra job left him no time for the hot shower or the steaming cup of coffee he had promised himself earlier.

He barely had enough time to towel dry his hair and put on dry clothes before it was time to pick Emmett up from tutoring. He didn't know how Ashley did it all every day. Not only did she work all day and take care of Emmett, she also managed to find time to clean the house, cook fresh meals every night, and take care of anything extra that came up. She was amazing.

Wade sat hunched over one of the dirt bikes with Emmett as he carefully disconnected its old battery. They had finished installing new brake pads, and his ratty clothes and hands were splotched black with grease. The rain had yet to cease and it pattered loudly on the roof of Wade's garage.

"You watched me fill the other battery yesterday. Are you ready to try this one yourself?" he asked Emmett.

"Yes," Emmett said, sounding determined.

Wade watched as he carefully opened the cartridge of battery acid. "Now, remember your gloves will keep you from getting burned from any rogue splashes, but they're not perfect so you still want to be as careful as possible when you're pouring it. Carefully turn it over and connect it to the battery. That's good, now push it down firmly to make sure it's secure. That's it. While the battery is filling up, you can check to see if there were any spills."

Emmett inspected the cartridge. "There might be a little on the outside of the battery."

"That's okay. You can use this rag to wipe it up. Just remember not to touch the rag again after you take your gloves off."

"What if the bikes won't start once we hook the batteries up?"

"Then we'll take a look at everything and try to figure out what's wrong."

"How scientific. No wonder you're in charge," Emmett said sarcastically.

Wade chuckled. "I'm glad you finally understand."

"So, do you like my mom?"

Wade stiffened at the abrupt question. "What makes you think that?"

"The way you act around her," Emmett said, taking off his gloves. "It seems like you like her."

"Would it bother you if I did?"

"I don't know. You're cool and everything, but it's weird to think of my mom dating anyone."

"I can understand that. It would certainly be a change that would take some getting used to. But think of it this way, if she never dates anyone, then that would mean she'd be alone for the rest of her life."

"Yeah, I guess I don't want her to be lonely. I guess if she wanted to go out with someone, then I might be okay with it eventually as long as I liked the guy. So… do you like her?"

Wade struggled to decide what the right answer was and decided honesty was the best option. "Yes."

"Do you want to go out with her?"

"That's kind of a personal question, Emmett."

"Come on, we're friends. Do you want to go out with her or not?"

"Yes, I do." Guilt bloomed in his chest. He hadn't lied, exactly, but he'd failed to tell Emmett the whole truth—that Ashley and he were already together. What if his omission of the facts came back to bite him later? He didn't want to lose Emmett's trust. But, he also didn't want to lose Ashley's. He hated being stuck in the middle. He silently prayed Emmett would leave it alone so he wouldn't have to make the hard choice.

"It looks like the acid cartridge is empty. Does that mean we can move on to the next step now?" Emmett asked.

Wade was grateful for the change of subject. "Yes. Take off the empty cartridge and close the cap. You just filled a battery! This one needs to charge overnight so we'll use the one I did yesterday. Slide it carefully into that space there. Now screw it down so it's securely in place. See those two black wires? The one closest to you is the positive cable. We'll hook that one up first. So carefully pick it up and attach it to the battery but be careful not to touch the terminals. Now attach the negative cable. Don't worry if there's a small spark when you attach it, that can happen sometimes. You did it! Nice work, Emmett. Let's put the seat back in place and try to start it. Would you like to do the honors?"

"I don't know what to do."

"I'll talk you through it." Wade explained to Emmett how to get on the bike, put it in gear, and kick-start it. After a few tries, the engine rumbled to life, shooting off a few puffs of smoke from the exhaust before puttering out.

"What happened?" Emmett asked.

"Try it again." Emmett did and the same thing happened.

"It might be the carburetor. Hop off so we can take a look."

"Is it broken?"

"No, it looks like it's just clogged. I'll teach you how to clean it out."

After Wade talked Emmett through all the steps, they put the cleaned carburetor back in place and tried to start the bike up again. This time, the engine started and kept running.

"It works! Awesome! Can we take it out for a ride?" Emmett asked. He was practically bouncing.

"Your mom would kill me if I let you ride in this weather. Don't look so disappointed. You'll get your chance soon. Besides, she'll be here any minute."

Right on cue, Ashley pulled up to the curb and jogged through the rain, holding her jacket above her head as a makeshift umbrella. She gave Wade a knowing smile before being bombarded by Emmett's excitement.

"Mom, we got one of the bikes running. Look!"

"Wow! That's amazing. You two must've worked very hard. I'm really proud of you, Emmett," she said.

"See you in a little bit for dinner, Wade," she said in between Emmett's excited chatter.

Wade watched as Emmett led Ashley to the car while he talked animatedly all about what they had done to the bike today. She turned to look at Wade over her shoulder and mouthed a thank-you before giving him a look that made him burn with anticipation for what was to come.

CHAPTER
TWENTY - FIVE

ASHLEY SAT ON her couch trying to read a book while she was actually just watching the clock. Wade had gone home shortly after dinner with the promise to return once Emmett fell asleep. As the minutes ticked past nine o'clock, the butterflies in her stomach transformed from a soft flutter to a raging swarm that had her heart racing with expectation. Thanks to his early wake-up time, Emmett was probably already asleep by now. All she had to do was check his room to be sure.

She tiptoed to his darkened room and mentally crossed her fingers as she slowly opened his door. In the darkness, she could hear him breathing soft and slow. She quietly closed his door and tiptoed away, careful to avoid the creaky floorboard in the hallway. Emmett was sound asleep, which meant she had the opportunity to do what she'd wanted to do all day. Only now that the moment had arrived, she found herself hesitating.

The last man she was with had been Jeff, and that was almost five years ago. What if she'd forgotten how or did something to make it awkward or weird? What if Wade didn't find her attractive? She wasn't as thin as she used to be. What if while they were doing it, she realized she wasn't ready? That could be terrible for both of them.

If she thought about it, there were plenty of reasons to put this off, most of which seemed perfectly valid as they raced through her mind. She could wait a little longer until she was positive she was ready, but what if that time never came? She didn't want to let her insecurities and worries hold her back. Besides, Jeff would have wanted her to be happy and Wade did make her happy. Of course she still missed Jeff, but that didn't mean she had to be alone. She wasn't sure if her heart could ever truly belong to someone else, but she wanted to try.

She liked Wade and she knew he cared for her. He was the type of guy who would try his best to do whatever she needed him to. Though she knew he wanted to, he had never tried to initiate anything intimate between them apart from kissing—which made her skin tingle just thinking about it.

No, tonight had been completely her idea. Wade understood how she felt and he would never try to push her into anything she wasn't ready for. He was giving and kind, he worked hard, and he was completely genuine. He was a good man and she couldn't deny that she cared for him. It wasn't love—it was still early yet—but maybe it could be if she let those emotions in. She needed to do this for herself; she had to see if there was a chance she could be truly happy with someone again. Even more so, in her heart she knew she wanted it. She wanted to be with Wade.

She pulled out her cell and typed the words: *Emmett is asleep. You can come over now.* As her thumb hovered over the *send* icon, her belly roiled with nerves. She could still change her mind, and part of her wanted to, but the other part of her, the part that ached for happiness, convinced her not to. She understood the nerves—anyone would be nervous if they'd been in her shoes—it was the emotion beneath that made her confident about her decision to hit *send*: excitement.

Almost instantly, her phone buzzed his reply: *I'll see you in a few.* She unlocked the front door, turned on the porch light and tried to wait patiently, but the butterflies just wouldn't quit. Unable to sit still, she paced around the room, pulling the curtains to check the street for movement every few seconds, training her ears to listen for the soft clump of boots climbing her front steps. Fortunately, Wade lived close and she didn't have to wait long.

Before he could knock, she opened the door and invited him inside. Her heart thundered in her chest as she caught sight of the warm gleam in his eyes and the crooked smile that curved up his lips.

"Hi," he said.

"Hi." A nervous silence ensued. She wasn't very good at this and knowing that had her practically pulling her hair out.

He must have sensed her unease because he said, "We don't have to do anything you don't want to do. We could just hang out or I could go home if you've changed your mind."

She forced her hands to still and removed them from her hair. "No. I want you to stay." Her gaze found the floor. "But you should know I'm not very good at this. I've been out of practice for a long time and I'm not sure I'll be any good."

He shook his head slightly and stepped forward to embrace her. He cupped her face and gently persuaded her to look at him. "I don't want you to ever think that about yourself. There is no way you could disappoint me tonight, okay? No matter what happens."

She melted into his hand and took a step toward him. She placed her hand on his chest and stared deep into his eyes. She could see his desire, along with some kind of raw and genuine emotion that had her leaning in to him. His eyes flickered to her mouth where they lingered, igniting a fire within her. Desire blossomed in her belly, quickly overriding her worry. She closed her eyes as his lips met hers, gentle yet firm, and inspiring a need that had been foreign to her for so many years.

As the kiss intensified, she forgot all the doubts and insecurities that had troubled her earlier. All she could think about was the heat that coursed through her veins and her growing need. She wanted Wade more than she ever thought she could want a man again. Her desire for him freed her and she surrendered herself to it.

He pulled at her waist as she ran her fingers through his hair. He pulled her body against his and ran his hands up her back until they reached the nape of her neck. He tangled his fingers in her hair and pulled gently, tilting her head back to expose her neck. Her breath quickened as he trailed kisses down her neck to her throat.

His breath was hot against her sensitized skin and it sent shivers down her spine as he spoke. "If we don't go to your room now, I might not make it there."

"I might not either," she said, before kissing him again.

"I don't think you want to chance Emmett waking up and seeing us out here," he said against her mouth.

She groaned and forced herself to pull away, to take his hand and lead him to her bedroom. After carefully shutting and locking the door, she turned to face him.

He took two steps to close the distance between them and pulled her against him as he kissed her deeply. He pushed her back against the door, trapping her in his embrace. Heat ran through her as his hands traced her curves down her body and cupped her behind. He lifted her to brace her against the door and she wrapped her legs around his waist, pulling his body flush against hers.

Her nerve endings were alive and sensitized as he rubbed his hips against her; all the while his lips moved fiercely and hungrily on hers. She threw her head back and let out a moan as she relished the sensation of his body against hers, his lips trailing over her sensitive skin.

He put her down on her feet and slowly pulled her dress down her shoulders until it fell to the floor. As he gazed at her in the glowing moonlight, he sucked in a breath. "You are so incredibly beautiful," he whispered.

His words gave her confidence and she slowly unbuttoned his shirt before running her hands over his strong chest. With a gentle touch, he slid his hands slowly down her curves, his eyes reflecting his admiration for her body. She closed her eyes and reveled in the feel of his hands on her and the sensations his touch elicited.

He lowered her onto the bed and placed himself on top of her, pressing her back to the mattress with his weight. He leaned down and kissed her passionately as their bodies met and she wrapped her arms around his neck to hold him to her. Under the light of the moon streaming in through her window, they got lost in each other as they made love.

Mended

CHAPTER
TWENTY - SIX

SWEATY AND SATISFIED, their legs tangled in the sheets, Ashley and Wade lay blissfully in each other's arms. She rested her head on his chest, his heart beating quick and steady. She kissed his chest and rolled onto her stomach to look up at him. He gazed at her with adoration, knowing it was more than that, something even deeper. She kissed him, one slow sweet kiss before laying back down.

"That was amazing," she said.

"That's because you're amazing."

"I was so nervous, but when you kissed me, suddenly I wasn't anymore. Thank you."

He chuckled. "You don't have to thank me. Believe me, I'm the one who should be thanking you. Like I said, you're amazing."

He brushed the hair out of her face and wished he had the nerve to tell her he loved her, that he never wanted to live without her. But, if she wasn't ready to tell anyone about them yet, then she definitely wasn't ready to hear the truth of how he felt about her. "All of this sneaking around makes me feel kind of like a teenager again. Sneaking in through the window when your parents are asleep and sneaking back out again before they wake up. Only in this case, the role of your parents goes to Emmett."

"You can use the window instead of the front door from now on if you want to make it more realistic." Her eyes twinkled.

"Very funny. I was actually kind of hoping we could stop with the sneaking altogether. It's been two weeks. Why haven't you told Emmett yet?"

She toyed with the covers. "I'm just waiting for the right time."

"When is that?"

"I'll know it when I see it."

"Come on, Ashley. Tell me what's really going on."

"Okay, fine. I guess I owe you that much. Emmett has been doing better in school and staying out of trouble lately. You guys have a good thing going right now and I'm afraid telling him about us might jeopardize that. I just don't want to go back to the way things were. I need him to stay on the right track."

"I get that, I do, but don't you think that if he finds out we've been keeping this from him, it will be a whole lot worse? I don't want him to feel like we've been lying to him. I don't want to lose his trust."

"You're right. I know you're right. I guess I just don't know how to tell him. And I will tell him soon, okay? But in the meantime, I kind of like our little secret. It makes me feel a bit naughty." She leaned down to kiss him breathless.

It didn't take much from her to get him geared up and he felt himself rolling her over to go again. *Don't let her distract you.* He needed to talk to her before she disabled all of his reason. He forced himself to pull away and moved to sit up. "When is soon?" he asked.

"I don't know. Soon."

"Like tomorrow?"

"I said I would tell him, and I will. Please just let it go."

"I can't. If you wait any longer, I'm afraid he's going to find out about us on his own. He's been asking me questions about us."

Her brow creased with worry. "Did you tell him anything?"

"I told him as little as I could, but he definitely suspects something. Today he asked me if I want to go out with you."

"What did you say?"

"I told him yes, but I left it at that. I hate not being truthful with him. It's only a matter of time before he asks me flat out if we're dating, and when he does, I won't lie to him, Ashley."

"I'll tell him tomorrow, okay? I promise. Now, will you please come back to bed?" Her voice was husky with desire as she trailed her fingers down his chest. Unable to resist her anymore, he fulfilled her request.

CHAPTER
TWENTY - SEVEN

WADE WOKE TO the early dawn light and the chirping of birds in the elm tree outside. As he slowly opened his eyes, still groggy from sleep, he looked around the room. Sheer curtains ruffled in the breeze through the open window. A ceramic vase filled with delicate princess blush flowers perched on a vintage summer green chest of drawers. This wasn't his bedroom. He sat up with a jolt, startling Ashley from her sleep. He wasn't supposed to have stayed the night. Emmett still didn't know about them, and having him find out by meeting him in the hallway this morning was not the way he wanted him to find out. "We must have fallen asleep last night," he said.

Ashley looked at the clock. "Oh no. It's already six thirty. Emmett is probably in the shower by now. You have to go before he gets out." She looked from the open window to Wade. "Now is your opportunity to relive the good old days of your youth."

"I'm not climbing out your window, Ashley."

"Okay, okay. Just let me check to see if the coast is clear. Although I don't mind the view myself, you probably wouldn't want Emmett to catch you with your pants down. You might want to get dressed."

"Believe me, I have no desire to experience the walk of shame, nude or otherwise, in front of Emmett this morning."

Wade dressed hastily as Ashley left the room. A few moments later she returned. "He's still in the bathroom. He'll head to the kitchen for breakfast next, so unless you want to climb out the window, I suggest you get going right now."

"I can't find my shirt."

She found it in a heap at the foot of the bed and threw it at him. "Now go! Please!" She gave him a shove toward the door.

"Maybe this is the walk of shame after all. Will you at least give me a kiss so I don't feel so cheap."

She gave him a quick peck and another shove toward the door.

"I feel so used," he teased.

She rolled her eyes and leaned in to him again. He pulled her the rest of the way and kissed her deeply, holding her against him. She pulled away first and gave him one last nudge to the door. "You'll be able to do that all you want after I tell him about us today. Just please go. I'm begging you."

"I can't turn down a begging woman. I'll see you later." He peeked down the hallway to make sure it was clear and tiptoed to the front of the house. He made it to the end of the hallway before he heard a voice that stopped him dead in his tracks.

"Wade? What are you doing here?"

Wade turned around and came face-to-face with Emmett dressed in his school clothes, his hair still damp from the shower. Wade gave him a tight smile. He looked to Ashley for guidance, but she merely shook her head frantically at him in a silent instruction to keep his mouth shut about their relationship. Her brow was creased with worry and her eyes wide with apprehension but she remained silent. With no help from her, he said the first thing that came to mind. "I'm here for breakfast."

"You've never eaten breakfast here before," Emmett said skeptically.

"I'm out of food, so I thought I'd stop by."

Emmett rolled his eyes. "They have grocery stores you know."

Wade shrugged. "You know me. I'm helpless when it comes to feeding myself."

"Come on, Wade. I'll fix you something," Ashley said as she walked down the hall and gestured for him to follow her to the kitchen.

Just when they thought they were in the clear, Emmett spoke again. "The kitchen is at the front of the house, so why were you coming from the hallway?"

Ashley looked at Wade desperately. "I... um... I needed to use the bathroom and you were in the shower, so I used your mom's bathroom"

"You guys are acting weird. What aren't you telling me?"

"Nothing, honey. Everything's fine." Ashley said, her cheeks turning pink.

"I want to know what's going on." His voice rose an octave as he looked frantically between Ashley and Wade. "Someone tell me what's going on!"

Wade looked at Ashley and started to speak but Ashley cut him off. "Emmett, there's something I've been keeping from you. I was scared to tell you. I didn't know how you'd react."

"Just tell me."

"Okay, here it is. Please keep an open mind and remember how much I love you." With barely a pause, she put it all out there. "Wade and I are dating."

His mouth dropped open. "What? For how long?"

"About two weeks."

"Two weeks?" Emmett shouted. "Why didn't you tell me?"

"Honey, I'm so sorry. I didn't know how to tell you. I was worried about how you'd react. But you're right, I should've told you sooner."

As Emmett turned his attention to Wade, Wade could see the betrayal on his face. "You lied to me."

"Emmett, I didn't…"

"You told me you wanted to ask her out, not that you had already been dating her for two weeks. You lied to me!"

"I'm sorry, Emmett. I wanted to tell you."

"He did want to tell you, Emmett. I asked him not to. I wanted to tell you myself."

"And when were you planning on doing that?" He shook his head furiously. "It doesn't matter. He still lied to me." He turned his attention back to Wade. "You lied to me earlier and you lied to me again just now because you didn't want me to find out why you're really here."

"Emmett, I didn't want you to find out this way. I was just trying to…"

"Stop making excuses! You promised you wouldn't lie to me again and you did it anyways."

"Emmett, I can see that you're angry and hurt. I know this is a lot to take in. But, Wade was only doing what I asked him to do."

With fists balled, eyebrows furrowed, his teeth exposed in a snarl, Emmett radiated fury. "Of course you would defend him. What about me? He betrayed me! I… I can't deal with this!" He let out an angry growl, turned on his heel, and stomped to his room, slamming the door behind him.

"I need to go talk to him. I need to fix this," Wade said desperately.

"He needs his space right now." Ashley placed her hand on his shoulder. "Give him some time to calm down and process this. Believe me, trying to talk to him when he's mad only ever makes things worse."

"I was afraid something like this would happen. What if he never trusts me again?"

"He will. Just give him time. I need to get ready for work. I'll check on him in a little while. Everything will be okay."

"I hope you're right. I'll see you tonight." Wade gave Ashley a quick kiss before heading out the door.

Sunbeams shone brightly through white puffy clouds, no longer dark and heavy with rain. The air was crisp and fresh, smelling of wet pavement and damp earth. Birds sang merrily and flicked droplets through their feathers as they bathed themselves in pools of fresh rainwater.

Yesterday's storm was over, replaced by a beautiful spring day. Wade couldn't miss the irony. Nature was mocking him. As his boots sloshed through puddles that shimmered with reflected sunlight, he couldn't stop thinking about the look of betrayal on Emmett's face. He had to fix this. He needed to make things right.

Mended

CHAPTER
TWENTY - EIGHT

TENSION FILLED THE car as Ashley drove Emmett to school. He sat in the passenger seat staring out the window, his arms crossed against his chest. His demeanor reminded her of their initial drive to Mason and she prayed they weren't headed back to that troubled time again.

Wade was right, she should've told Emmett about them sooner. He may have still been upset about the news, but finding out on his own and feeling like he'd been lied to for the past two weeks made it all the more worse. He'd climbed into the car this morning in complete silence and, minutes away from school, was still holding strong. She wanted to say something, to reach out to him, but she didn't know what she could say to make things better.

As they pulled up to the school, he made no move to get out. For several moments he merely continued his sullen stare out the window, giving her the opportunity she needed.

"I'm really sorry things turned out the way they did. That was my fault, not Wade's. I hope we can talk about all of this later," she said.

Emmett remained silent, his lips a firm line.

"So, I'll pick you up from Wade's house after work?"

"I'm not going to Wade's house today." His voice was calm and even as though he was talking about socks.

"What do you mean?"

"I'm not going to Wade's house today."

"Didn't you guys just get one of the dirt bikes running yesterday? I thought that meant Wade was going to start teaching you how to ride it."

"I'm not going to Wade's house today!" His calm had evaporated in the heat of irritation.

"Okay. You don't have to. I just want to understand…"

"Understand what? That he's a lying asshat and I don't want anything to do with him?"

"Emmett, he was only trying to keep his promise to me. He wanted to tell you. If you're mad at anyone, it should be at me, not Wade."

"I'll be here when you get off work," he said.

Ashley watched him climb out of the car and disappear into the school. A few short weeks ago, she would've been worried about the things he might do today—ditch school, destroy property, steal something, get drunk—but now, she was just worried about him, how this news had affected him. Emmett had been changing for the better since they came here, more specifically, since he met Wade.

He was doing better in school than he had in years, took interest in constructive activities, and showed no more signs of breaking the law. But, what would happen now that their relationship was strained? She wanted to think he wouldn't resort to his old ways so quickly, but what if he did? Could she handle going down that path with him again? Could she handle knowing it was because of the choices she'd made? She hoped she didn't have to find out.

***

The sky was now completely devoid of any sign of rain. The sun shined warm on the wet ground from its place in the cloudless blue sky, drying up the remnants of pools of water that had collected there during the storm. The only evidence left were the smells of damp earth, fallen leaves, and the occasional puddle. As Wade drove down the town's no longer slippery streets, he couldn't help but feel like they were mocking him. The conditions were perfect, they had a working dirt bike, but they no longer had a willing driver.

The news that Emmett refused to come by after school today rattled him deeply. Emmett had been dying to try out the dirt bikes for weeks, but apparently the appeal of riding the bike for the first time couldn't match his current aversion to Wade. He knew Ashley said to give Emmett space, but he couldn't do that without first convincing him to hear him out. Good idea or bad, he was going to his school to do just that.

Wade walked determinedly to the classroom where Emmett had his tutoring session. Inside, he could see him hunched over a textbook as his tutor, Austin, talked about some kind of math equation. Austin spotted Wade and smiled politely at him. "Hi, Wade. We're just finishing up here. Do you mind waiting outside for a few? I'll send Emmett out when we're done."

As Austin addressed him, Wade watched as Emmett looked up from the book, only to narrow his eyes in irritation. Not letting Emmett's obvious scorn get to him he said, "No problem, Austin. I'll just be right outside."

Ten minutes later, Emmett emerged from the classroom, shoulders tensed, jaw tight. Without sparing Wade a glance, he started walking briskly away from him in the direction of the school's back fields. Wade scrambled to his feet and jogged to catch up. "Hold on a minute!"

Emmett picked up speed. "Didn't my mom tell you I'm not coming over today?"

"She did, but I need to talk to you."

"I don't want to talk to you."

"Emmett, just wait. I need to say something." Wade closed the gap and put a hand on his shoulder.

Emmett angrily threw it off and whirled to face him. He shot Wade a murderous look. "What makes you think I want to talk to you?"

"I know you're mad, and you have every right to be. Just please hear me out."

"I'm not interested in hearing any more of your excuses."

"No excuses. I just want to tell you my side of things."

Emmett contemplated Wade for a moment. "Fine, you have five minutes. But if I smell bullshit, I'm leaving and I don't want you to follow me."

"Thank you. I'm really sorry I didn't tell you about your mom and me. Please believe me when I say I really did want to. Hiding something like that from you was tearing me up inside. But, I promised your mom I wouldn't say anything to you until she had a chance to talk to you. Then you started asking me all those questions about us and I didn't know what to say. I didn't want to lie to you and I didn't want to break the promise I made to your mom, so I was kind of stuck in the middle. I told you as much as I could without lying to you. I didn't like it, but that was the only thing I could think to do. I'm sorry how things turned out, and I'm sorry about this morning. We didn't want you to find out like that."

"That sounds like a lot of excuses to me," Emmett said as he turned to walk away.

"Think about it, Emmett. I was damned either way. If I'd told you, then I would've broken my word to your mom. If I didn't tell you, then you'd think I'm a liar. Either way, someone feels betrayed. I had to make a choice. I'm sorry the choice I made hurt you. I didn't want you to get hurt."

For several moments Emmett stood frozen in place, his back to Wade. When he turned around, his gaze was contemplative. "So, you care a lot about my mom?"

"Yes, I do. Very much."

"Is that why you agreed to let me come over after school? So you could get to her?"

"No, Emmett, of course not. I wanted to spend time with you because I like you. I didn't fall for her until after I'd already agreed to our arrangement."

"How do I know you weren't just using me to get to her? You lied before, so why should I believe you now?"

"I don't know what I can say to you, Emmett. You're just going to have to trust me. Yes, I care about your mom, but I also really care about you. I want things to be okay between us."

"I want to believe you, but I don't know if I can."

"Then, you'll just have to let me prove it to you. Will you please come with me? I'd really like to give you your first riding lesson today."

He shook his head. "I just want you to leave me alone."

Wade's shoulders drooped. "Okay, if that's what you want."

"It is."

"But, before I do that, in the spirit of being honest with you, I want you to know I have a date with your mom tonight. So, I'll be at the house around six. I just thought you'd want to know."

"So much for leaving me alone." When Wade didn't take the hint, he added, "You can go now." Wade didn't move and Emmett's voice rose to a shout. "Why won't you just leave me the hell alone?"

"I'm leaving now, but I want you to know I'm not going anywhere, Emmett. I'm going to prove that to you one way or another."

***

"I'm not going to go sit in some ancient dried-up old lady's stinky moth-infested house all night so you can go suck face with your boyfriend," Emmett said. He looked every part the stubborn teenage boy he was—eyes narrowed, mouth frowning, arms folded tightly across his chest.

"Wade got us some tickets to a show tonight and Myra was willing to watch you. Besides, it won't be that bad. She's a very nice lady," Ashley said.

"Why can't I just go to Carson's house?"

"Because the Millers aren't available tonight. It will only be for a couple of hours, Emmett. You'll survive."

"Well I'm not going and you can't make me!" Emmett threw himself down on the sofa and recrossed his arms stubbornly. "You know, sending me off to be babysat by some old hag so you can go out with Wade is only making things worse."

Thankful for the welcome interruption of Wade's arrival, Ashley moved to answer the knock at the door. "Hi. You look beautiful as always. Are you ready to go?" Wade asked from the entryway.

"Yes. I was hoping we could stop at Myra's on our way out to drop Emmett off. Is that all right?" She gave Wade a knowing wink. Her words probably sounded a bit too rehearsed, but luckily Emmett didn't notice.

"I'm not going!" Emmett yelled.

"Actually, I was wondering if it would be okay if Emmett came with us. I picked up an extra ticket to the monster truck rally tonight," Wade said. Ashley noticed how hard he tried to sound as though he hadn't practiced the words beforehand.

The words: "monster truck" piqued Emmett's interest and Ashley saw him lean in their direction.

"That's really thoughtful of you, Wade," her voice was too loud. She wasn't a good actress, but luckily her performance was good enough for their purposes.

"What do you say, Emmett? I'd love for you to join us."

Emmett tried his best to channel indifference. "Okay, I'll come. But it's only because I prefer monster trucks to smelly old ladies."

"I'm glad you're coming. I'm sure Carson will be glad too," said Wade.

"Carson's going to be there too?" Emmett said, failing to sound disinterested.

"You bet. Their seats are right next to ours."

"Cool." Emmett sounded enthusiastic, likely more so than he intended. To set things straight he finished with, "Just don't think this means everything is good between us."

"I wouldn't dare," Wade replied, his mouth twitching.

Before Wade could follow Emmett out of the house, Ashley caught his arm and held him back for a moment. "Nice going," she whispered.

"It's a step in the right direction at least."

"Just wait until you tell him you're giving him one of the dirt bikes. That, along with what you're already doing, should get you the rest of the way there."

Wade gave her an exuberant kiss. "Thank you! I can't wait to tell him."

"You guys better not still be in there because you are making out!" Emmett called from the front porch.

"I never would have thought I'd see the day my son would be chaperoning my date."

"Maybe if we're lucky we can sneak away for a few minutes."

"You were right. Dating when you have a kid really does make you feel like a teenager again."

"I'd be happy to sneak in tonight if you want to keep feeling that way."

"Will you use the window?" Ashley said with a grin.

CHAPTER
TWENTY - NINE

IN THE TWO months that passed the days grew longer and sunnier, the nights warmer, and the humidity beyond comfortable. Summer was just around the corner and the prospects of freedom, fun, and leisure filled the people of Mason with anticipation, the children, sitting in their classrooms, with impatience. In a few short days, summer would transform the town. Children would run free as they splashed in the river, the campsites would be filled with people on outdoor adventures, residents would sit relaxing on their front porches as they tried to stay cool in the heat, and beaches would be filled with locals and tourists alike as they basked in the warm Dixie sun.

Until then, Emmett was stuck in this stuffy classroom, sweat dampening his back—from both the heat and his nerves—as he finished his last exam. If he wanted to avoid having to sit in this classroom for the next two months in summer school, he needed to do well on this essay. His grades had been greatly improving all semester, but he wanted high marks on this essay to both guarantee his independence and to prove to himself he was better than he'd once thought.

Just last week, he'd received an early discharge from his probation for his good behavior. To Emmett that meant for the first time in what felt like a lifetime, he was free to put the past he'd grown ashamed of behind him. His mom was so proud of him and it felt good to finally feel worthy of her praise. He often didn't show it, but he was lucky to have a mom like her. She'd always been there for him, even in his darkest times, even when he'd been awful to her.

He remembered how upset he was by the news that his mom and Wade were dating. It wasn't that he thought she was betraying his dad or anything. His dad had been dead for a long time and he didn't want her to be sad anymore. It was something he thought he wasn't ready for, something he didn't know how to deal with. But, once he saw how happy Wade made her, he had let that go. It helped that he liked Wade. A lot.

Emmett was glad his mom was happy. She'd gone to hell and back over the past few years, and he'd added to that hell; he knew that. But those times were in the past and he was determined to keep them there. Of course there'd still be plenty times he would make things difficult for her or do things that drove her crazy—he was a teenager after all—but he promised himself he would stop breaking her heart. That meant no more getting arrested, no more being awful to her, and no more worrying her to her grave.

If you would've asked him four months ago, he would have thought it impossible. But it turned out, all he needed was someone beyond his scope to believe he wasn't the bad kid he saw himself as. Wade did that for him. No longer would his summers be filled with ditching summer school or day camp to smoke, drink, or get into some kind of trouble with the neighborhood kids. All he wanted was to go to the beach with his friends, ride his dirt bike, and work on whatever project Wade had for him next.

As Emmett struggled to write a conclusion for his essay, he listened to the subtle sounds of the quiet classroom—the steady ticking of the clock, the furious scratching of pencils on paper, and the occasional creaking of the old desks they sat in.

"You have ten minutes left." The teacher's voice resounded in the quiet of the classroom, momentarily startling a few students from their exams. Almost out of time, Emmett bent his head and joined the other students as he scribbled the best conclusion his brain could come up with, the hope of a real southern summer hanging over him, pushing him to excel.

***

Finally, the last day of school arrived. Exams and lessons were finished, which basically meant today was for signing yearbooks, goofing around—and for the eighth graders—graduation.

Ashley and Wade watched from their seats as Emmett strolled across the auditorium stage in his button-down shirt and black slacks. A pleased grin spread across his face as he found his mother in the crowd standing on her feet, clapping loudly, and wearing her proud smile. Wade stood beside her and gave him a thumbs up, followed by a loud whoop.

Not only had Emmett passed and was heading to high school in the fall, he'd earned all As and Bs this semester and he'd done it without cheating. To top it off, it was officially summer vacation. The boy had to feel pretty good right about now.

After the ceremony, Ashley and Wade caught up with Emmett and she wrapped him in her arms. He must've been happy because he didn't even try to shrug her off or wipe off the wet kiss she left on his forehead.

"Oh, Emmett. I'm so proud of you. You sure have turned things around the past few months." She said, as she wiped away happy tears. "What do you say we go get some pizza with your friends to celebrate?"

"Sure, sounds fun. I'll go ask them."

Once Emmett was out of earshot, Wade asked, "What if instead of having to go to day camp this summer Emmett spends those days with me? I could teach him some things and he could help me with some of the jobs I have this summer. He could be my paid assistant. I'd be happy to take him the other days too if he wouldn't rather be off with his friends."

"I'm sure he'd love that, but it's a huge commitment. Are you sure you want to take on something like that?"

"Absolutely."

"If you're sure, then I think it's a great idea. I'm so lucky to have you in my life." She gave him a gentle kiss.

"You think that, but really, I'm the lucky one."

"And you say all the right things. I'm never letting you go."

She said it lightly, like a joke, but he still hoped it was the truth. The last few months with Ashley had been like a dream. Every day they spent together he felt his love for her grow, to the point where his heart was full to the brim. He had never known love like this, and yet he still hadn't been able to tell her how he felt about her. He wanted to, he'd tried to many times, but he never seemed able to say the words. Three little words that he had never said to any woman other than his own mother. Three little words that could either make or break their relationship.

He knew Ashley had loved before, utterly and completely, like the way he felt about her. She had been so much in love that she stuck by her husband through the darkest of times, even when she grew afraid. He didn't know exactly what happened, but he knew that Jeff hurt her. That much was clear. Despite the fact that Jeff broke her heart, she loved him still. She had been so devoted to him that for four years after his death, she remained alone, untouched by another man with only her memories to keep her warm at night.

Even now, Wade knew she loved Jeff. He was the father of her child, her first lover, her rock for ten years of her life. No one could take the place Jeff held in her heart, and he wouldn't want it any other way. He just hoped there was enough room in her heart for him. He wanted everything with her: love, marriage, children, to grow old together—all things he'd never wanted until he met her.

He wanted to tell her how he felt, and he would do it. But, he respected that she needed time to heal, time to ease into this new part of her life with him. He wanted to wake up next to her every morning, to throw around the football with Emmett in the evenings while she watched happily from the kitchen window as she made dinner. He wanted to make love in the bed they shared each night. She would get there—at least he hoped she would—but in the meantime, he would take whatever she was willing to offer him. She was worth the wait.

***

"Here comes Emmett. Why don't you tell him about your idea and see what he says," Ashley said to Wade.

"Carson and the guys are down for pizza. Can I go see a movie with them after?" Emmett asked.

"Sure, you go have fun. Just keep your cell phone on you and tell me when to pick you up."

"Thanks, Mom. Let's go, I'm starving."

"Before we go, I had something I wanted to ask you, Emmett," Wade said.

"Sure, what is it?"

"I know you had plans to go to that day camp a few days a week this summer, but I was thinking if your heart wasn't set on that, maybe you'd be willing to spend those days with me. I have some jobs lined up for the summer that I could really use some help on. I could teach you what I know, and you could make some money."

"Uh, yeah! How much we talking?"

"How about five bucks an hour?"

Emmett stood up tall and squared his shoulders, always the negotiator. "The minimum wage in the state of Alabama is seven twenty-five."

Wade chuckled. "How did you know that?"

"It's called the internet. I know old people are afraid of technology and all, but you should really try it out sometime."

"Thank you for that. I can do five bucks an hour, cash. When you're old enough to get a work permit and a real job, you can make seven twenty-five per hour and have twenty-five percent of it taken by the IRS for taxes."

Emmett seemed to contemplate that. "Okay, five dollars an hour is good. Thanks, Wade."

"No need to thank me. I plan to make you work for it."

Ashley kissed Wade on the cheek and nestled herself under his arm. As they walked down the street to the pizza parlor, Wade's hand laced with hers, Emmett talking happily with his friends, she felt like she was finally a part of a family again—a family that was no longer broken apart by loss, heartbreak, or trauma. She was truly happy for the first time in years and she hadn't had a nightmare in months. Wade made her feel safe, cherished, whole.

For so long she had felt like she was in pieces, broken and shattered like a fragile vase. Wade put her back together again, filling in the missing pieces she thought were lost or unsalvageable. Maybe her chances of having love and family in her life didn't die with Jeff. Maybe her chance was walking beside her, looking at Emmett with the same joy and love she did.

CHAPTER
THIRTY

PINE NEEDLES CRUNCHED underfoot as Wade and Ashley walked along the dirt path. A warm breeze rustled the leaves in the trees. The hum of cicadas, buzzing like static, sounded in the space around them. Wade's hand clasped hers as he led her slowly through the undergrowth, careful not to let her fall.

"Can I open my eyes now?" she asked impatiently.

"Not yet. It's just a bit further."

She huffed her discontent but did as she as was told.

"I promise it will be worth it," he added.

"Are you bringing me all the way out here to kill me?"

"If I were, it would be a good spot for it. No one would hear you scream."

"Oh, I don't know about that. I've been known to have a pretty good set of lungs."

"Is that so?"

"Do you want me to demonstrate?"

Wade snorted. "That's not necessary."

They continued as they were, trudging carefully along the narrow path until they broke through the trees. Wade turned to face her and gently gripped both her shoulders to lead her the last few yards.

"We're almost there. Keep your eyes closed." Using his hands to guide her and instructing her where to place each step, he led her up a small bank in the clearing and walked her backward until the backs of her legs touched wood. "Sit down, but don't open your eyes yet."

"It feels like my eyes have been closed forever. I almost don't remember what it's like to see."

"Someone's being a bit dramatic tonight."

"What is sight? What are colors?" She said with a profound voice.

"Calm down, Socrates, you'll get to open them in a minute."

Wade guided her down until she was sitting on a raised surface, her back resting against the sturdy wood. With her eyes still closed, she ran her hand over the hard, flat surface of the wooden bench beneath her. Wade released her and sat down beside her, the bench swinging slightly as he did so.

"Okay. You can open your eyes now."

When she did, she gasped in awe. They were sitting on a cypress bench swing overlooking the wide expanse of the Alabama River. The view Wade had come to know so well was glorious. The calm waters of the river glowed orange and pink as they reflected the colors of the sunset that painted the sky. Crickets chirped and cicadas continued their static hum as they searched for mates in the summer night. A fish leapt out of the water, splashing upon its return and causing ripples in the smooth surface.

Ashley looked down at the bench they sat on. She rubbed her hand against the smooth grain of the natural-stained wood, her eyes wide with admiration. She clasped the chain closest to her and her gaze followed its ascent to the wood slat overhang it was attached to. She pressed her feet on the ground and pushed off, the smooth movement of the swing rocking them back and forth.

"This swing is perfect and the view is breathtaking. I had no idea you were even working on this."

"I wanted it to be a surprise," Wade said. "Eventually there will be a porch for it to hang from, but for now it just stands alone. I thought it would be nice to have a quiet place to sit whenever we're here. I hope you know that you and Emmett are always welcome to come out here anytime you want."

"It's perfect, really. This was definitely worth being blind for the past twenty minutes. What a beautiful spot. How long did it take you to make?"

"It took Emmett and me about three weeks in between our other jobs."

"Emmett helped you make it?"

"He's the reason the grain is so smooth. He did most of the sanding."

"Well, you guys did a great job. It will be a beautiful place to sit outside in the evenings. This is the perfect spot to watch the sunset."

"Just wait until dark. That's when the real show begins."

She leaned her head against his shoulder and he put his arm around her and pulled her close. They sat in silence, slowly swinging back and forth as they watched the colorful sky fade to a deep blue and the stars begin to make their entrance.

As Wade held her close, he pictured himself sitting here with her in the evenings, the lights from their home glowing in the growing darkness behind them. They would have a modest house with a big porch and room to grow. Wade would carve a path through the woods where they could all go for walks together and Emmett could ride his dirt bike. They could have barbecues on the riverbank and invite Emmett's friends, and when the heat became unbearable, they could go for a swim to cool off in the gentle river.

It was a life he wanted, but was it one Ashley and Emmett would want as well? Over the months he'd known them, he grew to love them both and never wanted to be without them. Whenever they were apart, he missed them. Even when they fought, even when Emmett acted like a teenager, he didn't want to be anywhere else. He'd found his family and he wanted to keep them forever. He just had to tell them.

He held Ashley close, swinging slowly to and fro as the last rays of the sun disappeared behind the trees. A light breeze ruffled her hair, brushing some loose strands against his neck. He kissed the top of her head and breathed in her scent, grateful they had this moment together. As dusk set in, he knew the show was about to begin, and his heart danced with excitement; he'd be the first person to share this with her.

"Watch the trees," he said.

"What's going to happen?"

"Just wait. You'll see."

It started gradually. First one and then another, until the trees were lit up with tiny dancing lights. Thousands of fireflies, glowing yellow in the night, covered the long strands of grass beneath the trees and floated in the air, their lights blinking in the darkness.

She gasped when she saw them. "Oh, Wade. They're so beautiful. I've never seen anything like it. Do they always come out at night like this?"

"Mostly during summer. You won't see much of them in the more urban areas, but out here they're quite a sight when summer comes around. It's another reason why I decided to buy this land."

"What a perfect spot to build a home. It would be so amazing to watch them like this from your own front porch."

"My thoughts exactly. I'm hoping I'll get to do that someday, hopefully with two people who are very special to me."

"So, you think about the future?"

"More so since I've met you."

"And I'm in it?"

"If you want to be."

She turned to look at him. Her eyes glimmered with the flickering yellow lights of the fireflies. Her expression was unreadable in the darkness and Wade feared he'd said too much. If she wasn't ready, if she couldn't picture a future with him, if she didn't love him… She lifted her hand to caress his face, cutting off his worried thoughts. He leaned into her touch as he closed his eyes to savor the moment. She kissed him lightly on his lips and he sighed against her.

***

When she saw the truth in Wade's eyes as he told her of his want for a future with her, she knew with utter certainty how she felt about him. It was in that moment she realized she was in love with him and had been for a while now. She didn't know exactly when it happened; maybe it was when she saw the way he looked at Emmett at his graduation today, or maybe it was when they first met at The Fried Pickle. She didn't know, but what she did know was that she never wanted to be without him.

He took away her nightmares, her feelings of self-doubt, and her fears. He made her ache for a future and gave her a reason to leave her painful past behind once and for all. He took Emmett under his guidance and brought out the side of him she had been missing for too many years. He made their lives better in every way.

Without a doubt in her mind, she loved him. She loved that he couldn't cook, that he built beautiful things with his hands, that he was understanding and compassionate, and that he cared so deeply for the people in his life. She loved his plaid shirts, his worn and ripped jeans, how he sometimes smelled of sawdust after he'd been working, and everything else that made him who he was. It was different than it had been with Jeff, but it was just as deep, just as

221

complete, just as real. It was the kind of love that made her want to dance in the rain, to unravel every molecule that made up who he was, and to commit herself to him—body and soul—for the rest of her days.

Sitting on the amazing swing he'd made with his bare hands—the swing he hoped would hang from the porch of the house they shared—watching the glorious mystery of the dancing fireflies by the tranquil river, made her see the life she wanted: a life with him.

She laid her head against his chest and let out a sigh of contentment as he put his arms around her. Her heart was filled to the top and she didn't want to waste another second of her life holding in how she felt. "I love you, Wade."

At her words, he tightened his arms around her and leaned his cheek against the top of her head. "I love you, Ashley. So much. I've been in love with you since our first date, maybe even before."

She looked up at him, her eyes widened with surprise. "Why did you wait so long to tell me?"

"I wanted to make sure you were ready. Besides, telling you I loved you on our first date would've been a little off-putting, don't you think?"

"I think it's sweet."

"Come on, you would have run screaming."

"I wouldn't have run. Maybe."

"See? I didn't want to rush you. And, I have to admit, I was a little terrified. I've never told a woman I loved her before."

Her eyebrows lifted in surprise. "Never?"

"Well, I couldn't very well tell someone I loved them unless it was true."

"You've never been in love?"

"There were a few times when I thought I could be, but I realize now that I was wrong." He shrugged. "I've just never met the right person."

She smiled and leaned her head against his chest again. "Until now."

"Until now," he said.

They sat in silence in each other's arms, watching the fireflies put on their light show. As they continued rocking back and forth, she suddenly needed to share something with him, something that had haunted her dreams and consumed her thoughts before he'd taken her pain away. "Wade?"

"Hmm?"

"Can I tell you something?"

"Anything."

"I'd like to tell you about Jeff. You know, the bad stuff."

"Are you sure?"

"I am. When you told me you loved me, suddenly I felt like I wanted you to know everything about me, even the horror from my past. But I won't talk about it if you don't want me to."

His shoulders relaxed and he leaned his head against hers. "I'm glad you feel safe talking to me about it. I'll gladly listen to whatever you have to say."

"Okay, but it requires going back a little ways."

"We have time."

She took a deep breath as she prepared to tell her story. The story she had never before told to completion, the story about the worst year of her life.

CHAPTER
THIRTY - ONE

JEFF WAS FINALLY home for good. That meant no more reaching out to him in the darkness of their room only to feel the cold, empty mattress beside her. No more spending every moment he was gone worrying whether he would come home alive. No more watching her son spend his days without a father. No more being afraid that every knock on the door was a soldier in uniform, coming to tell her that her husband would be coming home in a box. For the first time in her marriage, Ashley was no longer a wife of a strategic warrior in the Marine Corps and she had never felt more relieved.

Since Jeff's discharge two weeks ago, they'd been trying to make up for lost time. Family outings, barbecues with their friends, long showers, and making love every night in the bed they would share forever. It all had been almost perfect, except for one thing.

Jeff returned a different man. He startled if anyone came up behind him and became agitated at the smallest things. Sometimes he withdrew into the study for long periods of time, wanting to be alone. She understood that coming home after being at war for so long was a shock to his system, and soldiers like him needed time to adjust to civilian life again. In time, everything would be fine and the three of them would embrace the fresh start they'd been given. Jeff had come home in one piece and they were a family again. That was all that mattered.

***

She couldn't prove it, but Ashley knew something was wrong with Jeff. He hadn't been acting like himself lately, and she was starting to get concerned. Too often she woke up during the night to discover she was alone in bed. Sometimes she found him sleeping on the couch and was afraid of what that meant. For the ten years they'd been married, never had they intentionally slept apart. They were forced apart so much as it was that whenever he was home they made a point of sleeping together, even if they were fighting.

The fact that he was choosing to sleep away from her now only solidified her worry that something was terribly wrong. And then there was the night she woke up to find him standing next to the bed in the dark. When he lay back down, his shirt was wet and his heart beat wildly in his chest. She suspected nightmares or sleepwalking or maybe insomnia, but she couldn't know for sure.

Yesterday the three of them were going for a walk in their neighborhood when a car backfired as it drove by. At the sound, Jeff dove behind the closest parked car and flattened himself on the ground. For several seconds he lay there, his face to the pavement, his chest heaving as though he was under attack. He had started laughing then—a forced, fake sound—and insisted he was just joking around. His wide, fear-struck eyes and the sweat glistening on his brow told a different story, and when she confronted him about it, he became defensive and stormed away.

Wherever they were it seemed like Jeff was ready and waiting for disaster to strike. He was always on alert, his eyes and ears searching for signs of danger as if their neighborhood was a war zone and their home could be struck by an air raid at any moment. It seemed like he was always on edge, poised to react at a moment's notice and ready to go on the defensive if anyone confronted him.

Along with sleep disturbances and hyperarousal, came irritability. Lately, it seemed like anything could set him off. Earlier this week Emmett had come running up behind Jeff, excited to show him the good grade he received on his last test. The action startled Jeff so much he knocked over his cup, spilling his drink all over the kitchen table and himself. In the past, Jeff would've merely laughed at himself and grabbed a towel, but this time he slammed his fists on the table and screamed at Emmett to be more careful. He picked up the glass and threw it against the refrigerator, shattering it before storming out of the room.

She often saw him sitting in the plush chair in the living room, just staring out the window for what seemed like hours. Sometimes, he would stare into the space in front of him, his face like a statue. She wondered if he was depressed or maybe tired from lack of sleep. Whatever it was, he wouldn't talk about it. The most he would say was, "I've got it under control." But she could tell that even he wasn't convinced. Something was wrong; they both knew it, but instead of dealing with it, he shut everyone out.

Too often he disappeared for most of the day, locking himself in his study with a liquor bottle. She'd heard him talking to himself in there and heard a commotion a few times from inside. The first time she went to investigate, there were holes in the wall the size of his heel. The second time, the contents of the desk—papers, pens, notebooks, and the desk lamp—were scattered on the floor. Both times, he screamed at her to get out, his face distorted in agony. She'd scurried from the room scared and confused like a mouse when the farmer turns the light on in the barn. She didn't know what else to do.

She was walking on eggshells around him, always trying her best not to set him off. She tried to be supportive without pushing too hard, knowing the rage that would ensue if she did. Though her instinct was to face this head-on and try to fix whatever was going on with him, she knew that would only make things worse. So instead, she did her best to give him the space he desired. Not having many other options, she waited for it to pass.

***

Jeff hardly looked at her now. Whenever he did, he likely saw the bruises on her neck, an ugly reminder of what he did to her one night—that awful night when she'd awakened to find her husband gripping her neck, his eyes dilated to black and staring at nothing as she gasped and sputtered for breath. Jeff said he didn't understand what happened. One minute, he was having a dream—a flashback from one of his missions, he said—and the next, he was choking the life out of her.

Ashley was scared yet she tried to reassure him afterward. She was his wife and it was her job to be there for him. She asked him to get help, begged him even, but so far he refused. Jeff was never one to talk about his feelings—always thinking it made him less of a man—but this was serious. This went far beyond the typical group of hens clucking about the surface-level problems they had with their husbands and children. This was turning out to be a matter of life and death. If Jeff hadn't woken up that night... well, let's just say she was lucky to be alive.

He wouldn't talk about what happened that night. He wouldn't talk to her about anything anymore. All she could do was speculate from what she'd observed and she was tired of it. She was his wife. He wasn't supposed to be going through this alone. He was supposed to share his burden with her so she could help him, not shut her out of his life. If things kept going as they were she feared her marriage would be doomed. She wasn't going to give up without a fight and she knew there would be one.

Straightening her shoulders, she braced herself and knocked on the door to his study, where he now dwelled when he wasn't disappearing for days at a time. Only God knew where he was then. At first there was no answer so she pounded harder, refusing to cease until he opened the door.

"Go away!" Jeff called from the other side of the door.

"I'm not leaving here until you open this door."

"Ashley, please." His voice was a mix of strained and irritated.

"No, Jeff. We need to talk. You can't keep shutting me out."

The silence returned, so she started up the pounding again until she heard the click of the lock and the door swung open.

Jeff looked exhausted. Dark swollen circles lay beneath his bloodshot hazel eyes. He hadn't shaved in weeks, and thick brown stubble covered his neck and face, hiding the red scratch marks she'd inflicted there. His short brown hair was greasy as if he hadn't washed it in days, and he stunk of sweat and beer. His gaze flickered to the bruises on her neck and quickly shifted to the ground at his feet. He appeared broken and ashamed, so unlike the confident man she married.

"You shouldn't be here," he said to the floorboards.

"We need to talk."

"I don't want to talk, Ashley."

"Something serious is going on with you and we need to talk about it." On the desk behind him were an old fast-food bag and two empty bottles of beer next to a half-empty pint of vodka. Her mouth went dry. It was barely three in the afternoon. Things were getting worse.

Jeff ran a hand through his unkempt hair, leaving tracks in its wake. "I'm handling it, okay?"

"How? By ignoring your family and getting drunk? Because that doesn't work for me."

"What do you want from me?"

"I want you to be my husband and a father to your son. Do you have any idea how your behavior is affecting him? He's scared, Jeff and so am I."

"Why do you think I'm staying away? I don't want to hurt either of you."

"You already have."

He flinched at her words like he'd been struck.

She didn't want to hurt him, but he needed to hear the truth. He had hurt her, and not just physically. He'd turned her into a wreck and she couldn't survive much more. "Jeff, please look at me," she begged.

He shook his head in obvious pain. "I can't. Looking at you only reminds me of what I did.

"Good, maybe it will convince you that you need help."

Squaring her shoulders to keep her strength, she took a determined step forward. As she moved toward him, he retreated, as though fearful of what could happen if she came too close.

"Ashley, please don't. I don't want to hurt you."

"You won't. Look at me, Jeff." She took another step forward, only to cause him retreat backward again.

"You can't know that."

"I know you didn't do it on purpose." She moved toward him again and this time he stayed where he was, his shoulders slumped in defeat. "I love you, Jeff. I want to help you." One more step brought her to him and she reached out to gently touch his face. He closed his eyes at her touch and placed his hand over hers.

"I'm so sorry." His voice was shaky.

"I know you are. I also know you didn't mean to do it. I'm okay, Jeff. You stopped." She tried to sound confident, but her heart thundered and her knees quivered. She couldn't let him see she was afraid.

"But what if I hadn't?" He looked at her then, his gaze filled with agony, and pulled her hand off his cheek. "I could've just as easily killed you. I can't risk letting something like that happen. I'd never be able to forgive myself. I'm not even sure I can forgive myself now. It's better if I just stay away from you until I get a handle on this."

She took a breath to steady herself. "Abandoning us is not a solution. You need to get help."

"Talking to some shrink about my feelings isn't going to fix anything. Besides, do you know how embarrassing that is?"

"You don't need to be embarrassed. Lots of people have been in your position before. Talking to someone might help you move past whatever it is that's haunting you."

"Only crazy people and weaklings see shrinks, and I am neither of those," he scoffed.

"Getting help doesn't mean you're weak, it means you're strong enough to admit you have a problem. And you're not crazy."

"Which is exactly why I'm not going to see any shrink."

She felt her herself breaking. "Jeff, please. I can't keep going on like this!" Her throat was tight and she fought back tears. "I feel like I don't know who you are anymore. I'm scared all the time. I never know what you're going to do next or when it's going to happen. I want to help you. I want things to get better, but I don't know how much longer I can keep living this way. It's not safe for me or for Emmett."

"Then leave me. That's what you're saying, isn't it? That if I don't get help to fix what's wrong with me, you're going to take my son and leave?"

"That's not what I said. Just talk to me, help me to understand. What happened the other night to make you—"

"I already told you I was having a nightmare." His words were clipped, his temper lurking beneath the surface.

"What was it about?"

"It was a memory of something that happened while I was on a mission. They always are."

"Will you tell me about it?"

His mouth was a firm line. "No. You don't need to be burdened by the kind of hell I endured."

"I just want to understand—"

"Well, you can't understand, Ashley! You will never be able to understand!"

The anger had come out of nowhere, leaving her hurt and confused. "You don't need to yell at me. I'm just trying to help. You're sick, Jeff, and you need help. The sooner you admit that the better off we'll all be."

"You say you want to help? Then leave me alone to do what I need to do."

"Your solution clearly isn't working. If it was, then I wouldn't have this!" She gestured to the bruises on her neck, still painful to the touch.

He threw himself into the desk chair and scrubbed a hand down his face.

"Just listen. I've been doing some research and I think you might have post-traumatic stress disorder. It's a real illness and treatment can help. Please just think about it."

"Oh, so you're a doctor now? Then maybe you can tell me what illness you have that turns you into such a nosy bitch!"

Jeff had never spoken to her like that before and his words sliced through her like glass, cutting her into a thousand painful pieces. It would've hurt less if he'd slapped her.

He shook his head as if to clear the air. "Ashley, I'm sorry. I didn't mean that. I don't know what's wrong with me."

"Don't you think it's worth it to find out? You can't just keep ignoring this. Don't you realize that it's destroying us?" The words came out on a sob and he rushed to her, taking her in his arms.

"I know this has all been so hard on you."

"Of course it's hard on me. I'm your wife and I love you. You're acting so different. Angry one minute, depressed the next, and then you keep fading in and out like you're somewhere else. And the sleepwalking and nightmares. I'm scared, Jeff, and you won't talk to me about any of it." Her words were barely intelligible through her tears and her shoulders shuddered with her sobs. "I just want to help you. Don't shut me out. I want my husband back." A painful cry escaped her throat, and Jeff held her tighter.

"I'm sorry. I'll think about getting help, okay? I don't want you to feel like this."

"What is there to think about? Don't you want this to stop?"

"Of course I do. It's hell for me, too."

"Then please, do whatever it takes to make it go away. I don't want to lose you."

If only he had listened to her.

***

Days later, Ashley was roused from her sleep by a loud crash. It was pitch black in her bedroom, the light of the moon hidden behind dark storm clouds. Rain pattered loudly on the roof and smeared the windows, making it impossible to see anything outside. It was probably just thunder. She rolled over to go back to sleep when she heard it again. It sounded like it was coming from downstairs. Afraid that someone might have broken in, she moved to shake Jeff awake, but her hands found nothing but the empty mattress beside her.

She flicked on the bedside lamp and saw that she was alone in the room. She slid out of bed and entered the hall, leaving the hall light off as she crept to Emmett's room to check on him. When she opened his door, she was relieved to find him sleeping soundly, safe in his bed. As she quietly closed the door, she heard another crash followed by a yell of pain. Her pulse quickened. It was coming from downstairs. Turning on the hall light now, she silently crept down the stairs to the dark floor below where she froze, listening.

For a while all she heard was the rain outside and the pounding of her blood in her ears. But then Jeff's voice cut through the rain as he let out another cry of pain. Her heart beating wildly, she hurried toward the source until she found herself standing before the closed door of the study. Jeff was inside speaking in hushed tones as though he was talking to someone, yet she heard nothing but his agonized voice broken by his sobs. "I wanted to save you... I had orders... I couldn't... I didn't have a choice! I... I'm sorry... so sorry."

As she stood in the hallway, transfixed by his words, she heard the sound of breaking glass and a grunt of exertion, followed by continued sobs. Jeff was in pain. He needed help. She tried the doorknob; it was unlocked. Gathering her strength, she twisted it and stepped inside.

The room was in shambles. The contents of the desk—books, papers, pens—were scattered on the floor. The computer lay against the wall, its screen cracked from the impact. The lamp lay broken on the floor, its shade bent to one side, the light flickering from the partially unattached bulb. Shards of glass littered the floor at Jeff's feet where he crouched near the broken window. His back was to Ashley, and she was unable to see his face, but in his hand, she could see his fingers curled tightly around his black pistol.

His shoulders were hunched and they shook violently as he continued to sob. The room was freezing, and an icy wind blew through the broken window, billowing the curtains as it did so. Rain pounded against what was left of the glass and dripped inside, running down the wall and pooling on the wooden floorboards. He mumbled to himself, something about a girl he wanted to save, but a crack of thunder drowned out the words.

"Jeff," she called out tentatively, but he didn't respond. She walked slowly toward him, talking to him in the most soothing voice she could manage as though he was a cornered animal that might attack at any moment. A large gash dripped crimson streams of blood down his arm and onto the floor, matching the sounds of the pattering rain. "Jeff, you're hurt!" She reached his side and tentatively lifted her hand to touch him. "Jeff, it's Ashley. Everything is okay."

But it wasn't okay. Not by a long shot.

***

That was the night when Ashley's world came crumbling down—the night she sat on the floor of Jeff's study clutching Emmett to her, both mother and son sobbing. The gash on her head dripped blood down her face and turned her hair dark and sticky. Every breath was agony, her ribs screaming in pain from where she collided with the desk on her way to the floor. She looked at Jeff on his back, fear gripping her spine. Her ears still rang from the gunshot that had narrowly missed its target. How did this happen? What went wrong?

Jeff sat up, blinking in surprise. He looked down at his arm, which was bleeding badly and used his other hand to put pressure on it. Finally he glanced up and seemed to notice Ashley and Emmett for the first time. He stood and took a tentative step toward them, holding his pistol. Ashley flinched and Emmett whimpered in her arms.

Jeff's look of confusion turned to shock as he seemed to realize what he'd done. "I am so sorry," he whispered.

He tucked the gun into his waistband and, keeping his distance, moved past them to the door. Dazed, Ashley didn't say a word, didn't ask him where he was going. Instead, she waited until she was sure he was gone and carried Emmett to his room, where she spent the rest of a long night trying to soothe her scared little boy, unable to stop her own tears from falling.

In the morning, Ashley stood in her kitchen, gripping an oversized envelope. She trailed her fingers along its edges as she stared unseeing out the window. She'd found it on the kitchen counter when she went to make Emmett breakfast, but until now she had tucked it away, unwilling to read the message scrawled on the back until she was alone. She walked to the living room to check on Emmett and found him curled up on the couch, watching cartoons. She had kept him home from school today after their horrible night last night, more for her sake than for his. He seemed perfectly fine this morning—children were surprisingly resilient that way—but she was a wreck and she couldn't shake her feelings of dread that she'd almost lost him.

She walked back to the kitchen and sat down at the small table there, her chest heavy. She was afraid to read the note because she feared it would tell her that her marriage was over, that Jeff had left them and was never coming back. She never wanted this to happen. It didn't have to be this way. They could have worked through this if Jeff had been willing. But, here she sat alone in her kitchen, her side aching and her head throbbing in pain from where Jeff had hit her with the gun last night. She ran her fingers over his messy scrawl and began to read:

Ashley,
I'm so sorry for everything I've put you through this past year. My only job was to protect you and I've failed to do that. I have failed both as a husband and as a father, and I can't live with what I've done. It may hurt now, but it will get better. You and Emmett are better off without me and soon you will see that too. You will move on, Ashley, and Emmett will grow up

just fine without me. I will never let myself hurt either of you again. I could never forgive myself if I did. You're safe now. I love you and Emmett more than my own life and you will be the last thoughts I'll have. Please, don't be sad for long. Move on and live your life. Be happy without me, because I can no longer do that for you. I love you. You were always the only woman for me. Good-bye.

- Jeff

She reread the message over and over again, willing the words not to be true. They couldn't be true. She couldn't be a widow. This had to be a mistake. Jeff would come home, he always did. He was probably already on his way back. She would just sit here and watch for him.

She didn't know how long she sat there waiting—minutes, hours—before she saw something that drew her to the window. The flashing red and blue lights of a police car blinked in the morning light, dancing reflections on the glass.

She watched the car slow as it pulled next to the curb in front of her condo and came to a stop. Two police officers stepped out, dressed in navy and wearing somber expressions. For nearly a decade she had prayed this day would never come. But, here they were, making the final steps toward her front door to give her the news that would change her life forever. They may not have been soldiers, but they were still men in uniform coming to her door to tell her that her husband was never coming home.

CHAPTER
THIRTY - TWO

WHEN ASHLEY FINISHED telling Wade her story, they sat together in silence, rocking slowly on the swing as they had throughout. At times she had cried, at other times she had seemed almost angry, moving through a range of emotions as she relived that time in her life. All the while Wade listened to her story, trying to give her whatever she needed. What she needed now was silence and the knowledge that he was here for her, so he did just that; he sat in the quiet night beside her, not touching her, but simply rocking slowly forward and backward, waiting for her to speak again.

The waxing crescent moon was high in the sky now but offered little light to the surrounding forest. Ashley looked straight ahead. The dancing lights of the fireflies glowed in the trees and reflected on the surface of the river before them. Her expression was unreadable in the darkness, but Wade could tell she was okay. Telling the story out loud must have been difficult for her, but it also brought them closer together. As she'd relived the most difficult time in her life, Wade had remained beside her, unspeaking, forming no judgments or opinions, not putting any of the attention on himself. He simply listened and was there for her, being whatever she needed him to be. Now that he knew her story, he sensed they could put it behind them and move forward.

"For so long I convinced myself that Jeff killed himself to protect us, that he was some kind of a hero who sacrificed himself to save us. Maybe that was part of it, but in truth, he just couldn't live with what he'd done. To him, death was the only solution. I don't think I could ever feel that way," Ashley said as she stared out into the night.

"That's because you're an optimist. You look for the good in everything and everyone. That's one of the things I love about you."

She smiled at him and leaned her head against his shoulder. "I love you, you know? I don't want you to think that because I love Jeff, I love you any less. Jeff was my first love, the father of my child and I will always love him, but it doesn't compare to how I feel about you. What I feel for you is real, and it is deep, and I never want you to feel like it's less than what I had with Jeff. You have my heart, Wade."

"I know. I'm glad you felt like you could share your story with me."

She nestled into the crook of his arm. "I know that part of my life has been over for years, but tonight it feels like I've finally put it behind me. Thank you for listening."

They rocked back and forth, feeling safe and loved as they held each other in the night.

"Will you stay with me tonight?" Ashley asked, breaking the silence.

"Of course. But, I thought Emmett was going to be home tonight."

"He is, but I love you and I want you there with me. Emmett will be okay."

"Then I'll be there. How much time do we have until we have to pick him up?"

"Enough time to go home and get you out of those clothes." Her voice was husky with need as she trailed her hand up his thigh. An appreciative groan escaped his throat. "Besides, it wouldn't be a problem even if he called us to pick him up early. I've seen how fast you can get dressed when you want to."

"My balance and accuracy are to be marveled at."

She laughed. "It's true. I've seen you in action. You know, it's too bad you don't have a hammock or something set up here. That could really come in handy right about now." She leaned in to him and pressed her lips to his throat, making his skin tingle.

Despite the blood leaving his head at an incredible rate, his memory didn't fail him. "I have a blanket. I brought one with me in case we got cold while we were out here tonight."

"That will work," she mumbled into his neck.

He kissed her tenderly, cherishing her taste and the feel of her lips against his. He rubbed his hands up her back and ran them through her hair. He tilted her head back slightly so he could kiss her neck and she let out a soft moan. He returned his lips to hers, kissing her lovingly, passionately. She reached for the buttons on his shirt and undid them one by one, exposing his strong chest. She placed her hand over his heart, where it beat quicker beneath her palm. She pulled away for a moment to look at him, and he saw the love and devotion in her face, fueling his desire.

She picked up the blanket Wade had draped over the back of the swing and laid it on the soft grass. As she stood before him, she reached her hand out to him, silently asking him to lay with her. His heart raced with love for her as she led him to the blanket, her eyes never leaving his. She turned to face him and pushed his shirt over his shoulders, allowing it to fall to the ground behind him. She pulled her shirt over her head and brought his hands to her soft skin, begging him to touch her. Her eyes still locked with his, she unbuttoned the clasp of his jeans and grabbed his belt loops to pull him to her. Their lips met in a passionate kiss. Their tongues moved against each other wildly, heating his blood. She took him with her as she lay down on the blanket urging him on top of her. He closed his eyes and hissed out a breath as she wrapped her legs around his hips and rocked against him, barely managing to hold on to his control. He slid her panties down her legs until she was naked beneath her skirt. He moved his hand gently up her thigh, enjoying the softness of her skin.

For a moment he held himself above her, admiring her beauty and her strength. He loved this woman with all his heart and he would never let her go through something so horrible again. She placed her hands behind his neck and pulled him down to her for a soft kiss. As she whispered his name against his lips and confessed how much she loved him, he moved inside of her, joining their bodies as one as they made love beside the fireflies.

CHAPTER
THIRTY - THREE

WAKING UP NEXT to Ashley this morning, the sun lighting her golden hair as it streamed in through the window, had been a dream come true. They'd fallen asleep in each other's arms after making love in the softness of her sheets. As he'd drifted, he thought about all that transpired that night: watching the sunset and the fireflies as they professed their love for one another, listening to her heart-wrenching story, and making love on the bank of the river. Despite everything she'd gone through, she was able to love again, even stronger and deeper than before. It was a miracle, one that Wade was beyond grateful for.

To make things even better, when Emmett emerged from his bedroom this morning—bleary eyed and hair mussed—he gave Wade only a cursory glance before plopping himself next to him at the breakfast table and pouring himself a bowl of cereal.

"Can we go riding today?" Emmett asked.

"I wish I could, but I'm going to visit my brother today. It's a long drive so I probably won't be back until around two," Wade said.

"If we go somewhere close, that gives us two hours until the barbecue. Can we go then? I really want to try out a jump today."

"As long as I'm back on time I think we can manage that. The course by Carson's house has a few beginner jumps. We could go there."

"Cool. Thanks, Wade. Can I go with you to visit your brother? I'd like to meet him."

"I'm sure he would like that, but unfortunately they won't allow it. You have to be an immediate family member."

"That must be awful for him, being stuck in that prison for years of his life. Cut off from his family and friends. I don't think I could handle being in a place like that."

"It certainly is not an easy life. I worry about him. I want him to be okay."

"When does he get out?"

"He has five years left, but he has a chance of an early parole if he has good behavior."

"That's good."

"Yeah." *It would be, if he ever had good behavior*, Wade finished silently.

"I hope he'll be okay."

"Me too."

***

Wade watched from his seat on the cold metal bench as Ford filed into the visiting room with the other inmates. He appeared thinner than before: his denim jumpsuit hung looser than it had last time Wade saw him and his cheekbones appeared sunken and hollow as if he hadn't been eating. He looked as if he hadn't shaved in weeks and his skin and hair appeared oily and dirty as if he no longer cared about personal hygiene. Though the cut on his neck—once red and inflamed beneath the line of black stitches— was now only a faded pink line, there were fresh bruises on his face. The knuckles on his right hand were bruised as well. It looked like he'd hit something. As Ford lowered himself to the bench across from Wade, he winced with the movement in obvious pain. There was something in his eyes, something dark and terrible that hinted at some unforeseen horror. His face was set in stone, a bleak expression that you might find on the face of someone who has nothing left to live for.

Wade's voice flooded with concern. "Tell me what happened."

Ford waved him off. "It's not a big deal. I don't want to bore you with the details."

"You're not helping anyone by keeping this a secret. Tell me what happened, Ford. Please. I want to help."

"I don't want to talk about it. I'm fine, okay? Please just drop it. I want to hear about your sexy lady."

Wade pressed his lips together. He'd let it go for now, but this conversation wasn't over. "She's good, amazing actually. Things are really good between us. I've never been happier."

"How's the sex?"

"I'm not going to talk about that with you!"

"Wow, you're really serious about this girl."

"I am. I'm in love with her, and with her kid."

"I'm really happy for you, man. I'm glad you found someone who will put up with your ugly mug. Never let her go."

"I don't plan on it. I want to ask her to move in with me. At some point, we'll hopefully build a house together on my land by the river."

"That's a big step. I'm proud of you, Wade. I'm glad to see you're not wasting your life worrying about things you can't control."

"It's not a waste if I can help the people I care about."

Ford shifted on the bench, wincing as he did so. Before Wade could ask about it, he kept the conversation going. "How's Emmett doing?"

"He just finished school, pulled his grades up significantly. And he was released from his probation early for good behavior."

"I'll bet he's happy about that."

"I've never seen him happier."

"Do you worry he'll go back to the way things were before?"

Wade thought about it. "No, I don't. I believe him when he said that part of his life is behind him. He truly wants to do better, and he is. He's developed some positive interests and made friends with some good kids. I think that helps."

"It definitely can. How's the whole dirt bike riding thing going? I was amazed when you told me the two of you got those old bikes working. I never thought they'd run again."

"I had to put some money into them, but it was worth it for what we got out of it. Emmett has developed an interest in mechanics and he's good at it too. Maybe it will help him choose a career path in the future. He's improving quickly with his riding too. His first competition is in a few weeks."

"I'll bet he's excited about that. I remember going to your competitions with Mom and Dad when I was little. I was in such awe when I watched you ride."

Through the black surrounding Ford's eyes, Wade could see the sadness of the boy who missed out on the childhood he deserved. All he had left were fragments of happy memories before things went to hell. Wade's gut twisted with regret. "I wish I could have taught you. I always meant to, you know."

"I know. Life got in the way, it happens. So how is it going to work with Emmett out of school for the summer?"

"It happens." Ford had said it matter-of-factly, like it was no big deal. Wade wanted to believe him, but he couldn't ignore the fact that Ford's voice sounded so lifeless as he said it. Something was severely wrong. "You don't have to pretend like everything is fine, you know? You can talk to me if you want."

"I am talking to you. I asked you about Emmett. You're the one who didn't answer."

"I want to talk about you."

"Well, I don't. I want to talk about Emmett." His jaw was flexed and his arms were crossed tightly across his chest. "So, I'll ask you again in case you forgot. What's going to happen now that Emmett is out on summer break?"

Wade sighed. "Fine. Since Emmett has been doing so well he'll have more freedom to hang out with his friends, but I'm also hiring him on as my assistant for the summer. I'll pay him five dollars an hour to help me with whatever contracting jobs come up."

"That's a good idea. He gets to earn some money and do something constructive to stay out of trouble."

"Yeah. I'm looking forward to teaching him some things and spending more time with him."

"That's great, Wade. I'm glad to hear things are going so well and he's keeping himself out of trouble. I'm sure a lot of that has to do with you."

"I haven't done much except spend some time with him."

"You're there for him in whatever way he needs it. It's enough."

"It wasn't enough for you."

The emptiness in Ford's gaze intensified. "Nothing would have been enough for me. It wasn't your fault, Wade, so stop pretending like it was. Stop putting this whole thing on you. I'm not your problem."

"What if I want you to be my problem?"

"I don't want to be. So tell me more about Ashley."

"Ford, please tell me what's going on with you. I know something isn't right."

Ford sighed and his shoulders drooped as he lowered his gaze to the table. "Thank you for being concerned about me, but please let it go. I just want to hear about you and how happy you are. I

like hearing about it. I need to know things are good for you."
When Ford looked up again, his eyes were pleading. "Please do
this for me?"

Wade studied his little brother. He seemed so desperate, almost
begging. How could he say no to him? Although it went against his
better judgment, Wade obliged.

***

"That was so close! This time, push the throttle a little harder
to get more speed before you hit the jump." Wade stood on a
mound of dirt with Ashley as they watched Emmett put his dirt
bike in gear for another attempt at the smallest jump on the course.

Emmett revved the engine and took off, pushing the throttle
down hard as he picked up speed. He hit the jump and his bike
soared a few inches above the ground before landing with a loud
thump. He heard Ashley's gasp as Emmett's bike suddenly
wiggled from side to side. He hit the brakes hard—too hard—
causing his bike to skid and Emmett to go flying off.

Wade and Ashley both took off running toward him. By the
time they got there, he'd already removed his helmet and gave
them a thumbs up.

"Emmett, are you hurt?" Ashley said with obvious worry.

"I'm fine, Mom. Didn't you see the thumbs up?"

"I did, but I still have to make sure." After giving Emmett a
thorough inspection, she deemed him uninjured and let Wade pull
him to his feet.

"What did I do wrong that time?"

"It looked to me like you hit the brakes too hard and too soon.
Once you land the jump, if you have to brake do it gradually. If
you slam it you'll most likely wipe out. But, you caught some air
that time. I saw your tires leave the ground."

"Awesome! I'm going to give it another go," Emmett said.

"Right now? Emmett, you just took a fall. Why don't you take a break and try again another day?" Ashley suggested.

"Let him try. He wants to get it right," Wade said.

"Fine, but if he breaks his neck, I'll blame you."

"I'm sure if he breaks anything, it would be his wrist." At Ashley's horrified look, Wade added, "I'm joking. He's going to be fine. Just watch."

Emmett laid down the throttle as he accelerated toward the jump. This time he landed and kept going, before coming to a much smoother stop.

"Did you see that, Wade? Mom? I landed my first jump! I'm going to go again."

"Okay, that was worth it," Ashley said with a grin. "How did your visit with your brother go today?"

"It was okay. We mainly talked about you and Emmett. He wanted to hear every detail about the woman and her teenage son who stole my heart."

She studied his face. "It seems like there's something you're not telling me."

"You and Emmett both are so damn intuitive. He was injured again today, but he wouldn't talk about it. Usually he's so cocky about the fights he gets into, but this time was different. He seemed like he was ashamed of it, even scared to talk about it. I think he's really in trouble. He seemed so… hopeless."

Ashley placed her hand on his arm. "There's only so much you can do, Wade. I understand you want to be there for him, you want to fix whatever problem he's facing, but if he doesn't want to tell you, you can't make him."

"I know. I just wish there was something I could do for him."

"All you can do is keep showing up for him like you've been doing. Keep letting him know you love him."

"Yeah…"

"What?"

Wade kicked the dirt. "I've never actually told him I loved him."

"What? How can that be? He's your brother!"

"It's just not the type of relationship we've ever had. He knows I love him. There's never been any reason for us to say it to each other."

"That's absurd. Even if he knows you love him, you should still tell him. People like to be told they are loved."

He smiled his crooked grin at her as he grabbed her around the waist. "I love you, Ashley."

"Don't tell me, tell your brother." She gave him a playful shove.

"Fine, I will. But I'm warning you, he'll probably beat me up or at least threaten to do so. If you have to look at my marred face for the rest of your life, that's on you. I don't want to hear about it."

She laughed, a musical sound that warmed him from the inside out. She twirled her hair and batted her lashes at him. "The rest of your life, huh?"

"As long as you want me, I'll be here… and probably even a while after you decide you don't want me."

She laughed again and kissed him. "I love you."

"I like hearing you say that."

"I'm sure your brother would like it too."

He shook his head, amused. "I said I'd tell him."

"Good."

"Now try to keep your hands off me for a few minutes so I can watch your son nail his next jump."

CHAPTER
THIRTY - FOUR

WADE SEARCHED THROUGH his kitchen for breakfast. He had been staying at Ashley's house the past several nights and all he could find was a stale doughnut and some moldy bread. Opting for the doughnut, Wade preheated the oven to warm it up, hoping it would help hide the fact that it was days old. He wished he was at Ashley's this morning, or better yet, he wished she was here with him. He wished it was *their* house instead of just *his.* As the doughnut heated to what was hopefully an edible condition, he let his mind wander.

The enticing aroma of coffee brewing and Ashley's steak and eggs filled the house. Having been woken by the mouthwatering smells and his growling stomach, Wade traipsed down the hallway, his bare feet lightly slapping the wood floor. When he reached the kitchen, he saw Ashley standing by the stove, hard at work making breakfast. Emmett was at the kitchen table and he looked up at Wade's approach. "Hey, Dad. Mom's making your favorite this morning."

"I can see that. I smelled it all the way from bed. It smells delicious, Ashley," Wade said as he came up behind her.

She turned her head and smiled warmly at him, her devotion clear in the loving way she looked at him. Wade lifted her hair off her neck to kiss her soft skin and she leaned in to him, her back to his front. He wrapped his arms around her waist and gently caressed her swollen belly.

"How's our daughter this morning?"

"She's good. Of course now that I'm up and moving, she's finally quiet. But I know as soon as I lie down again she'll start up with her kickboxing routine. I swear she bruised my ribs last night."

Wade smiled against her neck. "Maybe she'll be a professional soccer player."

"Hey, Dad, can we go riding today?" Emmett interrupted.

"Sure, Emmett. I was also hoping we could finish sanding the crib today and maybe even put on the first layer of stain. Would you want to help me with that after our ride?"

"Sure thing."

"Breakfast is ready!" Ashley said cheerfully, only her words were drowned out by a loud beeping sound.

Wade was startled from his daydream by the piercing beeping of the smoke detector. As he opened the oven door, the smell of smoke and burned sugar hit him in the face, making him cough. He waved the smoke away and opened a window to air out the kitchen.

He was only supposed to put the leftover doughnut in the oven for a few minutes to warm up, but his daydream must have distracted him. Now his breakfast was burned beyond recognition and his kitchen was a smokers' lounge. *Great.* Maybe he'd get lucky and Ashley would bring something by for him when she dropped off Emmett this morning.

If only they lived together. Then, he could wake up to her every morning and be a more permanent influence in Emmett's life. It was one step closer to becoming the family he dreamed about. Not to mention that living together could save lives because let's face it, his cooking was a fire hazard.

He looked at the clock. Ashley would be here with Emmett in about fifteen minutes. Emmett had been working as Wade's assistant for the past two weeks, and he was proving himself to be a real asset. Work was coming in steadily and Wade was already booked solid through the summer. Even with Emmett working hard for him every day, his schedule was full. If this kept up, it wouldn't be long before he saved enough to start building his dream home by the river—the house he hoped his family would grow into. He just had to ask Ashley to take the next step with him.

As he silently worked out how he was going to ask her to move in with him, his cell phone buzzed in the pocket of his jeans. He thought it might be Ashley calling to say they were running late again this morning. He hoped it meant Emmett had overslept because that would mean he hadn't eaten yet and they could go out for breakfast before starting their work today. With fingers crossed, he pulled his phone from his pocket only to see a number he didn't recognize. Maybe it was another potential client. "Good morning. Wade Hudson here. What can I do for you today?"

"Mr. Hudson, my name is Virginia. I work at the Clarke County Hospital." Her voice was deep and rough and she had a slight lisp. "I'm calling regarding Ford Hudson. I have been informed he is your close relative. Is that correct?"

"Yes. He's my brother." His mouth suddenly felt as dry as ash.

"You're listed as Mr. Hudson's emergency contact and next of kin. You were his legal guardian until he turned eighteen, is that correct?"

"Yes… What is this about?"

"I'm calling you because you are also listed as his power of attorney, which means that in the event that Mr. Hudson is unable to make informed medical decisions about his care, then the decision becomes yours."

"I know what power of attorney means. What happened to my brother? Is he sick? Did he get hurt? Is it serious? I mean it must be serious if you're talking about him being unable to make his own medical decisions."

"I'm afraid I can't share any details with you about his condition at this time. I am calling you to—"

Wade cut her off. "What do you mean, you can't share any details about his condition? I'm his brother, his next of kin. You said so yourself!"

"Sir, I'm going to need you to lower your voice, please. Because Mr. Hudson is under the supervision of the Butterfield Corrections Facility, I'm unauthorized to provide you with any specific details about his condition at this time."

"Then what did you call to tell me?" Wade demanded.

"Sir, I do not appreciate your tone. I understand you are upset, but I'm just trying to do my job."

Wade took a breath and ran his hand through his hair. "I'm sorry. I just need to know what's going on. Please tell me what you can."

"I'm calling to inform you that Mr. Hudson has suffered a major accident and they are uncertain that he'll recover. We are calling to inform you of this and to also determine whether you would like the hospital to take extraordinary measures or to discontinue care if the situation should arise."

"Are you asking for my permission to let my brother die? How could you even ask me that? And how can I even answer that when I have no idea what the hell is going on with him or what happened to him?"

"Sir, I'm going to need you to calm down. I'm merely attempting to gather the information we need from you in order to determine how Mr. Hudson's medical care should proceed from here."

"Keep him alive. Do whatever you need to do to keep him alive."

"I'll note that in his file for now. But we're going to need you to come in and fill out some paperwork. His doctor would like to talk to you about some possible treatment options as well."

"Okay. I'll be there as soon as I can."

"When you arrive, come to the front desk and they will give you the paperwork you need."

"And then I can see him, right? I get to see my brother, who may or may not be dying?"

"I'm afraid that is for the corrections department to decide. Come in and fill out the paperwork and we'll go from there. Have a nice day, sir." The line went dead.

Have a nice day. Was she serious? He wasn't in the mood for someone telling him to calm down when his brother was in the hospital for some unknown reason, in some unknown condition. He needed answers—no—he deserved answers. Ford was his brother for God's sake. Where do they get off keeping this kind of information from him?

He was going down there, and he was going to find out what was going on. Ford was hurt, seriously hurt, or they wouldn't have bothered calling him. And, he was in the hospital—a real hospital—not just the prison infirmary. That most likely meant he was in grave condition or needed surgery.

Maybe he already had surgery. Maybe he was dying. What if he died and the crappy hospital staff couldn't even tell him why because of some stupid policy? He needed answers, he needed to see his brother. Racked with worry, and pissed at asinine policies and hospital staff that lacked people skills, Wade got in his truck and drove like hell.

CHAPTER
THIRTY - FIVE

WADE TAPPED HIS fingers impatiently on the information desk while the very unpleasant woman sitting behind it ignored him to continue her personal call. She had absurdly long acrylic fingernails painted blue and wore far too much makeup. Her voice was raucous and grated on his nerves, and she spoke at a volume that was too loud for a small lobby. As she cackled—an unattractive, piercing sound—at something the person on the other end of the phone line said, Wade's finger tapping turned into a full palm slap.

"Hold on a minute, Cora," she said into the receiver, turning her annoyed stare at Wade. "I'll be with you in a moment," she snipped, before placing the phone back to her ear to continue her gossip. After several minutes of finger drumming, foot tapping, and one long murderous look from Wade, the woman finally hung up the phone.

"What can I help you with?" she said with the enthusiasm of a rock.

"I got a call saying my brother was in the hospital. His name is Ford Hudson."

With the look of someone facing a four-hour lecture on soap, she turned her attention to the computer screen in front of her and tapped on the keys with her claws. "It says here, he's not allowed any visitors."

"I was told to come to the front desk to get some paperwork I need to fill out for him."

She made a sigh of the long suffering. "What kind of paperwork?"

"I don't know, something about ensuring he gets continued care or extraordinary measures."

She let out a grunt of annoyance and shot him a matching expression. "Just a moment." She punched a few numbers in the keypad on her phone and put the receiver to her ear. "Yeah, I have someone here looking for some papers to fill out for a Ford Hudson… Okay."

She put the phone back in its holder and with what seemed like great effort, rolled her chair over to a filing cabinet. As slow as humanly possible, she looked through the files and pulled out a small stack of papers before rolling back and handing them out to Wade without looking at him.

"Sorry I made your job so difficult for you," he said as he took the papers from her outstretched hand. She gave him a dirty look before he walked away, followed by a rude hand gesture behind his back, which he caught out of the corner of his eye. If everyone who worked at this hospital was as lovely and accommodating as she was, then he was in for a very long day.

Signed paperwork in hand, Wade found himself wandering the halls of the hospital, hoping he'd be lucky enough to stumble upon his brother's room. It felt like he'd been walking around for at least an hour, and the smell of disinfectant and death was starting to get to him. He glanced at the room to his left as he walked by. A small child lay with closed eyes—dwarfed by the size of the hospital bed and the shocking number of tubes connected to her tiny body. Her parents sat at the edge of the bed, stroking the child's impossibly small hand with dreary looks on their faces.

That was enough for now. Wade needed to take a break for a while, get some fresh air. As his mission changed from finding his brother to finding an exit, he rounded a corner and saw a man in a khaki uniform guarding the room at the end of the hallway.

Wade approached and the man with the badge took a more defensive stance—weight evenly distributed between wide legs, shoulders squared, hands free and at the ready, his body turned slightly toward Wade as he blocked the door. Wade tried to act casual like he belonged there, but his heart was racing wildly in his chest.

When he was one room away, the corrections officer turned to face him completely. "Sir, this is a restricted area. I'm going to ask you to please turn around and head back in the direction you came."

The green exit sign beyond the corrections officer gave Wade an idea. He clutched his chest and began taking exaggerated shallow breaths. In between short breaths, he gasped out the words, "Can't breathe… need exit… need inhaler… in car." Wade tried to look as panicked as possible as he doubled over and feigned a wheeze.

The guard seemed to assess him for a moment as Wade gave another strained wheeze for good measure. "Move over to the opposite side of the hallway and walk straight to the exit. Do not stop. Do you understand?" Wade nodded frantically and followed the guard's instructions. As he passed the room, he risked a peek through the partially opened blinds covering the window and stopped in his tracks.

Ford lay pale and lifeless in the hospital bed. Monitors beeped as they tracked his vitals, attached to his body through tangles of tubes and cables. He had a large white tube down his throat connected to a ventilator that made a whooshing sound as it compressed to push air into his lungs. Through the spaces in the hard brace stabilizing his neck, Wade could see a gruesome band of red, damaged skin.

Forgetting his charade, Wade turned to the guard. "What happened to him?"

"Sir, get away from the window," the guard said as he took a step toward Wade.

"That white tube means he can't breathe on his own, right? Why is there a red line around his neck? What happened to him!"

The guard used his radio to call for backup before turning back to Wade. "Sir, move away from this room or I will remove you by force."

"That's my brother in there. He's dying and no one will tell me anything. Why won't anyone tell me anything?" Wade took another step toward Ford's room and felt strong hands close around him firmly and pull him back. "Wait! I need answers. I need to know what's going on. That's my brother in there!"

But the hands kept dragging him back, away from his brother, away from the corrections officer standing watch outside his room. Wade felt himself being led down the hallway and pushed into a chair.

A beast of a man stood before him. He was all of six feet four inches tall, 350 pounds of muscle hidden beneath a round belly that protruded over his grey pants and strained the buttons on his oversized shirt. His skin was as black as midnight, making his shockingly white teeth stand out prominently. "Sir, I'm going to need you to wait here," said the giant security guard in front of him.

"I take it you are waiting here with me?"

He was met only with silence and a stare as hard as diamonds.

"I'll take that as a yes. Am I under arrest or something?"

Again, silence was his only response.

"Well, you sure are a chatty little thing aren't you."

This time he was almost certain he saw the corners of the security guard's mouth twitch upward, but he couldn't be sure.

As Wade sat in the poorly padded, atrociously uncomfortable chair in the hospital's waiting room, an angry elephant of a man glaring down at him from three feet away, every minute that passed felt like three.

He was worried about his brother, stressed about what he didn't know, and his arms hurt where Officer Rhinoceros had grabbed him to haul him down here. Plus, he was scared—scared for his brother and a little scared of the giant pachyderm in front of him—and Wade hated feeling scared. Being scared made him feel out of control and uncertain, which made him want to have a drink.

A man wearing a white lab coat and a stethoscope around his neck walked over to where Wade was being held hostage in his chair. "Thank you, Cecil. We should be fine on our own," he said to Wade's guard.

Cecil shot Wade a warning look before thundering away.

"It was nice chatting with you, Cecil!" Wade called out to his massive backside.

Kind grey eyes under bushy black eyebrows peered at Wade. "You must be Mr. Hudson."

"Call me, Wade."

"Wade, I'm Dr. Jackson. I'm Ford's doctor."

"Please tell me you can talk to me about Ford."

Dr. Jackson gave Wade a sympathetic smile. "I'm sure it's been very difficult for you to be kept in the dark regarding Ford's condition. Unfortunately we have to follow state policy regarding prison inmates who are brought to us for care, which means that we can only divulge the information they allow us to. I've been given authorization to fill you in on what you need to know about Ford's current condition in order for you to make sound medical decisions for him, but I'm sorry to say that is all I am permitted to tell you. Is that the paperwork the hospital staff asked you to fill out?" He gestured to the small stack of papers in Wade's hand.

Wade offered them to him and watched him look them over before tucking them under his arm. "Thank you. I'll make sure these make it into Ford's medical file."

"So, what can you tell me about Ford?"

"Ford is stable for now but he is in critical condition. He has suffered a small cervical fracture as well as some fractures to the bony and cartilaginous structures in his neck. We've stabilized his neck using a brace and we're hopeful there won't be any permanent damage to his nerves. However, he has significant damage to his laryngeal cartilage, which can easily compromise his breathing. In order to maintain his airway, we have intubated him, which means he has a tube running down his throat to his lungs. Currently Ford isn't breathing on his own, but we have him on a ventilator which is giving his body all the oxygen he needs."

"He also has acute pulmonary edema from the trauma that he received to his airway, which means that his lungs filled up with fluid. We have installed a chest tube to drain the excess fluid buildup and we are monitoring him closely. Do you have any questions so far?"

The information whirred through Wade's mind. His baby brother was in critical condition with a long list of scary-sounding health issues that might kill him. What had happened to him to put him in such a state? What if he died? Wade ran his hands through his hair and tried to collect himself. "He can't breathe on his own? Don't people usually die when they can't breathe on their own?"

"Sometimes, but we're monitoring Ford very closely. It's not his lungs I'm concerned about. Ford was unconscious when he arrived and he's remained that way since. A head CT informed us he has a buildup of fluid in his brain, which is putting a lot of excess pressure on the brain. He also has a large subarachnoid hemorrhage, which basically means his brain is bleeding. The hemorrhage, in combination with the fluid buildup and the cerebral hypoxia—or lack of oxygen to the brain during asphyxiation—may have caused Ford some irreparable brain damage."

Shock coursed through Wade's body. "Asphyxiation? Like he was choked?" Wade thought of the band of inflamed skin around his neck and the brace stabilizing it. "Oh my God. He was hanged. My brother was hanged!"

"Wade, I'm sorry but I can neither confirm nor deny your statement. I am not at liberty to give you any information about what led to Ford's current condition. I can only discuss with you his medical care."

Wade paced back and forth, blowing out huge breaths to try to stay calm. Ford had been hanged. He knew something was wrong the last time he went to visit him. He should've tried harder to get Ford to tell him what was going on. He could have reported whoever was threatening him. He could have prevented this... could have helped him. But he didn't. His brother had suffered a huge tragedy, and Wade hadn't protected him. How could he ever forgive himself?

"I'm very sorry, Wade. This must be difficult for you. I truly wish it didn't have to be this way."

"Difficult would be putting it lightly. Just think about if someone you loved was hurt or dying and no one would tell you anything. Someone hanged my brother. Wouldn't you want to know how something like that happened if you were me?"

"Of course. I'd want to go over every single detail. I'd be losing my mind not knowing. All things considered, you're handling all of this very well. Do you have any more questions about his medical condition?"

"You said my brother might have brain damage. What does that mean exactly?"

"It means we are uncertain he will wake up. In the event that he does wake up, he may have permanent brain deficiencies. I'm sorry, Wade. I know this is a lot to take in."

"There has to be something you can do."

"There are a few options, but they're risky and there's no guarantee they'll work."

"Tell me."

"We can wait and monitor him closely to see if the bleed in his brain stops on its own, or I can take him into surgery and try to see if I can find the source of the bleed and repair the cause. I would also put in a tube to drain any excess fluid in hopes of relieving the pressure in his brain."

"Will it work?"

"There is a chance it will work, and he will make a full recovery, but there is also a chance that once we open him up we will see that the damage is more extensive than we thought. There are many risks to a surgery like this, but in this case they are extrapolated because of Ford's current condition."

"What kinds of risks?"

"He could bleed out, suffer a stroke, or the surgery could cause permanent damage to his brain. Ford has been through a lot, and it has left his body weakened. There is a good chance the surgery will be too much more for his body to handle and his heart won't be able to take the strain."

"What would that mean?"

"There's a good chance Ford will go into cardiac arrest during surgery. If you choose to do the surgery, you'll receive more information about these risks and more paperwork to sign."

The ache in Wade's chest was growing with each passing second. "What are his chances of waking up if you do nothing?"

"In my professional opinion, I would say, slim. There's a good chance the bleeding in his brain will kill him. Despite the risks, I still think surgery is the best option."

"Do the surgery. Do whatever it takes to save him, please. He's my little brother."

"I assure you, I will do everything I can for Ford." He patted Wade's shoulder. "A nurse will be by soon to give you some consent papers to sign. As soon as we have those signed we can get started with Ford's surgery. I also have someone working with corrections to see if they can give you more information about what happened. In the meantime, I suggest you sit tight and stay out of trouble. You will do more for your brother here than you would from jail."

"Right, thank you, Dr. Jackson."

The doctor patted him on the shoulder. "I will keep you updated. Hang in there, okay?"

After Wade filled out even more paperwork, Dr. Jackson came back to let Wade know they would begin prepping Ford for surgery. As he waited, he mulled over the extent of Ford's injuries. Ford was gravely injured—he might not survive—and it was all his fault.

He knew something had been seriously wrong before, but he let Ford distract him. Wade had been so eager to talk about how happy he was and about all the great things going on in his life, that he failed to find out about Ford's obviously distraught mental state. While Wade carried on about love and his promising future with Ashley, Ford was trying to cope with something dark and horrible all on his own. And now he lay on an operating table, fighting for his life.

A familiar face suddenly appeared in the waiting room. "Reid? How did you? What are you doing here?" Wade asked.

"Ashley called me shortly after you called her on your way over here. She wanted to come herself, but they had some type of emergency at the clinic. She and Maggie will be here as soon as they can."

Ashley. Of course she would think of doing something so thoughtful as to call his best friend in his time of need. The only problem was, Wade would rather be alone right now. "Where's Emmett?" Wade asked.

"I spent the morning with him until Robbie's shift ended, and now he's at Carson's house."

Wade nodded his acceptance. He felt bad about bailing on Emmett today, but he was glad to hear things worked out.

"How's Ford?"

Wade updated Reid on Ford's condition and the doctor's plan to save him.

"So they haven't even let you see him?"

"I caught a quick glimpse of him from the hallway before they hauled me away, but that's it."

"Man, I'm really sorry. This must be killing you. How bad do you want a drink right now?"

"I've been trying to stop myself from going to the bar across the street for a good three hours now."

"Hang in there, man. You don't want to start down that path again."

"Is it okay if we just sit for a while. I don't feel much like talking right now."

"Sure, no problem."

Hours passed. Ashley, Emmett, Maggie, and Carson all showed up for support. Words of condolences, hugs, heartwarming gestures, and questions about Ford all came his way. Though they meant well, Wade didn't feel much like entertaining. Still, it felt nice knowing he had so many people in his life who cared so deeply for Ford and for him.

Ashley's shoulder pressed gently against his, her hand clasped in his, warm and gentle in his lap. She didn't say anything—she merely sat with him and held his hand—giving it a soft squeeze every now and then to remind him she was there for him. Her presence helped to ease the ache in his chest and his fear of the unknown. He was grateful for her—for her presence, her warmth, her support—just her. Wade gave her hand a soft squeeze. "Thank you for being here."

"Where else would I be?"

"I love you."

"I know, and I love you too. Ford is going to be okay."

A small squeaky voice caught his attention. "I'm looking for a Mr. Wade Hudson. Is he here?" Wade looked at the squat woman with the dark hair and the pale skin who had just entered the room. She wore black slacks, a billowy blouse in a bold geometric print, and an official-looking nametag.

"I'm Wade."

"Wade, hello. My name is Dr. Beasley. I am the psychiatrist at Butterfield Corrections. I'd like to talk to you about Ford. Is now a good time?"

Finally someone who was going to give him some answers. "Yes."

"Can we speak alone? I'm afraid I'm only authorized to discuss this information with you."

"Uh, sure."

"Splendid. If you would please follow me. I have secured a quiet place for us to speak."

Ashley gave Wade's hand a final squeeze, and he followed Dr. Beasley out of the room. She was so short that she barely came up to his chest. The way she waddled when she walked reminded him of a duckling, waggling its tail as it struggled to keep up with its mother. Wade followed her into a bland room with a long table and rolling desk chairs.

"Please have a seat anywhere you'd like." After closing the door behind her, she found a seat across the table from him and clasped her hands on the table top. "I know you are eager for information about your brother's injuries so I'll just get straight to it, but I warn you that you may want to brace yourself."

"Please just tell me."

"Very well. During a routine cell check, correction officers found your brother hanging by his neck, unconscious in his cell. Reports indicated he had made a noose with his bedding and tied it to a pipe on the ceiling. It was deemed a suicide attempt."

Wade's mouth went dry and he broke out into a cold sweat. "You're wrong. Ford wouldn't kill himself. He wouldn't have done that!" *Would he?* Wade thought about Ford's growing bleak outlook for his own future, his attitude of defeat, the dead look in his eyes. "No. I don't want to believe it."

"I know it must come as a shock to you, but I assure you, his injury was self-inflicted. He was locked alone in his cell when they found him. The cameras in the cell confirm it."

Ford tried to kill himself. Ford tried to kill himself. The words ran through Wade's mind over and over, but he didn't want to believe them. If it was true, then what did that say about Wade? Ford was his baby brother—his responsibility—and he hadn't even seen this coming. He should've been a better brother, a better listener. He should've visited more often, paid better attention. Even sober, he'd neglected his brother because he'd been so focused on himself and his own life.

Over the past several months his visits had become more and more infrequent. He had wanted to spend all of his time with Ashley and Emmett rather than burdening himself to make the drive out to see his brother. He might have been to see his brother two weeks ago, but before that he hadn't seen him for months. He neglected Ford, just like their father did, and he didn't even need booze to do it.

"I'm so sorry to burden you with this news. I can assure you that when he recovers, he'll be put on strict supervision and will receive regular counseling. We will do our part to make sure something like this doesn't happen again while he's in our custody."

"Do you have any idea why he might have done something like this?"

"The hearsay is that Ford had been getting harassed by a particular group of inmates. Officers reported breaking up fights and foul play directed at Ford. Has he said anything to you about it?"

"No, nothing. I could tell something was wrong last time I saw him, but he wouldn't tell me about it. A while back he did tell me he got into a knife fight with someone because a guy had been harassing him about his lunch. Could it be the same group of guys?"

"It's possible. It appeared that things had been getting out of control. There are multiple reports of violence involving Ford and this particular group of inmates, and the reports of violence seem to be in increasing severity. There's always a possibility that more incidents occurred than were reported as well."

"What does the prison plan to do to protect my brother? I guarantee he wasn't the one who started all this. If Ford hurt someone, it was only out of self-defense. My brother isn't a violent person."

"I assure you, we have the situation under control."

"Clearly. It only took my brother trying to kill himself on your watch for someone to do something about it. I need to talk to him. I know you have your policies and crap, but I need to talk to him when he wakes up. Please," he added hastily.

"I'm afraid that just isn't going to happen. You'll need to wait until normal visiting hours once he returns to the Butterfield Facility." She gave him a sympathetic smile. "State policy."

The anger—no, the fury—and the helplessness Wade felt was so overwhelming he almost couldn't bear it. As he returned to the waiting room, everyone's faces turned to look at him expectantly for information about Ford, but he couldn't talk about it. He couldn't say the words out loud. Suddenly, all those expectant faces turned to something behind him, urging him to turn around.

There stood Dr. Jackson, looking tired and grim. Wade held his breath. He didn't think he'd be able to handle any more bad news today.

"Ford is out of surgery and he's stable for now. I'm afraid there was a lot more damage to his brain than we initially thought. I was able to find the source of the bleeding and make the necessary repair, as well as install the tube to drain the fluid buildup in his brain, but we won't know if there will be any permanent damage until he wakes up."

"So, he is going to wake up." Though she was standing right next to him, Ashley's voice sounded far away, like he was hearing it from the other side of a long tunnel.

"We don't know. But we'll monitor him closely and we'll just have to wait and see. It could take days or more. You all should go home and get some rest. Wade, I will call you as soon as we have any news."

Wade felt himself nodding and Ashley's gentle touch on his arm. "Let's get you home. I'll make you something to eat."

"Thank you, but I think I'm just going to go home. I feel like I need to be alone tonight."

"Are you sure? I could at least bring something over for you to eat."

"No. I'm good. Thanks. I can manage on my own. I'll call you tomorrow, okay?"

"Emmett's still coming by tomorrow, right?"

"Oh, um. Actually, I may need to take a rain check on that. I think I might come back down to the hospital tomorrow."

"Okay. I'm sure we can figure something out for tomorrow. Let me know if you need anything, okay? I'm here for you. Ford is going to be just fine, you'll see." She gave him a kiss and gestured for Emmett and the rest of them to follow her out, leaving Wade standing in the hospital waiting room alone, his limbs tired and heavy, his soul numb.

***

The curtains were drawn, blocking out the last of the evening light. The room was dark where Wade sat alone on his sofa, but he made no move to turn on a light. In his hand he held a glass bottle, still frosted cold from the liquor store refrigerator. The numb feeling had left him long ago. In its place, guilt and misery dueled for control, leaving a well of pain in their wake. He twisted the cap off the bottle and heard the comforting hiss of a long-lost companion. He brought the frosty glass to his lips and savored the taste of the cool bitter liquid as it ran down his throat and warmed his belly. He drank until the thoughts that tormented him blurred and faded and his pain eased. He drank until his regret for going down this path again no longer plagued him. He drank until he felt nothing.

CHAPTER
THIRTY - SIX

ASHLEY'S STOMACH WAS in knots with worry. For the past week, Wade had locked himself in his house, only leaving to go to the hospital. Whenever she stopped by to bring him food, his clothes seemed progressively more wrinkled and dirty, his hair was mussed, his eyes were glazed and bloodshot, and his stubble grew increasingly thick. He would take the food she offered, give her a half smile and a quick kiss of thanks, and return to the shadows of his solitude. Most of the time he would dutifully answer her calls, but she found he never said very much. Lately, their conversations consisted of a bit of small talk, an occasional "I love you," and far too much silence.

She knew he was going through a lot, but she wished he wasn't so set on going through it alone. Though he wouldn't say, it seemed like something more was going on with him than just being worried about his brother. Something seemed different about him lately, something besides the grief. The distance he had placed between himself and the people around him, his constant disheveled appearance, and the overpowering smell of mint on his breath whenever she came by, all added to her unease. She couldn't shake the feeling that he was hiding something from her.

She'd seen the pain on his face and knew he felt guilty about what happened to his brother. He'd always felt responsible for Ford, but could he actually blame himself for this? She wanted to go to him, to cling to him and take away whatever was tormenting him. She wanted to be a part of this, if only he would talk to her. Why was he pushing her away? The way Wade was keeping everyone at a distance reminded her too much of how Jeff had acted in his final months. He may not be acting angry or jumpy or having nightmares, but he was acting strangely enough to fill her with unease.

Ashley pulled up to Maggie's house and stepped through the open front door. Since Wade hadn't been able to take Emmett the past few days—much to Emmett's dismay—she was forced to put him in a day camp. Fortunately she found one that Emmett wasn't completely put off by and—lucky for her—they still had two spots available so Carson could go too. It wasn't ideal and it wasn't a permanent solution—Emmett had made his feelings about the matter abundantly clear—but it would work for now.

"How much longer am I going to have to go to this lame camp?" Emmett whined.

"Until Wade feels up to going back to work with you."

"I don't like this. I'd much rather be with Wade."

"I know, but Wade is going through a lot right now with his brother and we need to be respectful of that."

His shoulders deflated. "I know. I guess it's just kind of weird not having him around lately. I like spending time with him."

"I know sweetie. I miss him too. But he wants his space right now and we have to respect that. He knows we're here for him if he decides that's what he wants."

"I hope he remembers my first race is this weekend. He promised me he'd be there."

"I'm sure he wants to be there, honey. But, things change when a loved one is hurt. I'll talk to him about it and see if he feels up to coming."

His frown said it all. "Can we at least practice tonight? I usually practice with Wade, but since he can't right now..."

"I'll take you out to practice tonight. Why don't we ask if Carson and Robbie will come too? I'm sure Robbie could give you some pointers until Wade feels better."

"Okay, I guess. Wade better snap out of it soon, though."

"I'll call to invite him to come with us tonight, but don't be disappointed if he doesn't feel up to it."

"Yeah, okay."

"Why don't you go in and find Carson. Robbie is going to drop you both off at camp on his way to work. Have a good day. I love you."

As Emmett jogged up the stairs, he passed Maggie on her way down. "Carson's in his room!" she called after him.

"Hey, Ashley. I'm just going to grab some breakfast and then I'll be ready to go. Robbie picked up these pastries from the bakery this morning. They're dangerously delicious. This is my second one this morning. Would you like one? It looks like we still have an apple streusel muffin, a chocolate croissant, and an almond Danish," she said, peering into the box.

Ashley's stomach roiled unpleasantly. "No thanks. I haven't had much of an appetite lately."

"Still worried about Wade?"

"I know he's hurting badly, but he won't talk to me about it. I'm trying to give him his space because he said that's what he wanted, but it's been a week now. I don't even know if space is actually what he needs right now. I just wish he'd tell me what's going on."

"Men are different from us, you know that. They don't like to talk about their feelings, Wade especially. If he asked you for space, you should grant him that. It's not like he's completely alone. You bring him dinner every night, you reach out to him and check on him throughout the day. He knows you're there for him. He knows that you love him. I know it's hard, but he'll come to you when he's ready."

"Have you talked to him at all?"

"I check in with him periodically, ask him if there's anything I can do. I know Reid has stopped by too."

"Has he told you anything? Like, any updates on how Ford is doing or why he was hospitalized in the first place?"

She shook her head. "He wouldn't say, and I didn't want to push him. He's having a hard time, and even I know not to pester him when he feels like crap."

"I think he's hiding something from me. Something bad is going on, but he's trying to make sure I don't see what it is."

"He's not cheating on you. He wouldn't do that."

"It's not that… What if he's drinking again? I know he's been sober for years, but he's going through a lot right now."

"I don't think he'd do that. But if he did, Reid would know. Wade always talks about that stuff with him. If you're worried, why don't you ask him? Or talk to Wade about it yourself."

"I don't want to invade his privacy. I'm probably just overreacting. I was going to call Wade to ask if he wants to watch the boys practice tonight. Hopefully he'll come and then I'll see that I have nothing to worry about."

"That sounds like a good idea."

She leaned on the counter, looking down at its soft gleam. "I just miss him. My bed is lonely without him."

Maggie took an oversized bite from her chocolate muffin. "I didn't need to hear that."

She pushed away from the counter to stand straighter. "That's not what I meant! I'm just saying I miss having him around. I'm so in love with him. What if he pulls away from me and I lose him?"

"If there's one thing I know, it's that Wade is head over heels for you. Nothing can keep him away from you, except maybe, you. Don't worry, okay? This is just a rough patch. The two of you will get through this. Then you'll get married and have lots of babies. So calm your nerves and eat a pastry," Maggie said holding out the box to her.

Ashley smiled, grateful for her friend's support. "Maybe just one baby," she said as she picked up a chocolate croissant.

"You're young enough for at least two more. Now, let's stuff our faces and go to work."

Mended

CHAPTER
THIRTY - SEVEN

ALL THE DAYS blurred together. Every day Wade woke up and drove to the hospital in hopes of being able to see Ford. Every day he was left disappointed when his request was denied and he was banished to the waiting room. There he would sit, pestering passing hospital staff for information, all the while chewing on his own fear and guilt until he couldn't take it anymore.

When that happened he'd find himself at the bar across the street. If one drink wasn't enough, he'd have two, and sometimes three. When his pain dulled and his thoughts quieted enough, he'd return to his chair in the waiting room until it was time to go home for the night. On his way, he'd pick up his nightly stash—usually a bottle of whiskey and a six-pack of beer—at a liquor store out of town and drink himself to sleep.

He wasn't working, he was ignoring his friends and family, and if it weren't for the food Ashley brought over every day, he wouldn't have been eating either. She was the only thing keeping him from falling completely apart.

He missed her so much—her smell, her smile, her laugh, the way her breath caressed his neck as they made love—but he couldn't let her see the wreck he'd become. She deserved a man who was stable, who could take care of her, but he was neither of those things. He was ashamed of the person he was becoming—a loser, a no-good drunk, someone who wasn't worthy of her. She was loving and kind, she was pure, and she loved him. She was the best thing that had ever happened to him, and he was screwing it up. He wanted to stop, but he was too weak to overcome the tidal wave of pain and self-loathing that called him to the bottle each day. He didn't deserve her.

Though he believed that to be true, he didn't want to lose her. So, every morning he'd get up and dump whatever liquor was left from the night before. He'd tell himself to be strong; Ashley was worth feeling any amount of pain. He could overcome anything to be with her. As the day wore on, the pain and the urge to drown it would chip away at his resolve until he crumbled and found himself heading to the bar again or buying a fresh bottle at the liquor store. If he didn't find a way to stop this destructive pattern, he was sure he would lose her. He couldn't tell her about it and he couldn't keep her away forever, nor did he want to.

Even now, the picture of her face in his mind was all the motivation he needed to dump last night's whiskey down the drain. To his dismay, the bottle emptied quickly this morning. Things had gone far enough. He wouldn't let his weakness overcome him today. Ashley deserved better than this and he so desperately wanted to be the man who deserved her. Gathering the strength he needed for another long day at the hospital, he grabbed his keys and headed for the door.

On his way out, his cell phone buzzed. His stomach lurched when he saw who was calling. "Dr. Jackson," he answered.

"Wade, I'm glad I caught you. I have some news regarding your brother. He came out of his coma last night. Our tests indicate he has no permanent brain damage and his other injuries are healing as well. If things continue this way it looks like he will make a full recovery."

Wade blew out the breath he didn't realize he'd been holding. Elation swelled inside him, making him want to sing a song of praise. Ford was okay. He was going to live. "Thank you, Dr. Jackson, for everything you did for him. Can I see him?"

"I thought you might ask that, and I wish I had a different answer for you, but corrections still isn't allowing him any visits from family members. But I assure you, he is doing well. I don't mind bending the rules a little and giving him a message for you."

"Can you tell him I'm glad he's okay and I'm sorry I wasn't there for him before. Tell him I'll see him as soon as I can."

"I'll tell him. You should take the day off, stay home, be with your family and friends. Share the good news."

"Thanks, Dr. Jackson."

"Take care, Wade."

Wade knew he was pressing his luck, but he had to see Ford. If he didn't get this off his chest he was afraid he'd have a drink again today despite the good news. He had to at least give it one more try.

***

Wade walked down the familiar hallway, the soles of his boots tapping the linoleum. Adrenaline pulsed through his veins as he approached Ford's hospital room. The corrections officer guarding the door spotted him and gave him an exasperated look, but he didn't make any moves to escort him away. "You shouldn't be here, Wade."

"I need to see my brother. Can I please just talk to him?"

"Do you realize that if I'd reported your daily visits to my boss, they would've already moved your brother to a different hospital?"

"I do. Thank you for keeping this between us."

"You should go home. Your brother is fine. Dr. Jackson gave him your message, which I am also pretending never happened. I was lenient with you before because his condition was critical, but this has to stop now. You need to leave."

"I promise I'll leave today and I won't come back if you just let me talk to him."

The officer's mouth was a hard line but his eyes were soft with sympathy. "You know I can't do that, Wade."

"My brother tried to kill himself and it was my fault. I wasn't coming around as much anymore, I wasn't paying enough attention. He almost died because of me. I need to talk to him so I know he won't try to do it again. Please."

The officer studied Wade for what felt like an eternity. The longer he looked at Wade's undeniable desperation, the more his eyes softened and his mouth relaxed. He let out a resigned sigh and shook his head as if he couldn't believe what he was about to do. "If I let you see him, you will leave today and you won't come back. You will wait until he's back at Butterfield and you will follow the prison's visiting guidelines from then on. If I see you back here, I will have you escorted out of the building and I will call my supervisor and have Ford moved to a different facility immediately."

"Understood."

"You have five minutes and I'm leaving the door open so I can hear you."

"Of course."

"If anyone finds out about this I will probably get fired."

"I swear I won't say anything. Thank you." Wade gave him a grateful smile.

After another moment of deliberation, the officer stepped aside to let Wade through.

Ford lay in the same hospital bed, but this time there were significantly fewer tubes connecting him to machines. His eyes were closed, but Wade watched with relief as his chest rose and fell steadily without the aid of any machine. He still wore the neck brace, but the red swollen band of skin around his neck, from where his makeshift noose had cut off his air supply, was now a healthier-looking pink. His head was shaved and there was a large laceration filled with black stitches across the side. His skin had enough color now to no longer be mistaken for the pallid skin of a corpse.

As Wade approached the bed, Ford's eyes fluttered open and widened with surprise.

"Wade? How did you get in here?" His voice sounded raspy like his throat was raw. "They said I couldn't have any visitors."

"I guess I've spent so much time here over the past week they agreed to break the rules and let me see you just so they can get rid of me."

"You've been here all week?"

"Of course I've been here. You're my brother and you were hurt."

"But you weren't even allowed to see me."

"That's not the point. You tried to kill yourself and I missed the warning signs. I wasn't around or observant enough or whatever to see it. I wasn't able to stop you. I'm so sorry I let you down."

"I'm not looking for an apology, Wade. Me trying to kill myself had nothing to do with you. I did it because I live in a prison cell and my life sucks in there. You had no effect on my decision, except maybe the fact that if I was gone, I wouldn't keep you from living your own life anymore. Have you seen Ashley or Emmett at all this week?"

"Ashley brought dinner over almost every night."

"Did you eat it with her?"

Wade was silent.

"Yeah, that's what I thought. I get that you worry about me, but you need to stop obsessing. I won't let you put your life on hold for me."

"I'm not doing that."

"Oh really? Before Ashley how many women had you gone out with since I started getting into trouble?"

"There were a few."

"That's being generous. How many of them did you actually care about?"

"What's your point?"

"Ashley is the first woman you've ever loved. I can see the change in you. You're happy with her. She makes you better. You have a chance to have a real family with her and I can see how badly you want that. But for some reason, you wasted an entire week ignoring them and keeping them away so you could sit in some disgusting hospital waiting room feeling guilty about something you had nothing to do with. If you have to find a reason to screw up what's good in your life, that's on you. But, I'm not going to let you use me as the reason."

"I didn't…"

Ford held up his hand with great effort. "Don't even try to deny it. I know that's what happened. If you're going to screw up your relationship with Ashley, do me a favor and leave me out of it."

"Fine. You're right. I did what I always do when I can't deal with something: I shut everyone else out and drowned my sorrows any way I could."

"Wait, you don't mean… you haven't been drinking again have you?" The shoulder shrug and resigned look Wade gave him was all he needed. "What the hell is wrong with you, Wade?" His voice rose. The extra strain must've been too much because Ford went into a fit of coughing. Wade handed him the cup of water on the tray by his bed. Ford drank greedily and cleared his throat before continuing. "Why would you do something so stupid? And, for such a stupid reason, too."

"It wasn't a stupid reason, Ford," Wade snapped. "You tried to kill yourself and I felt like I was to blame. I knew something was wrong last time I saw you, but I let you distract me when I should've been helping you with what you were going through. And then you go and try to hang yourself. You had to know I'd take this on myself. I love you, Ford. I couldn't live with myself if something happened to you."

Silence stretched between them. "That's the first time you've said you loved me."

Wade lifted one shoulder and dropped it. "Yeah, I guess it is. That doesn't mean I haven't always felt it."

"Look, I'm sorry I worried you. But you have to understand it had nothing to do with you. Prison is… hell." He stared at nothing, his eyes revealing only the tip of the misery iceberg lurking beneath the icy surface.

"Tell me what's going on."

Ford sighed. "Okay, I guess I owe you that. But you have to promise me, you'll just be there for me as a brother, okay? Nothing more. My well-being is not your responsibility anymore. Got it?" Wade was silent for a long time but eventually nodded in agreement.

"I need to hear you say it."

"I won't make myself responsible for you. I know you're a grown man. It's just hard for me to let go. I felt like I should've done more for you when we were growing up."

"I know. But, you need to let that go. I don't want you blaming yourself for the choices I make or the things that happen to me. Nothing that happened is your fault, except maybe getting drunk and screwing up your chances with Ashley."

"Are you going to tell me, or not?"

"Do you remember that guy I told you about? The one who tried to intimidate me and take my lunch a while back?"

"The guy who gave you that scar on your neck?"

"He tried to cut my throat, but luckily he missed. Well, it turned out he was pretty pissed that I stood up to him. He, along with his gang, have been giving me some trouble since then. Harassing me, beating me up, among other things."

"What other things?" Wade watched as a tumult of emotions clouded Ford's features: shame, humiliation, anger, suffering. Wade didn't want to believe the truth that was glaring him in the face.

"You flinched when you sat down at the table last time I visited you. How many times did they…"

"Once." Ford clipped. "Once was enough. I'm afraid it'll happen again." His bottom lip trembled. "I was afraid they were lurking around every corner waiting for me. It was hell. Death seemed a welcome alternative."

Wade's throat tightened. "Oh, Ford. Maybe we can…"

He held up his palm. "There is no we on this: there is only me. I will take care of it."

"I need to know you're going to be safe."

"There's no guarantee of that in prison. But I can promise you, I won't try to kill myself again. That sucked, and the recovery when I failed is even worse. You were right before, to push me like you did. From now on, I'm going to do my best to stay out of trouble and do my time so I can get the hell out of there as fast as I can. So, you can stop worrying about me and worry about your own life."

"Ford, I can't."

"Yes, you can. And you will. There's nothing you can do to protect me anyways. This is something I have to deal with on my own. So quit obsessing and go beg Ashley to take your dumbass self back."

"She didn't break up with me."

"But she doesn't sound like the kind of girl who's very keen on marrying a drunk, nor does she deserve that. You are going to marry her, right?"

"I need to get sober first. Now that I know you're alive, that part should be easier. The marrying part, well, that might be a little more difficult. I need to get myself together if I want to stand a chance."

"Tell me your plan."

"For starters, I'm going to call my sponsor and start going to AA meetings as often as I can. Then, I'm going to fight like hell to stay sober. I don't want to think about where I'd be if I lost Ashley to a bottle of whiskey."

"So go. Sober up, work your program, and stay sober. Go make it up to your woman and to Emmett because I can guess you've probably been blowing him off too. I don't want to see you screw this up and end up like Dad."

"Believe me, that is the last thing I want."

"Good, so go and don't come back here. I'll be fine. Remember our deal."

"I promise I won't come back here as long as you promise to take care of yourself."

"I already told you I would. Now go fix yourself up and get yourself a wife you deserve."

Just thinking about the prospect of having Ashley as his wife flooded Wade with a joy that warmed him from the inside out. He could hardly wait to have her in his arms tonight, to hear her musical laugh, to see her smile. One week had been too long without her. He never wanted to go that long again. Now that the veil of pain and suffering had lifted somewhat, he felt a surge of longing for her. He didn't think he could wait until tonight to see her. Maybe he'd surprise her at work. He'd send Maggie a text and see if he could steal Ashley away for the rest of the afternoon. Before plans for the day—some of them inappropriate for children—began consuming his brain, he turned his attention to his brother once more. "I'm glad you didn't die. If you ever try something like that again, I'll kill you myself."

Ford snorted. "You could try."

"Bye, Ford. I love you."

"Don't get sappy on me, man. Now get out of here!"

Wade rested his hand on Ford's arm and gave him one last longing look before walking out of the room.

CHAPTER
THIRTY - EIGHT

ASHLEY AND WADE lay tangled in the sheets of her bed. Her head rested on his chest, his arms wrapped securely around her, holding her close. A week apart had been too long for both of them and they were trying to make up for it. With Maggie's support, Wade had stolen her away from work yesterday with the intention of taking her anywhere she wanted to go. Since then, they'd been inseparable, neither one wanting to let the other go. A secluded picnic at their spot by the river, helping Emmett practice for his race tomorrow, a family dinner, and stolen moments together after dark had left Ashley feeling whole again.

She was happy to see that Wade was his old self again. Whatever plagued him when his brother was ill seemed to be gone. Once she saw him with his crooked smile at the clinic yesterday, all her stress from the previous week left her. She shivered as she thought about how he'd relieved any lingering stress with his expert touch since then.

It seemed silly now to have thought that he'd hid something from her. He'd just been ridden with grief, and being alone was how he dealt with it. Learning that your brother tried to commit suicide was a lot for anyone to take on, especially if you felt responsible for it. She was glad she gave him the space he desired, but now that Ford was better, she was going to make up for lost time.

Wade softly trailed his fingers up and down her back, leaving tingles in their wake. "I've missed you," he said.

Ashley giggled. "We've been together for the past sixteen hours."

"We were asleep for part of that."

"Barely."

Wade gave her his crooked smile and the look that made her belly do a flip. "How can a man possibly sleep when there's a beautiful woman in bed beside him? But, I was talking about how before yesterday I missed you for a whole week. I know I said I needed space, and I did, but it made me miss you too much. I don't want to be without you like that again."

"Me either."

"You know, we'd never have to be apart if we moved in together. I could fall asleep with you every night and wake up to you every morning. I could be here for Emmett more."

"I also wouldn't get any sleep if we lived together," Ashley joked.

"Is that such a bad thing?" Wade rolled on top of her and kissed her neck the way that made shivers dance down her spine and her belly quiver.

"Yes."

"Yes, that's a bad thing?"

"Yes, let's move in together."

A broad grin broke out over his face and he gave her an enthusiastic kiss on the lips. "You just made me the happiest man in this room."

"I bet I can make you happier," she said as she pulled his lips to hers.

***

When they finally pulled away—breathless and spent—gone was the early dawn light, the bright warm rays of the summer sun in its place.

"Are you sure you can't skip work today? I know your boss. I'm sure I could have a word with her," Wade said.

"She was kind enough to let me take a half day yesterday, I couldn't ask her for today too as much as I'd like to."

"Can I spend the day with Emmett then? He wanted me to help him make some last-minute adjustments on his bike for his first race tomorrow. I was thinking we could also go riding and then work on that bathroom remodel project. I'm pretty behind on work. I could use the help of my assistant."

"And, I'm sure he'd say he could use the money. I think he'd like that." She looked at the clock and groaned when she saw what time it was. "I need to get ready for work." She moved to get out of bed, but Wade pulled her back in for one more kiss that left her panting. "You're not making this easy. I really need to go or I'm going to be late."

"Okay, roomie. I'll go see if I can scrape together some breakfast for the three of us. Unless, you want some company in the shower?" He pumped his eyebrows twice and gave her a seductive wink.

She bit her full pink lips and fluttered her long eyelashes before shaking her head in refusal. On her way to the bathroom she tossed her thick golden hair over her shoulder and swayed her hips provocatively.

"Don't tempt me, woman."

She sent him a smug look and closed the bathroom door behind her. In the next moment, the sound of the shower running filled the bedroom. *I'm going to marry that woman*, he thought.

***

"You look tired and ridiculously happy. You were up all night having sex, weren't you?" Maggie asked as Ashley walked through the door to the veterinary clinic. Ashley's embarrassed smile was all the confirmation Maggie needed. "Well, I'm glad to see that things are good between you two again."

"More than good. This morning Wade asked if Emmett and I would move in with him. I wasn't sure if I was ready for something like that until he asked me, but then I just knew. We love each other and he loves my son. When Jeff died I never thought I would find that again. Sometimes I still worry that it's too good to be true."

"It's not. You deserve to be happy. How does Emmett feel about everything?"

"He's actually fine with it. I braced myself for the worst because of how he reacted when he found out we were first dating, but it didn't seem to catch him off guard. I think he actually might be looking forward to having another guy in the house."

"I bet that's a relief for you. It sounds like Emmett has come a long way."

"He has. He's really grown up since we've been here. I almost don't recognize him. That is until I ask him to clean his room or something. But, I can handle the griping and complaining any day. I'm just so grateful for the progress he's made. A lot of that has to do with Wade. He's been such a positive influence in his life and in mine." She thought about how she was no longer plagued by nightmares or depressing memories of the past and how he made her feel: truly beautiful, desired, cherished, loved, all feelings she never thought she would get to experience again.

"Do you still think Wade was hiding something from you last week?"

"No, I think I was just being overly dramatic. We talked about everything last night and I get why he reacted the way he did. Wade was practically Ford's father."

"I'm just glad that Ford is okay and everything is back to normal."

"Me too."

"But I'm not going to lie. I kind of hate you right now. You're way too happy and perky. I need to get myself another cup of coffee and then I'm going to try to forget that you were up all night having sex while I lay awake listening to my husband snore like a congested elephant seal."

"I guess I won't tell you about this morning then…" Ashley said, before holding up two fingers.

"And now I think I'm going to have to have a doughnut too."

***

Wade's good mood stayed with him all day. Not only did Ashley agree to move in with him, but Emmett was on board with it, too. When they told him the news this morning over breakfast, he barely looked up from his bowl of cereal to say, "Okay" between bites. Then he continued to ask Wade about their plans for the day, like the news was as mundane as hearing it was going to be another hot summer day. It felt good to be accepted into Emmett's life so easily and to know that he must've at least been doing something right with him.

After spending all day with Emmett doing all of the things he hoped to accomplish today, Wade sat at Ashley's dinner table with his soon-to-be-roommates, practically licking his plate clean.

"Your cooking was excellent as always, Ashley. Once we move in together, I may have to start exercising more."

"Why, so you can eat more?"

"You see right through me. So Emmett, how do you feel about your first race tomorrow?"

"I'm a little nervous. What if I screw up or crash or something? A lot of people are going to be watching."

"You won't. You've been practicing plenty. And if you do, just keep your helmet on so no one can see who you are."

Emmett snorted his amusement. "Helpful advice as usual, Wade."

"I try."

"You're going to be there, tomorrow, right?"

"I wouldn't miss it. I'll be the one holding the giant *Go Emmett!* posters and passing out T-shirts with your face on it."

"You're not serious."

"Why do you think I have to leave soon to meet Reid? He's coming over to help me make them."

"Yeah, right."

"I guess you'll just have to wait until tomorrow to find out," he said, leaning back in his chair. "Well, I better get going. Reid is probably going to need help unloading the boxes of poster paint and T-shirts from his car." He pushed his chair away from the stable and stood.

Emmett rolled his eyes. "You're not fooling me, so just give it up already."

"I'm glad you don't believe me. That means you'll be surprised tomorrow. I'm going to kiss your mom good-bye. You may want to avert your eyes."

Emmett rolled his eyes again and took his empty plate to the kitchen.

"You got the classic Emmett eye roll twice in thirty seconds." Ashley grinned. "Congratulations, you are officially family now."

"I'll take every eye roll and snort of derision for the compliments they are."

"I wish you were staying tonight," she said as she walked him to the door.

"Me too. But, I've ignored Reid for over a week now and I owe him. I'll see you tomorrow?" Ashley placed her hand on his chest and looked up at him, her ocean blues sparkling with desire. "You know, I could always blow him off. You're much prettier than he is."

With a throaty chuckle, she leaned in to give him a soft kiss. "Go be with your friend. I'll see you tomorrow."

He closed his eyes at her touch. "I might not be able to wait until tomorrow."

"Well, I'll be here all night. You know where the key is." Her warm breath caressed his ear as she whispered the words. He had to fight the urge to back her against the front door.

"You're a temptress, you know that? I better go while I still have the strength."

"It's kind of a warm night tonight. I might not wear anything to bed."

Wade let out a groan. "You're killing me. You're doing this on purpose, aren't you? Just because you can, it doesn't mean you should," he said playfully.

"But, it's so fun," she whispered as her lips lightly brushed his ear.

"I'm going to get you back for this. Good night, Ashley," he said as he forced himself to pull away and walk home. He hoped Reid realized what he was giving up for him tonight.

He thought of Reid having had and lost a love like this with Caroline and his irritation evaporated. He didn't know how Reid got out of bed in the morning. Ford was right, if he lost Ashley and Emmett now, there was a good chance he wouldn't recover. He thought of his dad drinking himself into a stupor every day to try to forget the woman he lost. He recoiled at the thought. He never wanted to end up like that.

He hadn't had any unbearable urges to drink since he left the hospital yesterday, but that didn't mean he wouldn't have them again. He needed to find a meeting and get to work on his 12-step program. He didn't want to risk relapsing again when Ashley and Emmett were living with him.

Reid would be on his way soon, but he had enough time to check on Ford. He hadn't talked to him since yesterday morning and he wanted to make sure things were still going well. He knew he'd promised not to go to the hospital again, but that didn't mean he couldn't still call to check on him. Ford would be none the wiser, and Wade would feel better knowing everything was still okay. He punched in the number and waited.

"Clarke County Hospital, how can I help you?"

"Hi, I'm calling for an update on a patient."

"What's the patient's name?"

"Ford Hudson."

"Just a moment please." The line went silent except for the faint sound of fingers tapping on a keyboard. "What's your name, sir?"

"Wade Hudson."

"I'm sorry, Mr. Hudson, but your brother has signed a privacy statement so I am not authorized to share with you any information about him."

"That's impossible. I just went to see him yesterday. I'm his next of kin."

"I'm sorry sir, but that's not what his file indicates. He must have signed the paperwork since you saw him last. There's a note here indicating the paperwork was filed at ten-thirty yesterday morning."

Wade was momentarily speechless. That was right after Wade had left the hospital yesterday, right after Ford assured him he'd be fine despite the horrors he was facing.

"Is there anything else I can help you with, sir?"

He cleared his throat. "Not unless you can tell me anything about Ford or let me talk to him."

"I'm not authorized to do either of those things, sir. The patient has stated his wishes outright. He doesn't want any contact with family members at this time."

"Then no, there's nothing else you can help me with."

"Have a good day, sir."

Ford had cut him off. Wade couldn't believe he would do something like that, especially at a time like this. Ford needed to have family around now more than ever. How could Ford face this alone? He convinced himself all wasn't lost. He would just talk some sense into him the next time he visited and Ford would realize he needed his support.

Wade's body realized the truth before his brain did. His belly bottomed out and his chest grew heavy as dread spread through him until he felt like he could barely stand. What if he couldn't talk to Ford?

His hands shook as he pulled out his phone and dialed. A short phone call to corrections confirmed his worst fears. Ford had truly cut him out of his life. He took him off the visitors' list, the call list, everything. There was no way for Wade to reach him now. He could try to send him a letter, but he doubted that would go through either. Ford had cut all ties and there was nothing Wade could do about it.

The realization pressed on his chest like a ton weight. He couldn't breathe. He was helpless and the feeling drowned him. Was Ford going to try to kill himself again? Is that why he shut Wade out? If he did, there would be nothing Wade could do to stop him. Dread crept down his spine and spread to every part of him.

His legs gave out and he found himself falling to the couch, the sound of the dial tone drowned out by his own pulse.

An overwhelming urge to drink came over him. He did a mental scan of his house, his trash, his truck, trying to figure out if he had any booze left.

Wade was still holding the phone up to his ear, listening to the dead line when Reid waltzed into his living room. "Man, I know you were grieving last week and busy making up with Ashley since then, but, damn, you could've cleaned up a little." Reid's lip curled in disgust as he kicked a pile of dirty clothes out of his way. "Man, you're really a slob when you're depressed. I think you're worse than me. Ashley is in for a real surprise if you ever get down in the dumps once you're living together." He caught a glimpse of Wade slumped on the couch and cursed. "What happened?"

"Ford cut me off." His voice sounded detached from his body.

"What are you talking about?"

"I mean he cut me off. Took me off the visitors' list, the call list. He signed some kind of privacy statement at the hospital to keep me in the dark about his medical condition. I'm not his next of kin anymore. He shut me out. I can't contact him. I won't get to talk to him again for years, or worse." Wade ran his hands through his hair as he clenched his teeth to maintain his composure. When he looked at Reid, he looked as worried as Wade felt. "What if he did this so he could try to kill himself again without me trying to stop him?"

"You don't know that. Maybe he just needed some space for a while. You said he seemed like he regretted what he did, that he wouldn't go there again."

"What if he lied? He also said he was going to start following the rules so he could do his time and get out, but he probably only said all that to make me feel better so I'd agree to back off. And now there's no way for me to find out what's going on with him or even if he's okay. What if I lose him?" Wade rested his head in his hands. "Damn, I want a drink so badly right now."

"Wade, take a second, okay? You don't know Ford is going to do anything and even if he does, it won't be on you. Maybe he just needs some distance from you for a while, a chance to not have to report to you. I know you mean well, but you can come on a little strong sometimes."

He shot Reid a dirty look. "You're not helping."

"He's probably fine. He's under constant watch at the hospital and he'll continue to be once he is back at the prison."

"It happened before, it could happen again," Wade said, as he stood and moved to the door.

"Where are you going?"

"To get a drink."

"The hell you are!" Reid said, moving to block Wade's path. "You're not thinking clearly. Just take a breath."

"Breathing is not going to help me. Only some whiskey can do that."

"Having a drink will only make things worse, you know that. I'm not going to let you do that to yourself." Reid braced his hand on Wade's chest, trying to hold him off.

"Oh, yeah? How are you going to stop me?" Wade's jaw was flexed, his shoulders square, and his chest puffed out like he was ready for a fight.

"What's going on with you? This isn't like you." Wade continued to stare at Reid, his chest heaving in and out until his shoulders suddenly deflated and he dropped back onto the couch. "Just tell me what's going on so I won't have to kick your ass." Usually a poke like that would elicit at least an *"I'd like to see you try,"* but Wade merely avoided his gaze and jiggled his knees in agitation. "Tell me," Reid urged.

Wade scrubbed a hand down his face as his knee continued its nervous rhythm. "I've been drinking."

"For how long?"

"Since that night we all went to the hospital."

"How bad is it?"

"On Wednesday I nearly polished off a half-pint of whiskey and a few beers, plus whatever drinks I had at the bar across the street from the hospital."

Reid cursed under his breath. "What about when you were with Ashley?"

"I didn't have anything. I had a few urges here and there, but nothing I couldn't handle. Nothing like how I feel right now." Wade's urge to muscle past Reid and drive to the nearest liquor store was so overwhelming that he had to clench his fists to try to remain on the couch.

"Does Ashley know?"

Wade shook his head. "I couldn't tell her. I thought if I could get it under control, then she wouldn't have to find out."

"Here's what we're going to do. You're going to call your sponsor and tell him what's been going on with you. Then you're going to find out when and where the next AA meeting is and get your ass there. I'm going to stay with you until you no longer feel like you need a drink. Got it?"

Or we can find out if you can stop me before I reach the door. Surprised by his own thoughts and not wanting to risk starting a fight, Wade decided it was best to stay seated. "I really hate you right now."

"You can hate me as long as you stay sober."

CHAPTER
THIRTY - NINE

IT WAS BARELY eleven, but the day was already stifling. The air was thick and wet with humidity, making the morning feel even hotter. The warm moisture clung to Ashley's skin in places she didn't want to think about. The air she breathed felt heavy and strange in her lungs like she was trying to breathe through a damp washcloth. Her hair—which she'd failed to tame with a tight braid—was a frizzy mess. Tiny hairs stood in all directions, looking like it had when she was a child, rubbing balloons on her head to see the effects of the static. Even in the shade, she was hot, sticky, and uncomfortable and she wasn't sure if the moisture that dampened her clothes was from the humidity or her own sweat.

Before her was a dirt track with small swells, sharp turns, and a few larger crests. The track was lined with ridges and bright orange cones to help the riders stay on the road. Silver metal stands, six rows high, surrounded it where spectators with sunglasses, hats, and battery-powered handheld fans watched the action. The high-pitched wail of dirt bike engines and the whistles and cheers of spectators filled the air.

Ashley sat in the stands with Maggie, Robbie, and Reid, watching riders zip through the course on their bikes. Her eyes were on the track but her mind was elsewhere, sorting through all manner of unfavorable possibilities of why Wade wasn't there with them. The tension from her unwelcome thoughts grew inside her until she heard the words spilling out of her mouth once again. "Has anyone been able to get a hold of Wade yet?"

She was met with the chorus of "nos" she expected. Emmett's race was about to start and no one knew where Wade was. He hadn't answered his door this morning and every time she called him it went straight to voicemail. She was getting seriously worried about him. He wouldn't have missed Emmett's first race for no good reason, which meant something wasn't right. She turned to look at Reid sitting beside her.

With each passing hour, Reid had become quieter and less relaxed. Presently, his knee was jiggling against hers something fierce and he was incessantly checking his phone. He looked over his shoulder again to scan the parking lot for Wade's truck for what seemed like the tenth time that minute. As he turned back, he caught Ashley studying him and gave her a forced smile before returning his attention to the race in front of him. He knew something, that much was clear, but why was he keeping the information to himself?

"Where's Wade?" Ashley asked him.

"Your guess is as good as mine."

"I would say your guess wouldn't be much of a guess at all."

"I don't know what would make you say that."

"You're a rotten liar. You were the last person who saw Wade last night, and you're sitting here like a toddler who had two cups of coffee. You know something and I want to know what it is."

"I don't know anything."

She was getting angry now. "You can see how worried I am about him. I've been calling him every few minutes and asking if anyone has heard from him more often than that. I have a bad feeling that something is wrong. I'm about to go over to his place myself and do whatever I need to do to get inside. I'm not above breaking a window."

"Don't do that. I'm sure he's fine. He probably just overslept. I heard he didn't sleep much the night before." Reid gave her a wink. The look she gave him had him holding up his palms as if she were an angry mare rearing to kick. "If it makes you feel better, I'll go over there to check on him."

"I'm coming with you."

"You wouldn't want to miss Emmett's first race."

Ashley still suspected he was hiding something, but the manipulation worked. She didn't want to miss Emmett's race. "Fine, but you better tell me if you find out something."

"I will. You sit tight and try not to worry, okay?"

If the way Reid was acting was any indication, she should definitely worry.

CHAPTER
FORTY

WADE LAY SPRAWLED on his bed, his head throbbing painfully. His mouth felt as dry as a hobo's elbow and tasted like bile and stale malt. There was a sour smell wafting from where he lay on the sheets and he hoped it wasn't coming from him. When he lifted his head to investigate, daggers stabbed his temples and he quickly flopped back down with a groan. His head was killing him, he felt foggy, and he thought he might throw up. The thunderous pounding on the front door wasn't helping, and the throbbing in his head quickly matched its relentless rhythm.

Wade groaned as he dragged himself off the bed and tried to stand. The room spun wildly and he lost his balance, his stomach roiling as he fell back down to the mattress. He blew out a few breaths, urging his stomach to settle before slowly trying to stand again. He wavered but remained standing this time and carefully made his way toward the front door, holding on to anything he could to maintain his balance. When he reached the front of the house, the pounding was so unbearably loud he feared his head would explode. Desperate to cease the punishing cadence, he threw open the door as fast as his unsteady body would allow.

The sunlight was excruciating. It pierced Wade's eyes and went straight to his head, intensifying his headache so much that he teetered on his feet. He threw his hands up to shield himself, but it did little to ease the destructive effect of the powerful rays. His nausea skyrocketed and he had to fight the urge to throw up all over his visitor's shoes.

"You've been drinking." Reid's voice cut through the ringing in his ears.

Wade started to close the door, but Reid put his hand out to stop him and pushed his way inside. "You look like shit, Wade."

"Makes sense I would look how I feel."

"I thought you were good last night. Didn't you call your sponsor? You told me he was on his way to pick you up and take you to a meeting. I would never have left if I knew that wasn't the case."

"Then it was a good thing I lied, or it seemed like a good thing until I woke up wishing I were dead," he said, gripping his roiling stomach.

"Good. I hope you remember this feeling so you won't do something so stupid again. How much did you have to drink last night?"

Wade huffed out a breath. "See for yourself."

Reid followed Wade's lumbering gait deeper into the house. There were half a dozen empty beer cans strewn across the floor and a small bottle of whiskey that was one-third of the way empty. "You had all of this after I left at midnight last night?"

"It appears so."

"You need help."

Wade sighed. "I know. At least last night's binge drinking kicked me on my way to recovery. I have no desire to feel this bad again anytime soon. Though, I'd kill for a drink or two just to ease this headache," he said as he slumped ungracefully onto the couch.

"Don't even think about it! You deserve every bit of your pain today."

Wade groaned and put his throbbing head in his hands. "If you don't stop yelling, my head is going to explode."

"You don't even realize what today is, do you?"

"Five minutes ago, I didn't even know where I was, so what do you think?"

"Today was Emmett's first race."

Wade cursed and tried to stand, but his dizziness overcame him and forced him to sit back down. "What are you waiting for? Go get me some water and some aspirin so we can get going."

"Do you really want Ashley or Emmett to see you like this? Besides, you're too late."

"Then why did you come here?" Wade growled.

"Everyone is really worried about you, Ashley especially, so I told her I'd come check on you, make sure you were okay. But I can clearly see you're not. Why are you doing this, Wade?"

"I had a moment of weakness and I gave in. You should know the feeling well. You do it often enough with all the meaningless sex you've been having," Wade snipped.

Reid took a breath and closed his eyes as if praying for patience. "Because I'm a good friend and you're having a hard time I'm going to pretend you didn't say that. This isn't about me. This is about you."

"I screwed up, okay? I know I did. But I'm done with that. I missed something really important today because I was too hungover from last night, and I won't let that happen again. I don't want to be that guy. I won't be that guy."

"I believe that's what you want, but your addiction might turn you into him whether you like it or not. Unless you get help."

Wade's shoulders sagged in defeat. "You're right. The drinking is way out of hand and it stops now. I'm going to call my sponsor today and go to a meeting. For real this time. No more lying. I'm ready to work to get past this once and for all."

Reid patted Wade on the shoulder. "I'm glad to hear it. Don't hesitate to ask for help, all right? I'm here for you." Reid's phone buzzed in his pocket and he pulled it out to read the text. "Ashley's on her way over here to check on you. You might want to get yourself cleaned up before she gets here."

Wade sat quietly, his head throbbing painfully with every beat of his heart as he thought about Reid's suggestion. His head hurt so badly he could barely open his eyes and he still felt like he was going to be sick. He couldn't remember a time when he'd felt this terrible. He caught a whiff of that sour smell again and realized it was coming from him. He was an utter disaster, an embarrassment. But, he had to do the right thing. "No. Let her see me as the mess I am. She deserves to know the truth."

"Wade, don't be rash. You're going to get past this. Seeing you like this could only hurt your relationship."

"Maybe, but she deserves to know. I love her too much to hide this from her."

A crisp knock at the door broke the silence.

"Do you want me to stay for moral support?" Reid asked.

"No, I can do this on my own."

"Okay, I'll let her in and wait outside."

***

The grim look on Reid's face as he opened Wade's front door to greet her caused Ashley to wring her hands with worry. Whatever had happened to Wade was worse than she thought. She felt her panic rising as her imagination took her to dark places. She couldn't handle losing him too. When she tried to speak, her voice was absent and she cleared her throat to force it back. Her fear must have been obvious because Reid placed his hand on her shoulder and smiled his reassurance.

"Wade is going to be fine, okay? He'd like to see you. Just please, keep an open mind. For both of your sakes."

Reid's words confused her, but she didn't have time to unravel them. She had to see Wade. She moved through the entryway, her footsteps lightly tapping on the hardwood floor until she stopped dead in her tracks.

Wade sat slumped on the couch, looking like someone else. His eyes were bloodshot and watery and blanketed by dark swollen circles. He wore nothing but boxer shorts and a white T-shirt that had a sour-smelling yellow stain across the front. His recently flat belly was swollen and protruded slightly under his T-shirt. He looked terrible and smelled even worse. At the sight of him, she rushed to his side.

"Wade, you don't look good. Are you sick?" she asked.

"You could say that."

"What can I do for you? How can I help?"

"Nothing, I'm okay."

"You don't look okay."

"I promise, I am. You don't need to worry."

Her concern narrowed into anger. "Then please tell me why you didn't answer your phone. I've been calling you for hours. I was so worried about you."

"Is that why you sicced Reid on me?" Wade said with a smirk.

She wasn't in the mood. She crossed her arms and frowned at him. "You're lucky Reid offered to come instead of me. I planned to break your window if you didn't answer the door."

"You sure do have a thing for windows, don't you?"

"This isn't funny, Wade! You missed Emmett's first race. You promised him you'd be there, signs, T-shirts, and everything."

He hung his head. "I know. I feel terrible. I really wanted to be there."

"Why weren't you then?"

He opened his mouth and closed it, floundering for what to say. "Ashley, there's something I didn't tell you last week, something I left out." He blew out a breath and rubbed his palms against his bare thighs. "Last week when Ford was in the hospital, I didn't keep everyone away just because I was upset. I also did it because I was drinking again."

"Why didn't you tell me?"

"I wanted to, but I was afraid of what you'd think of me. I thought if I could get a handle on it myself then I wouldn't have to risk telling you and having you look at me the way you are now."

He had kept something huge from her because of his pride. Wade's admission reminded her of a darker time in her life, a time when her own husband hurt her because he neglected his illness, a time when he chose to kill himself rather than seek help. The similarity chilled her bones.

"We were planning on moving in together and you didn't think this was something you should have told me?"

"I know I shouldn't have kept this from you and I regret it. But I'm telling you now."

"Were you drinking when you were with me the past couple of days?"

"No, I swear. I don't feel like I need to when I'm with you."

"So what, when you're not with me, you're just going to be off somewhere getting drunk?" She could feel her defenses rising.

"No. No more drinking. I'm done."

"You're done. Just like that?" she asked skeptically. She thought of Reid's unease at the races today and a troubling thought came to her mind. "Did Reid take you out drinking last night?"

"No, he wouldn't do that. I did this all on my own. Please, just listen. Last night before Reid came over, I called the hospital to check on my brother." He told her about what Ford had done and his fears about Ford's intentions. "Reid tried to stop me. He stayed

310

with me and insisted I call my sponsor and find a meeting. He was a good friend." Wade hung his head in shame. "I lied to him so he'd leave and I could be free to drink in peace."

She thought of Jeff, lying to her to try to cover up the symptoms of his illness, trying to keep it a secret, and a chill of dread trickled down her spine. "Why?"

"I didn't want him to stop me. I'm an alcoholic, Ashley. I always will be. The urge to drink is always there at the back of my mind, but sometimes when things get really tough, it becomes much harder to ignore. I tried to resist, I always do, but this time it was too much for me to handle. I should have called my sponsor or gone to a meeting, but I didn't. I wanted to drown in my own self-pity so I gave in. I regretted it instantly, but by then it had already been done."

"I made a really bad choice and I'm ashamed of it. It made me feel weak, a loser, like someone who wasn't worthy of you. That's why I didn't tell you before. I thought if I could overcome this on my own then maybe I could be worthy of you again, but it only turned me into a bigger fool."

"I want to move forward with you and that requires honesty"— he lowered his gaze to his hands—"even if it means you no longer want me." He paused for a moment, taking a breath as if to steady himself. When he looked at her, his gaze was pleading. "There will always be times when the urge to drink will threaten to overcome me, but I swear I'll never keep it a secret from you again. And I promise to get help, to do whatever it takes to stay sober."

Ashley didn't know what to say. He told her before he'd had a drinking problem in the past, but she never truly understood what that entailed. What if he couldn't stop drinking or what if he stopped now only to start again when things got hard? What if he became abusive or neglectful? She loved him, she knew without a doubt that she did, but could she deal with something like this?

What about Emmett? They'd been through hell with Jeff and she wouldn't put either of them through something like that again.

As if reading her thoughts, he continued. "I'll understand if you have your doubts about us or even if you don't want to be with me anymore. I know I'm asking a lot of you to accept this part of me. When Reid told me you were coming by, I could've showered, changed my clothes, played it off like I wasn't feeling well and forgot to turn on my phone, but I didn't. I probably could've even gotten sober on my own without you ever finding out, but I didn't do that either. Though a little late, I told you the truth because I love you. It was a risk I needed to take. You deserved to know and I deserved to know whether you would accept me for who I am, flaws and all."

Wade was silent then, giving her time to process everything. The minutes ticked by, the tension in the room growing with every passing second of silence. She hadn't looked at him since he last spoke. Wade's brow creased with worry and he shifted uncomfortably in his seat. "You've been quiet for a long time. Will you please say something?" he pleaded.

She looked at the man in front of her. He appeared a broken man—disheveled, ill, pathetic—but underneath all of that, he was full of determination. He'd put himself out there—raw, exposed, without a veil—and made himself utterly vulnerable for her. It was far more than Jeff ever did for her, but was it enough?

"Where will you go from here?" she asked.

"I plan to fight like hell to never drink again. Today I'll call my sponsor and tell him what a pathetic drunk I've been and we'll work out a plan to get my sobriety back. I'll go to AA meetings every day until I'm positive I won't fall back into my old habits, and then I'll keep going to them long after, because that's what I should've done all along. Above all else, I promise to be completely honest about my addiction from here on out: to you, to myself, and to those around me. I can't guarantee I'll succeed in staying sober, but I promise I will never stop trying. I'll do whatever it takes to make you feel safe in this relationship. I'll go to rehab if that's what you want."

"Do you think that will help?"

"I didn't need it before, but if it makes you feel better, then I will. What do you want?"

She was silent for a long while, processing his words. She loved Wade, but the truth of it was, she was scared. Sometimes love just wasn't enough. "I don't know. This is all just so much. I need some time to think things over. I'm sorry." She slid off the couch and hurried out the door without risking him a glance. If she'd seen the pain she knew had taken over his features, she wasn't sure if she would've had the strength to keep going. But she had to figure this out. She owed it herself and to Emmett to find out what was best for them.

***

Wade sat frozen on the couch. He knew he'd taken a risk, but at least now he knew how she felt about him. Maybe she just needed time to think like she said and everything would be okay in the end. Even though his heart said otherwise, his brain insisted this was a good possibility. He couldn't entertain any other scenario right now, not if he wanted to get sober.

He picked up his phone to call his sponsor. After making plans to meet him at an AA meeting in an hour, he rose to stand and trudged to the kitchen, the ache in his chest blocking out the pain from his hangover. He picked up the glass bottle of whiskey sitting on the counter, feeling the cool glass against his hand.

"Are you planning on drinking that?" Reid asked as he leaned against the kitchen entrance.

"No." Wade tipped the bottle and poured the contents down the drain.

Reid exhaled his relief. "So, how did it go with Ashley?"

Wade told him about their conversation.

"That's rough, buddy, but she'll come around. She needs some time to process everything and you need to prove to her you're serious about getting sober."

Wade nodded. "I know. I'm going to a meeting with my sponsor in an hour." He threw the empty whiskey bottle in the trash with an audible clink. With any luck, it would be his last. "I know I need to give her space, but I also need to apologize to Emmett for missing his race today. How can I do that when she doesn't want to see me?" He curled his hands into fists on the counter and rested his aching forehead against them "This is so screwed up. I need to talk to him, I need to fix this with both of them."

"You'll get your chance. I have a feeling they're not going anywhere. After you go to your meeting today, I think there's someone you should go see, someone who would gladly accept your leftover stash of beer."

Wade shook his head. "It's almost an hour's drive out of town. I don't know if my stomach can take it. I've had some close calls this morning."

"You'll be fine after you eat some breakfast. A shower might help too. I know I'm nauseated just breathing in your stink."

"Reid, it's just too much to deal with today, especially considering how much I hate myself right now."

"I think that's exactly why you should go. Stop making excuses and go clean yourself up because, damn." Reid pinched his nose in disgust.

Wade's shoulders sagged in defeat. He hated when Reid was right.

CHAPTER
FORTY - ONE

THE TIRES OF Wade's truck crunched on gravel as he drove through the Sunny Acres Trailer Park. Despite what its name implied, nothing about the park was cheerful. An oversized gravel lot surrounded by a chain-link fence was pretty much the extent of it. The only wildlife here were the determined weeds that sprouted from the dirt beneath the gravel and the aggressive hornets that hung around in search of food and unfortunate places to build their nests. Train tracks lay just beyond the perimeter, allowing the residents of Sunny Acres to be graced with the train's blaring horn and the screeching clickety-clack of wheels on rails as it made its twice-daily passes.

As Wade drove through the lot, he watched the trailers crawl by. Most of them were in halfway decent shape, but some—like the one he was heading toward—looked barely habitable. The trailer park was quiet for a Saturday. Most of the residents were probably either at the beach or the lake, trying to get any relief they could from the sultry summer heat. Only the biggest homebodies had stuck around today, and as he drove by, Wade saw the few sitting beneath their makeshift shade canopies outside their trailers, drinking booze to pass the time or feed their habits.

He parked his truck in front of a particularly decrepit one-man trailer but left the engine running to enjoy his final few moments of cool air. He didn't want to be here today—being here always took a lot out of him and he didn't have much left to give right now. He was exhausted and still felt like crap. The aspirin and the gallon of water he drank didn't completely cure his hangover, and he still felt queasy and a bit dizzy. Worse than that was the ache in his chest and the constant churning of worried thoughts. He didn't know where things stood between Ashley and him. She'd walked away, saying she needed time to think, which was never a good thing. He had a nagging feeling he was going to lose her. Maybe he already had.

He contemplated turning the car around and saving this visit for another day. Coming here would be easier if he was stronger and didn't feel like he might throw up on his dashboard. He yearned for a cool, comfortable place to take a nap or an ice cold beer or two to ease his troubles. *Don't go there.* That, right there was why he was here despite his ailments, to remind himself of why he'd quit drinking in the first place.

Though he would rather be anywhere else, Wade turned off the engine and stepped out of his truck. Hot air consumed him, momentarily knocking the air from his lungs. It was so sweltering outside, he could already feel himself getting dehydrated and weaker with every breath. He opened the door to the back seat of his truck and pulled out two paper bags filled with groceries. His arms full and already sweating, he walked the final few steps to the decaying trailer in front of him.

Though it had been more than adequate when he purchased it fourteen years ago, it was now a sorry sight, to say the least. The paint, once a sunny yellow, was now faded and peeling, revealing rust underneath. A number of dents littered the filthy side panels, which Wade could only assume were inflicted during a drunken rage. The screens on the windows were ripped and filthy and the windows themselves were so dirty you could barely see through them. At first Wade had kept up with the trailer's maintenance as best he could, but before long it's occupant no longer allowed it. Wade had tried to fight him on it, to make the repairs anyways, but soon he learned it was better to leave it alone. As long as the old trailer was still weatherproof and standing flat, Wade knew it was better to just accept the dweller's wishes.

Wade approached and studied the man slouching in the green-and-white-checkered lawn chair out front. He wore what was supposedly a white tank top that was now yellow with sweat stains and spilled beer. His cotton shorts were so filthy Wade wasn't even sure what color they were supposed to be. In his hand was a half-empty bottle of cheap bourbon that Wade guessed had just been opened this morning.

His thin limbs and sunken cheeks made his soft, round belly appear even more prominent as it hung below his dirty shirt. His once light brown hair was now almost entirely grey and the skin on his face appeared sallow and loose. Dark puffy circles lay under dull brown eyes that watched Wade with a glazed look. Cans of beer filled the trash bin outside and spilled over the top, leaving a pile on the ground and a trail leading to where the man sat.

He took a swig of his bourbon and gestured to the bags in Wade's arms. "I hope there's beer in there. I'm all out."

"Hello to you too, Dad. What happened here? It looks like your trash can barfed out a tailgate party."

"Did you bring beer or not?"

"Relax, the beer's in my truck. This is food. You remember food? You need to eat it to live."

"You always were a smartass."

"At least I'm a smartass who comes over to take care of your drunk ass once a week. By the look of this trash pile, I might need to start coming more often. Try not to get too drunk while I put this stuff away."

"It's too late for that," Roy said as he lifted his bourbon in a salute.

Wade climbed the two rickety steps into the old trailer and pulled open the door. He barely got inside before he heard the crunch of beer cans under his boots. Empty beer cans and empty glass bottles of liquor littered the floor of the small trailer and most of the available counter space. Empty food packages and takeout containers were strewn across almost every available surface, including the small couch that served as his dad's bed. The roll of giant black trash bags and the bottle of bleach he brought with him would be put to good use as usual.

As he put the groceries away, he took shallow breaths through his mouth and tried not to gag from the putrid smells of fermenting liquor and rotting food that filled the small space. When he was done, he studied his surroundings and noticed there was only one uncluttered surface in the entire trailer.

The small shelf by the makeshift bed held framed pictures of Wade's mother and some of her precious belongings. He waded through the clutter and picked up his favorite picture of her. Her dark hair framed her porcelain face and curled slightly at her shoulders. Her cheeks were a beautiful rosy pink, her naturally pink lips parted in a full smile. Her green eyes sparkled as she laughed at the camera.

Though his mom had been gone sixteen years, he could still remember the tinkling sound of her laugh. It had always lit him up with joy and made him want to join in. Even now the corners of his mouth turned upward. She was a great mom and he still missed her immensely.

She would have loved Ashley. She'd always wanted him to find a woman like her. The thought brought on a fresh ache in his chest. Not only had he lost the unconditional love of his mother, there was also a good chance he was going to lose the woman he loved more than anything in this world. Unable to bear the painful thoughts and the overwhelming stench enhanced by the stifling heat inside the trailer, he set down the picture of his mom and moved toward the door for some fresh air.

When Wade came back outside, he saw his dad had retrieved the case of beer from the truck and was already sipping his first can.

"Doesn't that taste better cold?"

"Probably, but I don't have time to wait for that. Plus, the fridge is broken."

"You could have told me that before I filled it with food from the grocery store." He sighed. "I'll take a look at it." He grabbed his tools from his truck and held his breath as he trudged back into the stifling garbage dump disguised as a trailer. By the time he came back outside his dad was well into his second can of beer and his face was flushed red from more than just the heat.

"It seems to be up and running again for now, but it looks like you're going to need a new one soon. I'll pick one up for you."

"You're a good son."

"Eat something other than beer today, Dad. I brought you some things you don't even need to heat up so you don't have any excuses."

"I will. Quit nagging me. How are things with you?"

Wade dropped to the chair next to Roy and his head spun from the movement. He closed his eyes and took a breath before answering. "They've been better, but they've also been worse."

"That's the spirit."

"Ford was in the hospital last week."

"Oh?"

"He tried to kill himself."

Roy cursed. "How is he now?"

Trying to avoid popping open one of Roy's warm beers for himself, Wade tried not to think about how his brother might be. "Last I heard, he was going to be fine."

"Good, that's good."

"I'm surprised you care. You haven't seen him in over ten years."

"He's still my son. I don't wish him any harm."

"No, you just don't want anything to do with him."

Roy ignored him. "Reid said you're seeing a woman and you've been spending a lot of time with her son."

"Yeah."

"Is that really the best idea, raising another man's boy? I mean, kids are a huge responsibility and the boy isn't even yours."

Wade scoffed. "Yeah, because you know all about raising children."

"I raised you!"

"If you say so."

"I just want to make sure you know what you're doing. I'd hate to see some other guy's kid come in and ruin your life just so you can get a little action. There are much easier ways to go about that."

Red clouded Wade's vision. He couldn't believe what he was hearing. Through teeth so clenched they could crack a crown he said, "If you say one more word about Ashley or Emmett I swear I will walk out of here and never look back."

"All right, all right. I didn't mean to offend you. I'm just trying to look out for you."

"Well, don't. You're not exactly in the best position to look out for anyone. You can't even take care of yourself." Wade could see that his words stung, but he was too angry to care.

Roy shifted in his chair with a creaking sound and cleared his throat. "Any paying jobs coming in?"

Wade was still angry, but blaming his dad's behavior on the alcohol helped calm him enough to answer the question. "They come and go. I get by just fine."

"Good, good. So have you been to visit Ford recently?" He was slurring his words now and he clumsily dribbled beer down his front.

"Dad, I just told you Ford was in the hospital last week, or are you too drunk to remember, already?"

"Right, right. Hospital. What about before that? How is he holding up in there?"

"Maybe if you went to see him yourself, you wouldn't have to ask me every time I come by."

Roy took a long drink of his bourbon and chased it with the rest of his beer. He crushed the can in his hand and tossed it to the ground as he let out a loud, wet belch. "What good would it do?"

"I can't believe you'd even ask that."

"What? He doesn't want to see me."

"Can you blame him?"

"I was a lousy father, is that what you want to hear? That he's better off without me? Maybe if I hadn't been such a lousy drunk, he wouldn't have been where he is now? Is that it, Wade? Huh? Anything else you want to say to me? Now's your chance!" Roy took another swig from the bottle before continuing. "He was better off with you anyways, so I guess it all worked out for the best." He hiccupped.

"He's in prison. How is that working out? Maybe if you'd pulled yourself together and actually tried being his dad, he wouldn't have ended up there. Ford needed you, Dad. I needed you. I was only eighteen. I didn't know how to be a parent! It was your job, not mine, but I did the best I could, no thanks to you."

"You try losing the person you love more than anyone in the world and then you can try to tell me how it is, but until then, you have no idea."

"I did! I lost my mom. But the difference is, I didn't become a worthless lifelong drunk like you. I had my own struggles, but I sucked it up and did what I had to because that's what you're supposed to do. Apparently you either weren't able to do that or you didn't want to try because you've pretty much missed out on Ford's entire life. How can you feel okay about that?"

"Congratulations, son, you get the gold star. You're better than me, that's what you're saying, right? What makes you think I feel okay about anything? I'm a drunk, Wade. A pathetic, poor excuse for a man who sits around here all day getting plastered just waiting for his son to come by to take care of him. Nothing about that is okay." A painful silence rang between them. When Roy spoke again his voice was a depressed drone. "If it weren't for you, I'd probably be dead by now. It's a good thing it won't matter for much longer anyways."

"What are you talking about?"

"I got the results back from that doctor you kept sending over here to pester me. You can probably guess it's not good news. My liver's shot, but that shouldn't come as a surprise. Doc says I've got weeks, maybe a few months at best. It's just as well."

Wade had a feeling something like this was coming; no one can expect to drink as heavily as Roy did for eighteen years without any kind of repercussions. Still, knowing it was coming didn't make it easier to take. As angry as he was at his dad, he didn't want him to die. "What are your treatment options? You can do dialysis, right? What about a transplant?"

"I'm too far gone for dialysis to do any good and there's no hope of a transplant for someone like me. Even if there was, I wouldn't want it."

"There has to be something. I'll call the doctor and see what we can figure out."

"You're not going to call him."

"I'm not just going to sit around and do nothing."

"I said, you're not going to call him! It's my life, so it's my decision. There's nothing left to do, anyways. You don't need to be taking care of the likes of me for the rest of your life or taking care of your brother for that matter. You're thirty-four years old, Wade. You're not getting any younger. You need to stop spending all your energy on lost causes like Ford and me and start living your own life. Don't waste any more time."

Through clenched teeth Wade said, "Ford is not a lost cause."

"Maybe he is, maybe he isn't. It doesn't matter. He's an adult and he's responsible for his own life, not you."

"Someone had to look out for him. You sure never did."

"And how are you going to look out for him while he's locked away in prison, huh? Are you going to be there to have his back in his next fight or be able to stop him if he tries to kill himself again?"

Wade couldn't do anything to help him now, no matter how badly he wanted to. Helpless to do anything, he clenched his fists to keep from losing control.

"Look, Wade, you can't change Ford as much as I can't make my liver work again. Ford is going to make the choices he wants. Let it go."

"I can't just give up on him." He hated to admit it, but what other choice did he have now that Ford had shut him out?

"It's not giving up if you never had any control to change things in the first place."

Though Roy spoke the truth that Wade had known for far too long, he didn't want to accept it. Wade had no control over Ford, yet he'd been killing himself trying to get it. He felt responsible for Ford because he felt like he owed him something, like his mistakes were the reason Ford had the life he did. But you can't be responsible for someone you can't control. Maybe what he was feeling was remorse. He hated the part he'd played in Ford's downfall and he was desperate to make it right. But he couldn't. That was the hardest part to take of all.

"But he needs me. He can't do this alone." Even as he said the words, he didn't truly believe them.

"Does he, Wade? Or do you need him to need you?"

"What is this, drunk philosopher hour?" Though Wade couldn't let Roy see that his words had hit home, he wouldn't lie to himself. He liked being needed; he liked knowing he was a part of someone's successes. That wouldn't be so bad, except sometimes he also blamed himself for the failures of others. That was why he had been reluctant to mentor Emmett and why he was so wrapped up in the way Ford chose to live his life. If they failed, then Wade would feel like he'd failed them. That was a lot of pressure for one person to bear. It would be such a relief to let that go.

In the silence, Roy finished his third beer and threw the crushed can toward the trash bin, missing by several feet. "I must be drunker than I thought," he said with a dazed look. "I can see your wheels are churning. What's on your mind?"

"I was just thinking about what you said. I guess maybe I do like being needed."

"It's okay to want to be needed, but it's not okay to get sucked in so far that you forget your own needs and your own life. I know I'm not the best person to be giving advice about what's healthy, but I just don't think it's good for you to put my, your brother's, or anyone else's poor life choices on your shoulders. You should spend your energy on your own choices and the things you can actually control. You like to help the people you care about. I admire that, but you can't forget to help yourself in the process."

If Wade wasn't so used to hearing the drunken way Roy slurred his words, he wouldn't have been able to understand what he said. Despite the booze haze, Roy's advice was actually good. "Well, aren't you full of words of wisdom today."

Roy shrugged. "I guess dying men have important things to say. I'm not done yet, so just listen. Mom would be proud of the man you've become. I know I am." Wade stared at his dad, struck speechless. Before he could say something in return, Roy continued. "I still miss her so much, but I guess I'll get to see her soon." He pulled out a new can of beer and solemnly raised it to the heavens.

Wade's heart broke at the look on his dad's face. Here was a man, so broken by loss and a growing sense of worthlessness, that he'd wasted nearly two decades of his life being someone he loathed. It was the loss that had started the drinking—and the incapacitating depression and anger it stirred in him—but it was his hatred for the man he had become that fed the disease all these years.

He never wanted to be like Roy—the man who ignored his family and everything that was good in life, the man who came to feel so worthless he'd let himself starve and rot away like his trailer if it weren't for his son, the man who would soon drink himself to death.

When Roy shifted in his chair, he clutched his side and winced in pain, his breath coming in shallow gasps. "You're a wise man to swear off booze, Wade. That way, it can never destroy you. I wouldn't wish my life on anyone, especially you. Dying is not very pleasant."

Wade felt like he had cotton wedged in his throat… like he was choking as he tried to swallow his sorrow, to push it back down into his heavy chest. He hated seeing his dad like this, but he was also still so angry at him for doing this to himself. They could've had so many more good years together and now he wouldn't even live long enough to meet his first grandchild.

It was in that moment—looking at the man before him who had nothing left—that Wade knew he would never let himself become him. Now more than ever, the urge to fight to stay sober overwhelmed him. He was willing to do whatever it took—one meeting a day, two, three, even rehab if it came to that. No matter how hard the recovery, he would do it, motivated by the image of Roy's pale, dying face burned into his memory. Wade never wanted to put the people he loved through this kind of woe. He remembered the way Ashley took a step back from him when he told her everything—so cautious, so uncertain. There was no time to waste. The drinking ended now. If only Roy had done the same.

Wade looked at Roy, whose sunken eyes winced in pain from his illness, and his stomach knotted. "I don't want to give up on you, Dad. I want more time."

"You're not giving up on me. I'm giving up on myself. My time's almost here and I don't want to prolong it. It's really okay, son. I've accepted it and I hope you will too. Hell, I would've ended things a long time ago if I had the balls. I want to be with your mom, even if she's pissed at me for what I've become."

"She wouldn't be Mom if she wasn't a little pissed at you."

Roy's chuckle turned into a fit of coughing, which he tried to cure with another swig of beer.

"I'm sorry I was hard on you, earlier," Wade admitted.

"You only said what was true."

"But that doesn't mean I should've said it."

"But I deserved it. Don't bother denying it."

"Well, I'm still sorry… and… and I forgive you, Dad."

Roy's eyes shimmered with tears as he gazed at his son. He cleared his throat so he could speak. "Thank you, son. That means a lot to me."

Wade nodded. "I should get going soon, but I'll get you something to eat and clean up a little bit first, okay?"

After heating up his dad's lunch, filling two giant black plastic bags with trash, checking to make sure the mini fridge was still chugging, and wiping every possible surface of the trailer with bleach water, Wade came back out to discover Roy was drunk beyond reason. Pretty soon he'd be completely passed out.

Wade helped him to his bed, took off his shoes, and put a bottle of water nearby. He looked down at the barely conscious man, who'd once upon a time taught him how to fix dirt bikes; played football with him in the backyard; and never missed a race, game, or a performance. Sadly, the dad he knew as a boy had been gone for a long time, and soon this version of him would be too.

With his heart heavy and a knot in his throat, he whispered the words his resentment had never allowed him to say. "I love you, Dad." His eyes burned and his throat tingled with forced-back emotion, and he promised himself he would visit again soon. Who knew how much time Roy had left. By the time he closed and locked the trailer door quietly behind him, he could already hear his dad's rumbling snores.

CHAPTER
FORTY - TWO

ASHLEY FEARED WALKING away from Wade had been the biggest mistake of her life. He had poured his soul out to her—revealed his biggest vulnerability, his biggest weakness—and she turned her back on him. All he asked for was her acceptance and she denied him that. She didn't walk away because of him, she did it because of what his truth stirred within her: a fear, an insecurity she thought she'd banished. Jeff had been ill too, but unlike Wade, he showed no intention of getting better. He let his illness overtake him until he became completely out of control, full of fear, and dangerous. Wade wasn't Jeff. Maybe she was wrong to compare the two.

The fact that he was a recovering alcoholic who'd experienced a relapse didn't bother her. Okay, maybe it bothered her some, but she'd mostly been upset that he kept it from her for a week, even though she understood why he did it. Once he recognized he had a bigger problem than he first realized, he came to her and told her everything. Putting himself out there in all his shame must have been so incredibly hard for him, but he did it because he loved her. She feared he would take her doubts personally instead of for what they were—demons from her past that had nothing to do with him.

She recalled the turmoil on his face, the way he slumped when she told him she needed time to think. She never wanted to hurt him. But, she had and she couldn't take it back. She owed it to herself to think this through. After all, he had lied to her. He seemed determined to get sober, but actions speak louder than words. Still, she didn't need to be so heartless. She could've done more for him than walk away.

The sun was setting, casting orange and pink hues against her white kitchen cabinets. As she watched the colors of the sky grow steadily darker, she replayed their last interaction over and over again, each time becoming more ashamed of herself. Wade loved her and trusted her. He had gone through so much, and all he'd asked for was her acceptance, her support, and she hadn't even asked him what she could do to help. By the time the sky took on a deep, dark blue and the first twinkle of stars shimmered in her vision, she feared their relationship was over.

***

It was Sunday morning, which for Ashley meant it was the start of a day filled with chores, errands, preparation for the week, and trying not to think about Wade. It had been over a week since he'd confessed his drinking and she'd walked out on him, one week without a word from him. She couldn't blame him. She was the one who'd said she needed time to think. She thought about calling him, but she didn't know what to say. She missed him. Emmett missed him too. He'd been moping around the house almost as much as she had, and had been asking about Wade relentlessly. What could she possibly say to him when she didn't even know where they stood?

Though her shoulder was sore from scrubbing shower tiles and her back ached from pulling weeds in the yard, trying not to think about Wade was proving to be the most difficult task of the day.

As the thoughts continued to push their way through her walls, she worked that much harder to distract herself with remedial labor. By afternoon the sun was blazing and she was sweaty and exhausted, her head still full of Wade. Giving up on trying to distract herself, she decided to take a shower.

The cool water cascaded over her and cooled her overheated skin, though it did nothing to cease her relentless thoughts. Frustrated at discovering the renown effects of a cold shower were merely a myth, she gave up and shut off the water. She towel dried her hair, which was already swelling with humidity, and put on fresh clothes that were, to her dismay, already sticking to her skin. When she was about to start organizing her closet, merely for something to distract herself from thinking about Wade, she heard a knock at her door.

Her heart swelled when she opened the door to find Wade standing on her porch, looking like his old self again. His clothes were clean, his face was shaven, and he'd gotten a haircut. If it weren't for the dark circles under his eyes or the sadness hinting at their sagging corners, she would say he was healed. Her face fell as he gave her a sad smile, revealing his uncertainty about their relationship.

"Wade…" she began.

"Before you say anything, I just want to say I know you told me you needed time to think, and I respect that. I'm not here to bother you. I was just hoping I could talk to Emmett for a few minutes. I want to apologize to him about missing his race last week. Is he here?"

"Yeah, he's here, but…"

He misread her hesitation. "Can I please talk to him? I promise I'll be out of your way soon."

She couldn't take it anymore. "Wade, just stop. Listen to me, please. I'm sorry for the way I reacted last week. The whole thing just reminded me too much of my past with Jeff and I panicked.

Even though I did need time to think, I shouldn't have walked away like that. I should've asked how I could help you. I should've been there for you. And I'm sorry for that."

"You don't need to apologize. I'm not your responsibility."

She continued, ignoring him. "The whole drinking thing just threw me off and when you told me you lied to cover it up, it made me think of what I went through with Jeff. But I realize that you're not Jeff and it was unfair to compare you to him."

"It's okay, Ashley. I understand your reservations. You didn't sign on to share your life with a drunk."

Ashley shook her head in frustration. "Wade, just stop. I'm trying to say something here. I wasn't there for you before, but I want to be there for you now. I miss you. Not talking to you has been hell. I don't even know how you are." When he didn't say anything, she pressed him. "How have you been?"

"I'm…okay," he said, sounding confident. "I miss you too, but I've been handling it. I talk to my sponsor every day and I've been to ten AA meetings in eight days. I haven't had a drink since the night before Emmett's first race. It's not much, but it's a start."

"That's great news, Wade. I'm proud of you. It sounds like you're really serious about getting sober."

"I am." After a few moments of silence, he pulled in a breath as if to draw strength before continuing. "I need to feel like I deserve you again before I can even hope there's a chance you might take me back." He squared his shoulders, exuding determination. "Even if I've already lost that chance, I'll keep working my ass off to stay sober. I don't want to be that guy who drinks his life away, his only companions the empty bottles that pile up beside him." He stood up straighter, his chin lifting slightly. "That's not going to be me."

She smiled at him. "I know." And it was true. She could see his determination, his sheer will to overcome the part of him he loathed. He was strong. Jeff had never looked the way Wade did standing before her now. "I went to an Al-Anon meeting this week."

He looked at her with shocked admiration. "You did?"

She nodded. "I told you, I want to be there for you. I want to help you overcome this so we can be together. I love you, Wade. I want to be with you."

His face softened and his eyes shined. His arms twitched as if he wished to hold her close, as she longed to be in his arms. Knowing he wouldn't make the first move, she stepped toward him and buried her face in his chest. He wove his arms around her, holding her close. She felt him melt into her, breathing a sigh a relief.

"I have a long way to go," Wade said.

"I know. But I also know you can do this. I believe in you. I believe in us."

At her words, he hugged her closer, breathing in her scent. She held him tightly, like a baby koala gripping its mother for dear life, listening to his heartbeat, strong and steady in her ear. She reveled in the love she felt for this man, how it filled her heart until it overflowed and coursed throughout her entire body, warming her down to her toes. Recovery wouldn't be easy, but Wade would make it, they would make it. They would take it one step at a time and eventually, everything would be okay.

Wade broke the silence first, his strength evident in his voice. "I need to feel like I deserve you."

"You do deserve me, Wade. You are a good man." When she pulled away she saw his disbelief. She placed her palms on either side of his face, forcing him to look at her. "Listen to me. You've done so much for me, for Emmett. You've given us a new life that we can feel proud of. I love you, more than I ever thought I could love again. You do deserve me. I know that because you're willing to do anything to prove to yourself that you do. You're fighting and I can see that you will never stop. We'll take this one step at a time and you will beat your addiction. Do you hear me?"

He smiled under her palms and placed his hand over hers. "You make me want to be a better man. And I will fight to be a better man every day of my life, or I'll die trying. But we need to take this slow. I need to focus on staying sober for a while."

Her vision shimmered as her eyes dampened. "I understand. Just know that you don't have to do this alone."

"Thank you." He cleared his throat. "Can I talk to Emmett?"

She dropped her hand and nodded. "He's in his room."

Wade gave her a longing look before making his way down the hallway to Emmett's room. He took a breath and knocked on the closed door.

"Come in." When Emmett recognized his visitor, his eyes narrowed before returning his attention to flipping through the magazine in front of him. "Oh, it's you. Let me guess, you came to tell me your excuses for why you missed my first race? Well, what is it this time?"

"I'm an ass."

Emmett stopped flipping pages and his eyes shot back to Wade. "Well, that's obvious. You promised me you'd be there. You could've at least let me know you weren't coming."

"I know. I'm sorry, Emmett. I really wanted to be there. I'm pissed at myself for missing out on it and I don't even have a good excuse. All I can say is I was really sick the morning of your race. The only reason I even woke up at all was because Reid was banging relentlessly on my front door."

"What do you mean, sick?"

"You really want to know?"

Emmett closed the magazine and moved to sit up on his bed. "I think you owe me that much."

"Fine, but don't get any ideas. I… I was really hungover."

"I thought you didn't drink."

334

"I usually don't, but I did the night before your race and I had way too much. I won't ever be doing that again."

"Yeah, hangovers are the worst. One time I threw up in one of my mom's flower pots. She was so mad. Well, madder than she already was when the cops brought me home drunk."

Wade reeled. "You're only thirteen, you shouldn't be drinking."

"I don't drink anymore. It was only ever fun for a little while, and it mostly just made me feel sick. Plus, it tasted so gross. I never really thought it was worth it. I mostly went along with it because my friends wanted to do it."

"Do me a favor and stay away from the stuff. When you're an adult you can make your own decision about it, but coming from me it's not worth it."

"I will. So where have you been all week?"

"Trying to get my life together."

Emmett nodded, silently contemplating.

"So, are we okay?" Wade asked.

"Yeah, we're okay."

"Good, because I'd love to hear all about your race."

"Maggie caught it on video. She gave Mom a copy if you want to watch it."

"Hell yes, I do!"

"Okay, I have it loaded on my computer."

Wade watched the short video of the race four times, each time with Emmett's original commentary. He listened graciously as Emmett reviewed himself and shared what he was thinking about on certain parts of the course. Wade added his own insights here and there, but mostly he just listened and enjoyed, glad to get to spend some time with Emmett.

His chest ached as he thought what might happen if things didn't work out between them. Ashley and Emmett were his family and he couldn't bear to lose them. He'd meant what he said. He would never stop trying to be a better man for both of them. He would do whatever it took to be worthy of having them in his life. He would fight and he would win, one day at a time.

CHAPTER
FORTY - THREE

SIX WEEKS PASSED and things returned to normal. Ashley had been to several Al-Anon meetings and she now felt confident about her ability to support Wade and cope with his addiction. Wade had been attending his AA meetings regularly and working with his sponsor. He'd been sober seven weeks now and was feeling more confident in his ability to stay that way each and every day. They'd been taking things slow for weeks, careful to make sure Wade stayed on track with his program, but Ashley was ready to move forward. It was time they moved in together as planned, and she hoped that was what tonight's surprise was about.

As she walked the two blocks to Wade's house, her belly fluttered with nervous excitement. Emmett and Wade had left hours earlier, whispering secretively to each other. They'd ordered her not to follow them and to go to Wade's house no earlier than seven so as not to ruin the surprise. After a quick kiss from Wade and barely a wave good-bye from Emmett, they were off.

Not knowing what to expect, she wore a casual black-and-tan party dress and her classic black heels that made her totter clumsily with every step. Two blocks didn't seem very far until she tried to walk them in heels. It didn't help that she hadn't worn them in years and was severely out of practice.

When she finally reached Wade's house, she carefully climbed the porch steps and knocked on the door. As Emmett answered, the smell of something burning reached her first, followed by the overpowering smell of air freshener.

"Is everything okay in there? It smells like something burned," she said.

"It's fine. We have it under control. Wade wants you to go around back, okay?"

Not wanting to get the full effect of Wade's kitchen mishaps, she didn't argue. Emmett disappeared back inside and she made her way to the back of the house, her heels tapping the pavers. When she rounded the corner, what she saw lit her up with a heartwarming smile.

Wade's round, plastic patio table was adorned with a white linen tablecloth and three place settings. In the center was a mason jar filled with freshly picked freesias—her favorite flower—surrounded by flickering candles. Black-iron-and-glass lanterns hung from the four corners of the pergola above, giving the whole setting a romantic glow in the dimming evening light.

The back door opened and Wade and Emmett—looking dapper in their semiformal attire—joined her outside, each carrying large plates and bowls covered in aluminum foil. Wade gave her a nervous smile and set his dishes on the empty spot on the table.

"You look beautiful," he said as he kissed her softly on the cheek.

"Thank you. You clean up pretty well yourself. I don't think I've ever seen you wear a tie. And, Emmett, wow, those freshman girls better watch out next school year. You guys did all of this for me?"

"We both wanted to give you a special night. You deserve it."

"That's very sweet of both of you, thank you. It looks amazing out here. Did you cook?" she asked Wade as she eyed the covered plates warily.

He grinned and shrugged apologetically. "I wanted to do something special for you."

"Well, it certainly is special. I'm sure it will be great. What did you make?"

"Have a seat and I'll show you." Wade helped Ashley into her chair before peeling the foil off the plates one by one. A pile of grilled-cheese sandwiches—some more blackened than others—a bowl of potato salad, slices of watermelon, and a plate of overbrowned chocolate-chip cookies lay before her.

"Wow, you guys really went to town. That's a lot of sandwiches."

"We would've had more but we threw away the burned ones," Wade said.

Ashley held in her smile as she eyed the thin black layer of char that covered the bread of 90 percent of the sandwiches.

As if reading her mind, Wade continued, "Well, the ones that were so burned they were unsalvageable. If we threw away all the ones that turned out a little dark, we wouldn't have much to eat."

"Is that what I was smelling when I came to the front door?"

"That, and the first two batches of cookies. Sorry about making you go around back, but it was pretty smoky inside." Ashley's lips twitched upward and Wade grinned back at her. "I know I'm not much of a cook," he said apologetically.

"No, it's perfect." And she meant it.

After eating one of Wade's acceptably burned grilled-cheese sandwiches, a few slices of seeded watermelon, potato salad that pretty much just tasted like mayonnaise and salt, and the crunchiest cookie she'd ever had, Ashley dabbed her mouth with her napkin and called it quits.

"Thank you, again. Everything was so... edible."

Wade chuckled. "That's the best compliment I've ever gotten for my cooking. Either I'm improving or you're the nicest customer I've ever had. Since I haven't done any cooking in months and everyone I know refuses anything I try to make, I think it's safe to say you're just being nice."

"We lie to protect the ones we love. But seriously, it was so sweet of you both to do this for me. Thank you. I feel so special. Can I help you clean up?"

"I'll clean up, Mom. You and Wade just sit and enjoy yourselves."

"What a gentleman."

Soon, it was just the two of them, sitting side by side. The candlelight flickered in the growing darkness, casting shadows on their glowing faces. Ashley kicked off her heels and rested her feet on the cool grass, appreciating the softness between her toes. They sat in silence, enjoying the gentle caress of the warm summer breeze on their skin and the chirp of crickets searching for mates from their hidden perches.

Wade tucked a loose strand of Ashley's hair behind her ear and leaned toward her until their lips were a breath away from touching. But, he didn't kiss her. Instead, he inhaled deeply as if trying to breathe her in. Her lips parted and she closed her eyes as she anticipated his welcome touch. Her breath quickened as his lips lightly brushed hers before pulling just out of reach again. Finally, she could take it no longer and he closed the distance for a fierce kiss.

All their love and desire, every feeling they had for each other streamed out into that one, passionate kiss. In that moment, it felt like their souls were connected, like they needed each other to breathe. Every doubt, every difficulty, every bad feeling melted away. The only thing that mattered was each other and how the depths of their love for one another poured into that one life-altering kiss. He pulled away just enough so their lips were no longer touching. Still, Ashley could feel the electricity pulsing between them.

They were still slightly breathless when he dropped his hand and pulled away. When she opened her eyes Wade was looking at her like he was the luckiest man alive. He reached for her hand and held it gently in both of his as he let his words come.

"Ashley, you said you were broken when we met, that you were beyond repair. Though your eyes were sad and your heart was heavy with grief, I didn't see someone who was broken. What I saw was strength, and despite everything you'd been through, hope. Even with your grieving heart, you were capable of love that I never even dreamed of—love for your son, your friends, your life, even for the man who left you behind. Even when you thought you were broken, I knew that you were the strongest person I'd ever met. Despite the damage, despite your pain, you still loved far stronger than I ever did."

"You opened my eyes to something wonderful, something that fills me up and makes me want to be a better man. My body and soul swell with it, my heart beats with it, and all I want is to show you how I feel about you. Though the words are not enough, I will say them anyway. I love you and I love your son, and I want us to be a family. If you let me, I promise to protect you and fight for you and our family all the days of my life. I will never walk away, I will never give up, and I will always try my best to be what you need me to be. If you let me, I will spend the rest of my life trying to be the man you deserve."

As Wade rose from his chair and went down on one knee, Ashley caught Emmett's grin out of the corner of her eye as he watched them from the window. She focused on the man kneeling before her, saying all these beautiful things that made her fall in love with him all over again. Wade was right to say she'd once felt broken beyond repair. She'd felt like her heart was ripped to shreds, its pieces crying out for all they'd lost. When he'd called her strong, she had felt her weakest, like her shattered heart would never be able to fall in love again. With a gentle touch, he'd coaxed the pieces back together until they stood reunited and beat as one, only for him. She'd been so sure that he saved her, but maybe the truth of it was, they saved each other. Wade mended her broken heart, making it able to love even stronger than before, but she showed him how to love, something that was equally compelling. Her heart was now whole and it beat for him steady and sure, just as his beat for her.

Wade pulled out a small square box and lifted the lid to reveal a modest princess-cut diamond on a white gold band. On each side of the stone were strands of small diamonds intertwined with a polished band, like a delicate twisted vine. The ring was beautiful and it sparkled in the flickering candlelight.

"Ashley Thomas, will you marry me?"

With happy tears sparkling in her eyes and a smile she couldn't have contained if she'd tried, she uttered the word that ensured her happiness for the rest of her life: "Yes!"

Smiling broadly, Wade slid the ring on her finger. Unable to contain her elation, she threw herself at him, wrapping her arms around his neck. The momentum of her body pushed them both over until they tumbled together and lay on the soft grass. He kissed her fiercely then trailed his knuckle down her cheek and gazed deep into her eyes.

"You just made me the happiest man in the world. I love you so much, Ashley."

"I love you too, as true as truth." A few moments of silence passed before she continued. "Sorry about pushing you over. I guess I got a bit carried away."

"You won't see me complaining. I just tricked the most beautiful woman in the world into agreeing to marry me. Don't ask me how I did it, because I couldn't tell you."

Ashley chuckled and leaned close, burying herself in his strength and warmth. The crickets sang their love songs into the twilight, and Wade wove his strong arms around her, holding her close to his heart. As she lay against him in the soft grass, listening to the steady rhythm of his heart, she knew she was home.

Thank you for reading

If you enjoyed reading *Mended*, please write a review on Amazon.

For more information on the author and her works, please visit Kayla Marie's website at www.kaylamariebooks.com
or
'Like' her on Facebook at
www.facebook.com/kaylamariebooks
and
'Follow' her on Twitter at www.twitter.com/kaylamariebooks

About the Author

Unless you know me personally you've probably never heard of me. That's okay! I wouldn't expect you to. I'm only important to a small number of people in my humble life and that's okay with me. I am first and foremost a wife and a mother, but just as true as that part of my identity is that I am also a writer. I've always had a love for reading and not a day goes by that you'll see me without my eyes glued to the page of a book. Writing has always been a passion of mine, but it took me until my late twenties to realize that the thing that was missing from my life was sharing my writing with the world. Except for my private blog about my family and the occasional Facebook post, my writing has never made it off of my desktop before now. Here I stand before you, (metaphorically of course) as I start on my exciting, though difficult venture as an author with my first novel, *Mended*.

I have to say that the learning curve is very steep in this business and I'm doing my best not to fall behind. I don't think I am better than anyone else and I know there are so many authors out there who are so far ahead of me that they aren't even visible specks on the horizon. But I have to start somewhere and this is where I chose to begin. My plan is to make *Mended* part of a contemporary romance series based in the deep south called *Sweet Home Dixie*. For now the rest of the books are merely notes scribbled in a notebook, but with any luck, they won't stay that way for long. In the mean time, please let me tell you a little bit about myself.

As a girl I wrote many stories and even fastened a number of them into books with hand-drawn pictures and covers made out of whatever cardboard and contact paper I could find in my house. Now, I write love stories and other creative fiction in the quiet hours of the early morning or the few cherished hours of my son's naptime, and I have to say that I am in love with writing. I love bringing my characters to life and discovering the life's choices and experiences they'll have as they go on their unique journeys. I love working through the plot while I complete my daily responsibilities and the feeling I have when I finally know the direction I want to take the story. It's those moments of clarity especially, that I can't wait until I have the opportunity to write it all out. It happens at random times, often at those times that are most inconvenient, but it's that feeling of pure joy as the words flow from my mind to my fingers as I type, that I know in my heart I am a writer.

Besides writing, the other major love in my life is my family. I live in a small house in a small town with my husband, our beautiful little boy, and our other furrier companions. What we lack in possessions, we more than make up for with the things in life that really matter. A few years ago I quit my job and left the world of adults to stay home with our beautiful son. Now every day is a new adventure and I have to say that I've learned more about myself, caring for the tiny person that I love more than breathing, than I had in my four years of college and my years in the workforce afterwards. Life is hard, but it's also beautiful and I am grateful for the time I have.

I know there will come a time when my son will no longer follow me around like my own shadow, hang on my every word, or seem like he just can't get enough of me. I know that time will come much sooner than I want it to. It is those thoughts that keep me grounded when things get ugly. For those of you who have met children, you should understand what I'm talking about.

My life is full of cleaning up messes, washing other people's underwear, getting bossed around by someone under three feet tall, and trying to gain enough control of the chaos so I can steal a moment for myself. No matter how severe the chaos, I always make time to write. It's the one thing I refuse to give up. At the end of the day I'm exhausted yet fulfilled, which is a feeling that I hope everyone gets to experience at some point in their life.

I don't want to be famous, or rich, or anything of the sort. I just want to be me: A woman who loves taking care of her family and who wants to share the joys of fiction with the world. I want to share the opportunity to get so immersed in a book that your problems and the hardships of your life seem to vanish as you're reading; that you become so connected to a character you can feel what they are going through; that you genuinely care about the outcome of a conflict in the story. That's how I feel when I read a book I connect with and I hope I can give some of you that experience.

I know I'm new to the world of professional story-telling and that I still have a lot to learn. But, a person has to start somewhere and I'm so grateful that you, my readers, have given me my first chance to achieve my dream of touching people's lives with my writing. I'll always be first and foremost a wife and mother and I would never want it any other way, but I'm also so excited to begin this new part of my life and I'm honored to share it with you.

Printed in Great Britain
by Amazon